SHEEP DOG AND THE WOLF

A Story of Terrorism *and* Response, *and the* Sheep Dogs Who Protect

CARL DOUGLASS

Neurosurgeon Turned Author Writes with Gripping Realism

PO Box 221974 Anchorage, Alaska 99522-1974
books@publicationconsultants.com—www.publicationconsultants.com

ISBN 978-1-59433-396-5
eBook ISBN 978-1-59433-397-2
Library of Congress Catalog Card Number: 2013-940674

Manufactured in the United States of America.

Dedication

To all Sheep Dogs

Other books by Carl Douglass

•**LAST PHOENIX**, A Story of the CIA's Phoenix Program in Viet Nam; A Story of Betrayal and Revenge

•**SAGA OF A NEUROSURGEON**, a Novel in Six Books
  ▫**THE YOUNG COYOTE**: Garven Wilsonhulme's Way to Success—No Quarter Asked and None Given
  ▫**ANYTHING GOES**
  ▫**HEAVEN AND HELL**: Garven Wilsonhulme Takes on All Comers in the Jungle of Modern Competition
  ▫**THE LONG CLIMB**: Young M.D., Garven Wilsonhulme, Engaged in a Social Poker Game of Winner Takes All
  ▫**ACADEMIA: LAW OF THE JUNGLE**: Surgeon in Training, Garven Wilsonhulme, Fang-and-Claw Competition for Glory
  ▫**THE VULTURE AND THE PHOENIX**: Neurosurgeon, Garven Wilsonhulme, the Final Great Fight

•**ALL IN JEST**: Renowned Neurosurgeon in the Fight of Her Life

•**GOG AND MAGOG**. Yawm al-Qiyamah, Yawn al-Din, The Day of Judgment

•**FINDERS KEEPERS, LOSERS WEEP**: A Novel of Innocence Betrayed and the Search for Restitution

William J. Bennett said in a lecture to the United States Naval Academy on November 24, 1997 that one Vietnam veteran, an old retired colonel, once said, 'Most of the people in our society are sheep. They are kind, gentle, productive creatures who can only hurt one another by accident or under extreme provocation—the regular people in society who go about their lives unaware of those who protect them or what they do. 'Then there are the wolves,' the old war veteran was quoted as saying, 'the criminals, foreign enemies, and terrorists; and the wolves feed on the sheep without mercy. There are evil men in this world, and they are capable of evil deeds. The moment you forget that or pretend it is not so, you become a sheep. There is no safety in denial.'

"Then there are sheepdogs," Bennett went on, "I'm a sheepdog. I live to protect the flock and confront the wolf." Bennett told the midshipmen about a sign in one California law enforcement agency, 'We intimidate those who intimidate others.'"

PROLOGUE

Betrayal is the only truth that sticks.

—Arthur Miller

Early January

In the aftermath, he hit the light switch and bathed his small room in *L'Ermitage Sacre Couer* with a shock of light. His chest was heaving from his exertions of the last few moments; his muscles ached; and he was confused at what had just happened and about the implications of the attack. His was an orderly mind and one that needed plausible answers. He knew he had been careful and was as certain as he could be that he had not been followed to the hotel. His brain cleared as his adrenaline rush subsided. He forced himself to think, to piece together everything that had just happened.

There was not that much to remember: He had been asleep—in that level of sleep below REM, beyond dreaming—benefiting from the deep levels of worry free restorative slumber. The hotel window behind its drawn drapes had suddenly crashed inward, and only with his finely-toned reflexive instincts had he saved himself by throwing his sleep benumbed body over the edge of the bed away from the window as the bullets from a silencer-muffled 9 mm automatic stitched a trail up the length of the mattress where he had been outstretched less than a second or two before.

The shooter had come up the fire escape from the well-lighted street five stories below intent on assassinating the sleeper—the wiry, late middle-aged agent code-named "Sheep Dog"—who was making a small contribution to his country's security. In a former life, that man had been a businessman with a family. That life was now irretrievably in the past.

The slender, lithe, well trained professional killer—secure with the knowledge that the element of surprise was in the intruder'sthe aggressor's—favor had smashed the way into the hotel bed room that was as dark as the bottom of a mine shaft. The shooter's young eyes had not adjusted to the blackness of the room as fast as Sheep Dog's reflexes had propelled him from the bed. The shooter had only a portion of a second to bemoan the fact that he had not been wearing night vision goggles.

The intruding killer moved with the speed of a leopard toward the side from which the sound of Sheep Dog's body landing on the carpeted floor had come. Sheep Dog balled himself up at the foot of the bed. The shooter whirled around the edge of the mattress and stumbled headlong over Sheep Dog's spring-coiled figure. Two more rounds pumped out of the silenced end of the gun as the would-be killer pitched toward the floor. Sheep Dog had three advantages now. The muzzle blast had momentarily blinded the shooter to the darkness in the room, and he was now badly off balance. And he was now in an equal battle with a consummate fighter and killer. Sheep Dog executed a smooth uncoiling to envelope the shooter's flailing legs which brought him the advantage of being prone on the shooter's back. He moved swiftly up the shooter's body and pinioned the intruder's gun arm before the shooter could turn back and fire. Two more shots spat out of the gun impotently into the side of the mattress.

Hunter and hunted locked in a deadly embrace. Sheep Dog knew that he had won when he realized how slightly built his attacker was. He lay on the intruder's back like a coiling anaconda inexorably squeezing the life out of its victim. Despite the attacker's violent struggles, Sheep Dog had been able to hook his feet around the attacker's shins and his right arm around the slim neck. He tucked his head against the side of the attacker's head and brought his left arm up to finish the slow death choke—the *mata leão* [kill the lion]. Sheep Dog patiently squeezed with all his might. His breathing slowed down and became more nearly normal. The attacker's struggles waned as the *estrangulamento* robbed the blood supply, then the critical oxygen supply to the attacker's brain. The struggles became feeble, then finally ceased. Sheep Dog released his compressing hold gradually and listened carefully to the attacker's breathing.

"*Buon dormo,*" [Sleep well] he had whispered soothingly, using the Portuguese of his Brazilian Jiu-Jitsu masters.

Wary that the attacker could have been playing possum, Sheep Dog had slowly begun to remove his arms from around the man's slim neck. His overworked imagination heard soft regular breathing. But there was no reaction, no movement. Sheep Dog let go slowly and cautiously. There was no response, no counter-attack. He grabbed the attacker's chin roughly in one hand and his occiput in the other and lifted sharply upward. There was still no reaction. Sheep Dog had then made a sudden violent lifting and twisting motion of a coup de grâce and heard the bones high and deep in the neck crack as loud as if he had broken a base-ball bat. The attacker's head canted at an impossible angle. Sheep Dog eased up on both hands and took the attacker's shoulders in his hands and shook violently. The thin muscular intruder's head moved independent of its body in a way that could only occur with a complete disconnection of the head and neck.

It was over. Less than fifteen seconds earlier Sheep Dog had been sound asleep. He became aware of his rapid cardiac rhythm pounding in his chest. Now that he could think, it occurred to him that there could be others. He scooped his Sig-Sauer Glock 9 mm from under his pillow and moved silently to the broken window. He peered outside from the window's edge quickly and then moved back out of sight again. No one. He stepped hurriedly to the hotel room door and peered out through the peep hole in the hotel door. The limited view indicated no one in the hallway. He undid the two chain locks and the bolt lock as quietly as possible and flung open the door and scrutinized the poorly lit hallway holding his Glock in a two-handed FBI crouch swinging it side-to-side. The hallway was empty. He closed the door, bolt locked it again, and re-attached the two chain locks.

Sheep Dog flicked on the hotel's room lights and was momentarily dazzled, but he moved swiftly to the side of the inert body of his would-be assailant. The slim figure was dressed in a one piece mat-black stretch nylon body suit, a thin Kevlar vest, a ski mask that showed only open dead eyes now, and black lace-up fighter's shoes with thick rubber soles. A black commando knife was attached to a heavy black web belt buckled tightly to the slender waist. Another, shorter, double-edged dagger was attached to the right ankle; and a sub-compact, semi-automatic 7 round magazine, .22 LR Beretta Bobcat in a concealed weapon holster was attached to the opposite ankle. He examined the larger handgun that had come too close to ending his life. It was a well-used 9 mm Belgian Fabrique National (FN) High Power contract manufactured pistol originally designed and made by Browning. The ID numbers had been expertly removed. Sheep Dog ejected the magazine and examined the bullets—VBR Belgium armor piercing projectile technology. He shivered a little.

"*Loaded for bear,*" Sheep Dog whispered to himself. "*Somebody was right serious.*"

His attacker was dead, and now Sheep Dog needed answers. Who knew about him? He did not believe in coincidences; this was no B&E gone wrong. Who wanted him dead? Specifically—and right now—who was after him? There were plenty of the compatriots of his own victims who would want him dead, but there was no reason to think that any of them—on their own—could have traced him to this country, to this hotel, during this night. He contemplated the answers and came up with a very disturbing train of thought.

He unsnapped and removed the attacker's Kevlar vest—a NATO Level IV Ballistic Vest with imbedded ceramic trauma plates—unzipped the sheath-like black suit and began to search the corpse thoroughly. His search produced two shocks. The first came immediately when he removed the ski mask from his victim's head. The attacker was a woman—young, attractive, and blond. The second came after he failed to find any identification in the pocket-less clothing. He removed her shoes and tore out the insoles. There he found a photo identification card which shocked him with its familiarity. The name meant nothing to him, but the card had been issued by the Central Intelligence Agency of the United States of America. Sheep Dog numbly put the ID card on the room desk top reacting as if he had been struck a violent blow to the center of his sternum. He was momentarily afraid that he would faint. He was a hunter who had become the hunted, and he was going to have to go dissect every event in his history with the Company to find his mistake; and, if he was going to survive, he could never make another one. He mentally kicked himself for not having the good sense to immobilize the attacker and to have extracted all the information she possessed that could have led to her masters. He had a highly honed skill set for extracting information from the reluctant, and it was useless to him now.

He took mental stock of his situation. His cover was blown. He had been betrayed. He was obligated to think the unthinkable. Only two people on earth knew his identity and his present location, and he had trusted each of them with his very life. One of them had been his friend for thirty years. Sheep Dog hated the implication of the evidence before him, but it was impossible to formulate an alternative that made any sense. Until a week ago, those two men had his back. A week ago, he had had two other men to whom he could turn for help. Now, there was no safety net for him—no one to call. Now, he was entirely alone; and the world had become infinitely more hostile.

PREDATOR AND HIS PREY

CHAPTER ONE

November, the year before

Camille and Genevieve bounded across the Jambo House Deluxe Villa to crash into their grandfather's hard legs and were deftly swept up into his arms and held aloft in his wiry powerful upper limbs. The game was so often repeated that the twin two year old girls squealed their delight at being tickled and frightened by their precarious positions.

Their grandma, Rosie, playing her required protective role, exclaimed as usual, "Put those kids down, Hunter Caulfield! You're going to break one of their necks, and then won't you be the sorry one?"

Hunter laughed. "Yes dear, just as you say," he said with a serious face and a mock chastened look.

His twinkling eyes said otherwise. He put down the little blond trouble-makers and gave each of them an affectionate pat on their diapered behinds that propelled them into the kitchen. Hunter moved quickly to his eldest grandson, Evan—age ten—and put him into a headlock and dragged the squawking boy into the kitchen. The rest of the family had already assembled at the table. Four year old Daniel, twenty-six year old Daniel, Sr. and his wife, Marie—young Daniel's mother and father and Hunter and Rosie's son and daughter-in-law—and Stephen and Donna—parents of Camille, Genevieve, and Eva—were dutifully seated at the breakfast table where a pot of steaming oatmeal full of whipped cream, brown sugar, and raisins waited. Donna was Hunter and Rosie's only living daughter. Their first daughter—Donna's elder sister, Pat—died in a car crash twenty-nine years ago, just after Hunter came home from Viet Nam.

Hunter had doted on, spoiled, and overprotected, his beautiful curly-haired blond daughter, Donna, throughout her life and had only relinquished her to Stephen Grandel when she was twenty-two; and Hunter was finally convinced that Donna was madly in love with the young man and that he was going to be as successful a young neurosurgeon as he was a resident at Johns Hopkins. Hunter and Rosie expressed their gratitude to God every day that Dr. Grandel was loving and fully supportive of his trophy wife in all of her rather dubious extra-curricular activities.

With the permissive upbringing Donna had experienced and the fully happy childhood they had provided, she was a brashly confident and very competent young wife and mother. She was an extreme-sport junkie and her parents complained regularly that she was in no position to put herself at such risk what with her marital and maternal responsibilities. Her husband smiled indulgently whenever the subject came up, and Hunter and Rosie shrugged in capitulation as they had done throughout Donna's privileged childhood and adolescence. For all of her daredevil character, she had developed an admirably stringent Protestant work ethic. She had an MBA from Princeton and a PhD in mining engineering from MIT. She had a great job with Consolidated Mines and could have supported her family quite without the meager salary Stephen brought home from his residency position. She was also a marathoner with an enviable record—and a parachutist, scuba diver, and free-hand mountain climber with an anxiety provoking list of broken bones. Her family, friends, business associates, and competitors all admired most her sparkling personality and quirky sense of humor.

The rest of the family found their places at the table. Daniel, Sr.—the Caulfield family scion—was the religious one of the family, having converted to the Mormon Churchlargely to please his wife-to-be Marie. He later developed a convert zealot's annoying immersion in his new religion. Hunter had a live-and-let-live approach to religion and was more amused than annoyed by his son's surprising choice since Hunter and Rosie had pretty much left religion up to their two children's choices as adults. Daniel had become a High Priest and a member of his local bishopric while his daredevil sister had become a quietly unobtrusive atheist. Marie had decided to join her husband in his somewhat pushy zeal for the church that she had taken more-or-less for granted before her marriage and Daniel's conversion. Marie was a rather plain young woman, but had blossomed into a church leader in the women's and children's organizations of her church once she had become activated.

"Say grace, please, Daniel," Hunter asked. At family gatherings, Daniel did almost all of the praying—both public and private—for the rest of them. He nodded an okay to his dad.

"Father in heaven, we thank thee for this fine meal and for the hands that provided and prepared it. Bless the food that it will nourish and sustain us through the day and help us to do good. Bless our family and keep us safe and free from illness, harm, or accident today. Bless the missionaries in the field and our armed forces that they, too, will be safe. Watch over those who are in harm's way to protect us and our liberties. Help the missionaries to find the pure in heart. These and all other blessings we pray for in the name of thy son, Jesus Christ, amen."

Hunter gritted his teeth slightly at the "pure in heart" reference knowing that his son was targeting him to take the missionary lessons which Hunter—the *paterfamilias*—had thus far gracefully dodged.

"Sorry, but I pretty much pooped out after a full day of rides and junk food yesterday at the Epcot Center, and I have to get some work done today." Hunter said after the prayer. "What's on the agenda?"

"Granpa, you have to come. Nobody else will take me on the tilt-a-whirl." Evan pleaded.

"Sorry, big grandson, that'll have to wait until tomorrow when we hit Tomorrow Land and Fantasy Land. We still have most of a week to do all of those throw-up rides again. Give me a little rest, okay?"

Evan frowned.

"You can join us at noon, dear," Rosie said. "We have the Crystal Palace on Main Street, U.S.A. scheduled for the whole family for lunch. We're going to meet the Swensons and their kids for their little Katrina's third birthday party. You can't miss it."

It was an order from the ship's captain, and Hunter knew better than to protest.

"I'm going to come back early this afternoon to get in some running time, and Marie is going to run with me for a while," Donna said. "Daddy, will you help watch the kids while we're out running?"

"When was the last time I ever refused you anything, Mizz Princess?"

Donna laughed affectionately. Both of them knew that he would do anything she asked because she would never ask anything he did not like or of which he really disapproved. She loved him deeply for his kindness and evident love for her—a love second only to that she shared with her handsome husband.

"So, I get stuck with the little monsters on the Family Magic Tour all morning," groused Stephen with an indulgent smile.

He was happy to be away from the hospital for the three days he could get off and did not begrudge any of the time he had with his children and his livewire wife.

"We ought to get an early start, get the quick pass tickets, and exhaust these kids early on; so, we can eat in peace without having to chase them all over the place," urged Daniel, Sr.

Marie started to clean up the breakfast dishes; Donna rounded up the children; and she and Rosie scrubbed their faces and hands, changed Daniel Jr.'s tee shirt that looked like he had strained his oatmeal through it, replaced the twins' sandals for the third time that day, and smeared all of the children with SPF 50 sunscreen. After a chaotic last minute set of plans and revisions and the women's fervent discussion about what they were going to wear, the party of nine made it out of the door and onto the Disney World shuttle bus. Marie ran back and got sun hats for Daniel and the twins and barely made it to the shuttle bus as its doors were closing. Hunter laughed heartily at the scene that suggested to him a hapless set of adults trying to herd cats. He watched as the shuttle bus drove off past the overly neat—but attractive—Lake Buena Vista in front the Jambo House.

He sat down on the couch with his top of the line Tecra laptop and began to review the encrypted Starbright Corporation's year end spread sheet and was pleased with what he was seeing. It had been a banner year for the company, and the best thing about it was that his son, Daniel—despite all of the distraction he put up with from his church activities—was proving to be an altogether competent CEO. Hunter had doubted that the company would be able to secure the top-secret Homeland Security anti-hacking computer contract, but Daniel had made a brilliant presentation to the secretary—better than Hunter could have done, he admitted—and they got the contract. Hunter felt like it was a Boeing type opportunity, and Daniel was shepherding the work along successfully.

Hunter had to smile about his son: he had a masters in computer science and was a world class programmer which made him a world-class hacker. He knew the world's major hackers by name, telephone number, and e-mail address. Most of them were young Russian free-lancers, and more than a few were part of the Russian Mafiya. Hunter had learned a great deal about those polar opposites from Daniel and was amused that his puritanical son helped the company along by quietly serving up information via both venues. His son had taught Hunter a great deal about the technology of hacking and the murky characters who lived in the electronic matrix.

It was up to Hunter as owner to determine the year-end bonuses; and he had to figure the appropriate sums to be handed out before Christmas, two weeks away. There were just over a four hundred executives, consultants, and employees to factor in. The first task was to set a total for the bonuses and then to haggle with himself about how much each was to get. It was a mildly daunting task, but the effort was made easier because of the significant profits Starbright was enjoying.

Once in the park, Rosie volunteered to chase Camille and Genevieve around, and thus to avoid the really gut wrenching rides that the girls and their older kids liked so much. She was amazed at how much repetition the two year olds could tolerate. She had grown accustomed to the fact by tending them as they watched the same inane Disney children's movies and cartoons over and over. The movies—and indeed—the resort's rides drove her half-crazy; but the chance to be with the little girls for three hours was a delight to the doting grandmother.

Camille was the physical daredevil, knowing no fear of injury. She did—however—have an amusing fear of the large Disney characters walking about the park. "Scawy" was her routine response whenever Mickey or Donald or Pluto came up to charm her. She wanted nothing more than to get on the Teapot ride one more time. Genevieve was less enthusiastic than Camille for the rides but was a follower and tagged along behind her vivacious identical twin obediently. She was—however—by far the more gregarious one of the pair, and was the one that worried her watchful grandmother the most. The pretty little curly-haired tow-head did not know the concept of stranger and went about blithely engaging total strangers in her two year old conversations and making them laugh. She raced away from Rosie at every opportunity and started talking to the first person she met: hippies, tattooed hip-hoppers, elderly men in wheel chairs, blue-haired over dressed matrons from Poughkeepsie, black people, South Americans, Africans, Catholic priests, Mormon missionaries, harried young mothers. The child was incorrigible, and her enthusiastic little face captivated almost everyone she encountered.

The family enjoyed a respite from the constant activity by going on Disney's Family Magic Tour of the Magic Kingdom, a two hour guided tour which was contrived as an inter-active quest to save Magic Kingdom theme park from the dastardly plans and bumptious actions of the day's Disney villain. The children were delighted by the tricky clues, rather transparent diabolical puzzles, and the zany scavenger hunt. As noon approached, Rosie was feeling the need to sit, and she wanted little more than to get to the Crystal Palace and sip a big Diet Pepsi until everyone else was seated and the vivacious young waiters and waitresses served the child-favored junk food to the young ones and a large Greek salad for her. The diet drink and the salad were orders from her internist because she was getting a substantial middle-aged spread. Her curves were becoming slopes; she was getting wrinkles where here laugh-lines once were; and, horror-of-horrors, she was beginning to see grey hair—silver threads among the gold.

Evan and Daniel, Jr. got along famously, and Evan took very careful care of his younger cousin. After the tour, Marie and Donna had only to sit on the park benches and keep a watchful eye on the two boys in their detective hats as they raced from one thrill ride to another. The day was balmy with clear skies and a gentle sun. It was a rare opportunity for the two young women to share confidences, family gossip, and concerns about their husbands' burgeoning careers, their sex lives, their worries about getting fat, what they were going to wear to the adults only dinner that night—everything except religion and politics. Their sisterhood—or more accurately—their deep cousin-hood, required tight lips about those subjects.

Both had to stifle deeply held sentiments, but each knew better than to broach such subjects or even to let slip comments that called attention to their well-known differences of opinion. Donna did not mention evolution, and Marie did not give in to her roiling desire to proselytize her heartfelt Mormon religious convictions. They were as physically different as they were philosophically. Donna was blond, firm, slim, and animated. Marie was soft, even voluptuous. She had black hair and enough of a Mediterranean look to be taken for an Italian. Donna displayed a good bit of skin and a tattoo of Hermes—the messenger of the Greek gods—on her left shoulder, and had two piercings in each ear. Marie wore long sleeve, high neck, ankle-length dresses and hardly wore make-up let alone a tattoo or a piercing—God forbid—which made Donna think of pioneers or fundamentalists, a thought that never passed her lips.

"Oh, good, it's quarter of," Donna observed.

"The boys have had enough. At least, I've had enough, let's hie ourselves to the Crystal Palace and pig out on a bunch of transfats and diet drinks," laughed Marie.

The cousin-friends each took her son in hand and started walking across Adventure Land towards the restaurant. They kept a sharp look out for Rosie—the universally beloved family matriarch and ever generous grandmother. Each young woman thought what a perfect day it was: carefree, safe, fun, and nondemanding. They were both hungry, and a big chilled macaroni salad, barbecue chicken and overloaded meat sandwiches seemed like the crowning quest to top off a delightful easy morning.

Hunter looked up from his laptop, and the time registered on him. It was eleven-fifteen; and he had not even showered yet. He reluctantly put away his work and locked the laptop with its serious corporate and governmental secrets in the special safe that the hotel had provided. He shaved and showered quickly, put on a loud flowered Hawaiian shirt, khaki cargo shorts, and sandals—'Jesus boots', he called them frequently enough to warrant a disapproving glance from his overcharged religious son—admired himself in the mirror, and laughed at the shirt that he would not have been caught dead in back home. It was quarter to noon when he rushed out of the front door of the hotel and caught the shuttle.

Rosie and her daughter and daughter-in-law met up with the Swensons and their four rambunctious children who ranged in age from three to eleven and were all handfuls even by their doting parents' admissions.

"How are you, birthday girl?" Rosie asked, kneeling to give a hug to the precocious elfin girl, Abby, whose birthday they were about to celebrate.

"I'm good," she said. "I'm fwee years old today. It's my birfday!"

"We all have really fun presents for you, sweetie," Donna said beaming at the friendly little busy-body.

"I wike pwesents," Abby declared as if it would be news to her listeners.

"Where's Hunter?" Bob Swenson asked Rosie as they looked for their reserved tables.

Evan was teasing the twins.

"Evan, stop that," Marie said. "We've got enough noise and chaos in here without you adding to it."

Evan sneaked one more rib tickle on Camille, then obeyed.

Daniel, Jr. proudly announced that he had found their names on the tables, and the two families trouped to find their places. The children of the two families intentionally intermingled so as to sit by their friends. Rosie sat by Janice Swenson who was looking pretty worn from her morning's duties of herding the "crazies", as she affectionately referred to her children. She and Rosie were both genuinely relieved to be able to sit and to bring each other up on the latest in their families. Rosie and Janice were as alike in their attitudes, aptitudes, and preferences as two sisters could be. Rosie was the quintessential mainstream WASP, and Janice was an African-American choir director in her AME church. Neither was all that religious; so, they got along splendidly. Race did not enter into it.

Donna sat by her brother, Daniel, Sr., after he had complained to her that she hadn't said a word to her since they had all arrived in Orlando.

"You prejudiced against Mormons, little sister?"

"Get over yourself, little brother, and tell me what's new in the secret dark corporate world nowadays."

Bob Swenson left a vacant chair for Hunter.

Rosie said, "He'll be here on the dot. He's nothing if not punctual, you know. It's because he was toilet trained too early."

Winnie the Pooh brought the children lemonades, and they all settled down to enjoy the unhealthy sweet drinks.

CHAPTER TWO

Hunter showed his pass at the entry bar of the Magic Kingdom, submitted to the cursory security inspection, and passed through the uplifted entrance bar and into the amusement park at seven minutes to noon. He walked briskly up Main Street, U.S.A. dodging the crowds. He rounded a gentle curve past the souvenir boutique and could see the Crystal Palace restaurant directly ahead. He would make it almost on the dot, and Rosie would not be able to give him the standard lecture on tardiness. Hunter watched as Pooh and Friends characters busily moved in and out of the entrance of the restaurant and scurried around among the seated guests. Hunter could see only one other person entering the pavilion. Odd—it was a very warm noontime—but the man was wearing a long coat—probably one of the strolling performers.

Ten seconds and ten yards closer, the pavilion disappeared in a clap of thunder unlike Hunter had ever heard or seen even in his military experience. The concussion of the blast lifted the two-hundred pound man and hurled him twenty feet away from the explosion. He crashed into a display rack of sombreros, sarapes, and Mickey Mouse hats, upending it. He was aware of being unable to hear despite seeing the expressions on people's faces that indicated screaming. He was also aware of intense heat which seemed to emanate from the foot deep pile of sarapes covering him. The last thing he saw was a mushroom shaped cloud, an indelibly familiar configuration which seemed altogether dream-like; then his vision went white; and he lost consciousness.

Hunter had brief moments of semi-consciousness during which he was dimly aware of needle punctures, the irritation of a catheter in his penis, of voices lifted in argument about when he would be able to talk, and of the clatter, hum, and smell of a hospital. For the most part he was unconscious, and only later he began to sleep. As he began to arouse, he became aware of the characteristic tick-tock hum of a cardiac monitor. As his consciousness began to increase, Hunter started to become restless and uncomfortable from a sphygmomanometer cuff on his arm, from the now out-right painful Foley catheter, and from being tied down. At times he panicked. He was back in the jungles of Viet Nam, tied down, and being tortured. He tried to shout out his name, rank, and serial number; but he knew that he was not making sounds. Finally, he furtively attempted to open his eyes but could not. The crack of vision he could muster was black, coal mine shaft black. He sank into despair knowing that he was alive and blind. The pain in his penis caused him to think that he had stepped on a brown-betty mine and was emasculated. He frantically tried to move his fingers and toes and strong hands held him down. He felt a warm flush in his vein, and sleep intruded once more.

After another long sleep, Hunter again gradually became aware of his body, then of the room, then of a hand on his shoulder. This time he remained quiet, having learned his lesson from the consequences of his previous outburst.

"Hi, I'm your doctor, Mr. Caulfield. I'm Dr. Risotti, one of Orlando Regional Medical Center's hospitalists."

"Hello, doctor, I'm Hunter Caulfield. But I guess you already know that."

"Yes, sir, I do. I have been taking care of you for the last eight days."

"Eight?"

"'Fraid so. You had quite an experience, my friend. What do you remember about what happened?"

"Not much. I was headed towards one of the Disney World theme restaurants to have lunch with my family. I heard a huge blast, felt like I had been hit by a cannon ball, saw a brilliant fireball and a mushroom shaped cloud, and that's about it."

"You were blown backwards some twenty or so feet and knocked a clothes rack over you. The clothes fell on you and covered you up; so, you didn't get burned to a crisp. You did get a pretty severe head injury. The neurosurgeons opened your skull and took out a blood clot called a subdural hematoma. They saved your life. You have been over a week in coming around, but you're going to do okay."

"I've got a couple of questions, doc."

"Shoot."

"Have my wife and kids or grandkids been by to see me? Were they upset seeing me all bandaged up and all of the tubes and stuff?"

"I'm sorry Mr. Caulfield, but I really don't know anything about your family. The city has been all but overwhelmed by the casualties from the explosion. I'll have to try and find out what I can about your family."

"Thanks."

"It's the least I can do."

"I have another couple of questions, Dr. Risotti."

"Go ahead."

"Will I always be blind? Did my pecker get blown off?"

The questions were so matter-of-factly put that it gave Dr. Risotti a start.

"Oh, that's right. No, no, you're not blind. We just haven't taken off the eye patches while you were awake. Your eyes got a flash burn, and we were protecting them and giving them a rest. Here, I think that's one concern we can get out of the way in a flash. And your penis is fine; it just has a catheter in it. All men hate catheters."

The young doctor quickly removed the taped on eye patches, and light poured into Hunter's sore eyes. He blinked and squeezed his eyes tightly closed and began to struggle with his wrist restraints.

"Hold on. I'll untie your hands."

The straps required a key, and Dr. Risotti had to leave to get one from the nurse's station. He undid the restraints and rubbed Hunter's wrists.

"Thanks."

"Sure. Sorry to have had to use them, but the last time we undid them, we thought we had hold of a wounded mountain lion. We weren't sure until right now whether we'd be safe to try it again."

"Sorry."

"No problem, just glad to have you back."

"I'm pretty sore. How about giving me the unvarnished version of what's broken, what's not working, and what's my prognosis."

"Nothing broken. Everything's working fine, at least I'll be sure about that once we get the Foley catheter out, but I don't expect any problems."

"Can't be too soon."

"And your prognosis is well-nigh perfect. You're in great shape, just bruised up pretty badly. If you don't mind me saying so, it looks like you've had more than your share of injuries. I have never seen anybody with more scars than you've got."

Hunter grew quiet.

"I guess some of what I see was from a pretty bad time. I don't mean to harrow up bad memories, Mr. Caulfield; and my questions are more than morbid curiosity. I need to know something of what you've been through to be able to give you the most informed care."

"It's okay, doc. I have spent most of the last thirty plus years trying not to think about it."

His eyes had adjusted to the light.

"Okay, maybe this's more than you really wanted to know; but here goes with the short version. These two are bullet holes."

He pointed to round scars on his chest.

"So're these six on my thigh."

The strain of reaching down to point them out made Hunter slightly light-headed.

"You don't have to overdo. Take a breather."

Hunter sank back into his bed and turned his head aside in his pillow.

After a moment, he felt better and continued his guided tour over the rough topography of his scarred body. "Burns here."

Ten perfectly round scars—the hall marks of cigarette burns, of torture—indented his wrists and the dorsums of his feet and behind his knees.

"Bayonet stab wound."

He pointed out a large deep scar in his flank.

"Just about did me in. The face scar came from a different fight, different bayonet. And these are knife cuts."

Those scars could not be missed. There were two neat rows of knife cut scars, one on each side of his chest. Hunter rolled up on his side to reveal similar rows on his back. Dr. Risotti winced at the thought of what the man must have been through.

"How did you get those?" he asked respectfully.

"Death of a thousand cuts. I was captured by the Viet Cong."

"I...I'm sorry, Mr. Caulfield. All I can say is thanks for what you did for us. I'm sorry to bring it all up again."

"It's okay. I survived. Too many didn't."

"Well, the whole country owes you a debt of gratitude, anyway."

"Not really. I just did my job. But, you want to know what was the worst wound of all?"

Hunter's face was dead serious.

"I would."

"I came back out of country in May, 1975 after being in-country for most of ten years. I was walking through San Francisco Airport in my full dress uniform, the only clothes I had. Some young men and women walked up to me and yelled, 'Baby killer! baby killer!' Then a nice looking soccer-mom type lady came up and spat in my face."

Throughout the rendition of his terrible physical woundings, the patient had not showed any self pity, anger, or pain of recall, but now he was fighting back tears. His teeth were gritted tight and his jaw clenched to prevent himself from being humiliated. The doctor, remembered his own rush to judgment as a teenager reared by liberal parents. He had been one of those budding hippies who had marched against the Viet Nam vets and shouted the same kind of slogans. He was ashamed for having abandoned thinking and for having behaved so badly in dishonoring the returning soldiers. What a difference there was now; every veteran was being treated as a hero.

"I'm sorry, Mr. Caulfield, I didn't mean to pry."

"I'm sorry, doc. I haven't spoken about any of this to anyone but my wife, and I soon learned that even she couldn't bear to hear about it. I guess I'm in a weakened condition, and I let down my guard. Sorry."

"I'm glad you told me. You probably have some left over PTSD. Maybe it's good for you to unburden."

"When can this horrible Foley catheter come out?"

"How about now, my friend. Mind if I call you Hunter?"

"You can call me Harriet if you want, if you just get rid of that torture device."

Dr. Risotti cut off the input tube to the fluid reservoir and released the pressure of the bulb in Hunter's bladder. The Foley slipped out on its own accord. It felt like a porcupine was being pulled backward out of his raw urethra. The burning did not let up for fifteen minutes.

"Thanks a million," Hunter said sarcastically.

"Think nothing of it," Dr. Risotti said giving a mock sadistic smile.

Hunter laughed and felt a dozen new pains from the movement.

"I'll go and see what I can find about your family. Were they in the park for sure?"

"Yeah—in the…what is it?...the Crystal Palace restaurant."

The doctor blanched in recognition.

"I'll look into it and get back to you, Hunter."

He gave a brusque little wave, picked up his clip board and left.

Hunter was surprised at how tired he was after the talk. He fell back to sleep almost against his will. It was early afternoon when he awakened. Dr. Risotti and a late-middle aged man in a reverse collar shirt and black priest's suit and utilitarian black lace-up shoes were standing in the room when he opened his eyes. He waited expectantly knowing their presence, especially with the solemnity of their facial expressions, could not be good news.

"Tell me the worst," he said looking directly at Dr. Risotti.

"Hunter, I'm sorry, but the information we have is sketchy at best, but I'll tell you what we know. You say your family was in the Crystal Palace. There have been no reports of them so far."

He paused for a pregnant moment.

"Here it is, then. There is nothing left of the restaurant. Nothing. Where it was sitting is a crater ten feet deep and fifty-five feet across. The cops think it was a suicide bomber with two vests on, one front and one in back. The fire ball you described took out all buildings in a circle a hundred feet across. It was all gone in about five seconds. No bodies have been recovered…or even seen in that hundred feet diameter circle. Forensic teams are sifting through the bits of wreckage that are left. There're no reports back yet, but it looks like it will be a matter of finding bits of DNA like what was done after 9-11. Incidentally, this was the deadliest attack on U.S. soil since the Twin Towers came down."

He was rushing now, anxious to get it out before he choked up from looking into the stricken man's eyes.

"The authorities have a preliminary guesstimate that as many as six hundred people or even maybe as many as a thousand were killed, another two thousand seriously injured. I'm truly sorry, Hunter. I can't tell you how much I wish I could give you better news. But, with all of the confusion, who knows? Maybe they'll turn up."

"My nine and a thousand more," Hunter said in a flat resigned voice.

Dr. Risotti and the chaplain put their heads down. They watched the life light go out of Hunter's eyes. His face turned as gray as a stone, and he turned his head to the wall. The two men left the room sorrowing.

Father Umberto said, "I think that is the first time I ever saw a soul die in a man still living."

Hunter was released four days later. His long-time secretary, Constance Nickelson, the COO of Starbright Corporation, Conrad Devlin, and a nurse met him with a limousine for the ride to the airport.

"Sorry about what happened," Conrad said as soon as they were in the car. "What kind of info do you have about the family, boss?"

Hunter was looking at the floor. He responded with a lifeless calm. "No final news, yet. Looks bad, though."

"We'll do anything we can to help. You know that."

"Thanks Conrad, but there's not much to do for the moment. I'd just like to get home and to try and sort things out."

The plane ride back to Denver International Airport was disconcerting for the COO and the nurse. Hunter did not volunteer any speech, and only answered questions perfunctorily. He was obviously lost in his thoughts, and from the look on his face, they must have been dark ones. At DIA, Hunter politely told the nurse his services were not needed.

"Conrad, do you think you could find who Daniel's Mormon bishop is… was? I am going to have to think about a funeral."

It was three weeks before three naval officers appeared at his door. The ranking officer, a Seals captain, introduced himself.

"Captain Caulfield, I'm Bob Withers. The SecNav asked us to come to directly with some news. May we come in?"

"Of course, where are my manners?"

The three men stood awkwardly facing each other.

"Give it to me straight, Captain."

"Captain Caulfield, we have the sad duty to inform you that your family members are casualties of war. It has been proved beyond any doubt that a Muslim terrorist suicide bomber blew up a double improvised explosive device in one of the most crowded areas of Disney World. We have positive DNA confirmation from some tissue fragments that match your wife, Rosie, one of your granddaughters—sorry, we can't be sure which one—and your daughter, Donna. We don't have confirmation for anyone else in your family. I'm sorry for your loss."

The phrase sounded stock.

Captain Withers looked down, "God, man, I am so sorry."

Hunter maintained his composure.

"Thank you Captain, Commanders. I'm sorry you caught such hard duty. I've been there and done that, and it never got any easier."

"No, sir," one of the two commanders said gently. "No, sir."

The funeral was held two weeks later in the chapel of the Denver ward of the Church of Jesus Christ of Latter-day Saints to which Daniel, Sr., Daniel, Jr., and Marie had belonged and where they had been so involved and happy after Daniel's conversion to the faith. The ward bishop, a quiet, soothing, kindly man conducted the funeral with dignity, promises for a better future in the celestial kingdom—which Hunter took to be the Mormon heaven— and the assurance that Hunter would see his family again in the hereafter.

Hunter had never been much of a believer; and, after the fatal explosion, he had lost all faith in God, religion, in the goodness of his fellow men, and even in hope. He was not bitter exactly, but had an empty core. Where love had been, was now resignation. Where hope had been, was a deep void. He could not cry, whether because he was cried out or because his defenses had driven the pain into a compartment of his brain beyond reach.

Hunter had requested that no flowers be given. Instead, he requested that any donations be given to the survivors' fund of the Disney World disaster. After the bishop's short eulogy and funeral sermon, Hunter asked that anyone who knew the family might give a eulogy if they wished. The Elders' Quorum president and the Relief Society president gave short reassuring talks which were glowing with praise for the members of their congregation and brief apologies for not having had the opportunity to know the other departed family members.

There was a feeling of unfinished business in the lone remaining member of the family. When the Relief Society president sat down, Hunter stood and walked slowly to the lectern and gripped the sides of the microphone base hard enough to turn his knuckles white as he composed himself for the upcoming ordeal.

"My friends, I can't thank you enough for all you have done for my family. As I sat there listening to the beautiful eulogies, I felt like you should know all of the family that is no longer here. I am a practical man and not one for euphemisms; so, let me tell you about these people whose lives we honor today. On Saturday, December 14, at precisely the stroke of noon, a terrorist suicide bomber snuffed out the lives of about 729 total innocents in the name of his or her despicable religion."

He paused to let that sink in, and the assembled funeral goers were silent, unused to funeral orations that were not full of sweetness and a blissful trust in the great beyond that beckons us all.

"There will undoubtedly be more once the forensics teams are finished with their work. Besides myself, there were nine members of my family. Here is a brief sketch about each of them; at least, in this place they can be known as human beings, not just statistics in an ongoing war of attrition that appears to be without end.

"I will go by families, starting with Daniel Caulfield, Sr., his wife Marie, and his son, Daniel Caulfield, Jr.."

Hunter moved quickly through the accomplishments of each of the three knowing that their ward member family already knew almost everything about them.

"Next is the family of Stephen Grandel, M.D., his wife, and my beloved daughter, Donna Caulfield Grandel, PhD, their son Evan, and their twin daughters, Camille and Genevieve, age two. Stephen was chief resident in neurosurgery at Johns Hopkins University Hospital. In six months he was slated to join the faculty at Cornell University where he would combine the practice of surgery, surgical teaching, and research in his chosen subject—mathematical computer models of epigenetic memory processes with an eye to attacking the root causes of dementias such as Alzheimer's disease. His wife…" Hunter's voice faltered for a few moments, and he fought back tears. "his wife, my little girl, was a PhD computer genius employed in mining engineering and security protection for computer networks. She was a loving wife, an outstanding extreme sports athlete, and a doting protective mother. The birth of Donna was the greatest joy of my life.

"Evan was a club soccer player and a rascal, full of fun and mischief. He was bright, obedient—most of the time—and full of curiosity and questions. He had his whole life in head of him. Who can say what heights he was going to climb, what service he would render? And he is gone, murdered for the sake of a cruel, mistaken, bigoted religion—for nothing. The two little twins, Camille and Genevieve, were funny, exasperating, loud, demanding, amusing, loving sprites who brought humor and affection wherever they wandered. And they are gone—all of their beauty, grace, enthusiasm, and wonder… Gone." He paused again fighting for control.

"And finally, there is my Rosie, my wife, my love, my support. She was an uncommonly loyal, supremely decent woman. She was bright, had a steel spine, and was a down-to-earth hard worker, loving mother, grandmother, and friend. She was *my* friend, and she meant everything to me. I have been robbed. I want to believe in your God and your after-life survival and purpose if only so that that good and beautiful woman can obtain her just reward. Perhaps one day when there is a measure of peace on the earth—and the vicious attackers stopped—my frozen heart will thaw enough to let in the concept.

"I have heard much today about the goodness of God and his holy plan. The bishop spoke eloquently about forgiveness and about going on and triumphing over adversity. I have to say to him that I may someday be able to forgive, but that will only be after there is justice. I may one day feel that I have triumphed and can move on, but now there is a cavernous hole in me, a wound that will not heal. I am not a religious man. Pray for me. I have lost touch with the heavens.

"Again, thank you for all you have done. I will see those of you who plan to attend the short ceremony at the gravesite right after this service."

There was a closing prayer and a plea to the congregation's Heavenly Father to attend to the spirit of Rosie and her family to let them rest in peace and to be welcomed into the presence of the Lord one day. Hunter's short speech had made almost everyone in the audience very uncomfortable. He had said things that one did not say in funerals. But—after all—he was not enlightened in their happy forward looking faith. They pitied him, more for the threat to his soul than for the admittedly terrible loss he had suffered.

CHAPTER THREE

December

The internment site ceremony was very brief—a dedicatory prayer and a brief eulogy by Earl Dactel, CEO of Consolidated Mining. It was a cold December day with an added unpleasant wind-chill index, and only a handful of friends of Stephen and Marie's from the ward, and of Daniel and Donna's from their respective university and business attended. There were no caskets or even urns—only a simple brass plaque engraved with the briefest of summations of their lives: their names, dates of birth, dates of death—chillingly, nine memoria all with the same date—lined in two serried rows. Hunter was all but oblivious to the words of the bishop's counselor's prayer, to the cold, and to the few people left to shake his hand and to repeat their condolences. It was too cold for anyone to stand around, especially since Hunter was pretty much noncommunicative.

He stood silently and alone in the cold reading again and again the names and dates on the plaques until the visual impact was forever indelibly implanted on his psyche and in nonerasable brain tracts. It was growing dark when he finally turned and reluctantly walked away towards his car.

From behind the shadow of a large Colorado spruce, a tall patrician figure stepped into view.

"Hunter," the man said softly, but just loud enough to be heard in the stillness of the growing evening dark.

Hunter recognized the voice; but, at first, could not attach a name to it.

"Hunter, it's Oliver. I wanted to catch you alone to tell you how terrible I feel for what you have suffered. I was at the funeral. Your talk was powerful. I'd like to talk to you about it."

"Oliver? Commander Oliver Prentiss, the friend who had my back all those years. It has been a long time. It's too bad that we had to get together on this occasion. I'm not up to much socializing, I'm afraid. Forgive me."

"There's nothing to forgive. I very much want to talk seriously to you when you have had a chance to collect yourself. Here's my card—has my home address and number. Natalie and I would like you to come to dinner at our place in Georgetown. Could you fly out the next week or so?"

"Let's make it the first Sunday in January. I have to get all of my nine departeds' business in order. I should be able to do that by then. How would that be?

Oliver checked his Blackberry.

"The 6th. That would be great. Call me if there's a problem. I will understand perfectly. We should get together. We have a lot to remember, a lot to talk about, and I have a proposition for you."

Hunter raised his eyebrows.

"Not now. You need to get some rest. What I have to talk to you about will require that your mind be clear. It can wait."

"Thanks, Oliver. I admit to being curious and that my mind is far from clear right now. I'll be better company by then."

The two men shook hands warmly and separated into the darkness.

CHAPTER FOUR

Early January

With six seconds left in the first half of the annual rivalry between the Minnesota Vikings and the Green Bay Packers, the score was tied 14 to 14. Both NFL teams were unbeaten; and the Las Vegas odds makers had them at even money for the game; but the betting was 6 to 4 that the winner would be in the Super Bowl. Minnesota failed twice in the previous minute to be able to run in for a touchdown or to make a field goal because of a holding penalty and was set to kick the second time. It was fourth down. As the center hiked the ball, and the placer set it; Donovan Parks, the eleven year veteran kicker stepped twice; and the Packers called a time out, its third and final for the quarter. Mall of America Field at HHH was packed to one seat shy of full capacity—64,110 seats filled. The fans and the scores of officials, coaches, and players waited with cacophonous anxiety for play to commence. Minnesota ran back and lined up quickly. Green Bay took its time. The referee blew the starting whistle, and the play clock began to count down—10-9-8. Almost no one noticed as two men walked out onto the 50 yard line.

They raised their arms and screamed the Takbir, "*Allahu Akbar! Allahu Akbar!*"

Simultaneously each man depressed a metal switch on the front of a thick vest, and MOA stadium exploded into a fireball caught on film, then the television reception went dead.

President Tom Storebridge turned to Secretary of State Jeffery Southem and asked, almost afraid to hear the answer, "Owen, what just happened? Tell me it wasn't what I think."

"I'll find out," Owen Paxton-Reems, chief of staff, said, and dialed a number on his Blackberry.

All eyes in the Oval Office were on the chief of staff. Shock and dismay spread over the rapt faces as they saw Paxton-Reems' face turn a deathly white and his face contort in disbelief and pain.

"Preliminary, but looks like a terrorist. Minneapolis will get back to us as soon as they have anything real to tell us," he said tersely.

President Storebridge knew that his worst nightmare was about to come true. He was going to face his first real presidential test. The bombing in Disney World was a shocker, but both the government and the press had downplayed it as the work of a disgruntled nut or of a fanatic of one stripe or another. There was no absolute proof that that one had been caused by an Islamic extremist. This one could not be explained away even briefly or slightly without him being labeled an appeaser, or worse, a wimp. He was already composing his speech for prime time, all channel, national television and dreaded the very thought of doing it.

The families' lives had been remarkably orderly. Wills, trusts, disposition of personal property, property deeds, persons to contact in the event of disaster or death, durable powers of attorney, and the transfer of guardianship from one sibling to another were up-to-date and readily available. With a few visits to his own and his son and daughter's attorneys and with certificates of death in hand, submission of some paperwork, legal forms for life insurance agents, and a few remaining odds and ends of his nine family members' lives, Hunter's work was complete. He gritted his teeth when he determined that he was the sole remaining beneficiary of all that his son and daughter and their respective spouses had to bequeath, a sum that approached five million dollars. He would have given all that he had in the world to be able to go back to seven minutes to noon on that awful day and have it all turn out to be nothing but a passing dark fantasy. It was sobering to realize that he was the last remaining member of his family and his genealogical line. He now had no real personal ties to anyone; his and his family's history would end with him.

He arranged to have the houses and their contents sold at auction, had his lawyer and bank take care of the money, and took a leisurely car trip from Colorado to Virginia. He could not yet bear to sleep in his and Rosie's bed—too many memories, too cold without her, too much anger at the Muslim world generated by those familiar things. He could not watch television, listen to the radio, or enjoy his favorite iPod music. He avoided friends and acquaintances.

He found a hotel in Washington D.C. and took tours of the district, the D.C. area, including the 288 foot tall brilliantly white six spired LDS temple that seemed to grow up from the ground as he approached it headed south on the Capitol Beltway. He wandered the capitol grounds, the mall, and the memorials of the center of the city. He loved seeing the tiny red light shining atop the Washington monument. He spent hours sitting in front of the Viet Nam War memorial, fingering familiar names engraved on the shining ribbon of black stone. The experience kindled a few fond memories and many that seared his emotions. He left the mall in a deep depression.

Early in the evening on the 6th, Hunter called the Prentisses and got directions from Oliver's wife, Natalie.

She said, "Hunter, I'll wait until you get here to really talk. You don't have to feel pressed to talk about the disaster. We'll understand. Come early."

"I'll be there a little after six-thirty if that's okay, and the traffic permits."

"See you then, Hunter. It'll be nice to get together again."

"Good, see you then, Nat. Good-bye."

"Bye, Hunter."

The traffic going out to the semi-rural Virginia countryside was only moderate; the directions were excellent and detailed; and Hunter was able to arrive at the Prentisses at six-twenty-five. A thin African-American woman dressed in an old-fashioned maid's uniform answered the door at Hunter's second knock. She greeted him with a smile, took his coat, and escorted him in. The entry hall was three stories tall and lined with variegated slabs of marble. The effect was of incredible richness but, to Hunter's unaccustomed eye, more than a trifle beyond gaudy. The entry hall chandelier hung a story above the marble tiled floor. It was made of two thousand very small tear drop crystals and illuminated by hundreds of tiny brilliant lights artfully situated among crystals giving the effect of light coming from the crystals themselves. The floor reflected the brilliant light which illuminated a splendid mosaic tile showing Hercules straining to hold up the world. The obsequious maid directed him into a spacious room located to the right of the main entry hall and silently backed away out of the room, closing the door behind her.

Oliver and Natalie Prentiss arose from their seats on a brocade divan and moved swiftly across the large octagonal room to embrace him.

"Hunter, oh, Hunter, we're so glad to see you and so sad about your loss. It is as impossible to convey the level of our sympathies as it must be for you to try and comprehend it," Natalie said softly into his shoulder.

Natalie was a tall, handsome, aristocratic woman of thirty-five. She was a slender blond with perfect delicate facial features and translucent skin. She had a distinct aroma of rich perfume. From fantasy shopping sprees with Rosie when they had gone on business trips to Paris, he thought he recognized Baccarat Perfume Los Larmes Sacrées de Thebes—priced at something like $1700 for a quarter ounce bottle. He and Rosie had laughingly decided that they could not afford even the empty bottle. Natalie's hair was perfectly coifed in a long page-boy. She wore a simple black Vera Wang silk dress with a deep décolletage. The thin material of her dress caressed her lithe body and accentuated her impressive physical attributes. The hem came to a point just above her knees and set off her long legs in a calculatedly tantalizing way. She wore small diamond earrings; and on a slender platinum chain, she had a single pear-shaped Leo Schachter diamond pendant which Hunter estimated at six carats. He made an effort not to stare at the diamond, particularly since it rested comfortably between her partially exposed breasts which had probably required nearly equally expensive plastic surgery to achieve such perfection. She was a good fifteen years younger than her husband.

Oliver Prentiss held his old friend in a firm embrace with his left arm and his wife with his right.

"Hunter, we'll only talk about what you've been through if you want to. We're good listeners, if you want to unload."

"Thanks, you two. I'm still pretty raw. Maybe it would be better if we stayed away from the subject until I'm in a little better control."

"I assume you heard the news, Hunter. Terrible. The second outrage in a month," Oliver said.

"I've been completely self-absorbed the past month, I'm ashamed to admit, Oliver. What now?"

"Let's turn on Fox News. It'll be on. There's nothing on the tube but that right now."

He reached back for the remote lying on the large custom made Philippine mahogany desktop, pressed the "on" button, and a 55 inch screen slid silently from its niche in the ceiling. Oliver put in the numbers for the conservative national news channel and shortly the HD pictures began to illuminate the screen with terrible reality.

Hunter gritted his teeth in poorly suppressed anger. His eyes narrowed and his lips thinned to a mere straight line below his nose.

Frank Dewitts, one of the daytime anchors narrated: "That's all we know for sure to this point. Let me repeat the verifiable facts that we have been able to obtain from reliable sources. A massive bomb—or more likely two bombs—was set off in the middle of the Minnesota Mall of America Field by what appears to be a pair of suicide bombers dressed in Arabic clothing. The bombs had both high explosive and powerful incendiary components which were powerful enough to bring down the superstructure of MOA stadium almost completely. There have been only a relatively few survivors from among the nearly seventy thousand people in the stadium and in nearby buildings, and almost all of them are critically injured. The injured number in the hundreds, and it is obvious that the medical teams responsible for their care would take exception at my characterization of them as 'few'.

"Spokespersons on the scene expect the death toll to rise with time. As we speak, the fires are still burning in the stadium and in several adjacent buildings. All available emergency response team from a five state area around MOA field and from two Canadian provinces are on hand. The Red Cross has sent out an emergency request for money and blood. The regional National Guard reserves have been called out and have set up two dozen emergency medical triage centers. Needless to say, the region's hospitals and clinics are swamped, and every physician and nurse in the area has been mobilized in accordance with the FEMA and Homeland Security plans. This is the first major test for the relatively new plans; and thus far, they seem to be functioning at great speed and efficiency. Critical burn centers in the five state area are overwhelmed, and many victims have been life flighted to distant states.

"The president is slated to address the nation in the next ten minutes or so. He is expected to announce sweeping security measures. As of right now, all air flights have been ordered to touch down at the airport nearest them.

"I warn you that the footage that you are about to see is appalling, and viewer discretion is advised. This cannot have happened in the United States, but it did. Here is the grim reality of this unconscionable attack."

Vivid still photos, cell phone footage, and digital video motion pictures showed fire, destruction, and carnage beyond anything any American had ever seen in his or her country. It was sobering, frightening, and profoundly disturbing.

"I'm especially sorry that you should be exposed to such pictures and such awful news, Hunter," Natalie said, placing her manicured hands with the piano player's fingers, on his forearm. "It is too much after what you've been through."

Hunter did not reply. He looked at Natalie by way of acknowledgement; but she was right, it was indeed too much for him for the moment. He stared numbly at the horrors, unable to look away from the television.

Through the rest of the day, Hunter and the Prentisses returned to the news for brief updates, but otherwise made a studied attempt to engage in light conversation. At ten, Hunter begged off from another platter of expensive gold wrapped chocolates and said that he needed to get some rest.

"Of course, Hunter, let me show you to your room."

The silent African-American maid appeared—as if she had stepped out of the wallpaper—and picked up Hunter's overnight bag. Hunter, Oliver, Natalie, and the maid climbed the spiral marble and inlaid precious wood staircase to the second floor guest room. The maid set down the bag, turned down the sheet and blanket, and unobtrusively left the room.

"Get some rest, my friend. We'll talk tomorrow," Oliver said.

He and Natalie nodded goodnight and left him to get his rest. Hunter stripped, had a quick shower to rinse off the tension sweat, climbed into bed, and was asleep in less than five minutes.

He came down to breakfast at ten the next morning, having avoided watching the news on the television in his room.

"The president spoke last night. You didn't miss much. He just repeated pretty much what we already knew. He did say that he has mobilized the National Guard. This is a big hit, I'm afraid. There were likely multiple bombs scattered throughout the stadium in strategic locations in addition to the two suicide bombers. "

"And the crowning failure of the libs' pushing through the death of the Patriot Act," Hunter said with an undercurrent of suppressed anger.

"How do you feel this morning?"

"I'm okay."

"Up to some serious talk?"

"The proposition you suggested on the day of the funeral?"

"Yes. Then, I have some friends I want to bring into the conversation; some of whom you may know; and some you should know."

CHAPTER FIVE

White House West Wing Cabinet Room, 1000
PRESENT: POTUS, ALL MEMBERS OF THE CABINET

While Hunter, Oliver, and Natalie were spending their morning breakfasting and watching television news, the cabinet room at the White House where news got made was the scene of tension in anticipation of the subject most of them dreaded to broach. As usual, the president asked for each of the cabinet secretaries to voice their opinions beginning with The secretary of State.

"Mr. Secretary of State," The president directed, beginning the discussion, "there is but one item on today's agenda. What do we do with the indisputable intelligence we have from the CIA that the responsibility for both the Disney World and the Minneapolis attacks began in Saudi Arabia, moved to Syria for supplies and transport, and to Iran for execution? Israel is pressing hard for a definitive response by us."

"Mr. President, I have given the matter my focused attention for the past month with little else getting done. The knee-jerk reaction is to let anger determine our course of action as did George W. Bush. President Obama took the high road and worked tirelessly to rebuild the bridges between us, our European friends—and now we can genuinely call them our friends and vice versa—and, in fact, with our, uh…counterparts in the Middle-East. While it is incontrovertible that the perpetrators were Saudis, Syrians, and Persians, that does not necessarily mean that their governments initiated or ordered the actions or even supported them. I strongly…most strongly…urge that you adopt a soft spoken diplomatic approach. No public disclosures of evidence; no threats or bellicosity. There is no need to pander to the radical right who hate you anyway. They will never vote for you, no matter what."

"What about Israel? How dangerous a game of brinkmanship do you think they will play before taking decisive action on their own?"

"Israel is our product, Mr. President. We sustain them. We keep them. They do not do anything without our approval that is of a significant nature in the Middle-East. They know which side of the bread has cheese on it. We should continue to remind them of the golden leash that they wear, and we hold. Let me deal with them."

"There are plenty of students of the Middle-East, including the NSA, CIA, Homeland Security, members of the Congress and the Senate, and even some outspoken members of the administration at State, who beg to differ with you."

"The dissenters do not represent the government of the United States, sir. As the head of State, I am telling you right now that there are going to be a passel of new faces in the State Department come tomorrow. I am quite sure that you will be pleased with the tenor of communication coming from there. As I said regarding Israel, I say about the foreign service of the United States: let me handle it."

"These are times that call for a firm hand, Jeffery. Make no mistake about that. I know what you think about Israel and your tilt towards Palestine in the ongoing…may I say, eternal, negotiations about the establishment of a Palestinian state; but I, for one, am not so sure that the Israelis have the same opinion about themselves that you have about them. At the very least, they bear watching. Let's hear from Defense. Michael?"

"I don't think we are about to recommend war or any facsimile of it any-time soon; but, to state the obvious, we have had acts of war committed against us. We can hardly ignore the acts or their implications. We have put the defense forces on Orange Status."

Jeffery Southem, secretary of State, almost leaped out of his chair.

"You what!!?? Without a word to me?! I can hardly imagine a diplomatic signal more provocative than that short of actually firing a cruise missile!"

"Easy Jeffery. I okayed the order," The president said, "We cannot come across as complete wimps. Maybe the meek will inherit the earth; but I, for one, would like it to be something more than the remains of a post nuclear holocaust world."

The secretary of State said, "'Terrorists want a lot of people watching, not a lot of people dead', is a realistic aphorism made in the 1980s by Brian Jenkins of the RAND corporation, work triggered by the hostage killings at the 1972 Munich Olympics and continued for decades. With the exception of 9/11, most of the Muslim Jihad demonstrations have been for show and to sow disruption of governments, usually their own or their neighbors."

"That is an aphorism which thousands of bombing victims would doubtless dispute, Mr. Secretary," Michael Chisholm, The secretary of Defense said pointedly. "Mr. President, the Joint Chiefs and I would like to do a whole lot more; but we have held off until after this cabinet meeting. At the very very least we strongly recommend that you and The secretary of State meet with the foreign ministers of Saudi Arabia and Syria and the Swiss who are handling matters for the Iranians and come to an understanding that our patience can only be strained so much. The American people will be up in arms if we do nothing. I have to tell you that I have been hearing serious officers suggest that they will resign if we roll over and play dead after another attack."

"I agree with both of you," said the president. "You are both recommending a firm diplomatic approach although Jeffery wants it softer than you do, Michael. Jeffery, please make arrangements to have the foreign ministers of Saudi Arabia, Syria, and Israel meet with the two of us today, and have the Swiss get on the horn with their Iranian friends; so, we can get some sort of dialogue going with them as well."

"Do you think it wise to meet with Ehud ben Cohen's people so soon and so openly, Mr. President? That could never be kept a secret, and the Arabs and the Persians will know about the meeting before we even have a chance to come up with a mutual statement. They will be furious at what they will perceive as an insult and a veiled threat," Secretary Southem queried earnestly.

"I can't sit back and let them all think I'm a wussy. More importantly, I can't let the American voters get that idea into their heads. Our fine right wing friends are already worrying that horse to a froth."

"So let them. We have control of both houses, all but four of the governorships, and more than 70% of the state legislatures, to say nothing of our most helpful friends in the media. We can control any attacks from the loonies on the right."

"I have an appointment with the CIA at four. This is apparently something that they didn't bring up in the morning briefing. I'll let you know what they've learned or what mischief they've been hatching up. I think we've done about as much as we can here. Let's all get out and reassure the public that we have the situation under control and that we have a plan that concentrates both on diplomacy and preparedness, ladies and gentlemen."

The president stood up effectively adjourning the cabinet meeting. All members stood and waited until he left before collecting their papers and beginning to file out of the room. Jeffery Southem gave Michael Chisholm a frosty diffident look, and The secretary of Defense failed to return the gesture with even a convincing diplomatic smile.

The friends to whom Oliver referred were conveniently waiting in the Prentiss's spacious third floor office. They had been there since nine-thirty, and were becoming mildly antsy before Oliver finally got around to letting Hunter know they were already present and were looking forward to talking to him. It was ten forty-five.

"You seem to be taking me for granted, my friend," Hunter said good-naturedly. "I have the feeling that I'm about to learn a bit more about your world than I picked up in the better part of ten years in 'Nam with you."

"Withhold judgment until we've had a chance to talk."

"I always weigh motivations, recommendations, and decisions seriously, Oliver. You should know that."

"I do know that, Hunter. You certainly know how much respect—even admiration—I have for you. Frankly, you wouldn't be here, and this meeting would never take place if I didn't have that well-founded impression of you and if I had not been able to convince the others of your bona fides."

Oliver led the way up a set of back stairs that were the equal of the impressive spiral stair case leading from the entryway to the sitting room where he and Natalie had greeted Hunter. Natalie—for her part—had unobtrusively disappeared through a side door. Oliver's office was neat and everything was expensive, but unlike the rest of the house it was all function with form following function all the way. The chairs were comfortable, but designed for people to do serious work and not to be entertained. The rest of the house was expensive wood and stone; the office was chrome and glass and technology. There were several computers, a bank of television screens, security cameras, recording devices, and locked wall safes. It must have been patterned after the presidential situation room. Hunter thought it must be somewhere on a par with what the president himself could command.

"Hunter, I believe you recognize the DCIA."

Hunter nodded to Gerald Lang, impressed that he was meeting one of the most powerful people in the world.

"I don't think you've met Mac Withers. He's involved in some of the less public aspects of our work, you might say."

Hunter shook hands with both the DCIA and Mac Withers.

"Happy to meet you, gentlemen," Hunter said with a note of caution in his voice.

"And this is the brains of the outfit, Olive DeSanctis. She's an MIT PhD in computer science, one of the world's foremost cryptologists, and an organizational genius. She is also particularly shy of the public eye, and I'm sure you will be discrete about having the opportunity to meet her."

Oliver gave Hunter a meaningful glance. Hunter nodded, and shook the proffered hand of the senior agent, a dour appearing study in grey and black. She was not at all physically attractive, but she had penetrating deep brown eyes that could see through a man and into his inner computer. Not a one to cross, Hunter decided.

"Well, Hunter, to coin a phrase, perhaps you're wondering why we called this meeting," said the DCIA, a commanding presence for all of his nondescript appearance—balding, short, fat, and dressed in a three piece black suit, tie, belt, and shoes right out of central casting for a KGB puppet master.

"It had occurred to me to wonder, sir."

"Let's cut to the chase. I know you're a straightforward person, and so am I. So are all of us for that matter."

Hunter could just bet.

"The three of us and the head of NSA and Homeland Security are going to meet with the president at four this afternoon about some thoughts we have about dealing with the recent spate of terrorist hits on this country. We don't like them, and we don't feel like sitting on our thumbs while those nice Arab peace lovers blow our country and our citizens into oblivion. We all know that you are more aware of the consequences of their actions than anyone else in this room, and we unitedly and very sincerely offer our condolences."

Hunter gave a small nod.

"Okay if I call you Hunter?"

"Sure."

He was not about to call the man Gerald, however.

"I'll get right to the point; then I have to leave. I presume I can count on your strict discretion, Hunter?"

"Certainly."

The DCIA nodded his satisfaction with Hunter's laconic answer.

"This president will not order any kind of military action unless he is absolutely pushed into it—say by a frank nuclear attack on U.S. soil. That's not the opinion of a politician, but my studied professional opinion. We have to have another means of resetting the scales with the members of the peaceful religion. What we are going to propose is the recruitment and training of some, what shall I call them?...equalizers. We are fully aware of your work in the Phoenix Program. Both you and Oliver were highly instrumental in the defeat of the Viet Cong, and neither of you flinched at doing your duty. We won that war, and the hippies and liberals threw it away. The whole thing was very public and—in retrospect—very stupid. We intend to be as obscure as spider web this time around. We want you to be one of our agents. We are prepared to renew your status as a full-fledged agent of the Company, and we are prepared to offer you a full navy captaincy as a legitimate—albeit covert—status. What do you think?"

"I've got a lot of questions, like why me since I'm getting a bit long in the tooth, and what if I decide not to go forward at any point?"

"You don't look particularly 'long in the tooth' for a forty-two year old. You pose good questions. We have full faith in you, and guarantee you every protection and resource we can offer. I'll not be coy. While we will train you, supply you, find you safe havens and safe entrances and exits, you will largely be on your own. You know the drill: if you get exposed or captured, we never heard of you."

"Fair and honest enough. I'm in, at least to hear the proposition out."

"Good. I'll take off. This meeting never happened, of course; and no one ever suggested that you might operate a bit to the side of the law, so's to speak. Okay?"

"I understand. I appreciate the head's up."

DCIA Lang stood up and moved his bulk out of the room without further explanations or pleasantries. Hunter turned his attention to Olive DeSanctis and Mac Withers.

Oliver spoke first, "Hunter. For the record, as I'm sure you've recognized already, I stayed with the Company after 'Nam. I have a cushy desk job somewhere in the bowels of the Langley building. If you get on board, I'll have a hand in your operation on the daily ground level, but we won't be corresponding pen-pals or e-mail buddies."

"Fine with me."

Olive DeSanctis spoke next, "Hunter. Please call me Olive. One thing I have to get straight with you is that we don't have any further conversation without you signing a limited official secrets act agreement. By so signing you will be bound in perpetuity not to divulge anything that you hear in our meeting. As the director said, so far as anyone else might be concerned, our get together today didn't occur. Agreed?"

"Agreed."

Mac Withers produced a brief and simple but no-nonsense document. Hunter read it quickly. He could never talk about, publish in any form, or in any way divulge information regarding what was said during the meeting. The date, time, and location of the meeting were accurately described, and Dr. DeSanctis had already affixed her notary seal to the bottom of the page below where Hunter was expected to sign.

Hunter shrugged and signed with alacrity.

"Good, Dr. DeSanctis said. "Now let's get to it. Without going into detail, we intend to recruit and train a core of dedicated assassins to rid the earth of a number of particularly venomous creatures who either commit or support terrorist activities against our country and our allies. I am sure you know that many of the niceties of international law are going to be circumvented. As Sir Winston Churchill said when the British took over Iran in 1941, '*Inter arma silent leges*—In times of war, laws are silent'."

Hunter nodded his understanding.

"Your participation in the Phoenix Program was stellar. I'm not a flatterer, Hunter, we just don't have the time or patience for that sort of thing. You have a set of experiences and skills that seem altogether apt for our needs, for the needs of our country which is in trouble. You won't be a big shot, anymore than any one of the three of us are. We all make a small contribution, and we are asking you to make one as well."

"If I can do something other than sit behind a desk, I am pretty much sold. I have to tell you that, although I can be professional about my work, this is definitely personal. It won't get in my way; but I have a deep and abiding conviction that those people must be stopped; and, frankly, most of them eradicated."

His face, body language, and stone hard eyes left no doubt of the intensity of his declamation.

"Can you take orders?" Mac asked.

"I can."

"You'll get some that will give you a moment of pause, if all goes as we hope it will."

"I can handle it."

"Can you work on your own without direct assistance?" Dr. DeSanctis asked.

"You know my background and experience. My résumé—my real résumé—speaks for itself."

"It certainly does," Oliver interjected. "I can personally vouch for that."

"I have a couple of questions before we get too far into this."

"Go ahead," Mac said. "Better to get it all on the table now than to have regrets later."

"Okay, I wanted to find a way to get at the terrorists. Until today I hadn't the foggiest notion how to get involved. I'm so long out of the loop that I have something of a hard time believing that the CIA would pay attention to me as an applicant since there are some 14,000 other applicants for this year alone."

"Probably true. But we know something about you; and, frankly, we have clout. We also have secrecy. We would rather have a seasoned vet who knows the ropes about real secrets than some new enthusiast who might well feel like becoming a whistle blower if the heat gets turned up. Look, I am going to be straight with you. We have stuff on you. It shouldn't take a lot of thought on your part to know what I mean. You and the rest of the PRUCs have been lying low since 'Nam. You all are afraid that you would be branded as criminals and probably tried…probably found guilty of a significant number of felonies if the Company ever got real put out about you and let some records accidentally leak out. In the hard core short of it, you would be in a terrible position to make a fuss."

Hunter's face became grim. "You are still something less than the Christians In Action, I see. So, am I to understand that you are going to extort me into being your hit man?"

Oliver started to speak, but Mac held up a quieting hand to him.

"Not at all. You can walk out of here tonight and never hear from us again unless you think it would be a lucrative opportunity to sell the story of this meeting to *The Enquirer*. That would upset some very unforgiving people. You are looking at three of them, and you saw one of them earlier. We are not people to mess with, Hunter. We can and expect to be very good friends of yours; but turn on us, and you will wish you had never been born; and that is not just a trite turn of phrase."

"Hunter, I'm your friend. I will do anything in my power to help you, to protect you. But you recognize that this is war, just not a war that will make the news. No one in or out of this room can be allowed to have the kind of information we are going to give you and to betray the Company without prejudicial consequences," Oliver said. "That's not really a threat so much as it is a fact. The stakes are too high."

Hunter reflected on the precise terminology Oliver had used. 'Prejudicial', as in to 'terminate with maximum prejudice'. He had been ordered to kill people by such orders and had given those same orders to other men and women. Hunter Caulfield was not a new guy who had to learn the ropes, not those ropes.

"If you are interested and want to go on, we will have to have a contract, and you will have to be sworn. You can still back out; but you will be bound by the Company's secrecy policies; and in this case they would be most stringent and watchful of you for years to come if you did," Dr. DeSanctis said quietly.

Hunter laughed, knowing that he was being swept into an entangling net like an unsuspecting fish, but the opportunity to make a contribution—even a small one—towards getting justice, or, call it by its real name, revenge, for the deaths of all nine members of his family was sufficient bait.

"Okay, I'm still in even after the beating you all just administered. What's next?"

Oliver said, "My friends, I think we've covered enough for one night. Let's get to Langley tomorrow and make all of this official and get onto serious work. That all right with you, Hunter?"

"Yes."

"Olive?"

"Let's get Hunter to my office by eight tomorrow. I like an early start."

"Mac?"

"The sooner the better."

"I'm pooped," Oliver said, "and I'm sure Hunter needs his beauty rest before tomorrow's work. Let's call it a day. It's quarter of one, and I have to meet the director then brave the lion in his oval den."

Mac and Olive nodded and took their leave.

When they were alone, Oliver turned to Hunter and said, "You are perfect for this. Don't be put off by the hard approach; it just underscores the seriousness of what we're asking you to do with us. If this project goes south, we'll all lose our heads. We want you to succeed. It is in our best interests at the Company, and we believe in you. You realize that we have vetted you from Able to Zotz. You are the man for the job. These are your qualifications: you are unattached, rich, bored, and looking for something worthwhile to do. You have no familial attachments. Your businesses can run by themselves and provide a good cover for you. You are as fit and strong as men half your age. You are good with weapons and scary in the martial arts. You are bright, a fast learner. Above all—and this I remember best about you—is that you are able to keep secrets. We both have some things we did for the Phoenix Program that we have never divulged and in all frankness don't dare tell anyone for fear of prosecution or worse."

"Thanks," Hunter said softly knowing that he was not being flattered.

Oliver's rendition of his qualifications was factual, and his friend's presumptions about his motives were right on.

"Here's the dossier we have compiled on you. I gather that you want to do something to even the scales against the terrorists. You can think on it overnight. I leave for work at six. If you want to get back in, we can drive in together and get the ball rolling. That sound reasonable?"

Hunter nodded his assent.

CHAPTER SIX

White House Oval Office-1100
PRESENT: POTUS, SECRETARY OF STATE, FOREIGN
MINISTERS OF SAUDI ARABIA, SYRIA, SWISS
REPRESENTATIVE FOR IRAN

Neither man spoke in the Oval Office as President Storebridge and Secretary of State Southem sat waiting for the foreign ministers of Saudi Arabia, Syria, and the Swiss representatives of Iran to arrive for their strongly requested appointment. It was two twenty-five and the ambassador then the foreign ministers were due begin arriving in five minutes. The secretary did not voice his serious misgivings about the whole concept of having the meeting. He saw it as at least a partial unraveling of all of his efforts to bring the United States back into the good graces of the moderate Arab world and a mistaken unnecessary provocation of the crazies from Iran.

There was a soft knock on the door.

"Come in," The president said.

"Mr. President, the Swiss Ambassador-at-Large, Jeremy LeFevre," Sally Rose Mathews, the appointments secretary announced.

President Storebridge stood up and walked to the door to usher in the representative of Iran.

"Glad you could come, Ambassador LeFevre. We are most appreciative of your government's willingness to act in our behalf."

"It is a pleasure and a privilege, Mr. President, but unfortunately, I am the bearer of bad tidings."

"We're not altogether surprised," Secretary Southem said dourly. "So what does President Sofrekheneh have to say about this latest provocation? We certainly have the Persians dead to rights with all of our evidence."

"It will come as no surprise, I'm sure, that the president of the Islamic Republic of Iran doesn't much care about your opinions, your evidence, or the lives of your people. His exact words were, 'So, once again The Great Satan, gets his comeuppance. They shift the blame from themselves to the peace loving people of Islam—the true victims. You can tell them for me that we will not lower ourselves to reply to this insult.'"

Ambassador LeFevre read the statement from a typed note.

Secretary Southem shrugged in disgust.

"How nice of him to reply," The president said.

"Sorry. He was implacable. I couldn't get him to budge a millimeter."

"We know it's not your fault, Mr. Ambassador. I am quite sure that this is not the last of it," President Storebridge said with resignation.

"I'll take my leave, then, Mr. President, unless you have more need of the services of my government."

"No, and thanks."

The president and secretary shook hands again with the Swiss ambassador, and he turned crisply and exited the room.

The two men looked at each other somberly.

"The question of the day is going to be, 'now what?' I'm afraid, and I predict that we will have much the same question after meeting with our next two guests."

The president's interoffice phone lit up with a flashing light. He pressed the speaker button and said, "Are they here?"

"Yes, Mr. President."

"Bring them to the office then, Sally Rose."

"Right away, Mr. President."

Less than a minute later the familiar soft knock on the Oval Office door sounded again.

"Come in."

"Mr. President, the foreign minister of Saudi Arabia, His Majesty Prince Muhammad ibn Saud, and the foreign minister of Syria, Dr. Amjad Zia Abuzia Kutchemeshgi."

The president and the secretary personally ushered the two men to their chairs. The prince seemed slightly uncomfortable in his expensive Western suit, but neither man betrayed the slightest hint of being ill at ease or the impression that they felt as if they were being called on the carpet.

"Mr. President, it is a pleasure and an honor to be invited to this great seat of power," flattered the prince.

"The Syrian state is similarly honored to be here today, sir. And, Jeremy, it's nice to see you again. What has it been, two months?"

"I'm afraid so, Amjad, too long."

"Well, gentlemen, we realize that the request for this meeting is a bit abrupt, and we are well aware of your busy schedules. Why don't we get right down to the business at hand," said the president with what seemed to be an uncouth abruptness to both of the Arabs.

Prince Muhammad thought to himself that this undereducated man—who had somehow gotten elected to the most powerful office in the world—could be excused for not appreciating the fine points of courtesy. *Praise be to Allah that we have Jeremy Southem to deal with on a regular basis.*

"Yes, Mr. President, that would be most efficient."

Only Jeremy Southem of the two Americans took note of the irony in the prince's response and the implied insult. He thought it more than likely that the man would next offer his left hand for the president to shake.

"What can we do for you, Mr. President and Mr. Secretary?" asked Dr. Kutchemeshgi.

"You are no doubt aware of two recent suicide bombings perpetrated on our soil, gentlemen."

The Arab foreign ministers nodded.

"What you may not know, is that the criminals who committed these heinous crimes had direct ties to both of your countries."

Both men knew perfectly well that the suicide bombings were linked to their countries. They remained impassive.

"We are sure that your governments had nothing to do with the crimes, of course, gentlemen; but we need assurances from both of your governments that steps will be taken to interdict the criminal elements in your countries that are responsible, and that the radicalist networks are dismantled."

"We are shocked to learn that there could be any involvement by our countrymen, Mr. President. Can you share the intelligence you have regarding the cases?"

Jeremy Southem had to fight the urge not to roll his eyes.

"Jeremy?" The president asked, glancing at the large portfolio in front of the secretary.

"Yes, sir. Here is the evidence, gentlemen. I'm afraid it is abundantly evident that cells in your countries and in Iran cooperated to commit these murders in our country."

He passed the prepared evidence statements and photographs to the two Arab diplomats. They perused the data briefly without altering their expressions.

The prince spoke first.

"I will look into this promptly, Mr. President and Mr. Secretary, of that you can be assured. If our investigation corroborates your evidence, we will bring the criminals to justice swiftly and efficiently."

Southem recognized the diplomat's between-the-lines communication: a scapegoat would be delivered up, and the very likely involvement of the Saudi General Intelligence Directorate—the *Al Mukhabarat Al A'amah*, or the Syrian Political Security Directorate would never be mentioned. At least the message had been delivered.

Dr. Kutchemeshgi said, "My government looks on such actions as particularly grievous, and you can rest assured that, if indeed our nationals were involved, they will find no place far enough, deep enough, or obscure enough in which to hide. We will keep you well informed."

Prince ibn Saud coughed gently.

"There is a small problem. We hate to ask, but we trust that our usual arrangement will remain in force. It is most difficult, as you know, for some conservative members of our governments to admit to such goings on and will balk at the costs to be incurred."

"Of course, gentlemen. Our intelligence services will be at your service in the usual spirit of cooperation. We have already set aside a sum of five million dollars to assist in the investigations. Here is the account number for our usual Bank of China account used in these matters."

Secretary Southem handed one of his cards to the prince who merely glanced at the handwritten password numbers and letters on the back.

"Good, then we should really get to work," said Dr. Kutchemeshgi.

"I agree," said the president and showed the foreign ministers to the Oval Office door personally.

When they were gone, Secretary Southem gave a small sigh that at least neither of them had offered his left hand.

"I think that went pretty well, don't you, Jeremy?" the president asked.

Southem answered with a shrug.

The two Arabs left the West Wing escorted by and under the watchful eye of Anders Ketchum of the Secret Service.

Dr. Kutchemeshgi whispered to Prince ibn Saud, "By Allah and the Prophet, may he be blessed forever, can they be as simple-minded as they appear?"

The prince ran a long index finger across his aquiline nose in a dismissive gesture, pointed back down the hallway and answered tersely, "We'll see, Amjad. Give it some time."

The two men left unsaid that the Westerners had not grasped the truly important aspect of the meeting which was that two Arab nations who were regularly at considerable odds with one another met together and in full concert with the U.S. leaders who were blithely unaware of the potential consequences. Furthermore, neither American had taken note that the foreign minister of Syria had an Iranian name, was a Shi'ite in a Sunni country, and had family ties in Iran that went back ten generations, perhaps the most significant oversight on the Americans' part of all.

The scrambler phone light blinked again after a five minute period of time elapsed.

"Yes, Sally Rose?"

"The Ambassador of Israel, Mr. President."

"Bring him in, Sally Rose. I presume you made sure our previous two guests did not meet with Ambassador ben Moises."

"Most assuredly not, sir. They came and went through entirely opposite corridors."

The soft knock came again, and Mrs. Mathews brought the Israeli diplomat into the office.

"Come in and take a seat, Daniel. Some coffee?" Secretary Southem offered.

The Israeli declined. He was an old soldier and a reluctant diplomat famous for his brusqueness and for cutting to the heart of issues without preliminary small talk.

"Mr. President, Mr. Secretary, I know you've had the Saudis and the Syrians come by today. I trust that you had a forthright discussion."

"More forthright on our end than vice versa, I'd say."

"Not surprising, of course. I'll be direct."

"As if we would expect anything else of you, Daniel," said Southem.

"We received your intel on the terrorists..."

"Since President Obama, we don't call them terrorists. They're now Persons Who Facilitate Man-made Disasters," chuckled Southem.

"We have more vigorous descriptors," responded General ben Moises.

"So, Daniel, what is Israel's take on our bombings? What, if any, response is Israel contemplating?"

"The same as always, gentlemen. We will defend our existence. Iran is near to making a viable nuclear war head. They already have a medium range missile that can put a bomb in downtown Tel Aviv. We intend to see to it that no bombing such as you suffered takes place in our little country. We certainly will not stand by idly until a nuke is launched."

"Isn't that overreacting?"

"You know it isn't."

"We'll be most reluctant to countenance a preemptive strike, you know that, Daniel. That is the take home message from this meeting," said the secretary of State. "It is not politically defensible."

"With all due respect to you and your most generous country, gentlemen, we are not running for office; we are dealing with issues of outright survival. It is as primal as that, and no kind of political correctness is going to be allowed to make us a bit of collateral damage in a larger sphere of interest."

The general's face betrayed his determination if not the expression of the diplomat that was required of him.

"Let me remind you, General, and you need to take the message back to Prime Minister Cohen: we will not, and I repeat *not* agree to or support any unilateral action on your part."

Southem's face had reddened and the stress in his voice was more than he had intended; but it was the bottom line in the contract between Israel and the United States in his estimation; and it was better said now than to pick up the pieces after some half-baked attack by the arrogant little nation.

"I predicted this conversation almost to your choice of wording, Jeremy; and Ehud Cohen and I discussed our response; so, this is the official line of the State of Israel: We cannot, and we will not sit by and be destroyed. We hope you will take action. We will work with you. But if we come down to an imminent lethal threat, we will act with or without you. If it takes a preemptive strike so be it."

The president listened as the Israeli hawk scratched a figurative line in the sand.

"Don't be overly hasty, Daniel, give us some time to work things out. We are going to have to consider all the options before we act. From our end, we cannot obtain the support of the American people for another foray into the Middle-East unless the 'facilitators of man-made disasters' force our hand unequivocally by another attack or especially by a more extensive one."

"Mr. President, yours is a huge nation with over 315 million people. You might be able to argue that a few million casualties here or there can be overlooked in the grand scheme of things, but Israel cannot. There are less than eight million of us. One can see our entire country by looking out the window of an airline jet. We cannot afford the luxury of such thinking."

The meeting ended cordially enough. The men shared demitasses of thick bitter Turkish coffee and some biscotti before taking their leave of each other. The president and the secretary knew that Israel meant every word the general had said; and with the help of the U.S. Jewish lobby, the determined little nation would call the bluff of the administration if it threatened to withhold the usual foreign aid or even direct military assistance. The two senior officials of the United States government were beginning to feel their backs being pressed up against the wall.

At precisely four in the afternoon, Sally Rose Mathews showed the DCIA and the ADCIA, Oliver Prentiss, the secretary of Homeland Security, Jensen Dräger, and the DIRNSA, Walter Owen Miller, into the Oval Office.

The president was tired and not in the mood for small talk. He focused his attention on the director of Central Intelligence who had requested the meeting.

"What is so important that it couldn't wait until tomorrow, Director?"

"Mr. President, our intel circuits from satellites to mano-a-mano are hot with indications that our nice Muslim friends are hatching not just an attack but a series of them. We work with one hand tied behind our back since the Patriot Act was cancelled, but we are still getting most worrisome indicators. Here is the folder on what we have so far."

The manila folder was marked: TOP SECRET, EYES ONLY POTUS.

President Storebridge took a cursory look at the voluminous set of documents.

"I obviously can't go through all of this now. I will get at it today, but give me the highlights."

DCIA Gerald Lang launched into a precise and efficient assessment, a talent for which he was famous. He presented only the most important pieces of raw evidence, but what he had to say had a telling effect.

"I hate it when you come in with one of your confounded briefs, Director. I wish that just once during my presidency that you could come in and give me some good news."

"Mr. President, you know what it says over the door."

His reference was to the inscription over the entrance to the CIA Building.

"'Ye shall know the truth, and the truth shall make you free' I know I can't work without the truth; but I have to tell you, there are times like today when I hate the truth."

Lang gave the president a small sardonic smile.

"So, any suggestions short of launching a preemptive thermonuclear strike, Director? any of you gentlemen?"

"We've put a lot of thought into that."

He looked at the director of NSA, The secretary of Homeland Security, and his own ADCIA for the National Clandestine Services who all nodded their assent.

"We are not naive about the political situation, Mr. President. Any kind of overt or public attack would be inimitable to what your administration has been advocating since you were a candidate. So, covert is the only way to go."

"How can you blow up a bomb plant covertly or attack a radical mosque or a Saudi government directorate covertly? I have racked my brains. This very day, the Saudis, Syrians, and Iranians have all denied categorically that their governments have been involved in the atrocities in America and have demanded some time to do their own investigation. An act of retaliation would be a major international incident; and in so saying, I am the master of understatement. The provocations have been dreadful; and we all know they are lying through their teeth; but our country is in a state of seriously poor relations with Europe and the Middle-East. Any move would solidify the world-wide stereotype of us as George Dublyawar-mongers. You've got to come up with something we can do and deny. Plausible deniability. That's an absolute."

"I think we can do better than that, Mr. President. We'd like ADCIA Prentiss to give you an outline of what we have in mind."

"Please do enlighten me, Mr. Prentiss."

"Yes, Mr. President. We are trying to wage—and hopefully win—a very real war without accurately identifying the enemy or its motivations for seeking to destroy us. This defies common sense and past military experience. The old rules don't apply. However, one fact is the same as existed prior to and during our major conflicts during the twentieth century; we once again face a relentless totalitarian ideology bent on our destruction. These enemies have a fervent belief that they have a divine mandate to wreak destruction on all of Western civilization. In a word, we are talking about "*Sharia*"—the path to God—an all encompassing legal, traditional, and educational theocratic way of life that at its core is totalitarian, virulently intolerant, and absolutely bent on establishing a global Islamic state. They are a threat around the world through their *Sharia* based concepts of *dawah* or stealth jihad—insinuation into every facet of Western life to undermine the foundations—*Dar al- Islam*—subjugation of nonIslamic states, and *Dar al-Harb*—the house of war. Every bit as importantly, there are substantial numbers of them living undetected in our own country.

"What we are going to suggest is something like what Rudi Giuliani enacted shortly after he became the mayor of New York City and every one from the cops to his own staff thought it was impossible to stem the rise in crime throughout the city. He ordered the police to focus their attention on subway crimes, everything from jumping the turnstiles to rape and murder. The apparatus of the crime wave depended on guns and informants. The minor criminals were found with guns, saved their skins by ratting on the higher ups; and the crime wave began to unravel.

"We want to try a variation on Guiliani's theme; except, of course, we plan to have a small scale scheme that is as secret as the Manhattan Project was in its day. We will have an assassin like perhaps no other in history. He or she will be given every possible assistance but at more than an arm's length. He or she will work with complete anonymity—false passports, identities, cover stories, passports and IDs from a dozen other countries, weapons and technology that are not U.S. in origin, and no records at CIA or in any other U.S. governmental entity."

"So, I presume you have already found such an agent?"

"Yes, sir, we have. But this agent will be our test weapon. If he or she is as effective as we think he or she can be; and the nice folks who 'facilitate man-made disasters' begin to howl and cry foul; we will have our answer. We can then turn up the heat with some more agents until the real facilitators—the Saudis, Syrians, Iranians, and our allies, the Egyptians and Pakistanis—sue for an armistice. They will never be able to prove that we are behind the assassinations; but they will be sure; and they will be afraid. They will realize that the U.S. is as Khrushchev described us when the Cuban Missile Crisis had brought the U.S. and the Soviet Union to the brink of world war three: 'The Americans will take hit after hit and insult after insult, and will look like paper tigers. Then they will suddenly shoot you in the heart'. He backed off, and we think that—faced with a personal threat from a phantom—so will our current..."

"I hate secrets. You know that. They always seem to come back to bite the president's butt. How can you be sure, I mean absolutely sure that the secrecy can be maintained; so, we can deny the existence of our phantom without being humiliated?"

The DCIA interjected, "By having the fewest possible people in and out of the government know who he or she is, what he or she does, and by what authority and with what resources. The right hand will not know what the left hand is doing. No person other than the phantom will know exactly what is happening, who the targets are at any given time, and when and where our attack will take place. We are even going to obscure our own vision by a series of cutouts. Finally—and I hate to say this—if the phantom becomes a liability, we will remove him or her."

"I'm not sure I care for this veiled reference to he or she, him or her. I presume that I will have a full set of information about the project, the phantom, and the missions before, during, and after the fact."

"No, sir, we thought long and hard about that. The DCIA will not have any further information passed to him after today. We will not give you information in order to keep you squarely in the position of having full plausible deniability. You won't have to flinch when you tell the media that you don't know a thing about any assassinations. Our stance is going to be that those bloodthirsty 'facilitators' are having an interfamilial fight; you know how violent they are against each other. The Sunnis and the Shi'ites are at each other's throats as usual, or the Egyptians are taking out the Syrians, or the Iranians are trying to take over the whole movement, or Al Qaeda is having a quiet war with Hamas, whatever."

The president steepled his fingers against the bridge of his nose and was lost in silent thought for a full three minutes.

"I am reluctant—most reluctant—but I guess this is only the worst possible plan except for all of the other possibilities. Go ahead, but nothing in writing. Not a thing."

CHAPTER SEVEN

E arly the next morning, Oliver and Hunter drove in Oliver's black Lincoln Town Car with overly tinted windows into the District. Oliver moved briskly across the George Washington Memorial Parkway Bridge to the Virginia side of the Potomac and to the CIA building in Langley—technically, in a part of McLean, Virginia, an unincorporated area of Fairfax County a few miles west of the District of Columbia. There was no need for the two men to talk; Hunter had already given a firm 'yes', that he would take the intelligence job as they met over coffee at Oliver's breakfast table an hour earlier in the morning. Oliver pulled into the South Gate entrance, showed his credentials to the gate guard—who checked it thoroughly even though he had seen Oliver two hundred times a year for the past fifteen years—and were waved through. They drove through a beautiful, lush, green forest to the Original Headquarters Building [OHB]. Oliver parked his official vehicle with its brilliant green parking permit sticker in the covered parking area for ranking officers in a space that read *Deputy Director, Central Intelligence, NCS.* Oliver made a short detour to the OHB courtyard; so, Hunter could see the statue of Nathan Hale. Then he and Hunter walked up a short flight of stairs and into the main lobby. Oliver led him to the north wall where the memorial to fallen CIA heroes was placed. On the wall, in neat rows, were engraved 83 black stars with no names. On one side of the wall of stars was an American flag and on the other a CIA flag. In the center was a book with, again, 83 stars, but only 48 names.

Hunter looked at Oliver's face for answers.

Oliver said, "The others are still classified."

The two men returned to the center reception desk, walking across the 16 foot diameter inlaid CIA seal. Oliver asked the attractive middle-aged woman for a visitor's pass for Hunter and was given one with alacrity. The receptionist asked for Hunter's name. Oliver put up his hand in a stopping motion.

"We won't need to record that, Penny," he said in a friendly voice of authority.

"Yes, sir," the receptionist said and waved the ADCIA and the visitor on.

They ascended the elevator alone to the seventh floor to the DCIA's suite of offices. It was too early for the regular workers to come in. Oliver asked Hunter to sit in a small well-appointed conference room while he went to find the other participants for their upcoming formal conversation.

Oliver was right at home in the inner sanctum of the house of power and secrets. Hunter quietly assessed his friend who had risen to such heights. He was a little older, considerable thinner and more athletic in appearance, taller; and he still appeared to be very fit and not a man to mess with, owing in no small measure to the fact that he had been in special ops in Viet Nam for several tours—not as long as himself—Hunter reflected—but long enough to be a formidable individual.

Hunter envied the man his comfortably worn good looks. He still had his full head of curly black hair; Hunter was well on the way to being the poster boy for the male-pattern-baldness-is-sexy campaign should it ever get started. As a result, he wore his hair very short cropped in a military cut. His eyebrows were too full; and his eyes too close together for him to be handsome; and his large nose had a hook shape that cried out for a cosmetic nose job. He had acne scars pits on a tanned face, full lips, and a strong chin. He also had a strong Adam's Apple, a prominent feature. He was not displeased with himself despite his lack of the genetically inherited or surgically enhanced handsome facial features; and he had that distinctive facial scar.

Unlike Oliver, he did not have a tennis player's nice tan. Also unlike Oliver, his teeth were neat, but not perfect, yellowing slightly in contradistinction to Oliver's pearly whites standing in perfect even condition; he had had work done that Hunter could not afford early on and later could not find time to take to get the cosmetic changes. He was quite ordinary—six feet tall, but the definition of his trained muscles showed even under his well-fitted white Van Heusen dress shirt. Hunter had the body of a man shorter than six feet in height—more like a prize fighter than a business executive—and he carried himself in an habitual protective posture. He wore a black three piece suit and a patterned red bow tie. His black wing-tip shoes gleamed from a recent polishing. His outfit was not in the same class as Oliver's, but he felt like he was dressed as if he belonged. He had been a slob in country when the two of them ran around Hué and its environs and especially when they had moved their irregular PRUC troops around the Mekong Delta riverine country.

The Provincial Reconnaissance Unit Cadres were CIA created and directed hunter-killers, the like of which the world was not likely to see again. Both he and Oliver had been PRUC officers. Hunter was definitely impressed that his friend had come so far after 1975—deputy director of the National Clandestine Service [NCS]—as it was now called officially—a position to be able to make a real difference.

Hunter took a moment to look in the mirror on the south wall. He evaluated himself as objectively as he could and concluded that he had progressed from a young average looking man to a middle-aged face-in-the-crowd, one of the gray people to whom no one paid attention—everyone's dad—maybe even young grandpa—with his only distinguishing feature being his facial scar. His hair, he admitted, was past being thin; and it was greyer than it should have been. He had hazel irises like practically everybody else and in most respects was pretty much average, he thought. Maybe that was an advantage in his prospective new assignment. He probed and pinched the skin of his face. His facial features were definitely blah, not large or small or crooked or marked, or hairy, and definitely not a head-turner for the ladies. Despite his stint in the navy, he had stayed sober enough not to get a tattoo, not even a large Phoenix bird on his back or the "Sat-Cong" on the pectorals that most of the members of the small fraternity of secretive men with whom he had served had had needled onto their skin in order to show their allegiances.

"Oh, well," he sighed, chalking it up to the rest of his mediocre life of late.

Oliver returned in ten minutes accompanied by two other fashionably suited men, one older and one younger than himself. They were preceded into the room by a mousy little Eastern European woman in what had to have been a government-issue blue serge suit. She was carrying a court stenographer's recording machine.

Oliver made introductions: "Lady and gentlemen, this is an old friend of mine who, for the moment, we will call, T. You are the only people with any knowledge of why T is here, and it would be best if you did not know his name, address, and the like. Please confine your questions to other areas. T., these people are CIA officers from the Counterterrorism Unit of the NCS. They want to know a lot about you, except they don't want to know who you are. It would embarrass them if you were to slip and give them your name or personal particulars, okay?"

"Okay."

"Everything is going to be recorded, and a transcript printed. It will be 'eyes and ears only' for four people—the three of us and the DCIA. When this interview is over, you will take a lie detector test. While you may—in the course of your work for the Company—lie upon occasion; of necessity, you must not lie in even the most trivial instance today or ever to the four people outside of yourself who know your mission. I will be the only person who knows who you are, where you live, and the full details of your missions. That understood?"

"Yes, sir," Hunter answered without irony.

Oliver smiled at that, knowing as Hunter did, that they had slipped easily back into old navy roles.

"Then, let's begin. I'll go first. Mr. T., that's not your real name, correct?"

"No, sir."

"Tell me about your military service briefly. We want to know mostly about your time in Viet Nam, your work with the CIA, and how you felt about it. You don't need to give us your unit numbers since they could be used to trace you."

Hunter told him—them. It took forty minutes.

Oliver turned to the older of his three companions, "Your turn."

"T., tell us something about your life as a business man after you got back from Viet Nam, please."

Hunter told him about getting his first job after retiring from the service with Unified Export/Import Limited which he had obtained because he spoke French—with a Vietnamese accent—Vietnamese, and Spanish, having been born and reared in New Mexico. He carefully omitted the name of the company. He mentioned that he also had an MBA. Hunter's narrative included that he had climbed the corporate ladder rapidly and correctly read the tea leaves about his future in the company. He was granted a sabbatical and obtained a law degree from Stanford with a specialty in international law. Thereafter, he spent most of the remainder of his career in Europe where he married and sired three children, learned Italian and German, and became as familiar with the streets of Budapest and Leipzig as he was of those in Albuquerque and Washington D.C. where his daughter lived. Hunter omitted any mention of his daughter or of anything more of his family than that they existed—had existed.

As the stock market began its meteoric rise in the early nineties, Hunter went on, he opted for a stock option rather than a significant pay raise. He rose to the position of first vice-president, and when he sensed that the market was very over inflated, he cashed in on his stock options with a profit of well over ten million dollars and resigned from the company. That was in the last week of December, 2000, and the market began its calamitous decline less than a month later.

For the next five years, he developed his own company with the best and the brightest people from his former company—he told his inquisitors without telling them the name of the company—which earned him considerable enmity from several of the top officers of the former company. Loyalties were nonexistent in the corporate and legal world by then, and they soon forgot their antipathy towards him and moved on to more pertinent enemies du jour. Without boasting, Hunter informed the three agents that his timing was excellent; and the people he chose to work with in his new company were superb. In five years, they were able to merge with Fed Ex and became Fed Ex's European arm. The senior officers of Fed Ex wanted their own man in my place, Hunter said, and made him an offer he could not refuse.

"I retired," Hunter said, concluding, "for real this time, with a total nest egg of nearly seventy-five million dollars. I am now forty-two years old."

"Tell us about your activities outside work. Your dossier says you are quite the hunter," said the younger of the two men with Oliver.

"I started hunting as a kid and became more interested in the weapons and in competition shooting than in hunting per se by the time I was thirteen or fourteen. I have hunted all over North America, Mexico, Africa, in parts of the Middle-East—especially Turkey and Pakistan—and in the mountains of the 'stans—Uzbekistan, Tajikistan, and north eastern Iran. I collected trophies from all over and had them mounted in a new house—the house I shared with my family until recently."

The three agents other than Oliver raised their eyebrows in a question to which Oliver shook his head.

"Did you prefer one kind of hunting over another?"

Hunter was not quite sure what he was getting at; so, he took a small chance to get a step ahead of him.

"I tried archery but wasn't very good at it. I did get quite adept with a cross bow, but the hunting fraternity has a positive snit if you even bring up the word 'cross-bow'. What I liked best was to make long shots. After a while, I sort of lost interest in hunting per se and took up long range competition shooting. There is quite a fraternity of wanna-be snipers, and all of us are fans of fifty caliber rifles. I probably wasn't the best among my peers; but I could hold my own; and I even won a few tournaments."

The older agent nodded, and Hunter was sure that he had provided the information for which the man was looking.

"What's this business about you wanting to do your bit for the country in the War On Terrorism?" Oliver asked and glanced at his note pad. "I think your exact words were that you wanted to make some sort of a 'small contribution'."

"I don't know, maybe it's just a mid-life crisis; but yes, I am frustrated with the monstrous things the terrorists do; and I would love to be part of the effort to thwart them. I don't fancy myself a James Bond type, but my bet is that there are people behind the scenes—even way behind—that do a lot. I guess—if the truth be known—that is my secret fantasy."

Oliver asked, "How about a not great paying, hazardous, uncomfortable, and unsung hero type job that just might make a difference?"

"You are a super salesman, Oliver. How could anyone resist such a tantalizing offer with such a golden future?"

"I'm serious," he said. "We need someone to fill a special niche. I'll be right up-front with you. Our last guy got killed."

"Encouraging."

"And you remember those black stars on the wall in the lobby, the ones with no names attached?"

"I do."

"That agent doesn't have one, and neither will you if you die in the line of duty. You will never have happened so far as the NSC and the rest of the government and the country know. You understand that, right?"

"No ticker-tape parades, then."

"Not even an obituary."

CHAPTER EIGHT

After Oliver's cheerless description of Hunter's slim prospects for becoming a hero, the older mana humorless cold-fishsaid, "I think we've learned enough for the time being. T., we'd like to have you take a polygraph test, and then talk more definitively with you about a contract."

He got up abruptly—nodded to Oliver—and the two of them left. The younger man motioned for Hunter to follow him. They went to a room with an obvious one-way mirror. A colorless, expressionless man in a gray suit and gray tie with blue stripes nodded to Hunter and the older agent as they entered and motioned for Hunter to sit. He took the seat proffered—one with an obvious sensor pad on the seat—and sat facing the functionary across a small table which was covered with medical appearing paraphernalia. The officer who had accompanied Hunter to the polygraph laboratory turned and left the room.

The technician seated in the chair opposite to Hunter got up and said, "Please take off your shoes."

Hunter did. He then placed a mirror next to Hunter's left foot and proceeded to affix a sphyngmanometer to his right arm, a plethsmygraph band around his chest, electrodermal galvanic skin response electrode patches on his right hand, and had him lift his shirt while he placed ECG leads on his chest. He wheeled a computer screen up to the table so that Hunter faced it directly, then he placed a P300 wave analysis electrode headband on his forehead. Lastly, he placed a PSE machine next to Hunter's mouth—a psychological stress evaluator for voice stress analysis.

The technician had Hunter fill out a bio form and did not indicate surprise or even change expression when Hunter made a point of not filling in his name or other identifying information. While Hunter worked on the bio, he moved his chair to Hunter's left side.

He spoke again after his set-up was complete, "You are about to take a polygraph or lie detector test. I direct you to tell the truth to every question asked since the polygraph equipment will detect every lie by showing even the slightest stress. You cannot alter your responses in any way to trick the machine since your responses are automatic. The machine is sensitive to all of the fight, flight, and freeze mechanisms of human physiology. I will ask a series of questions—some of which may be repetitive—in order to verify any responses that indicate falsification on your part. I am a trained and qualified expert and have done thousands of these tests. I will be aware of any effort on your part to lie or to evade the truth.

"You have the right to refuse to take the polygraph test; but if you do, you will not be hired. The polygraph test is not the sole determiner of whether you are hired or not. If you elect to proceed, you will be given questions that deal with your life's experience, any criminal record, your employment record, medical information, and your intentions. By agreeing to proceed, you are agreeing to allow the information from the test and from the forms you filled out to be passed on to any agency the CIA deems necessary. Have you any questions?"

"No."

"Do you wish to proceed?"

"Yes."

"Hereafter, answer only yes or no. Answer truthfully, and keep your mouth open and your hands on the table at all times between answers."

Hunter nodded his understanding and agreement.

"Did you sleep more than six hours last night?"

"Yes."

"Did you eat breakfast this morning?"

"Yes."

"Have you had corrective eye surgery?"

"No."

His numerous questions dealt with known truths, facts about Hunter's life that he had placed on the forms, his general honesty, suitability, and integrity. He asked about Hunter's criminal record—nonexistent—his general propensity to lie, whether he had ever lied for any reason, any drug use, whether he had ever committed and gotten away with arson, murder, assault, sexual exposure, sex with a minor as an adult, forgery, or had any weapons violations not recorded. Did Hunter cheat, take credit for work done by others, cheat at cards, ever do anything he was ashamed of, withhold necessary information in an investigation, or had he ever done anything for which he could have been fired? Hunter paused on a few of them, but did try and tell the truth as best he could knowing that some of his answers required more than a simple 'yes' or 'no'.

Then the technician got to the nitty-gritty questions.

"Do you know anyone who is involved in espionage or sabotage against the United States?"

"No."

"Have you ever copied or removed classified material without permission?"

"No."

"Have you ever made unreported visits to foreign countries or embassies?"

"No."

"Have you ever been approached, trained by, made plans with, or been compensated by any person involved in espionage or sabotage against the United States?"

"No."

He went through a long list of closely related questions about Hunter's possible contacts with organized criminals who associated with terrorists, any unauthorized contacts that could pose a threat to the country, any compromising sexual and pornographic proclivities, and did Hunter have any belief in a religion or philosophy or group that espoused injury to the country.

The test took three hours. Hunter was very tired at its conclusion.

"That is all," the technician said and dismantled the equipment from Hunter.

Before he could stand up, the young agent who had been with Oliver during the introductory interrogation stepped back into the room and said, "Come with me please."

He had obviously been watching from behind the one-way mirror. That had to be one of the world's most boring jobs, Hunter thought. They returned to the conference room where lunch was served.

CHAPTER NINE

White House Oval Office-Noon
PRESENT: POTUS, CHAIRMAN JCS,
ATTORNEY GENERAL, SECRETARY OF HOMELAND
SECURITY, DFBI

President Storebridge sat at his desk facing The chairman of the Joint Chiefs, The attorney general, The secretary of Homeland Security, and the director of the FBI. After coffee, small scones, and brief small talk, the president turned to the subject that had been gnawing away at him ever since he had given the order to proceed to the intelligence officers the previous afternoon.

"Give me a plan for dealing with these wretched attacks on our soil that does not involve mobilizing for a major war, covert assassinations, or public diplomatic confrontations. President Obama got the Nobel Peace Prize without changing a thing except some aggressive terminology used by his predecessor. I see us in a bind that won't be solved by such innocuous measures."

General Simons wriggled in his chair and grimaced before giving his answer, "Mr. President, the Joint Chiefs Planning Division has been on this since the Disney World attack. Here's our folder."

The president thumbed through the sections as General Simons gave a brief summary: "Our options include, first, watching and waiting. That's what Europe wants. They are scared to death that what we do will change a sad disaster into a war that they will inevitably be dragged into. Second, as we were immediately following the 9/11 attack, we would be entirely within our rights to launch a crushing attack on the Saudis, the Iranians, and the Syrians which would be an actual war from the get go. The political consequences would be disastrous, but the great appeasers across the pond would get over it so long as they could claim a complete arms-length distance between them and us and the war. Those are the two extremes. Third, we can leave it to Secretary Southem and the diplomats. Speaking as an old soldier, it seems to me that we have been trying that since Obama was president, and we have had no positive results other than the French think we are nice again. Fourthly, as a military plan, we could launch many—say something on the order of several dozen—small surgical strikes by the Seals or the rangers which would be a sort of low level *lex talionus* approach. It would be readily evident that we were launching the attacks; but the moderates around the globe except the Muslims would come to see such responses as just—even conservative—and we could stand to garner a few grudging kudos. It is the most sensible and the most limited assertive response we could make, but our critics would have a field day with the fact that we would once again be acting as the bully. After some debate, the Joint Chiefs have decided that that is the preferred approach. However there is one more option, sir:"

"And what could that be, General. I'm hungry for a palatable solution."

"Establish a kind of fifth column in the aggressor nations—saboteurs, covert assassins, very careful and covert drone attacks—any kind of nonpublic, deniable, highly secretive, small disruptive actions that would wear the enemies of the U.S. down over time."

"I don't know if our country is much good at that sort of thing, General; and it is a bit late in the day to start a major and top secret training program, no?"

"Well, sir, we do have the precedents—the Revolutionary War and Civil War intelligence operations from both sides, the OSS during World War II, the Phoenix Program during the Viet Nam offensive—all of which were quite successful."

"But not secret enough, I'd say, General. I have to admit that I have only the vaguest recollection of the Phoenix Program. You say it was a success? How so? If I recall correctly, we lost that war, big time."

"With respect, sir. The Phoenix program was extremely successful; and until our press and left leaning politicians—and here I mean no reflection on you personally—Mr. President, but until *they* lost the war for us. We had all but obliterated the Viet Cong, and the NVA would not have advanced had we bombed Hanoi and Haiphong Harbor and sent the message that we were done with the one-arm-tied-behind-the-military's-back policy imposed by the public opinion slash media consciousness that dominated our political establishment. Militarily, that war was won. I admit that the secrets were not well enough kept, and anything done by units like the PRUCs in the Phoenix Program were obviously instigated and carried out by the U.S. military and intelligence establishments. Secrecy was considerably less than was needed; it is obvious in retrospect. In my opinion the worst that could have come out of us capitalizing on our Tet Offensive victories is that the Europeans would not have liked us. That would not have been a big change, nor would it have been one we could not have weathered if only the nonmilitary elements of our government had had the spines to persist."

"Probably some truth in what you say, General; but that was a missed historical opportunity; and we can't go back in time to change anything. One thing you mentioned was an organization called the PRUCs. What was that, exactly?"

"That is just the designation of the officers of the Phoenix Program who saw to it that the actual work got done. It is an acronym like everything in the military—Provincial Reconnaissance Unit Cadres—some pretty rough customers. Like Harry Truman said of Patton, 'he's a son-of-bitch, but he's our son-of-a-bitch'. Or what George Orwell—I think it was—said, 'men sleep peacefully in their beds at night only because rough men stand ready to do violence on their behalf'."

"The concept is all well and good, General," The president said thoughtfully, "but the problem seems to me always to have jammed up on the secrecy issue. I have every respect and confidence in our young and superbly trained military people and in the tough paramilitary elements of the CIA, but to me they always look the part. They look and act like Americans, and we cannot afford for anything to look like our country was involved."

"Well, sir, all I can say is that our Delta Force, the Navy Seals, and Force Recon Marines have done a lot of those 'in the night operations' without their activities coming to the light of day. I tender the offer that we are ready, willing, and able to come up with the personnel and the wherewithal to get the job done whenever you give us the go-ahead. In fact, as you have been reading, we have fairly well worked out plans for any one or all of the options we have discussed."

"And it's good work, too, General. I'll mull it all over pretty thoroughly before giving any final okay to a plan of action. Thank you for coming by."

"My pleasure, sir. We work at your orders and await them."

General Simons recognized that he had been dismissed, stood up and gave a polite nod of his head to the president and exited the Oval Office.

CHAPTER TEN

"Not too hard on you, I hope," Oliver said after Hunter returned from the lie detector vetting. "We'll have the results in about an hour, and we can discuss them together."

"No complaints," Hunter said between mouthfuls of chicken salad sandwich.

"Good. In the meantime, let me tell you a little about the training program we have in mind for you if all goes well in the vetting process, as I'm sure it will. Actually, the polygraph is the last step. We have already had the FBI investigate your every move since you got out of the service. You are clean as a whistle, incidentally."

"You are nothing if not efficient," Hunter said, genuinely impressed if a bit uneasy at the ability to keep the investigative activities a secret from himself until now.

Oliver nodded.

"The standard training these days at the Farm is even more vigorous than when you and I were young, my friend. The physical stuff is about the same, but the sophisticated technological training has advanced by geometric progression. Given your age, no one is going to expect you to keep up with the kids, although you will have to put in a vigorous effort to get back in top shape. You will also have to train with both new and old weapons and in the martial arts, and there you will have to measure up along with everyone else. That will occupy the first month of your stay, and then we will concentrate on mission specific training for a couple of months. The trainers are good, specific, and pretty patient. You'll get the hang of it. I'd like you to stay here in an apartment in the building until you are either approved or disapproved.

Then you can either let your business people know that you are off on an extended vacation; or you get to go home; and none of us ever speaks of the events of today again."

"Okay," Hunter said, although he had not come prepared to be incarcerated for any extended period of time, and mused that he did not even have a toothbrush.

Oliver smiled. As they finished lunch, he explained some of the mundane realities of getting into and working for the Central Intelligence Agency. His main emphasis was on the nondisclosure requirements. Despite the straightforward and direct absolutes of the CIA, it took Oliver half an hour to detail the obligations of agents. He told Hunter that he would be given a contract. That alerted Hunter because he remembered the fundamental differences between contract agents and fully commissioned agents of the agency.

"Hold up, Oliver. I very well recall the difference between contract agents and regular agents. And—at your house—you and the director gave me a promise. I don't think I would be all that interested in having the contract status. I recall from the Phoenix Program that the contractors got hung out to dry when we all went home in April of '75. I won't soon forget that poor smuck, Anders Bergstrom—you know, the one everyone called the white giant ghost—*con ma da trang khong-lo*. Not only did he get screwed royally, but he escaped and did a number on several high officials, according to the scuttlebutt I heard."

Oliver spoke with reluctance, "Hunter. It's the best we can offer. Especially early on. Sorry."

Hunter ignored Oliver's apologetic tone, "Oliver, you can offer what you want. I saw that much today. I'm not some kid just waking up. Try again."

There was a significant pause. Oliver steepled his fingers under his chin and appeared to be in deep thought.

"Maybe I could arrange a probation period, say a year, for you to prove your worth to the higher-ups. Then we could talk full agent status."

"How about three months after training. I either perform, or I'm out. If I perform, I get full benefits of membership—as they say—at the country club."

"You haven't lost your business negotiator's edge, I see, Hunter. I think I can swing that, but there is a problem. The work we have in mind for you will have to be off ledger. So far off that you will never be officially listed in the regular accountings as an employee of any stripe. You will have to be on the books at the Department of Agriculture or some other safe place. That complicates the arrangements."

"I have every confidence in your abilities to arrange, to delegate, and to overcome obstacles, Oliver. Why don't you work on that sort of thing while I languish in your comfortable jail here in the mother-ship building."

Hunter did not like the back-sliding on the deal he had been promised verbally. He looked directly into Oliver's eyes to let him know that that was the final bargain so far as he was concerned. Oliver took note of the fact that his old friend did not mention pay or retirement, or perks. He was making only one demand, and that had to rate well when he took Hunter's proposal back to Homeland Security.

Hunter thought that so long as he was going to take great risks, as all of the indications were that he would, then he wanted to have at least that much status and the very real protection it afforded as opposed to being only a contract agent. His focused eye-to-eye demand somewhat unnerved Oliver, as if he were being threatened.

The ADCIA looked away first.

When the two men parted the next morning, both of them made promises of continuing friendship and strong interest in each others' families, Oliver by expressing his condolences once again, and Hunter by asking after the Prentiss's only daughter, Heather.

"She's the smartest kid in her class, and her class is the sophomore one at Yale. But to say more would be boasting, and that would be unseemly."

That small confession of jingoistic fatherly pride signified the depth of the bond between the two men. Hunter was glad that he had a friend who would watch his back.

CHAPTER ELEVEN

Hunter was bored to tears for three days. On the evening of the third day a sharp knock came on the locked door to his room.

"Enter."

A uniformed marine gunnery sergeant entered and said stiffly, "You are requested to come with me, sir."

Hunter put on the clothes that he had entered the building with the first day and walked to the elevator with the gunny. They descended four floors, and GySgt MacKay led the way into a medium sized office which was well appointed and comfortable.

"Take a seat, sir. The officer will be along shortly."

He turned and left—another man of few words in an organization of tight lipped minions. Oliver Prentiss walked into the office less than a minute later and sat down with familiarity in the desk chair.

"Your office, I presume, Oliver," Hunter said. "Nice."

"Don't get any ideas about taking my office, Hunter. I'll fight for this space...I already did, come to think of it."

Both of the men laughed.

"All right," he said. "Here's what I worked out. You were in the navy and a little note can be slipped into your jacket that says you were in the reserves all the time and have been called up for active duty as a consultant. That is good and nebulous, and it keeps everything strictly on the up and up for paper trailers. It will get a bit more difficult when they try and figure out what it is you do, should they ever take a notion to do that. All of your pay and perks can come through the navy via the Department of

Agriculture. Specifically, you will be on assignment in the NASS; that's the USDA's National Agricultural Statistics Service working on RSS—Rich Site Summary feeds—which means that you will ostensibly be doing research and sending in reports from Web sites that contain article headlines, summaries, and links back to full-text articles on the Web. Your specific interest will be the FAS—Foreign Agricultural Service—searching for anything that can benefit U.S. agricultural markets abroad. Your office—or more accurately, your cubicle—will be a chair, a computer table, and a computer in some large room filled with similar cubicles in the Albert R. Mann Library at Cornell University. In case you don't have a clue—and particularly if you should have some weird hankering to know—that building is located at 260 Tower Road, Cornell University, in Ithaca, New York. If you can't remember any of this you can always look it up on-line. I assure you that there is no need for you ever to see the place or to be seen there."

Hunter laughed out loud. So much detail for so little substance. So much cloak and dagger to guarantee obscurity. It seemed absurd to him, even though he had no disagreement with the purpose of the convolutions.

"Your pay check—in your real name—will be mailed to the Commercial Federal Bank on 17th and Welton in downtown Denver. I'm sure it's familiar to you, and it won't be necessary for you to fill out any papers. If curiosity gets the best of you; and you make the effort to read the documents on file at the bank; you will, no doubt, be surprised to see who you are, where you live, and your place of employment. Except for your name, nothing else will bear the slightest relationship to the truth. You have chosen to forego receiving regular bank statements. You may check your account status by phone or on-line if you are so inclined, but I advise against it. If you really must go in person; go in disguise-a different one every time. Don't plan on making friends with the folks at the bank or even nodding acquaintanships.

"The bank has a number of nice services, including a free one to send all of your checks to an obscure post office box located in Rifle, Colorado. I have all of the details in this folder. You can peruse it at your leisure.

"You'll have to have an alias, or more accurately, several of them. We will make the first one for you for the training period, and then if you survive that; we will get down to cases. Probably, you will get a new cover for every assignment."

"What about my status in the Company?" Hunter asked unwilling to let him talk so long and seductively that Hunter would forget to get that clear.

"Sorry. CIA brass and the president, himself, would not budge on the question of having you be appointed a full fledged officer or even a contract officer. They are never going to allow you or anyone who searches for you to be able to find anything that traces you to The Company. The navy is willing to take you back at the rank you had when you resigned at the end of the war. Incidentally, on your official records as they currently read, that never happened. You'll be a commander with hazard pay. For the training period, you will be kept in the reserves. If all goes well, you will go over to regular navy. When you complete a mission satisfactorily, the CIA brass will contact the DOD, and you will be quietly promoted to captain. From time to time, the Company will give an evaluation report, but it will always appear that it came from somewhere within the Pentagon. It is the best of both worlds for you and for the Company. I can't tell you details, but having the navy connection provides deep cover, so deep that you won't appear on any CIA records; and the navy will have no knowledge of your mission. Your cover will be layers deep. Very few people care what the USDA does except a few farmers in East Cowlip, Iowa. Even fewer care about the NASS. *Nobody* cares a whit about the NASS. You will be about as obscure as it is possible to get.

"Along that line, let me tell you that I will be your only contact in the Company. I can be reached by name at my office here at Langley, or you can get me anytime at the number I'm going to give you. Memorize it and never write it down anywhere. Give the person who answers your code name— Sheep Dog in numerical format 19-8-5-5-16-4-15-7—and add the numbers of today's date, 01-22."

"Sheep Dog?" Hunter asked.

"The DCIA's idea. Something William J. Bennett said in a lecture to the United States Naval Academy on November 24, 1997. He related that one Vietnam veteran, an old retired colonel, once said, 'Most of the people in our society are sheep. They are kind, gentle, productive creatures who can only hurt one another by accident or under extreme provocation—the regular people in society who go about their lives unaware of those who protect them or what they do. 'Then there are the wolves,' the old war veteran was quoted as saying, 'the criminals, foreign enemies, and terrorists; and the wolves feed on the sheep without mercy. There are evil men in this world, and they are capable of evil deeds. The moment you forget that or pretend it is not so, you become a sheep. There is no safety in denial."

Oliver continued, "'Then there are sheepdogs,' Bennett went on, and said, 'I'm a sheepdog. I live to protect the flock and confront the wolf.' Bennett told the midshipmen about a sign in one California law enforcement agency, 'We intimidate those who intimidate others.' Finally, Hunter, you'll be one of the sheep dogs—the warriors, doctors, nurses, and cops—the hard men and women who in the night quietly do what needs to be done—including the unpleasant things—to protect the sheep and to get rid of or at least control the wolves. You have had a good turn at being a sheep dog in the past, and I suspect that your time of malcontent at being one of the sheep is about to stop. That's where it came from."

"I'll try to live up to it."

"I have no doubt."

CHAPTER TWELVE

Hunter's real orders came by telephone, nothing written. The Navy sent official orders to report to Yukusca, Japan. He ignored that and did as the telephone voice instructed him. He was given two weeks to get his affairs in order; and then, he made his way to The Farnthat void on the map in Virginia where CIA, special ops forces, and various foreign forces train in the latest and best weaponry, tactics, attacks, and defenses. Hunter already knew the way, having spent nearly three months there before he shipped out to Viet Nam. When he entered the gate, his mind was inevitably and unpleasantly drawn back to those hard days. He remembered the toughness of the training and the very real rivalries and betrayals that had occurred then. The men and women with whom he had trained and from whom he learned had—more often than not—come from checkered pasts. It had been best not to ask questions or to become too chummy with anyone. They did not send each other Christmas cards.

The best man Hunter knew in training was a young giant of a fellow. He knew him by one name in training, but when he encountered him again in Saigon, he was called by another, Karl Isaacson, and later Anders Bergstrom. He was stronger, faster, smarter, and tougher than anyone else during the training. He had gotten into some sort of deadly fight with the Frenchman, Jean-Luc DuParrier who was born a snake, and hopefully had died as one; and the resultant bad blood between the two of them had outlasted even the war. If even half of the things he had heard about what the Giant White Ghost, or Isaacson or Bergstrom—as he was later called—had done were true, Hunter hoped to avoid running into another one like him, but he quietly determined to be as competent as the guy was before he went bonkers and killed some high ranking U.S. officials after it was all over.

Camp Peary as it is named officially—but better known as The Farm by insiders—is located northeast of the city of Williamsburg, Virginia on the west bank of the York River off Route 5, close to Allmondsville and Croaker. It is an official secret of the CIA, but to no one else apparently. It is enclosed in a twenty-five square mile section of wilderness Virginia running between the highway and the river that serves as a huge training site for CIA agents, infiltrators, covert operators, and for special ops military units as diverse as SEALS, Army Rangers, and Special Forces, Viet Nam war PRU leader trainees, and the Delta Force. Its location is openly discussed by locals and pointed out to tourists. About the only persons unfamiliar with its location are those totally devoid of curiosity, newly arrived, nonpolitical, nonmilitary immigrants, and ardent right-wing religious zealots who accept the fiction of a benign U.S. foreign policy.

The first day at The Farm was casual. Hunter and the other newcomers got moved into simple one-room college dorm living quarters. Every person had a room to him or herself, and nearly half of the new trainees were female and about a quarter were black, a sea change difference from the first time Hunter had trained there—not much political correctness back then. They met in front of their dorm at 0400 the next morning in their running clothes and started the day with a nerve testing cross country run. Despite his personal opinion about his own level of physical conditioning, Hunter was done in by the time they finished, and started coming to grips with the depressing realization that he was not quite the man he had once been and had a great deal of catch-up to do before he could measure up to the extraordinarily fit instructors and young men and women trainees with whom—like it or not—he would have to compete.

For three months, he joined in the traditional training demanded of all new recruits arriving at Camp Peary: harsh runs; grueling calisthenic workouts; weapons training that was triple the speed and quadruple the mind strain that he remembered from navy boot camp or officer training—in the dark, blindfolded, with one hand, etc., etc.—drills to sharpen memory of things seen and things heard; paramilitary stalking, orienteering, GPS reading; communications and computer readiness classes that were as thorough and impatient as those at MIT, or Cal-Tech; quickie language courses to learn the very basics of twenty languages just in case; and courses in a full dozen martial arts from around the world taught by the best of the best—not just the highest ranking black belts, but the most accomplished killers.

The only course where Hunter excelled was the advanced mixed martial arts full contact course which led to a quarter of his trainee class either quitting or being sent away. On a sunny afternoon, he was singled out for a full fight wearing helmet and pads by the Israeli Defense Forces unarmed combat instructor in Krav Maqa, the official IDF commando special units/special forces defense and attack system. Lev Moises was a hard mana hard teacherand a man without patience for those who could not hold their own. He had a very impressive personal record in street fights in Palestine.

Hunter's opponent was a 280 pound body builder from Houston, who bore scars of his own urban battles and was no stranger to real violence. He laughed at Hunter who had graying and receding hair and was outweighed by 80 pounds. Lev brought them to the center of the mat and gave the men his few instructions: they were prohibited from biting, eye-gouging, testicle kicking or tearing, and techniques designed to break an opponent's neck. Otherwise, each man was on his own.

Clinton Ivory rushed at Hunter to terminate his defenses in a blinding explosion of energy and violence. Hunter deftly used Clinton's mad rush to throw him in a graceful somersault to his back. As Clinton rolled up to a semi-sitting position preparatory to going to his feet, he had his back turned to Hunter. The smaller man had an explosive energy of his own. He flew onto Clinton's back, put his neck in a powerful *mata leão*, and applied monkey-feet control of the huge man's legs. Clinton—for all of his superior strength, youth, and agility—was unconscious in less than ten seconds.

Lev brought out five more competitors that afternoon. One was rendered unconscious by a front choke; one suffered a broken leg, one suffered two clavicle fractures; one had a fractured nose and knee; and the final opponent, a woman, lasted nearly three minutes with Hunter until she was knocked unconscious by a spinning back kick. In all, Hunter was on the mat for less than ten minutes. Lev discussed his performance with his superiors; and thereafter, Hunter was one of the instructors, until his three month stint as a regular recruit was finished.

CHAPTER THIRTEEN

April

There was no graduation ceremony and no certificate. On his 91st day at Camp Peary, a soft-spoken, elderly, fit man knocked on Hunter's door, helped him collect his meager belongings, and drove him to a far corner of The Farm to a medium sized rock sided cottage with bars on the windows, terra cotta tile roof which bristled with antennae, and a kennel of the largest, most vicious dogs Hunter had ever seen. Guards patrolled the perimeter regularly with one and sometimes two such dogs on leashes. They were very effective dissuaders for the curious.

His guide opened the door to the cottage and waited for Hunter to enter.

The guide stood in the doorway and said, "Goodbye, agent. You will be joined shortly," turned and left.

Hunter looked around. The front room was rustic but comfortable with hand quilted throws on the furniture, a few white-tail deer shoulder mounts on the log walls, and shiny pale gold stone tiles on the floor. In front of the overstuffed chairs and a divan were two bear skins and a cougar skin. Hunter walked into the kitchen. The cabinet tops and work areas were covered with expensive appearing granite; sinks were pewter colored steel with Grohe faucets. The floor was tiled with sealed and polished blond limestone. Everything was neat and in its place with a proverbial place for everything. The refrigerator was full of fruits, fresh vegetables, lean meats, whole grain breads, European cheese, milk, and orange juice. All health food, Hunter observed—no sweets, no cans, and no packaged foods. The cabinets contained a full stock of cooking utensils, pots, pans, grill ware, cutting and table utensils, glass tumblers, and ceramic cups. Canisters of flour, salt, sugar, brown sugar, coffee and brewable tea stood in neat order against the splash boards on the walls of the cabinet tops. Everything in the room was what was required with no waste and no frills.

The four small bedrooms each had a twin bed that appeared comfortable but was made up with militarily Spartan correct spit and polish. The tables, lamps, and chests of drawers were alike in each room—simple and adequate, but no sense of hominess. The bathrooms likewise had nothing fancy, but were spick-and-span neat and clean as if no one had ever lived there after the house was built in the 1930s.

As he was checking out the pantry, a gruff male voice behind him said quietly, "You John Smith II?"

"I must be," Hunter said, laughing, "but no one told me so."

"Everybody here is John Smith, including me. That would make you really John Smith the 55th, or thereabouts."

Both men laughed. Hunter turned and shook the man's hand. He was tall, very fit appearing, and had a ramrod stiff military bearing. His hair was steel-grey; his skin leathery, and wrinkled. Hunter estimated his age to be about sixty, but it was hard to tell. He had what appeared to be a dueling scar on his cheek, not unlike the one on Hunter's. His eyes were a striking silver-grey with flecks of luminescent green, and he focused them to good intimidative use. He was dressed in olive drab heavy canvas pants and shirt and a regulation army belt and buckle. His shoes were regulation army brown—from a bygone era.

The two men studied each other for a few moments before the other John Smith spoke. "I am your trainer. You and I will live here alone. Hope you're okay with that. I'm not queer; and I hope you aren't either; but if you are, we'll keep our distance."

"Nothing queer about me," Hunter said.

"I will be your mentor, teacher, trainer, confidant, and god father for the next few months. You and I will be pretty much on our own most of the time, but occasionally we will have guest teachers like the marine sniper who will arrive here for lunch with us. He doesn't need to know who you are, what you do, why you do it, or who for; and he won't ask. He will expect you to be a qualified expert marksman already—which you are—then this afternoon he will teach you to really shoot. We will drill on every aspect of being a sniper every day from here on out."

"Sounds good," Hunter ventured.

"He is good—the best. Although you and I will do a lot of physical training together and a lot of martial arts stuff, from time to time we will have other guests who are experts with killing and maiming with bare hands, fingers, feet, knives, little guns, you name it. I know you have had a considerable amount of experience, at least, I presume so; but don't underestimate what these guys will have to teach you. When you leave here in three months, you will be genuinely surprised and pleased at the skill set you have garnered and how much more effective you have become. You would not be one to meet in a dark alley any night after you graduate from the John Smith academy. There have been very few people in the history of this country or any other who have had such in depth training in so many areas related to doing harm to your fellow men and avoiding such harm being done to ones self as you will. You up for it? It'll be a tough course for mind, spirit, and body."

"I'm looking forward to it, John."

"Good, let's eat. You are going to need lots of protein during this three months. We'll have steak, eggs, a veggie, and milk for lunch. Suit your fancy?"

"Yeah, I'm starved."

John and John worked side be side quickly and efficiently to serve up a heavy duty meal.

As they ate, John—the teacher—said, "Oh, there's a rule you need to know and obey. I don't know or care what you did in your former life; but here with me, there's no tobacco, recreational drugs, or alcohol. Can you live with that?"

"Sure. You sound like a Mormon. My son lived like that for twenty years after he converted to their church. I guess I can do that much."

"That was more than I needed to know, but I know their ethic. I've worked with a few of them and liked their lifestyle. Especially the part about having as many wives as you want," he smiled wryly.

Hunter laughed and sighed, "That's history. Too bad for you and me."

At 1300 sharp, a rap came on the door. John opened the door for a twenty to twenty-two-year-old Hispanic man dressed in camo from his hat to his boots. He was barely five-seven, dark and wiry, with a two millimeter haircut. He had dark, intelligent eyes, the high cheek bones of a Mayan, and strong, sinewy arms and hands. He was carrying a rifle case and had two different style gillie suits draped over his arm. In his other hand he had a small brief case. He did not venture a smile.

John—the teacher—said simply, indicating John—the student—"This is the sniper. We'll go out on the range now."

The sniper nodded a greeting. The two Johns nodded back, and the three men hiked up a low hill behind the house. On the top, Hunter viewed a full rifle range and a government-issue grey building on the east that he presumed to be the pistol range. John Smith I handed Hunter—John Smith II—a pair of binoculars and pointed at a target 800 meters in the distance. It was shiny brass an—despite the distance—it was readily visible through the binoculars. Hunter took note of the paper cutout of a man who was pointing a rifle at them. Hunter nodded his understanding. Then John Smith I pointed further up the far hill above the 800 meter mark at a second target which was painted a brilliant blaze orange. Similarly that target had a paper cutout of a menacing character.

The sniper spoke next, "There are two targets—one at 800 meters and the second at 1600 meters. We will work on the closer target first. When you can put five shots consistently in the heart at .5 MOV, we will turn our concentration to the further target and repeat the exercise. Next, we'll practice, practice, practice on hitting the sniper's T Kill Zone; that's the imaginary T formed by a horizontal line half way across the eye brows on each side and vertical line straight down the nose from the horizontal to the chin."

He opened the gun case and took out what appeared to be a pile of leaves and branches and handed it to Hunter.

"This is your ghillie suit poncho. I have a second one for you in a desert pattern. For the work I understand you need to do, this offers the best chance to move quickly and to avoid being seen in the camo. Please put it over you and assume the prone position."

Hunter was familiar with the ghillie suit—a type of camouflage clothing that is designed to break up the human outline and help the wearer blend into nature—but had not seen the poncho style. He remembered that the jump suit and the two piece style he had used in Viet Nam were somewhat cumbersome to put on and take off and were a real impediment to running. He could stow the poncho quickly or ditch it at a moment's need and could see the reasoning in the trade-off with the poncho allowing more mobility and the other styles' somewhat more effective camouflage. The poncho, made of military grade synthetic thread, looked remarkably like heavy foliage. It consisted of an inner shell of sound-insulated, soft, nonitchy cloth covered with netting and the synthetic string in a piled leaves woodland pattern.

Hunter took the poncho, lay down prone, and pulled the camouflage gear over his body with his head in the fitted pouch at one end. The sniper lifted an immaculately clean and recently oiled Steyr-Mannlicher SSG-69 PII sniper rifle and placed it carefully in Hunter's hands. The SSG-69 is the Austrian Army's standard issue sniper rifle, the PII is the police modified civilian version of the same weapon. The SSG is extremely accurate and several international competitions have been won with it.

The sniper said, "This is the best sniper rifle money can buy which is not made in the United States. I personally tested and set the sights."

He affectionately patted the ZF69 scope.

"I guarantee that the weapon can shoot with an accuracy of sub .5 MOA; and in the last three days, I've personally fired five round sets which were consistently sub .25 MOA. The ZF69 scope is graduated for firing out to 800 meters; but of course, you can still hit a target at 1600, although your spread will increase; and you will have to be content with a chest shot. I like the PII because of its heavier contour barrel with no iron sites, and it has an enlarged bolt handle."

Hunter remembered the definition of MOA—a minute of arc or arcminute is a unit of angular measurement, approximately one inch at 100 yards, a traditional distance on *target* ranges. The usual use of the term refers to *shooting* an average of 1-inch groups at 100 yards with greater accuracy being expressed in fractions of the standard inch groupings. He was aware that the groupings would spread the greater the distance of the target from the point of firing and that adjustments of the scope would be required to compensate for the distance factor, but he could not remember the formula for compensation for distance and/or windage. He was pretty sure that the sniper would refresh his memory; so, he did not advertise his inadequate knowledge and memory.

The sniper opened his brief case and took out three Boze over-the-ear sound suppressors, and each man put one on. He mimed to Hunter about loading the sniper rifle's magazine, and Hunter took the proffered 10 round box magazine of 7.62 X .51 NATO ammunition and snapped it into place. Hunter then took a moment to adjust the length of pull from 12¾ inches to 14 inches by adjusting the removable spacers in the butt of the ABS Cycolac synthetic half stock. This helped him to compensate for the moderate weight—4.6 kg—of the weapon with its long 25.6 inch barrel. He gently fingered the triggers, double set for extra control and accuracy, and waited for the command to fire, trying not to hold his breath.

"Caution on the range," the sniper ordered although none of them could hear his voice.

"Fire five rounds at will," he said and gestured to Hunter with five upraised fingers.

Hunter took a breath, let it out slowly and fired the first round.

The sniper shook his head as he watched through field binoculars as the first round connected two inches to the side of the paper target cut-out's head. Hunter looked up at the sniper who held up two fingers and shook his head. Hunter fired the second round and looked up again to see two fingers. He was flinching. He took care to squeeze the triggers for the third shot rather than to pull on them as he had been doing which obviously was creating a jerking as he fired and was unacceptable.

The third round gained a gesture from the sniper of an O formed by his thumb and index finger of his right hand and a finger passing through the O. Bulls eye. Hunter set his teeth in determination and fired the next two rounds in quick succession. The sniper handed him the binoculars. Hunter found the holes in the target for all five rounds. There were the two holes to the left of the target's head and three in the head with a spread of about two inches between each of the three. He knew they would have been kill shots, but he was also quite sure that the sniper would scoff at his limited accuracy.

The sniper and John Smith II removed their sound suppressors and indicated to Hunter to do the same.

"Not bad for a rookie," the sniper said with a grin.

Hunter shrugged, chagrined.

"Do it again."

Hunter lay in the uncomfortable prone position firing round after round. As he did, he was annoyed by the relative effort required for cycling the bolt action, but realized that his accuracy was not impaired so long as he concentrated. After each five rounds, a new paper man automatically snapped into position on the metal target. After two hours of firing, Hunter's last five sets were grouped in .50 to .25 MOA distances apart, and the sniper nodded his grudging approval.

It was now 1515 hours, and Hunter's powers of concentration were wearing thin. The sniper recognized his pupil's problem and called for a rest. The three men ate candy bars, and Hunter closed his eyes for a power-nap. The sniper and John Smith II nodded their approval of their student's ability to fall into a brief refreshing sleep, a trait that would likely stand him in good stead during arduous times while he was on mission assignments.

Hunter slept for fifteen minutes, then abruptly awakened and was fully alert.

"Okay, sleeping beauty," said John Smith II, "let's get back to work."

"Sorry, I guess my eyes got tired."

"No need to apologize, John, you need to be able to rest when you can. Later, we'll do drills to push you to the point of exhaustion and force you to perform; and that will be a real test of your powers, believe me."

"Okay, John," said the sniper, "now let's go for the 1600 meter target. Same drill. You'll shoot until you can at least make a good head shot, but preferably, you should be down to .50 MOA, all right?"

"I'm ready."

The men replaced their over-the-ears sound suppressors; Hunter cloaked himself in the camouflage poncho, adjusted his telescopic sights as best he could estimate for the distance to account for the expected errors of parallax, and fired off three rounds in rapid succession. None of them hit the head, but all were close and all were grouped to the left of the target's head. Hunter reworked the adjustments and fired off two more. One was dead on between the target's eyes, and the second was slightly above and to the left of the first.

"*That was pretty good shooting,*" he said to himself.

The sniper lifted Hunter's sound suppressors and said quietly, "Bad job, John. You fired three useless misses, alerted your target; and he wasn't there for the fourth and fifth. By the end of that series of shots, the enemies had tri-angulated in on you, fired off a rocket; and you were toast. You and me have to go back to school; so, you can get the adjustment formulas down pat and can make the alterations fast. Otherwise, you are going to be a useless dead sniper. In the real situation you'll need to make chest shots."

Hunter's temper flared, but he held his peace. His rational mind told him loudly that the sniper was altogether correct. There was no room for error in this lethal game. A miss here and there on the range didn't get you killed; but the real world was most unforgiving; Viet Nam had taught him that, if nothing else. He gritted his teeth, made minor adjustments, and fired the next five rounds. All of them placed in the head, three in the T Kill Zone. He estimated the MOA as less than 2 and maybe as close as 1 for a couple of them. Not perfect, but the target was dead, not him.

The sniper took the rifle, lay beside Hunter, and did a few quick mental cal-culations, then tweaked the adjustment knobs. He fired sets of two, checked the accuracy with his binoculars, tweaked again after each set, and on the last set put three shots at less than .50 MOA in the T. Then, he handed the rifle back to Hunter.

Hunter was impressed. He had always been a good shot, but never that good. He was determined not to be beaten by the young upstart. He sucked in a big breath, let it out, did it again, and fired off five shots into a fresh target's head. The grouping was less than two inches top to bottom and three inches side to side and was centered on the middle of the target's forehead.

The sniper lifted Hunter's sound suppressors and whispered, "beginner's luck. But you'll get the brain stem if you fire a trifle lower."

Hunter flashed him a good-natured finger, reloaded and re-fired. The sniper finally stopped him after five more near-perfect sets, all near enough to the T to have killed a living target.

"Okay, good job. But you're lucky there's no wind. Tomorrow, we are going to have a big wind machine up here, and we're going to use a sound suppressor for your shots. Both of those factors will add a measurable degree of difficulty; and we will be at it all day, I'll bet. I'll also have you concentrate on the chest for a lot of your shooting."

Hunter remembered that John Smith I had said that he had his marksmanship medal, but that the sniper would teach him how to shoot. That was certainly an accurate prophecy. He was pleased with himself, and was gradually beginning to feel that he was getting back into the groove.

Back at the house, the men showered, made a hearty stew and a salad, and drank diet sodas. After they rested for an hour, the sniper and John Smith II led Hunter into a projection room. There were no comfortable overstuffed chairs there, just regulation metal desks and chairs.

The sniper delivered a lecture on sighting and shooting.

"Here is a book on my lecture; so don't worry overmuch about taking notes. I'm sorry to say, but to do your work well and safely, you are going to have to know this stuff. I'll start at the bottom line for simplicity's sake. Your beautiful rifle has a beautiful, but modified scope. It is a Zeiss 6-24 X 72. The SAM, or Shooter-supporting Attachment Module, which measures and provides aiming and ballistic relevant data and displays this to you in the ocular of the sight it is developed for."

The instructor detailed the relevant information about the SAM's has different integrated sensors integrated and how it calculates the actual ballistic compensation.

"It memorizes up to four different ballistics and four different firing tables and displays the info into the ocular. So it is possible to use one SAM with four total different weapons without an additional adjustment. It will do most of your work for you. The scope is mounted on the tough Zeiss ZM/VM mounting rail system in case you bang your weapon around, which you will. The BDC—Bullet Drop Compensation of ballistic elevation feature—

we have had incorporated assists you in compensating for wind drift, air density, and for different cartridges."

He smiled. Hunter shook his head and smiled back.

"*Go ahead and gloat, sonny, your day will come,*" he muttered inwardly.

"Of course, you have a mil dot reticle for stadiametric rangefinding; so, you have a personal visual means of estimating ranges in addition to the fancy automatic stuff. You will be a trained user, and trained users can relate accurately the range to objects of known size, the size of objects at known distances, and can compensate for BDC and for wind drift at known ranges which allows you to make a mental note about the accuracy of what the gadgetry is telling you."

The sniper and John Smith I alternated during a three-hour lecture on reticles, parallax compensation, bullet drop compensation formulae, integrated laser range finders, preferences for scope bases, rings, mounting rails, and rail interface systems, optical parameters including magnification and objective lens diameters, the value and problems of variable lens, field of view, and exit pupil size.

Hunter looked quizzically at John when he said 'exit pupil size' because he had never heard the term.

John said, "That's defined as the objective lens diameter divided by the magnifying power. All you need to know is that ordinarily, that number should equal the diameter of the dilated iris of the human eye, about 7 mm. That is usually reduced by factoring the age of the shooter, and yours would be closer to 6 mm. However, a larger exit pupil size makes it easier for the shooter's eye to find the light source and to fix on the target more quickly, especially if the target is moving. Yours has been set to 9 mm for that reason, and the diminution of focus is compensated for, we think, by all of the other features of the telescope, especially the best lenses in the world, in our opinion."

Hunter was astounded at the specificity that had gone into customizing his sniper rifle. He knew that it had to have cost the government a mint to produce such a one-of-a-kind rifle and sighting system.

John went on to tell Hunter that the government had also provided three other rifles and that all of them were manufactured outside the United States for plausible deniability. The other rifles were of more common occurrence and even less suggestive of the U.S. origin than his highly customized gun.

"Tomorrow and the next day we'll fire your standard issue 1891/30 rifle from the former USSR, and the Beretta M501 from Italy. We have some silencers for you to get used to. They are much improved from the Viet Nam era. In particular, the new ones allow a much more effective range. You look beat. Grab whatever you want to eat. At the crack of dawn tomorrow we'll go on our little constitutional run with a few twists, then the three of us will indulge in a little boyish fighting to warm up for the day's shooting."

"Sounds great to me," Hunter said.

It was getting late. He had never been a late-nighter, and this night he was so worn out that his speech was slowing and in half an hour would be slurred. He forgot to brush his teeth or to take off his clothes and fell asleep lying prone cross-wise on his bed.

CHAPTER FOURTEEN

Hunter awakened before the 0630 witching hour and was proud of himself for being out of bed when John Smith knocked softly on his door.

"Nice day for a run," John said.

"I'm ready," Hunter said and quietly cursed the shoelaces on his running shoes for getting knotted.

He was fully alert and out of his room in half a minute with his shoes tied with an extra knot. The two men set a hard pace as soon as they left the house. The dogs snarled and barked, and their K-9 keepers snarled orders to be quiet which the dogs obeyed instantly. John led the way along a twisting path through the adjacent elm tree woods which required them to concentrate to avoid running into trees or branches. John abruptly turned and headed straight up a fifty yard incline and waited for Hunter on the ridge top. Hunter hated to admit it, but he knew when he was beaten.

"So, I have more work to do," he said, mildly chagrined by his deep inspirations.

He fought the urge to put his hands on his knees to help him to catch his breath and to prevent syncope. That would be the ultimate humiliation.

"Any idea why we just took that path?"

"Sure I do. I have to be in better shape in the case where I have to run away to avoid capture or being shot in the back."

"Bright fella."

John smiled, and Hunter laughed.

"We'll see," Hunter said. "this isn't over. We'll have this conversation again at the end of the three months."

It was John's turn to laugh.

"Ready for more lessons?"

"Show-off."

He knew that he had just been subjected to his first object lesson of the day.

John set off again. This time he sprinted from one large tree or rock to another, stepped out of sight, then burst out again. Hunter took the hint and copied him. After half an hour, he was sweating profusely, but found himself becoming more able to capitalize on the brief periods of rest afforded by the momentary hiding efforts. That was a lesson—number two.

John led Hunter back to the cottage's lawn at a sprint, then stopped abruptly, and stood waiting for Hunter to catch up. Hunter was puffing and nearly out of breath. John suddenly whirled around and performed a deft hip throw—*Osae-Komi-Uki-Goshi*—putting Hunter cleanly on the ground and straddled the still very much out of breath Hunter in the Jiu Jitsu mount position.

Hunter was afraid he would suffocate or black out or have to tap out. He held John off from getting a choke utilizing the minimum of effort while he caught his breath. He moved elbows and knees and bucked his hips to keep John off balance. He remembered his Brazilian Jiu Jitsu instructor's lessons on breathing and staying in the fight and living. He took in short small breaths and exhaled in long slow breaths through pursed lips. Gradually, despite his struggles and the skill of his opponent, Hunter grew aware that he was able to breath normally again. His heart rate slowed even though his defensive efforts were still only about three-quarters of his full energy capacity.

He now made a display of being short of breath, reached up and laid his fingers softly on John's tree-branch hard arm, the preparatory motion to a tapping which would signal Hunter's submission. He felt the vice-like grip of John's strong thighs on his lower chest relax ever so slightly. In an instant, Hunter threw his hips up to full extension then dropped them back to the ground even more quickly. He rolled quickly but minimally to his left side while John's body was separated from his by a fraction. He was able to throw his right knee under John's thigh and to hold him away from his own torso effectively. Hunter could feel that John was off-balance. He locked his hand on John's right wrist, scissor-kicked upward and to his own left and turned John over. Now he was in the guard position—not a full advantage, but light years better than where he had been two seconds previously.

John smiled benignly up at Hunter, "Nice," he said as he tapped Hunter's arm.

It was no tap-out, but Hunter had learned lessons two and three: Never let down your guard and get caught with a sucker move, and work to get time to regain your breath and to let your brain and body find the energy resources earned by hard training and to use the skills you worked into your muscle memory. Oh, and there's no such thing as a fair fight; that would only be a failure of your tactics.

Hunter nodded.

"Thanks. I will try not to forget the tutorial. It won't be as easy for you to sucker me next time, and you might pick up a bruise or two."

"Give me a minute to stop trembling," John mocked.

"Time for breakfast…unless you're too tired," Hunter said as he stood up and offered John his hand.

They ate cooked oatmeal fortified with brown sugar, raisins, and cream. Hunter downed two glasses of orange juice and a piece of toast with crunchy peanut butter and apricot-marmalade jam. The sniper arrived ten minutes late, and both Hunter and John raised a quizzical eyebrow as he came through the doorway.

"Had some stuff to round up," the sniper said laconically.

Through the open door, Hunter and John turned to see the sniper's 1038 version HMMWV four man troop/cargo carrier with an attached small covered trailer. The vehicle had a very large winch on the front and a very high ground clearance owing to having had a sixty inch deep water fording kit applied after manufacture—by the sniper himself, it turned out.

"Sweet ride, no?"

"Whatever gets you off," John replied, remembering his own experience with the rough ride related to the absence of shock absorbers or cushions on the seats as he recalled.

"Ready for a big day?"

Hunter answered, "Sure. We've had a restful morning, who wouldn't be?"

John just smiled.

The three men piled in and headed to the same rifle range as the previous day. The hill they climbed then was clearly not navigable to any ordinary truck or car, but the humvee moved sprightly up the 60% [31º] slope as easily as most trucks moved up a 5% grade. Near the top, the sniper turned to the right and traversed the side slope which was approaching a 40% [22º] incline. Hunter was sitting on the downhill side and made it a point not to look down. The humvee moved along as if it had claws. For the fun of it—boys will be boys—the sniper took off along the ridgeline at the vehicle's maximum speed of 55 mph powered by the 6.2 liter, 3,600 rpm engine, presumably reworked by the sniper in his copious free time. Hunter was sure that he would pee blood before this day was out. He decided that he was too old for this sort of fun as it was apparent from the sniper's face that this was something approaching ecstasy in the fun department.

The sniper made an overly sharp and bone jarring turn and put the three men at the same location where they had had the marathon shooting drills the day before.

"We're here, gentlemen. Everybody out."

Both Hunter and John breathed theatrical sighs of relief and hobbled out as fast as their stiff and sore muscles and joints could move them.

"Today we're gonna do the same as last, but today we're gonna work a little fast to quote Harry Belafonte," the sniper quipped, "and we're gonna do some quite different stuff. After today, you'll be on your own to practice. That's how you get to Carnegie Hall—practice, practice, practice," he laughed.

John rolled his eyes.

"Bring your weapon, John?"

"Whatta you think?"

"Good man. But I brought an updated version. I'll trade you."

He reached into the trailer and brought out a very long camo gun case. Hunter pulled out the sniper rifle and noted the attachment of a silencer.

"This is the best there is," the sniper said, "the same SSG-69 PII sniper rifle but this time with a permanently attached chrome molybdenum 4130 steel sound suppressor. Chrome moly steel is hard, tough, very durable, and holds its zero so long as it's properly attached. It takes non-reflective surfaces—Parkerizing—and holds paint very well. Paint is now the coating of choice, since it is corrosion resistant, and can be easily changed to camo. Baked on polymers are great as well, but I thought it would look too much like American manufacture; so, I went with paint. Incidentally, a suppressed rifle should be stored and carried in its assembled, ready-to-go configuration.

"We've all have seen action thrillers in which a spy or a sniper carries a fitted case full of components—stock, action, barrel, forearm, scope, mount and silencer—which was then assembled quickly in the field, and then used to complete an important assassination, sometimes with more than one shot. That is pure *Hollywood*. No military sniper or law enforcement officer in his right mind would ever assemble a rifle on the spot on an assignment and expect the weapon to hold its zero. It might, but such an occurrence would be a rarity. Some suppressors cause shots to stray with various degrees of tightness or looseness on a rifle's barrel. My testing indicates that a rifle with a suppressor fixed permanently in place with a properly executed, two-point, conical, tensioned barrel mount will remain in zero. This zero remains even after the suppressor has been removed for cleaning and replacement. As long as the replacement torque is close to the same, the zero will be unaffected—and I mean no discernable, cold shot shift after a day, a week, or a year, at 180 to 2000 m.

"If you're going to suppress a sniper rifle, that rifle should he totally dedicated to suppressed fire. Using a rifle which is only occasionally silenced is an invitation to either a lawsuit for law enforcement or to poor field shooting, which is the crucial issue for you who will not likely be able to get off more than a couple or three shots in as many seconds, since any rifle will carry a different zero without a suppressor, as opposed to its zero with one."

Hunter nodded his understanding and said, "So, let's shoot."

"Let's."

The weapon was heavy, considerably heavier than the comfortable rifle he had become fairly proficient with the day before. The sniper briefly described the particular suppressor he had chosen for Hunter's sniper rifle.

"The suppressor—and that's the politically correct term—since the public sees hit men and other murderers as the only people who would use a 'silencer' is a modified LRM M1 169 upper on an AR15/M16 type platform. The modification is for the NATO supersonic ammo you'll be using instead of the 9 mm used in the regular production. It's long—12.75 inches—and weighs 4 pounds, 4½ ounces. With the suppressor plus the upper half, the whole set-up comes to 21.5 inches. It is admittedly cumbersome, and you will have to practice, practice, practice to get used to it and to be effective. I'll tell you, though, this thing keeps its zero through any amount of shooting and most abuse. You won't be able to sneak it through TSA or customs; so, your friendly Company friends will have to get it to you in the diplomatic bag."

The sniper was right. The weapon was unwieldy in Hunter's unpracticed hands. He could not fire it with any hope of accuracy standing cowboy style. He fired round after round from the prone position and from a semi-sitting-one-knee-up position. He felt himself getting discouraged as he fired dozens of rounds that were no closer than 2 MOA. After a two hour stint, he took a breather, wiped the sweat from his brow and hands, clenched his teeth, and determinably started again. Finally, half an hour later, his shots on the 800 m target were coming fairly consistently in the sub 1 MOA area for five consecutive shots. After another half an hour, something clicked in, and he ceased finding it such a strain. It was like learning how to drive a stick-shift vehicle. Once you understand the feel of the clutch lifting up and the accelerator pushing down smoothly together, it is difficult to remember why it was so hard to do earlier. He had been at it for four and a half hours before the sniper called a lunch break.

"How do you think you're doing, John?"

Hunter answered the sniper with his learning-to-drive analogy. The sniper smiled his understanding.

"Let's chow down and then work on the 1600 meter target, okay?"

"Yeah. I'm beginning to feel like I get it. I'll have to shoot a thousand rounds before I get really confident, though."

"More like two thousand."

The three men ate two BLTs each and downed a couple of liters of bottled water. Hunter took a twenty minute power nap and awoke fully refreshed. He was gradually getting back into his LRRP form from Viet Nam and remembered his long range reconnaissance patrol experience with more fondness than he had at the time.

John I announced, "It's time to get on with it. I know you've got more toys than this in your little vehicle and trailer."

The sniper nodded his agreement, but he said, "first our novice sniper has to learn to shoot a man on the run. I've arranged for a cardboard man to dart between two walls. His trip will take two seconds. There was a sniper in Fallujah who killed something like 32 men in five days at 800 yards, a significant number of which met the conditions you are going to be in during the next hour or so. When you can hit five targets in a row in a kill zone, you graduate."

CHAPTER FIFTEEN

White House, 0630: Daily CIA Briefing
Present: POTUS, DCIA

The sleepy president, still in his white pajamas with a White House emblem pattern, gestured to Gerald Lang to sit in front of The presidential desk while he settled into his own large leather swivel chair.

"I have some early appointments, Director. Let's get right into the meat of the briefing."

The jowly DCIA began in the quiet, precise, monotone for which he was known, "Mr. President, we have two items that matter. The first is that overnight two arrests were made. Our operatives apprehended a terrorist..."

The president shook his head.

"A facilitator," Director Lang said, working to suppress his disdain for the euphemism, "was apprehended attempting to board a flight from Lagos Murtala Muhammed International Airport to Detroit Wayne County Airport. Our people had been watching him for the past five weeks. He's on the TIDE list—along with 550,000 other...uh, facilitators—and has been active in a mosque known to be a recruiting site."

"Refresh my mind, director, what's TIDE?"

"It's a mouthful. It's the National Counterterrorism Center's massive Terrorist Identities Datamart Environment database. Our friend, Umar Betullah Moussaoui—no relation to the famous Zacharias—lives in a section of Lagos called Akinogun. Early last night, we watched him go into his house looking slim and come out in a trench coat looking fat. Our operatives there—who are, incidentally, indigenous folks—followed Umar's beat-up 1950 Russian "ZIS"—Zavod Imieni Stalina—Model 110 in their equally beat up 1940's Ford pick-up along Idimu Road to the Abeokuta Express and off onto the Agege Motor Road. There, a cut-out unit followed him onto Airport Road. They parked a couple of spaces away from him and followed him into the terminal. He headed directly into the exit way bypassing security without a soul bothering him, and our guys tackled him. He had on a suicide vest and carried a very sharp Yoshi Blade ceramic knife. He had no ID, no passport, and no ticket; but somehow, he had gotten what appeared to be a valid boarding pass. Fortunately for all concerned, the surprise was complete; and he was unable to detonate his huge bomb made of high grade PETN. We had a discussion with him before turning him over to the Nigerian authorities, and he was quite forthcoming."

The president raised an eyebrow.

"I haven't gotten the details of the level of intensity of the discussion, Mr. President," the director lied.

"Maybe it'd be better if I didn't know."

"Might well be, sir."

"Good work."

"Indeed…this time, but it is worrisome that still something like half of the world's major airports have not initiated our demands for their security. Anyhow, that is the first arrest. And incidentally, our Nigerian counterparts took a dim view of Mr. Moussaoui's activities. It appears that they intend to be somewhat more direct with the fellow than we were. Perhaps we will gain some more insight into the underbelly of Nigerian politics."

"You said there were two arrests."

"Yes, sir. The second one is somewhat more of a problem. Faizah Batool al-Faisal—the name means victorious ascetic virgin—a young, very well educated girl, a physician—was rounded up in a raid by the National Security Agency, one of Yemen's two main intelligence organizations, in a basement bomb making factory in Sana'a. She was caught in the very act as the Bible would say. She had a sophisticated fuse in her hand and several bomb making guides in her clothing when she was grabbed by the Yemenis. They have not laid a hand on her and have not interrogated her beyond learning her name, since then for a couple or three reasons."

"Which are?"

"First, she looks like she has a lot of information; second, she has extensive contacts with Hamza Ali Saleh al Dhayani, AKA Aldhaini and al Dhajani, who is a prime suspect in the September 17, 2008 suicide attack on the U.S. Embassy in Yemen that killed 16 people, including an American citizen. Yemen also named him as a suspect in mortar attack on the U.S. Embassy in March of the same year. Our sources indicate that al Dhayani was the recruiter and driving instructor for the suicide car bomber who murdered eight elderly Spanish tourists in Mareb in July 2007. Dhayani is a Mareb under the protection of the Jahm tribe and is immune to Yemeni prosecution—it's sort of like diplomatic immunity; third, and most important—although we can't establish it beyond doubt—Dr. al-Faisal, appears to be closely related to the Saudi royal family. We think she is a niece of King Abdallah; and, further, we have reason to believe that she may be married to a brother of Prince Nayef bin Abdulaziz."

"Head of *Istakhbarat*, the Saudi Intelligence Service?"

"The very same."

The president's face visibly blanched.

"Fourth, she was educated at Vassar as an undergrad, Yale for a masters in nuclear physics, Harvard Medical School for her M.D., and at Johns Hopkins for her radiology residency, largely a research type of post grad program.

"Aren't you full of good news."

"I'm just the messenger, Mr. President."

"Now what?"

"I'll have to send that ball back to your court, sir. Everyone everywhere is handling this with the utmost secrecy and delicacy. The Yemenis have said point blank that they want nothing to do with her, and want you, Mr. President, to tell them what to do next. They insist that she is an American citizen. She insists that she is a Saudi and therefore cannot be extradited. She is confident that she will not be subjected to Yemeni interrogation, and demands to be sent to Saudi Arabia where she can face any criminal charges that might be in the offing. She is no dummy, sir; and she is sure that she has us over a barrel."

"I'll have to ponder a bit on this, Gerald. I'll get back to you."

"Yes, Mr. President. I'll await your instructions."

The president shuffled a few papers, the usual signal that the daily briefing was over; and Director Lang made his exit.

CHAPTER SIXTEEN

The three shooters all assumed prone positions on the low rise that looked over the field of fire between them and the two distant targets. The sniper insisted that Hunter cover himself all the time he was shooting to help him to get used to the somewhat uncomfortable camouflage cloak. Hunter was then ordered to fire at a moving target with his now familiar SSG-69. It took an hour before he could kill 5 targets in a row. He asked to continue with five more before he was satisfied.

"Do I graduate?" Hunter asked, smiling at the sniper.

"Not quite. I have some more toys for you."

"Hey, you promised."

"I lied."

The three men laughed, and the sniper fetched two well-worn old canvas gun cases and handed each of the men a handsome, but obviously old, sniper rifle.

"This is the model 1891/30 Sniper rifle. These rifles were used all over the world for much of the 20th century and are still available to killers in under-developed areas because they are cheap, accurate, and reliable. The weapon is no match against your SSG-69, but it is very useful. It has the distinct advantage to you—John—in that it is unquestionably of Russian—even Soviet—origin and cannot be traced to the U.S. To create the sniper version of these rifles, high quality examples of the 1891/30 were pulled off of the Russian stock production line in the early 1920s. The Sovs specifically looked for high quality barrels. They took these hand picked rifles and then turned the bolts down for operation while using a scope. They mounted a scope using either the PV (4x) or PU (3.5x) version. There was no bayonet issued, and the trigger was lightened. The 1891/30 Sniper proved to be exceptional, probably the best in World War II. The rifles were mass-produced, with as many as 330,000 of the sniper variants being produced between 1941 and 1943; and, therefore, there are tens of thousands of them floating around the world unregistered and uncontrolled. If either of you were in Viet Nam, you might have seen them around, since the NVA used them as their preferred sniper rifle.

"We have put in a new trigger because the originals had a lot of trouble, and the original wood of the stock had warped from use in wet conditions; so, we replaced it. The rifles are long and heavy and a bit awkward in the field. Nevertheless, these rifles were very accurate and remain so—average accuracy is about 1.5 MOA. This particular one tests out at below 1 MOA."

Hunter admired the handsome long rifle and recognized it from among the weaponry he had taken from dead NVA during his years as a LRRP, and from occasional captures in the later Phoenix Program.

"So, lock and load. John, let's see you put in five sets at 800 yards. We'll move on when you can get to 1.5 MOA or better."

Hunter examined the rifle carefully, worked to get the heft and balance adjusted to his needs, and found it longer and heavier than his SSG-69. His first set of five were all placed in the head of the target cutout, but at about 2.0 MOA. He steadied himself, and his next five were at 1.5 MOA, and the next three sets of five after that were all close to 1.0 MOA.

"Good enough, John. Go for the 1,600 meter target."

Hunter took three sets to get to 1.5 MOA and could not improve on that. However, his self-esteem was preserved by seeing through the spotting scope that every shot was in the head. It might not win a shooting contest, but every shot would have been a dead terrorist.

"That was good and fast. Keep practicing, but I doubt that you are going to be able to get to 1.0 with any consistency. We'll try another rifle now."

The sniper brought out a Beretta M501.

"This sniper rifle is the Italian Army standard. It has a five round detachable box magazine and a heavy-duty free-floating harmonic balancer with four grooves which is contained within a tube hidden in the front end of the stock, a nice piece of technology which is used to reduce the vibrations of the barrel, helping to improve accuracy. It fires 7.62 X 51 mm NATO rounds. I prefer synthetic stocks, but this wood stock has a nice feeling contour. The rifle is issued to Italian snipers with 1.5-6 X 42 mm Zeiss scope. It is not available outside the Italian army. This weapon comes to you courtesy of the company you work for."

"Let's test it out," Hunter said enthusiastically.

If nothing else, he admired the rifle's beauty. It was the most comfortable of all of the rifles he had thus far handled. It was lighter and easier to move about and to fix on a target. The best thing about the gun was that after an initial five round set of 1.5 MOA, Hunter developed a feel for the weapon and shortly was able to put nearly every set at 0.5 MOA at 800 meters and after the very first attempt at 1,600 meters, he was able to score 0.75 and 0.5 MOAs every set. All of his shots would have been lethal, and half were in the T Kill Zone.

"Like that one, amigo?" asked the sniper.

"This baby is downright fun. Let's be sure it gets into the bag when I go someplace."

John I said, "Already on the official list, John. You have three beautiful weapons at your disposal, and none of them is traceable to you or even to the USA. Hard to beat that."

Hunter nodded his approval and appreciation. Next, he shot at moving targets; and like his stick-shift driving analogy, he was comfortable with the new rifle and missed only one rapidly moving target, having overestimated the required lead time on that one. It was now only 1430.

"Ready for a change of pace, my friends?"

"Bring on the rest of the toys," urged Hunter. "This is getting to be the most fun I've had in years."

The sniper went to his HMMWV and pulled out a boxy looking weapon with multiple barrel ends visible, something like a small Gatling Gun barrel and a Tommy gun magazine. He held them out for the two Johns and said, "This is my personal favorite for relatively close range. It is a crowd clearer and a house vermin exterminator. It has a tremendous fear factor. You can't dodge it, and most of the stuff the bad guys want to hide behind is useless for them.

"This is an Atchisson Assault Shotgun or Combat AA-12 Combat shot gun. This drum magazine holds 32 rounds. It is a fully automatic, gas operated, and can fire 300 rounds per minute. The standard issue shotgun can use many different types of cartridges such as hardened 00 buck shot, #4 bird shot, 12-bore lead slugs, or less-than-lethal rubber stun batons. It can also fire flares or special Frag-12 18.5 mm fin-stabilized HE, HEAP, and sensor fused HEAB air-burst fragmentation shells that can detonate in mid-air and are accurate to 175 meters. It is light enough to carry around, and a strong man can fire it one handed, conceivably even fire one in each hand."

"Like old Arnold Schwarzenegger!" quipped John I, and Hunter laughed.

"Just like. One stop shopping—high explosive, high explosive armor piercing, high explosive air burst, and regular shot. Who could ask for more? The grenades I have here are Frag 12 armor piercing little monsters which can be fired at a rate of 120 per minute bursts and clear everything in a nine foot radius—that's a circle 18 feet across. This little missile here is an HE, armor piercing, fragmentation grenade with wings—flechettes."

"We need a suitable target for our Buck Rogers sci-fi gadget." Hunter said.

"Let's get aboard the hummer, and I'll take you to the perfect target."

The three drove to another section of the shooting range. 100 meters from where they parked sat three ugly three story concrete buildings with standard size window openings from which the glass had long since been blown away. The walls were thoroughly pockmarked with impacts from a large variety of fire power. The entryways appeared to be made of solid steel.

"This was delivered to me last night from the Black Hawk Training Center in Moyock, North Carolina. Watch this," the sniper said with a malevolent grin.

He loaded and locked the magazine, aimed at the first of the buildings then fired 20 rounds through the windows and doors in the next four seconds. The noise was deafening, and the incredible amount of damage inflicted on the building impressed even the two seasoned veteran militarists. The sniper set down the gun and started walking towards the hapless building, beckoning his two pupils to follow.

The building was structurally unsound, and the three men gingerly picked their way in for a cursory look. The target had been outfitted with furniture and mannequins in every room. The furniture bore no resemblance to anything that could once have been useful to people. The people—mannequins—were blown to pieces, tiny fragments. It was evident that many of them had essentially been vaporized.

"Like I said, gentlemen, this weapon has an incredible fear factor attached to it."

"Amen," said both Hunter and John I at the same time.

Both students gave the remarkable weapon a thorough workout. It fired flawlessly, accurately, and with a convincing devastation.

"And I get one of these?" Hunter asked like a little boy viewing the chance to get his first real .22.

"Yup. Part of the standard armamentarium for you regular spy folks," said the sniper when the din and dust died down. "There is a catch."

Hunter frowned.

"Yeah, you have to clean it after every 10,000 rounds."

They all laughed at the absurdly effective, nearly indestructible, and incredibly durable science fiction weapon Hunter was now holding.

Hunter shook his head in wonder and appreciation. He was convinced that Oliver was as good as his word. Any mission he was about to undertake would be at least equipped as well as was possible. He still had more than two and a half months of this kind of training left and had some difficulty in imagining what would be in store for him for the rest of the time.

The sniper smiled at Hunter and said, "you did good. Not as good as the average marine, but good."

"Thanks for all that faint praise."

The sniper gave Hunter an approving nod and left the two Johns to prepare his lecture for the evening.

John I said, "You know, John, you really got high marks and serious praise from that guy. I shouldn't tell you this, but he's the top instructor at the Quantico Marine Sniper School."

Hunter's expression stayed placid, but he was quietly very pleased with himself. He had always liked to be a respected man among men, and it was heady stuff to be praised as a shooter among shooters.

CHAPTER SEVENTEEN

After the long day of shooting, and another lecture by the sniper, Hunter settled on his bed, picked up a copy of *Middlemarch* that had been on the coffee table, turned on the radio to a country music station, and drowsily began to read. He knew it was a mistake for him to listen as the first twangy nasal voice came on.

The disc jockey, said, "And now all my friends out there, here's an oldie and a goodie. Let's give a listen to Dickie Lee's *Rocky* from the *Country Gold 1975-79* album."

"Alone until my eighteenth year, we met four springs ago.
She was shy and had a fear, of things she did not know
But we got it together in such a super way
We held each other close at night, and traded dreams each day
She said Rocky I've never been in love before, don't know if I can do it
But if you let me lean on you take my hand I might get through it
I said baby, oh sweet baby it's love that sets us free
And God knows if the world should end your love is safe with me"

Hunter listened in spite of his better judgment; it was too close to the bone; and he should turn it off.

"...And she said Rocky I've never had a baby before, don't know if I can do it
But if you let me lean on you, take my hand I might get through it
I said, baby, Oh sweet baby it's love that sets us free
And God knows if the world should end your love is safe with me"

For months, Hunter had gritted his teeth to avoid the heart wrenching images of his family that he had hidden deep in the recesses of his mind. The lyrics brought to the fore sweet Rosie and her fears as labor started with and of beautiful Donna as a baby girl. He began to cry silently but with a river of tears as the dam that held in his tightly held emotions began to crumble. He fought to control himself, but there was a poignant and close truth to the man in those lyrics he could not defeat.

> *"We had lots of problems then, but we had lots of fun*
> *Like the birthday party, when our baby girl turned one*
> *I was proud and satisfied, life had so much to give*
> *Til the day they told me that she didn't have long to live*
> *She said Rocky I never had to die before don't know if I can do it"*

The floodgates of the dam opened and the entire contents of his misery, loneliness, and pain poured out. He grabbed his pillow, crushed it against his face, and ran into the bathroom; so, John I would not hear him. He wept inconsolably.

> *"...Rocky you know you've been alone before, you know that you can do it*
> *But if you'd like to lean on me, take my hand I'll help you through it*
> *I said baby, Oh sweet baby, it's love that sets us free*
> *And God knows if the world should end, your love is safe with me."*

The emotional catharsis was draining but strangely restorative. When the great waves of grief finally ebbed away and back into their hidden place in his wounded mind, Hunter felt exhausted and finally able to face what had happened to him. He was surprised that the song had triggered such a spontaneous outpouring but; as he fell asleep, he recognized that he might well be starting to heal.

His dreams were both beautiful and profoundly disturbing. Over and over, he walked on a shining beach holding Rosie's and Donna's hands and smiled down at young Daniel as he trotted along side, hurrying to keep up. There was warmth, light, and a great feeling of peace and of all being right with the world as they walked along barefoot in the warm sand. Then, repeatedly, in the distance, Hunter saw a tall bearded Arab in a kaffiyeh and thobe walking towards him and his family. As he drew closer, the dark hawk-nosed Arab waved a *Qur'an* and shouted; but the Arabic words were incomprehensible to the family. At the end of each repeat of the dream, Hunter woke up sweating and angry, only to fall asleep again and to experience the same scene.

When the alarm went off at 0630, Hunter awakened and said, "I will never stop hunting them, Rosie; you and Daniel and Donna and Stephen and Marie and the little ones will have justice if I have to kill every "peace loving" member of that twisted religion in the world.

CHAPTER EIGHTEEN

White House Oval Office, 0630: Daily CIA Briefing.
Present: POTUS, DCIA

Gerald Lang was ushered into the Oval Office unceremoniously and without formalities or pleasantries.

"Give me the latest, Director. Anything more about the attacks on U.S. interests in Israel—the visa office at the embassy in Jerusalem, the FBI legat office in Tel Aviv, and the Brigham Young University Center for Near Eastern Studies on Mount Scopus in Jerusalem?"

"There is one more occurrence that you did not get called about last night, Mr. President. There was a fourth attack planned against Israel by Hamas on the Grand Oasis Hotel and entertainment center on the Israeli-Jordanian border between Eilat and Aqaba. It is best known as The American Partners Tourism Project which made it a prime target. But that facilitator of man-made disaster's suicide vest malfunctioned. He took off the vest, tried to fix it and failed, then his compatriots took it away from the hotel and gave it a go and were privileged to achieve martyrdom. He was captured intact. Mossad had a discussion with him—quite a vigorous one, apparently—although the details of that were not forthcoming. The bottom line is that the gentleman gave a plethora of information about the entire plot, to wit: Hamas, under Adel Abu-Darzi—ostensibly a citizen of Gaza, but in fact a citizen of Tehran—was the tactical commander. The other direct participants—now vaporized—included two other Iranians—a woman, Ronan Hussain, and a gentleman, Muhammad Ali Khomeinil; a citizen of Saudi Arabia, a ranking operative of the Saudi General Intelligence Directorate—the *Al Mukhabarat Al A'amah*—named Sheik Abdullah el-Faisal; and a true Palestinian Arab, Abdulkhaleq al-Shibri."

"Any significance to the individuals you've named?"

"Indeed so, Mr. President. Abu-Darzi is an Iranian agent, a representative of the government of the Republic of Iran who probably answers directly to President Ahmadine-jad. The Sheikh came to Israel directly from the Saudi government bearing operational money. Al-Shibri was the nephew of Oumar Abu al-Shibri, who is the finance director of the *Palestinian* National Liberation Movement—*Harakat At-Tahriri Al-Filistiniya*—or FATEH. The directness of the involvement of the Shia and Sunni official worlds—generally assumed to be at complete logger-heads with each other—could hardly be more explicit or worrisome."

President Storebridge was contemplative, and there ensued a thoughtful silence that lasted a full three minutes before he spoke, "Director, I think you are drawing somewhat of an overly tight conclusion based on the facts you have presented, and I want you to squeeze every bit of intel out of anyone and everyone involved before the government of the United States can accept at face value the full impact of your conclusions. Second, you serve at my pleasure, Gerald. I acknowledge your great contributions to the intelligence service and to the country, but your penchant for sarcasm irks me. Since President Obama, our country has made dramatic strides in regaining our popularity among our allies and even among those with whom we differ. Get used to the idea that this is no longer the War on Terrorism, that it is not a war, and that we do not, repeat, *do not* publicly refer to the perpetrators as terrorists any longer. I want you to get used to the new reality. George W. Bush is gone along with his bellicosity. There is a new president and a new attitude, a hard won diplomatic state of mind. The members of this administration shall hue to the new line; so, we can continue to function in the world. *Capisce?*

"*Capisce*. But, Mr. President, the events of yesterday are serious. Israel cannot tolerate such outrages on their soil any more than we can afford to let our consulates be attacked in any country. Those attacks are every bit tantamount to acts of war on our soil. The use of euphemisms like "violent extremism" suggests that there are only a few, fringe, semi-lunatics acting with some warped definition of *Sharia*. When al Qaeda is identified as the culprit in some heinous outrage, the reporter or politician is quick to refer to the organization and its acts as somehow being a "corruption of Islam". That way of thinking and behaving on our part flies in the face of two stubborn realities: first, these people are doing nothing more than implementing the *Sharia*. Second—and more important—they have literally tens of millions of sympathetic and supporting adherents, far more than a diminutive term like 'fringe-group' suggests. We are seeing a significant upturn in jihad by the sword—one of the core tenets of the religion. What would you have The Company do?"

"Can you send your Sheep Dog people to create some mischief?"

"Not yet. Our operatives are just not ready. That will have to wait for three or four more months, and the targets will have to be chosen very carefully. Actually, while diplomatic efforts are underway, the U.S. can appear to be acting in a measured way. When we do hit, the perpetrators will not be able to make direct connections between action and reaction. Our preparations are moving along very well. We are pleased with the progress being made, and the Sheep Dog program will be a finely tuned machine when it is fully up and running; you have my word on that, Mr. President. And, I apologize for being snide. I am frustrated—as I know you are—about the growing intentional chaos."

"Apology accepted. I am going to dispatch Jeffery Southem and his team to Israel this afternoon and have him call on the Palestinian authorities tomorrow. He can spend a couple of days with the Saudis. Maybe he can spread a little oil on the troubled waters. Miracles do happen."

"It would seem that we need one, sir."

The president looked down at the large pile of papers in his inbox, and the DCIA gave a small nod and left.

As he left the room, President Storebridge pushed a console button and said, "Sally Rose, please get The secretary of State and Daniel ben Moises in for a meeting before noon."

CHAPTER NINETEEN

Hunter's anger from his dreams had dissipated by the time he and John I completed breakfast. The residual adrenalin energy generated by his emotional outburst and angry pronouncement in his room lingered as the two men did a double long, double difficult run which left both of them trying to catch their breaths.

"What's on for today, John?" Hunter asked when he could talk.

Let's do a half day's worth of gunnery practice, then, this afternoon will be dedicated to some sophisticated martial arts training. I think you'll actually learn something today, my friend."

"Sounds good."

The shooting went well with Hunter's growing expertise showing the benefits of practice. After lunch, the dogs barked; and one of the paramilitary guards knocked on the front door.

"Enter," said John.

The guard opened the door and admitted a diminutive oriental woman and a burly muscular man.

"Mai Ling, nice to see you again. Thanks for coming all the way out here. Lior, ready for a little brutality?"

Mai Ling Chang bowed slightly, and Lior Batushansky nodded.

John looked at Hunter, "Mai Ling is the most deadly knife fighter in the world. Lior is the most deadly hand-to-hand fighter you never heard of in the world. He is the grand master of Krav Maqa and comes to us compliments of the Mossad."

Hunter shook each of the fighters' hands.

"We should probably get to work with Mai Ling first so you aren't too tired and sore to throw knives and to learn the delicacies of knife work—incidentally, an art called 'lightening and silent death' in Mandarin."

The four walked to the rear of the house where a set of four targets were set up at a distance of ten meters from where they stood. Each target was a cut-out of a human figure, all assuming different postures. Mai Ling opened a case of double edged throwing knives and laid them out on a folding table which had been set up by the staff earlier in the morning. She positioned them in an overly neat row, then behind the precisely engineered throwing knives, she lined up two rows of knives of assorted sizes and shapes. She picked up four of the throwing knives and swiftly and effortlessly threw each of the four hitting each target cutout figure in the center of the neck. She then picked four knives at random from the assorted size knives and threw them at lightening speed into the left side of the chest of the target.

She turned to Hunter and said, "Now, you."

Hunter had had no experience throwing knives. He was pretty sure that he was about to play the fool. He picked up four of the razor sharp throwing knives gingerly to spare himself the ignominy of cutting himself. He drew back and threw the first one missing the target altogether. Mai Ling giggled quietly and placed her four delicate fingers over her mouth. The second throw put a knife in the left thigh. The third clunked handle end first into the target's abdomen. The fourth actually stuck point first in the area of the target's solar plexus. Hunter shook his head in embarrassment and looked at delicate Chinese woman for an okay to proceed. She nodded yes.

He picked up a Bowie knife and bounced it off the target. A small bladed Sgian Dubh kilt knife hit the target mid-sternum point first.

"That's a little better," he thought.

His third throw was a forward curved black bladed Smithwess bush hog Kukri knife; it was a clumsy, ill-balanced weapon, a poor choice under the circumstances, and was poorly thrown. The knife handle and blade landed horizontally on the right side of the frame holding the target. Hunter winced. For his fourth throw, he picked a German Fallkniven military survival knife—sighted carefully—drew back his arm and made a quick forward flexion of his wrist pointing his finger at the neck of the fourth target. He was dead on and heaved a sigh of relief. He was sweating.

Mai Ling clapped daintily while wearing a faint enigmatic smile. Hunter grinned sheepishly at her and lowered his head in self-effacement. John I roared in laughter. Hunter blushed, and that made John laugh all the harder.

"Okay, smart guy, let's see you do better."

He should not have said such a silly thing. John I made a small courtesy bow to Mai Ling, picked up four throwing knives and in less than four seconds centered four points in four vulnerable target necks. He picked an assortment of four different shaped knives: a French dagger, a Camillus medium boot knife, and an Indo-Malay Kris ceremonial knife. The first hit the target mid-left thorax; the second impaled the right mid-chest; the third hit the solar plexus dead center.

John I then smiled impishly at Hunter; and, like a billiards hustler, said, "Fourth target, Adam's apple."

Hunter groaned aloud.

The knife flew as precisely as if it had been on a guide wire.

"Now, secret agent, allow me to demonstrate the proper technique of throwing a knife successfully," Mai Ling said, all business.

She chose only throwing knives this time and showed Hunter how to hold the knife, how to aim it, how hard to throw it, and how to follow through. He was able to begin hitting the target in lethal parts even if not exactly as precisely as he would have wanted after the sixth throw.

"You will have to practice. I will see you again tomorrow to monitor your progress."

She smiled kindly, made a graceful about face and walked back to her waiting vehicle.

"Doesn't look like this is going to be my forte," Hunter observed, glumly.

"We are going to practice an hour a day for two months," John I said. "You'll be an expert before then. Have some faith in yourself, my friend."

Hunter shrugged.

While Hunter had been intent on learning to throw knives, big Lior Batushansky had been to the house and carried back three duffel bags of heavy protective gear. Each of the three men donned the gear which looked like jointed Kevlar football padding by the time the parts were all in place.

"We will play rough," Lior said, his voice betraying that his native tongue was Hebrew despite his short-cropped red hair.

Hunter was pretty sure that Lior meant what he said.

He was right. For the next two hours, Lior pummeled, threw, kicked, bruised, and battered Hunter and John I alternatively. Hunter had previously thought that either he or John I was the best fighter pound-for-pound that he knew. Now he knew different. It was full contact all the way and all of the time. The only breaks came when Lior pointed out the reason for Hunter's errors and even those of John I. By the end of the session Hunter was so tired that he could no longer really defend himself, and his battered lateral thighs could hardly hold him upright.

Lior said, "You are not in good enough shape. You should be able to fight successfully two men for three hours. Until you can, you are most vulnerable. I come from a land that has been shown no mercy. Meeting Palestinians mano-a-mano is a real test. When a Jew and a Hamas killer go into a dark room together, only one comes out. Before we are done with you—my friend—you will be the only one who is still standing. I think I am a good fighter; in fact, I have proved it. However, you know much; and I predict that by the end of our work together, you will be able to beat me. At least, you will have no match in the terrorist world. You won't be learning any moves sanctioned by the Marquis of Queensbury, and your reflexes won't allow you to underestimate or be a single step behind any actual or potential enemy. You will not survive if you do not learn all I know. See you tomorrow and every day thereafter while you are vacationing at The Farm."

He gave a friendly nod, and walked alone back to the house.

"I can't imagine surviving a daily beating like that one today."

"Lior assures me that this is the only way to become the best. You and I have had some good work-outs, but this has been the hardest fighting I've done outside actual combat, and I never went up against anyone like Lior. Think of it as a special opportunity."

Hunter gave John I a weak 'I'll-try' smile.

It was four-thirty in the afternoon, and they realized their hunger. The two men—who were developing a real friendship—trudged back to the house and made a bountiful proteinaceous lunch and had a nap to restore themselves for a brief shooting practice. For the rest of the time Hunter spent with John I, their daily routine became one of cross country running, big meals, hours of shooting, hand-to-hand combat, knife-throwing, and a late afternoon teaching session from one of a variety of experts in every aspect of clandestine and violent life.

126

CHAPTER TWENTY

White House Oval Office, 1118
Present: POTUS, SECRETARY OF STATE, ISRAELI AMBASSADOR

Secretary of State Southem and the president met briefly at eleven o'clock to prepare President Storebridge for his meeting with the Israeli ambassador. The meeting took fifteen minutes and did not result in a meeting of the minds of the two strong-willed American leaders. Southem left in time to avoid running into Ambassador ben Moises. Sally Rose Matthews waited carefully until Southem was gone from the West Wing before escorting ben Moises into The president's office.

"How are we to deal with this recent set of unfortunate circumstances, my friend?" The president asked as soon as the ambassador was seated.

General ben Moises was not at all fond of euphemisms, but let it go.

"You have your problems, and we have ours, sir. Yours, it seems to me, absolutely require an upgrade in your own security procedures and a hardening of the physical defenses. I know Secretary Southem has a different position: that heightening efforts sends a negative signal, but Israel has been in the position of having to do so for as long as she has existed. However, more importantly, your nation must devise a plan to get better intelligence and to do some pre-emptive strikes at the heart of your enemies if you are going to avoid another all-out war."

"You know as well as I do that we have this pesky rule against racial profiling which is not a problem Israel shares. My hands are tied there. We also have become a nation of doves, and any president who overreacts is a political goner. We do have a program which will likely bear fruit, but we are not ready to implement it yet. When we do, I am confident that it will be effective. The things we have planned will demonstrate our capacity to get at the terrorists where they live and work and will strike fear into the hearts of even the most hardened of those killers."

"*The Sheep Dog Program*," ben Moises said to himself.

He had known about it for a month, but the Mossad had not been able to get enough information about it to do the ambassador any good in negotiations with the Americans.

He said to the president, "Mr. President, I am directed to tell you that Israel has lost its patience. We have our own sources, and we will be putting appropriate *lex talionis* measures within the week. We cannot and will not allow any of these atrocities to go unanswered."

"Please encourage restraint, General. No one wants to ignite the spark that propels the entire region into another true war."

"I'll convey your wishes, Mr. President. However, our answer will become apparent within days. Our many enemies will feel a sting that they will remember for some time. In addition, the IDF is on red alert. Security is going to be the tightest it has been in decades, and the Mossad's in-place operatives around the world will become active as never before."

"I wish you and your country every good thing, my friend. Keep the faith with us. Our response will be quieter and less apparent, but I am indeed confident that it will have a meaningful impact."

The president noted that he had his fingers crossed when he said it. General ben Moises and President Storebridge shook hands and ended the meeting. Both were dissatisfied but realized that they were in a quandary, and the best solution was not yet apparent.

CHAPTER TWENTY-ONE

April

Hunter Caulfield's routine now consisted of a brutal morning of running, weight lifting, and mixed martial arts training followed by a full afternoon of shooting and knife throwing, and evenings occupied with didactics from John Smith I regarding a wide range of spy craft: encryptions, codes, safe houses, exit strategies, and who to contact—how and where. John's lecture program was punctuated with fascinating practical special courses in the finesse of spying, betrayal, and the art of killing—at a distance and up close and personal—essentially the gamut of man's inhumanity toward man for king and country.

Two days after Mai Ling Chang and Lior Batushansky met with and intimidated both Hunter and John I, a curious, somewhat effeminate, scholarly man with 1950s horn rim glasses and wearing a heavily starched white button-down shirt, a black suit, and a very narrow tie suited to the same era, arrived after supper for that night's and the next four night's didactic sessions.

John I introduced the man to Hunter, "Hunter, may I present Dr. Heinz Bühler-Rothe. Dr. Rothe this is John Smith. I'm sure you have heard of him."

Dr. Rothe laughed politely and said, "I'm pleased to meet you, sir. You are the thirteenth John Smith I have had the pleasure of teaching at The Farm. Either the name is common, and I am seeing a more than statistically probable number of men of your same name, or you come from a large, unimaginative family."

Hunter laughed with the man who—for all of his fussy appearance—had a fetching sense of humor and eyes that gleamed with intelligence reflecting a brain full of a wealth of valuable information.

"Shall we get started?" asked John I.

"Indeed. Could I get one of you fine physical specimens to help me bring in my teaching materials."

"I'll do it, John, why don't you help the good doctor start setting up."

Dr. Rothe sat at a long rectangular government-issue steel table looking across at his two pupils. He spread an assortment of vials, partially filled syringes, a cupful of snails, three academic volumes on poisons and antidotes, and a three inch high stack of published acad-emic papers across the table.

Breaking his attention away from the collection of the tools of his trade and his apparent paramount interest, he said, "Johns…I am a poisoner. But that is false modesty. I am, in fact, the foremost expert on poisons in the world. I am an eminently practical man as well; and I will convey to you the best, most effective, the most cunning, and the least detectable toxins known to history and modern science." He looked into Hunter's eyes. "I have prepared a collection of useful tools and materials for you to take on your adventures. Our purpose for the better part of a week will be to acquaint you with these deadly things. I consider it better that the evil-doers should perish for your purpose rather that that you sicken or die by an accident of your own making."

Hunter nodded his agreement.

"Please take notes. When you leave this august training facility, I will have encoded copies of what you have deemed pertinent plus what I consider pertinent for you to take with you. First, we will learn about snails, frogs, newts, snakes, and fish. Take notes please; we have a lot to cover.

"All of the some 500 cone sea snails, family *Conidae*, are poisonous. The creatures of concern are the large ones—especially those whose various conotoxins are lethal—including a venom that contains a pain-reducing toxin which the snail uses to pacify the victim before immobilizing and then killing it. Some cone snail venoms—the ones we have an interest in—contain tetradoxin—TTX, for short—the paralytic sodium channel blocker neurotoxin found in pufferfish, the blue-ringed octopus, and the Oregon rough-skinned newt, which are about as deadly a set of creatures as ever evolved. We have taken a few liberties with the components of the toxins and *voila!*, we have produced a toxin that—unlike the naturally occurring peptide—when it is rubbed on the skin or ingested in amounts comparable to a droplet the size of a pencil eraser results in death before the victim takes two steps…You no doubt know of the vicious little Vietnamese green tree snake?"

Hunter nodded his unpleasant memory of the notorious two-step snake up close and personal from his stay in the lovely jungles of Viet Nam and Cambodia.

"That is, in fact, a myth; but this toxin is quite literally the real thing. You have a vial of it. Don't make a mistake and get some on yourself—no fingers in the mouth or rubbing your eyes; those are fatal errors. In addition to oral or transdermal installation, the newly improved conotoxin can be injected, just as the nasty marine gastropod mollusks do with their ghastly tooth that they use like a harpoon. Makes one shudder. Since the worst creatures are endemic to California, we are able to harvest a truly impressive number of poison sacs; so, you can be downright wasteful; but I remind you again, you can only be careless once.

"In this second amber-glass stoppered vial, we have the batrachotoxin of *Phyllobates terribilis*, the beautiful golden poison frog native to the Pacific coast of Colombia that has been used to poison arrow heads by the indigenous hunters for centuries. The toxin is a particularly poisonous steroidal alkaloid secreted from the frog's skin glands. A minute amount of less than 140 micrograms is sufficient to kill a 70 kilogram man. That is about three grains of ordinary table salt. This file contains enough poison to kill about 500 men, give or take. One need only place a drop of the colorless, tasteless, viscous liquid in an alcoholic drink or on the tongue of a sleeping person, and the victim will experience almost immediate neuromuscular transmission blockade followed by muscular and respiratory paralysis and a quiet death. Unless the toxin is specifically suspected, the cause of death will be written off as being of natural origin such as a heart attack and further investigation will produce such negative findings that the poison will not be suspected.

"Now, snakes and a little evolution. The cone shell snail and the black mamba evolved separately; but remarkably, they each evolved an amino acid sequence in their genomes that was very, very similar in effect; and each developed a potassium channel blocking neurotoxin that is also extraordinarily similar in action although different in chemical makeup. I won't bore you with the DNA sequence details, but I do stress the fundamental nature of the neurotoxin. In my lab, we have been able to manufacture mamba toxin in quantity which will serve you well in your work; so, I have been informed. A black mamba bite is usually fatal in thirty minutes unless the victim of the bite receives the antidote almost immediately. Incidentally, the victim meets his doom from respiratory paralysis—a particularly hideous way to go, I am told. A physician would have to know that his or her patient had been envenomated in order to initiate treatment. That would border on being an impossible intellectual leap for a doctor encountering a dying person who had no history of contact with a mamba. Furthermore, unless specifically sought in a competent lab, no evidence of such poisoning would be forthcoming. And you, sir, have a fairly large vial of the stuff with which to ply your trade."

Dr. Rothe smiled benignly. Hunter thought that the man was the very picture of the mad scientist or the soulless serial killer. But then, who was he to cast the first stone?

"As fond as I am of black mambas, it is interesting to note that the world's most poisonous snake is the rather unassertive hook-nosed sea snake or beaked sea snake [*Enhydrina schistose*] Mouse LD50 (mg/kg) 0.02, generally considered to be the most venomous sea snake in the world. That poison compares to the Inland Taipan [*Oxyuranus microlepidotus*] Mouse LD50 (mg/kg) 0.03 generally considered to be the most venomous land snake. We have a supply of the venom from each of these lovely creatures, but we have not yet been able to manufacture synthetic venom; so unfortunately, you will have to be more frugal in your choice of persons to inject."

Dr. Rothe's tutorial demeanor was the very picture of bland. He could have been reading from the *Geodetic Survey* for all of the emotion he was expressing.

"Any questions so far, John Smith?"

Dr. Rothe allowed himself a faint wry smile.

"Being a pragmatist and not an academic, Dr. Rothe, I need to know the nuts and bolts of how to deliver these poisons."

"But of course you do. You will note in the packet of instructional materials sitting before you, a quick and dirty description of directions and a small note sheet telling you where you can obtain extra supplies beyond those I will send you away with. I needn't say—I am sure—that these instructions and the names and contact information you will have in your possession are not to be seen by anyone else; and I mean *anyone* else. *Capiche*?"

Hunter nodded his understanding of the obvious.

"Now, let me conclude with a description of Ciguatera—ichthocarcotoxin—a form of fresh fish poisoning produced by tiny marine organisms—dinoflagellates—which grow on marine algae and accumulate in the fatty tissue of the fish—barracuda, grouper, amberjack, and snapper. This obnoxious toxin produces severe stomach distress, a variety of neurological symptoms including aching joints, metallic or peppery taste, mouth and throat dryness, skin itches, dizziness and nausea, and especially, a reversal of cold and hot sensation. Death results from ingestion of high concentrations. It is difficult to detect as an intentional poison, especially in a person who has consumed a fish dinner. I rather like this natural chemical because, with proper planning, the murder can appear to have been only a mishap from eating an infected fish."

Dr. Rothe concluded his lecture for the evening with the fish toxin and showed Hunter the fairly large vial of the poison prepared for Hunter's collection. He then collected Hunter's personal notes and seemed pleased with his student's work.

"Tomorrow evening we will deal with more conventional chemical poisons. I appreciate your attention, John Smith. I assure you that the information you are receiving in addition to the actual poison and toxin materials will give you a distinct advantage in the land of smoke and mirrors and assorted things that go bump in the night."

"Thanks. It was interesting, Dr. Rothe. I look forward to the rest of your lectures."

The next three evenings, Hunter and Dr. Rothe were alone. John Smith I left directly after supper on those days and was enigmatic about his whereabouts and activities. Dr. Rothe presented extensive descriptions of Sarin, the deadly nerve gas and Ricin, from the common shrub *Ricinus communis* oil, which is considered so highly poisonous that the very activity of squeezing the oil from the seeds leaves powdery dry pulp that requires elaborate measures to protect the manufacturers and has been abandoned even by chemical warfare operatives as being too dangerous.

"The gas is 6,000 times more toxic than cyanide," Dr. Rothe stressed. "You have been given a hermetically sealed canister. You must—absolutely must—wear protective gear if or when you use it, which is likely to put a damper on your enthusiasm for this agent. My suggestion is that you plan to use it in conjunction with a small explosive to disperse it in a building. You—of course—will detonate the bomb from a safe distance."

The poisoner went on to describe atropine [Deadly Nightshade]; Bryony berries, noting that as few as 10 berries can kill a large man, and hemlock leaves—six leaves of Great Hemlock [*Conium maculatum*] are fatal in even a large man, he told Hunter.

"Piperidine alkaloids are identified by their saturated heterocyclic ring, that is, the piperidine nucleus. The best known piperidine alkaloid poisons are those of poison hemlock. Socrates is reputed to have been killed by being forced to choose to eat a poison hemlock extract.

"Death Cap mushrooms contain two poisons," he continued, "and produce initial vomiting and a coma-recovery-relapse series of symptoms with death coming a few agonizing days later."

Dr. Rothe advised, "Our especially nice mushroom potion might be reserved for someone you would rather like to have suffer for a time."

He concluded the didactic portion of his lecture series on day four with presentations on strychnine—from the Indian Koochla tree [*Strychnos vomica*], a poison that usually acts so rapidly that there is no effective antidote and curare—distilled from the bark of two South American trees [*Strychonos tosifera* and *Chondodendrum topmentosum*]—a paralytic used as a muscle relaxant in surgery. Dr. Rothe explained that death comes from inability to breathe or move but with retention of full brain function until the very end.

His last presentation was on Furadon.

"Furadon is probably your government's favorite choice since it is cheap and almost impossible to trace to its source. It is used to kill lions."

He showed Hunter a baggie of purple/blue granules.

"Furadon is tasteless, colorless and is sold in Kenya in Agri-Stores at a cost of two dollars per bottle. It is considered to be a pesticide and is sprinkled on a carcass to kill lions. It has all of the poisoner's favorite properties, and we are giving you a hefty lot to use. There is no American connection to this poison; so, you can use it freely. It dissolves in most solvents including water, and is undetectable unless some intrepid Kenyan physician happens to be on the scene, an unlikely scenario."

He and Hunter shook hands, and the fussy professor of secret death handed over a neat little zippered brief case containing the vials and laminated instructions, and Hunter's own notes that had been neatly typed onto five by six inch color-coded cards.

"Thanks."

"My pleasure. Good hunting, John Smith. I hope this helps."

They parted, and Hunter began to wonder what John Smith I had been up to the past three evenings.

CHAPTER TWENTY-TWO

White House Oval Office: Daily Briefing, 0630
PRESENT: POTUS, DCIA, SECRETARY OF STATE,
SECRETARY OF DEFENSE, CHAIRMAN JCS

"Do we have a laudable military and intelligence success or a lamentable snafu, Michael?" The president asked without preamble.

The secretary of Defense paused a moment before answering.

"Some of both, Mr. President. Let me explain. Our intelligence was good." He gave a small appreciative nod to Gerald Lang, the DCIA.

"We had essentially perfect intel about the shipment including unequivocal evidence of its origin, destination, contents, and the names and bios on the participants. We knew the route they were taking from Saudi Arabia into Yemen. That's the laudable success part. However, the truck made a totally unexpected stop at the southern edge of the *Ar-Rub'-al-Khali*—the Empty Quarter—near Sabya, shortly before our Predator Drone was about to launch its missile. The perps got away in the desert. That's the lamentable part; we lost the chance to get even more intel from them; and we lost the bargaining chip they would have represented in the diplomatic arena. On the plus side—however—we removed a large truck load of high explosives from future use by the "facilitators"—Semtex, RDX, PETN, dynamite, blasting caps, fuses, disposable cell phones—the whole magillah."

"That's good work, but I'm more concerned about how and why the perps were able to evade the Predator," President Storebridge asked pointedly, looking at Army General Lemuel Simons, The chairman of the Joint Chiefs of Staff.

"It happened because some rag head paid twenty-five bucks to SkyGrabber for a satellite card to be able to intercept all of the drones' communications," General Simons said almost gritting his teeth in anger.

DCIA Lang interjected.

"Mr. President, please allow me to explain. The fundamental problem lies with budget cutbacks and our new world friendly diplomatic policy."

The secretary of State, Jeremy Southem, glared at the DCIA, but held his tongue for the moment.

The DCIA continued, "We have not taken the necessary measures to scramble the signals being received by SkyGrabber to and from our drones. Although U.S. military personnel sitting stateside can program and direct a drone aircraft halfway around the world to deliver a missile or a bomb on a specific target, the Pentagon has not encrypted the signals going to and emanating from the drone. Six years into the war in Iraq, the very capable hackers of the insurgency were able to use SkyGrabber technology to pinpoint flight paths, moment-to-moment locations of the drone, and the timing and location of planned attacks. Incidentally, the technology is available for $25 at retail software dealers around the world and is perfectly legal in every country on the planet."

"Co-opting the incredibly sophisticated computer and communications of the Predator Drone just can't be that simple. Can it?" The president had a bemused look on his face. "How on earth does such a technology work?"

In his driest monotone, the DCIA explained, "SkyGrabber is an offline satellite internet downloader. It accepts free-to-air [FTA] satellite data like movie, music, or pictures by using a digital satellite TV tuner card called a DVB-S/DVB-S2 which saves information onto a hard disk. You don't even have to keep an online internet connection. The company can customize the customer's digital satellite TV tuner card to a satellite provider to start accepting free-to-air data. There are different types of internet connections, such as Dial-Up, ADSL, Leased Line, etc. Satellite internet is a kind of internet connection and is used mainly in remote areas like the Empty Quarter of Yemen or in areas where internet access is problematic because of its not being available at all, or is only available in nearly useless slow speed or where budget conscious terrorists resist the high cost of local internet connections.

"Besides, the local internet hook up is fraught with hazards of traceability, a taboo for our Muslim "facilitator" friends. The hookup from a mud hut somewhere out in the desert where an illiterate Bedouin al-Qaida flunky sits waiting is to the internet through various geostationary satellites, which are located at an altitude of 35,786 km above the equator and provides a zone coverage which allows our Bedouin to have access to several satellite transmitters with no more knowledge of the computer that to use the point-and-click moves his handler taught him. Our Bedouin's set-up is almost impossible to locate. The high value of the signal—48dBW—used by al-Qaida allows an antenna of only 60 centimeters in diameter. That is only 23.62 inches, no bigger than his cooking wok."

"Well, Director, you have quite evidently done your homework. So, how do we stop this intrusion into our communications?"

"Let me answer that, Mr. President," The secretary of State interrupted. "We don't. We have international agreements that are iron-clad in which we have agreed that we will never jam internet connections. Moreover, it is not in our best interests to do so. We can intercept internet messages better than can our Bedouin friend, and we obtain a ton of useful intelligence by doing so. I could not, and will never approach the UN or any individual country to push such an agenda that would jeopardize our hard-won friendships. President Obama staked his and the country's reputation on a program of change in our diplomatic relations to one of friend and ally from the abysmal communications of his predecessor. It has worked and could only be countermanded at our peril."

"So, we're just stuck, then, you say, Mr. Secretary?" Michael Chisholm asked testily.

"Your clever techies at the Pentagon will have to come up with a better way, it appears, if you are going to get around this inconvenience."

"Inconvenience?!" Chisholm snarled.

The secretary of State responded with an irritatingly avuncular small smile of one-upmanship.

"What happens now, Director?" The president asked.

"Not a lot. We now have a nice store of explosives. Perhaps our agents can find a use for them. I would not advise turning them over to the Yemenis. Al-Qaida has infiltrated the Yemeni law enforcement, military, and security forces so thoroughly that the lethal shipment would be in their hands within the week."

General Simons spoke up, "I'd like to suggest with some emphasis that we initiate the Sheep Dog program in Yemen first."

"I will make that a presidential order, General." Turning to the DCIA, he said, "Director, consider that as of this date, the order stands for Sheep Dog's first orders are to visit Yemen."

"Yes, Mr. President. We will accelerate the preparations."

CHAPTER TWENTY-THREE

May

Hunter became aware that there was a developing acceleration and a harder edge in his training program. He guessed that the powers-that-be were becoming impatient.

"You're pushing a lot harder, John," he said. "What's up?"

"The DCIA, himself, called in an order to push you harder, to cram more training into a shorter period. Must be some source of urgency us peons don't really know much about. I had wanted to let you work on all of the skills we have been practicing; but now, we are going into overdrive on the schedule. Today, we're going to get into explosives, bombs, and IEDs. Before we do, I want to show you something I did for you. You remember how, about three weeks ago when you and Dr. Rosen were working together without me; and I was gone for several evenings?"

"Um-hmmh."

John walked to his desk and extracted a large manila envelope, opened the clasp, and dumped the contents on the kitchen table.

Hunter saw something like two dozen passports. He gave John a quizzical look.

"All for you. Several of them are Belgian, you'll note. Since 1990, well over 20,000 blank passports have been "stolen", actually sold by crooked civil servants on the side. They were easy enough to come by, and you can think of them as use-once-and-discard passports. All of this is offline and wouldn't be appreciated by the Great Ones, but I've been around a bit; and I know something about what happens when the winds of fortune and political wisdom shift in D.C. Someone takes the blame or becomes the tethered goat. It's usually not the generals or the president. The stuff still rolls down hill, and I think there's a possibility that you might find yourself in the valley. So, I have gone out on a limb for you. I guess it's unprofessional; but I've taken a liking to you; and I want you to survive this up-coming adventure of yours."

"Thanks," Hunter said quietly.

"You're quite welcome. First, let me tell you about the passports. They are from a dozen different countries, and they are altogether genuine, right down to the multiple entry and exit stamps. Your picture has been very expertly photoshopped; so, you look every bit the businessman from France, the aging English Duke, the gruff union boss, the consulting engineer, the soldier, and the Arab sheik, etcetera. We'll put in long hours with a make-up artist to make you an expert in altering your appearance to fit the passport photos. And, if you have the good sense I credit you with, you will keep mum about all of these passports and about the disguise program.

"I advise you—my friend—to take every opportunity to amass money and salt it away in secret accounts in the Caymans or Vanuatu or wherever. You can steal or extort from your victims. You can purloin their caches and burglarize their safes without Uncle Sugar becoming the wiser. Remember that a secret is something only one person knows. Whatever you think about your handlers, always keep something back from them. Always have escape routes, exit strategies—not only from your assignments, but also from them. You work for the CIA; it shows on your face. They don't care a whit if you are dishonest or queer or enjoy perversions so long as it does not threaten The Company or the United States. God help you if you do become a perceived threat. You have to prepare for that day and hope that it never comes as much as you have to be an absolute expert on the deadly arts and the arts of subterfuge, being an imposter, and escape."

John's face was grimmer than Hunter had ever seen it in the months they had worked together. He was clearly serious, and Hunter paid serious attention.

"So, tonight, we'll work on make-up and disguises. You might be amused to know that I have a Hollyweird com-symp pinko who became converted to the true gospel after spending some quality time with me. I saved her backside when some government types, who could not get over their enthusiasm for McCarthy's doctrine, came after her. She's good people—a bit weird, call it eccentric—but she keeps the faith. I meet her at the main gate at eight when it's pretty dark. She'll stay with us for a week, and she's got a boxful of make-up and disguise goodies for you."

"I appreciate all of that, John."

"You can show it by being indefatigable and by putting up with my pushing you. I'm on your side, but for the next couple of months; I'll seem like your worst nightmare."

"And that will be different how?" Hunter smiled.

"You can't even imagine. We'll start in half an hour with a whirlwind course in explosives. The Company is bringing in a Company expert—an NYPD bomb squad vet of thirty years experience—and the *piece de resistance*—a reformed Palestinian bomber. Should make for interesting conversations at supper."

Hunter nodded.

"Oh, carry a notepad and pen all the time. You are likely to live or die by the quality of your notes and your capacity to memorize. When you're done, you will be given some sophisticated and untraceable fuses, det-cord, and concentrated HE materials."

Twelve hours a day for the next two weeks, Hunter exercised his brain like he had never done before. His only respite came with the early morning run and hard martial arts practice and with an hour each day in rifle, hand gun, and cross-bow shooting drills and repetitious knife throwing. His skills were at a peak, and he needed only to keep them there without burning out.

The explosives training was exhaustive and exhausting: how to handle explosives ingredients—PETN [Pentaerythritol tetranitrate], RDX, or cyclonite [Cyclotrimethylenetri-nitramine], Semtex, sodium cyanide, nitric acid, diisopropyl fluoro-phosphates [for nerve gas]; dynamite, TNT, and ammonium nitrate—a common fertilizer component which is cheap and abundant and therefore a favorite of terrorists for their bombs.

The Palestinian gave him *The Terrorists' Handbook*—169 page document with detailed instructions for making chemical weapons and high explosives. The retired NYPD bomb squad detective gave him a dog-eared copy of *Silent Death, Improvised Explosives*, by "Uncle Foster".

Hunter memorized an encyclopedia of explosives information, the equivalent of a college semester in a month. He added to his mental repertoire such arcane bits as: PETN has a vDet—velocity of detonation—of 8,400 meters/sec, explosion energy of 5810 kJ/kg (1390 kcal/kg), an explosion temperature of 4230 °C. RDX has a vDet of 8,750 m/s and is safer, more stable, and more castable than PETN. Semtex is a general-purpose plastic explosive containing RDX and PETN which is used in commercial blasting, demolition, and in certain useful military applications. Semtex became notoriously popular with terrorists, the Palestinian told him, because it was, until recently, extremely difficult to detect, as in the case of Pan Am Flight 103.

Hunter developed a practiced and practical working knowledge of how to program a throw-away cell phone detonator, how to lay an undetectable line of bouncing bettys along an approach of a target, how to make improvised explosive devises out of fertilizer, baking soda, and agricultural acid; and incendiary devises fashioned from water bottles, chemical toilet cleaner, and aluminum foil. He was instructed in how to make a shaped charge out of pentolite, how to initiate a PETN explosion with a laser beam, how to employ detonating cord such as brightly colored or transparent Primacord, and what type of fuses, and fuzes.

A fuse is a simple pyrotechnic initiating device, like the cord on a common fire cracker. A fuze is the sophisticated ignition device employing both mechanical and electronic components; examples shown Hunter included proximity fuzes for an M107 shell, magnetic-acoustic fuzes used on sea mines, spring-loaded grenade fuzes, pencil detonators, antihandling devices, visco fuzes—which are simple fuses consisting of a burning core coated with wax or lacquer for durability and water resistance. The commercial and military version of a burning fuse is commonly referred to as safety fuse—a textile tube filled with combustible material and wrapped to prevent external exposure of the burning core. They are colored black in military ordnance and fluorescent orange in commercial usage. Safety fuses are used to initiate the detonation of explosives through the use of a blasting cap and to provide a time delay, a fact of which Hunter took particular note.

Hunter was shown—with mind-numbing repetition—how to use the fuses and fuzes, and particularly, blasting caps, safely. With equally tedious repetition, Hunger learned which explosive materials to use in any particular situation and how to avoid being blown up. He developed a very healthy respect for unstable components like trinitrotoluene—TNT. The demolition squad team taught Hunter about avoiding detection. Fire debris submitted to forensic laboratories which employ sensitive analytical instruments with GC-MS capabilities for forensic chemical analysis can readily detect hydrocarbon-based fuels [petroleum distillates—gasoline, kerosene, turpentine, and butane—and various other flammable solvents like acetones, carbon disulfide, and even ethyl alcohol—the common ingredient in drinkable spirits], and solids such as white phosphorus. Ignitable liquids leave evidence in the fire debris, including irregular burn patterns. HPD-type accelerants—Heavy Petroleum Distil-lates—

such as diesel fuel and number 2 fuel oil—the common home heating oil—are very difficult to detect as are certain types of rocket fuel.

Being pragmatic, the team taught Hunter how to use common household items and objects which can accelerate a fire and are difficult to detect unless the arsonist uses excessively large amounts. They demonstrated how to get an arson fire going without using the more commonly detectable and almost prima facie evidence kind of hydrocarbon and other highly volatile liquids. They set fires near household heating units and electrical units with paraffin, insecticides, carpet and carpet padding, tar paper, shingles, wood, insulation, paper, sheet rock, vinyl flooring, and plastics. They showed their student how wicker and foam have high surface to mass ratios and favorable chemical compositions and thus burn easily and readily. Hunter learned to spread the non-petroleum distillate accelerants about the area of intended arson to mini-mize the evidence of the fire having been intentional. The methods the bomb squad experts showed their student demonstrated how to use large fuel loads to increase the rate of fire growth as well as spread the fire over a larger area, thus increasing the amount of fire damage.

Each day he rested during supper—which he devoured voraciously—and had a short power nap. Then, beginning a week after the explosives lectures started, the strange elderly Hollywood make-up artist John had told him about arrived to teach him her magic for a week.

"John, this is Hedy Lamarick, the famous Hollywood make-up artist," John Smith I said, and Hunter could not help but detect the obvious fondness John had for the eccentric little woman.

Hunter wondered what her real name was but knew that he did not need to know any more about her than she should be privy to about him outside their teacher-pupil relationship. He was looking at a wizened tiny woman of no less in age than her seventies. She could not have been more than four feet tall even in her entirely utilitarian black lace up orthopedic shoes. She had obvious scoliosis, with enough of a serpentine set of curvatures that no one would require medical training to recognize her deformity and to sym-pathize with the pain she must have had to live with her entire life. Her face was wrinkled and intense but artfully made-up to give the impression of a much younger woman if seen at a distance. She had crooked, unfetching teeth, a drooping mouth line, and horsey features; but her sad eyes were an intense grey, the intensity reminiscent of his own. Her hands were gnarled with Heberden's arthritic nodes and crooked joints, but the nails were assiduously manicured and painted a tasteful shade of glossy maroon. Hedy wore an attractive matching maroon velvet dress and a wide, 1940s belt. She smiled at him, a smile that he felt to be more practiced than genuine.

Hedy—her real name—looked briefly at the powerful, sinewy man with the scarred face standing over her. John Smith, indeed, she snorted to herself. But then, every person she dealt with in her work for The Company was John or Jane Smith, Pepe or Maria Gomez, or Chang Lee or Mary. In her work for John Smith I over the years, she had encountered some intimidating characters, but John had assured her that this one was the most frightening of them all. He had admonished her not to seek to know anything about him, and to forget having every seen or even heard of him. The man had icy hazel eyes that seemed to penetrate her brain stem and a nasty facial scar that had to have come from a machete or a bayonet. She gave a little shiver.

"I'm pleased to meet you, Ms Lamarick," Hunter said both politely and kindly.

"Please call me Hedy."

"Then, I'm John, Hedy."

"Would you like to get started?"

"I'm ready and interested," Hunter replied, which was the truth.

The odd little woman was interesting to say the least; and he was convinced that what she had to teach him was crucial to the success of his missions to come and—probably—to his very survival, as much as the martial arts or weapons training.

"Today, we will deal with the more mundane principles and practical steps in the use of make-up and easily applied disguises, some of which you can improvise from materials you encounter in daily life.

"First, let us consider minimalist disguises. You can become one of the invisible people—the people who are there but are not seen. Consider a busy urban setting and going through the mundanities of every day life. You—like most people—are busy and focused on your own activities, goals, and contacts, both those with whom you are presently engaged and those with whom you expect to interact during the course of the day. The people around you—like the streets and buildings themselves—are ignored and do not become part of your memory bank. There are a great many chairs, sidewalks, buildings, and automobiles that must be occupied, it would seem; but the occupants are invisible. We simply do not register the servants, waiters and waitresses, housewives, gas station attendants, construction workers, post office workers, UPS drivers, and police in their respective uniforms, businessmen in their dull colored suits, or black and Asian people who all look alike. Jewish orthodox people, observant Muslim women in burqas, Indians in turbans, hippies with their tie-dye shirts, tattoos and piercings, the smelly and dirty homeless people…are all invisible; they are—as we say in the makeup and disguise world—in a state of 'not-being'.

"By and large, they have some invisibility characteristics in common including: they are what people expect to see—stereotypes; they all appear in context and therefore do not draw attention to themselves; they keep their heads down and avert their eyes; for the most part they are neither sexy nor colorful. Most of your contemporaries do not generally strike one as especially rich or poor; they do not flaunt jewelry or extravagant watches. They avoid seeing you or you seeing them. Most of them do not speak out in public—fool's names and fools faces are often found in public places, an adage they recognize and make every effort to eschew—and they are loathe to be thought of as fools or to be thought of at all. They are invisible, as innocuous as wallpaper.

"Your teacher has been good enough to bring in a few trunks of my rather extensive costume collection; so, you, too, can learn the subtle art of being invisible."

For the rest of the evening, Hunter and John I submitted to Hedy's ministrations and rapidly changed from short-haired tough guys into bums, nuns, observing Muslims, police officers, janitors, mailmen, and a variety of ethnic people. She showed them how to apply just the right amount of coloration of make-up and dirt, how to wear various uniforms and regional clothing, and how to blend into the ebb and flow of everyday life by becoming another person, but an invisible one.

The next evening after a long day's session with the bomb makers and a quiet supper, Hedy returned, this time with a scruffy young man as an assistant.

"Gentlemen, this is my young friend, Emmanuel. He is a reformed car thief…I think."

She gave the young man a slight affectionate smile.

"Why a car thief, you might legitimately ask? Because the characters we created last evening are seen in public with their props, and those props are often automobiles. The cop has his squad car; the UPS man has his van; the construction worker has his pick-up with a logo on the door and equipment in the bed; and so on. Neither you nor your employers can readily come up with the appropriate vehicle from a prop department—that is the function of a movie studio crew working in a large warehouse. No—gentlemen—you will have to learn to steal and to do so quickly and without being detected. As a result of his unfortunate childhood, Emmanuel learned how to steal cars; and now is in the employ of your Company. He is very well traveled and has experience with just about every kind of vehicle in the world. Emmanuel, show the nice gentlemen how it is done."

A car-carrier pulled up in front of the house, and Emmanuel quickly and expertly drove the vehicles off the truck's ramps and onto the lawn, locked the doors and placed their keys in a cardboard box on the porch. He then proceeded with a tutorial on the fine arts of bypassing car door locks using simple tools that included wire clothes hangers, thin metal bars, and on one new Cadillac, resorted to a drill to remove the lock with brute force. Then, he patiently showed the two men how to bypass the ignitions of all of the vehicles and explained which cars could not be jumpstarted because of their computerized locking and ignition systems.

"Just stay away from them," he said.

When—after an hour—he stopped demonstrating and talking, he took a break to roll himself a cigarette, adding finely crushed dry leaves from a sandwich sized baggie. The resultant smoke was pungent, aromatic, sweet, and familiar to John I and Hunter; but they avoided making remarks.

"Now, it's your turn," Emmanuel said, looking at Hunter.

The next hour, Hunter spent breaking into cars and trucks. He was frustratingly slow, and Emmanuel was a harsh critic. The third time around, Emmanuel used a stop-watch to time Hunter's progress; and the adage of 'practice-makes-perfect' proved apt. Hunter was able to put himself in the driver's seat of a locked car in less than thirty seconds, and to have the car running in less than a minute 90% of times. Hunter was not overly surprised to see that John I was completely familiar with this nefarious art, and was able to move his vehicles with less wasted motion and faster. However, Emmanuel finally pronounced that Hunter had passed the course with an A- and was declared fit for service.

During the last hour of the evening, Hedy made Hunter dress the role of police officer and UPS driver, make his way with convincing nonchalance into the appropriate vehicle, and to drive it away across the lawn three separate times.

The next three evenings, Hunter practiced the nuances of makeup application, choice and use of wigs, use of props like canes, crutches, boxes, and bags for his role as a derelict, and how to dress, move, and how to speak like a pregnant woman, a mature woman, an Eton educated British businessman, a cockney, an Indian subcontinent salesman, and an oil executive from Iceland—which proved to be the most difficult accent of all to master. Hedy taught him a few catch phrases in a dozen foreign languages that he could use to avoid the incriminating embarrassment of not being able to match his speech to his character role at all.

"In your nice little make-up bag, John, I am including suntan inducing cream, color sticks for African Brown and Ivory White, which is useful to help you look sick or old or just pathetic."

She had him apply color with a makeup sponge and taught him how to use translucent powder and setting spray, how to darken portions of his nose and to lighten others to create the illusion of larger or smaller facial features, how to put on a bra and to fill it so it looked natural, what kind of glasses, hats, and veils to choose, how to make wrinkles and blemishes, or to take them away. They spent sessions on the application of temporary tattoos.

Hunter was clumsy with the transition to being a woman. Hedy gave him a myriad of tips.

"Women are more careless and sexy today. They show more skin. So, even though you will best play the role of a mature woman, wear a dress or blouse that shows some chest skin."

Hunter started to protest.

Reading his mind, Hedy said, "So be sure to shave thoroughly and to apply body makeup. Cake it on. Wear a black bra which calls attention to the very fact that you are wearing one and are—therefore—what you are generally trying to appear to be—a woman. Let a bra strap show. Men and women expect it. Women now show thong straps on purpose, but maybe you won't want to go that far."

Hunter laughed and nodded his agreement.

"And for heaven's sake, don't try to wear real high heels. You walk like a cowboy who fell astride a fence pole when he was a boy. In heels, you'll wobble around like that same sailor who's had too much to drink. Stay with sensible shoes. Wear reasonable earrings. Every woman wears earrings; and they are expected; but don't get gaudy."

She produced a small jewelry box and gave it to Hunter. He gave the contents a cursory glance, enough to see that she had provided a sensible collection of conservative jewelry.

"Your hands are hopeless. Wear jewelry whenever you are a woman. Keep your hands demurely folded or in your purse, or busy fumbling with papers; so, no one has time to scrutinize those big paws."

Hedy made a MoldGel alginate dental impression and from that created several sets of false overlay teeth which she gave him. He was impressed with the alteration that occurred in his appearance with just the change of teeth. The teeth in the dental prostheses were of different sizes, variations of white, yellow, and brownish hues, degrees of orthodontic symmetry, and apparent levels of periodontal disease.

She also provided him with a dozen pair of different colored contact lenses.

"Your eyes are very much too striking, John. Make liberal use of the contact lenses to soften their impact and to make you less identifiable and memorable. Choose the right color for the role you intend to play. Don't minimize the importance of details and nuances."

Hunter could not shut off his mind that night. In his dreams, he frantically applied makeup and disguises and berated himself for his ineptitude.

CHAPTER TWENTY-FOUR

White House: Presidential Family Quarters, 0235

The red phone at President Storebridge's bedside rang with its irritating unfriendly jangle.

The president often said to his wife, Afton, that "no good news ever came by telephone."

He was pretty sure that this time would not be the exception.

"Hello," he said brusquely.

"Lang here, Mr. President, sorry to awaken you. This is a secure line. NSA Director Miller is on a second line with us."

"What is it Director?"

"Yemen, sir. Since ten D.C. time, we have been intercepting all kinds of traffic from the Middle-East, especially from Yemen and the Saudi-Yemeni border area about a major strike in the offing. It is unclear exactly what the target is, but this sounds like the real thing."

"How sure of the authenticity of these intercepts are you, Director Miller?"

Walter Owen Miller spoke for the first time.

"About 92%, Mr. President. The signals are in clear Arabic, and in some instances there have been no attempts at encryption. They seem to be communicating, and presumably acting in some haste."

"What do we do about it, Director Lang?"

"An attack seems imminent, Mr. President. Even if the Yemeni government would permit an American invasion, we could not possibly get anything there for three days that would be useful; and we are hamstrung by the probability that the perpetrators are Saudis and are currently on Saudi soil. The Company's on-the-ground assets think that what we are hearing is still planning, but they are convinced that something big is about to happen unless we can disrupt the planning and logistics of the plan."

"Where do you think they plan to hit?"

"I would bet the farm that it is in Yemen, and it will either be the embassy or a major Yemeni governmental institution, probably the presidential offices."

"Director Lang, I see no viable alternative. I want the operatives of Sheep Dog in Sana'a within the next forty-eight hours ready to act. No more discussion of 'preparation'. Understood?"

"Perfectly, Mr. President. We have some intel about a major confab being cooked up somewhere in the Rafad region. We should have better information by tonight, and we can make that meeting our main target."

"We can't send in Delta Force or Recon Marines—nothing that shows our colors, remember that, both of you."

"We are well aware," the two directors said at once. "We'll get it done our own way."

CHAPTER TWENTY-FIVE

John I knocked briskly on Hunter's door at 0322. Hunter was instantly awake.
"Come in."

"John, get up. It has hit the fan. You will board a jet for your first assignment at 2300 hours, and there is a lot to get done before you do. Hedy and some of her worker-bees will be here in about ten minutes. I have a crew coming in to get your gear packed; so, it will be on the plane when you get there. You ready for the big time, son?"

"Um-hmmh," Hunter said, sure that John I could hear his heart thumping.

He fought to sound casual, and found that his training was kicking in, and, instead of getting more excited, the prospect of moving into the field was actually helping him to calm down.

Following John I's directions, Hunter was lying supine on an examination table that had been brought into the house during last night's heavy meal. Hedy and her crew moved into the house and took over, scarcely speaking to either John.

"We are going to get a life-cast mold of your face and neck, John," she said. "You are going to need a very effective disguise for where you are going, my boy, and don't bother asking; it is not at my pay level to know where that might be."

A technician harshly scrubbed Hunter's face and neck with soap and equally harshly dried them off with a towel with the texture of number two sandpaper. Then he scrubbed it again with rubbing alcohol.

"Good enough," Hedy told him.

Hedy and the tech gelled Hunter's hair flat then glued a theatrical bald hair cap to the margin of skin under the cap's edges with surgical glue. They applied protective petroleum jelly to his eyebrows, eyelids, ears, and lips, inserted drinking straws into Hunter's nostrils then put a thick coat of alginate dental impression material to begin the process of making a life-like mold. As soon as the alginate impression hardened, they applied several coats of orthopedic fracture web plaster bandages with lime to the alginate, waited twenty-five minutes for it to harden into a mask, and removed the perfect impression of his face. Other technicians hurriedly coated the model with release agent, then Hedy and her main assistant covered the model with professional grade plasticene to permit the eventual creation of a flexible elderly face. Hedy carefully scratched multiple wrinkle lines into the plasticene mask in strategic places.

The team of other technicians set to work on the mold, and Hedy and her assistant repeated the process four more times to make a total of five facial masks. Each mold was then treated to separate the plasticene from the plaster leaving a flexible piece of very believable skin for the artists to work with. The technicians applied surgical glue five separate times to Hunter's now raw and burning face, cut the prostheses into three large pieces, and applied the prosthetic pieces to his prepared face. Hedy cut a hole in the chin area so that a separate chin piece and separate lip pieces could be attached later. Hedy carefully laid the pieces in place, cut off the excess edges with a surgical scalpel, and glued the edges together. The forehead, nose piece, and neck pieces were glued to the chin piece giving Hunter a complete, but rather featureless new face. Hedy and her assistant applied lower eyelid bags with tweezers and glued them in place to the rest of the mask. They then gave Hunter a set of wrinkled eyelids.

Two young makeup artists began applying makeup, one on each side of his new face. First they put heavy amounts of darker colored makeup on toothbrushes and flicked the paint onto Hunter's new skin to create the irregularities of aged skin. They used several different colors typically found on the skin of the elderly. They smudged those paint spots with their nimble and practiced fingers. Then, they used very thin little brushes to add darkening to the wrinkles in the mask, added some freckles and age spots. Hedy added some subtle color to the aged lips to increase the authenticity and pronounced her work, "superb" in a characteristic piece of Hollywood modesty.

Hedy fussed over the available choices of wigs and found a neatly coiffed silver- haired one that gave Hunter a completed handsome, dignified, albeit aged, Aryan face. She and her crew worked feverishly to create faces of an elderly woman, a vigorous middle-aged African-American man, and a wind and sun leatherized Arab. The process took twelve hours, one which Hedy told Hunter approached the miraculous, since the usual process took the better part of a month with a single prima donna artist doing everything and closely protecting his or her work. The prima donna charged as much as $10,000 for one mask, and Hollywood producers were happy to pay it.

"You can bet that the big producers in the capital are glad to give us double that for the production of five masks. That is for each mask. We may be over budget, but we are on time."

Hunter was very tired, but was still impressed to see the remarkable transformation the masks provided him. Even he would have been fooled by the disguises he saw in the mirror had he not known that the image he saw was himself. Hedy packed the masks in protective bags. John I had already seen to the removal of his baggage to the airport, and had exited about three hours earlier without so much as a good-bye to Hunter, which caused a pang of disappointment for the fledgling Sheep Dog. As they parted, he gave the diminutive make-up genius a peck on the cheek, and she protested politely and returned his gesture with a firm embrace.

An envelope lay on his bed. He opened it to read:

Top Secret, Eyes Only, Sheep Dog
Report 2230 in the Shoreham Hotel lobby, D.C. to meet handler for operational orders.
Signed, DCIA, POTUS.

CHAPTER TWENTY-SIX

CENTRAL INTELLIGENCE BUILDING,
Langley, Virginia, Office of the ADCIA, 2000 Hours.
PRESENT: ADCIA, CIA OFFICER EDWARD LIAM SALINGER

Ed Salinger took the seat in front of Assistant Director Prentiss. "Time is tight, Ed. Is he ready?"

"I'd like another three months."

"Can he do it? This has become an urgent problem. We have to get him into Yemen by tomorrow and ready to go. Is the Sheep Dog going to prove to be a weak link?"

Salinger thought for a moment before answering.

"He's ready. I guess I just don't like to send one lone agent into the middle of that hornet's nest, and I'm being protective. But, yes, he's ready."

"Meet him at the Shoreham; give him his instructions; and get out to Andrews; so, he can be on the flight at ten. You did a great job with him, and now it's time for him to step up."

"All right. I'd better get over there. I'll let you know."

"I'll need a real time update as often as you can get news to me. And remember that you and I are his only links; nobody—but nobody—gets to know any operational details. Dast-rup gets just the info he needs to assist Sheep Dog—no more, no less."

"Neal is a good head. He'll put two and two together, you know."

"Tell him not to stick his nose in. The Company, the U.S., and the president cannot have enough information on this renegade to let any of us get into an international incident."

"Good old plausible denial," Salinger said.

"You've broken the code. Now get on with it."

CHAPTER TWENTY-SEVEN

E d Salinger sat across from the shiny mahogany bar in the darkened room. He had chosen a booth in the back that gave him a view of the entire room without letting him be seen by anyone who was not standing immediately in front of him. He fidgeted with his watch—checking the time—trying not to count the minutes. By two minutes to ten, there was no sign of John II, and Salinger was becoming tense. He could see two yuppies and a businessman sitting at the bar, an elderly silver haired gentleman in an expensive tailored suit who sat two stools away, and Oliver Prentiss, who was sitting in the first booth keeping an eye trained in the direction of Salinger's booth.

At eight sharp—with Salinger's nerves beginning to fray—the two yuppies and the older man got up from their bar stools and started walking towards the exit archway. The yuppies continued out towards the reception desk, but the old gentleman snapped his fingers and turned about to return to the bar. Salinger could see that his wallet was still sitting on the smooth shiny surface. Salinger looked away in the direction of the entrance ignoring the forgetful gentleman.

As a complete surprise, a man's voice—a familiar one—addressed him. The elderly man was standing right in front of him.

"Pardon me, sir," the reedy, well modulated voice said, "I'm new in the city. Could you possibly direct me to a less expensive but still comfortable and safe hotel? You seem to know your way around…If it's not an imposition."

The accent was unusual, but not significantly so. Salinger tried to place it—sounded mostly Scandinavian, but not Danish, Norwegian, or Swedish.

In a minor feat of mind reading, the speaker said, "I have just arrived in the capital from Reykjavik, and I do not know the city."

Finally, it dawned on Salinger.

"John?!" he said, greatly amused.

"No, John, it's Svein Magnus Thorsteinsson," the Sheep Dog said suppressing a laugh.

"Sit."

The Sheep Dog slid into the booth with Salinger. The senior agent glanced down the barroom and caught the eye of the ADCIA. They shared their surprise at both having been fooled.

"You got me. I have to admit that. If you had been an assassin, I would be slumped over by now. I am getting lax in my old age. That disguise is just about perfect."

"Hedy and her boys are geniuses."

"They are. We don't have a lot of time. Take the mask and the monkey suit with you. Wear it as soon as you get off the plane and as long as you are fully operational. Leave the country in it. You will meet our agent, Neal Dastrup, and his son, Dusty, at The Company's private airstrip, and they'll drive you to your take-off point; but they won't accompany you beyond that because they are too well known. Otherwise, you are not to have the slightest connection with CIA personnel or any other Americans of any stripe while in Yemen.

"Now, you can be privy to a secret. It may come as a shock; but my real name is not John; actually it's Edward Liam Salinger. That's my real name. I want you to call me Ed. Don't tell me your real name or anything else about yourself. Here is a card with my sat phone number and ID code. You can call me anytime, and The Company will find me. However, don't contact me unless you have been compromised or are in imminent danger or some other extraordinarily important thing comes up. I will not be able to contact you."

Sheep Dog nodded his understanding.

Salinger handed over a manila envelope.

"Don't open it now, but it contains the particulars of your mission. I have sent on a 9 mm sound suppressed automatic hand gun, your Steyr-Mannlicher SSG-69 PII sniper rifle with all of its attachments, the AA-12 Combat shot gun, plenty of ammo, your ghillie suit, a good set of BDUs, running boots, and the best spotting scope you ever saw."

"And Dastrup will have all of that waiting for me?"

"Yeah. Look, John, I wish I could do more. I really wish I could be there with you, but you know I can't. So, all I can do is wish you good luck and God-speed."

"I appreciate everything you have done already. I'll send you something to let you know of the success of the mission."

Salinger liked the positive construction of the Sheep Dog's last sentence, nothing about the possibility of a failure.

"Let's get on out to Andrews. You have an exciting ride in head of you. Ever been on an F-22?"

"Can't say that I have."

"Well, all I can say is that you'll have to buckle up."

CHAPTER TWENTY-EIGHT

At quarter to nine that evening, Sheep Dog and Ed Salinger reached the private Company hangar at Andrews Air Force Base. Their journey across the extensive tarmac required a two car escort. The hanger was pitch black. Two armed guards stayed with the two visitors all the way into the hangar. Their supervision was transferred to a burly, unsmiling, fully armed African-American Chief Master Sergeant and an equally dour Russian Federation Air Force *General-leytenánt VVS "aviátsii"* [Lieutenant General of Aviation]. The Russian officer—the equivalent of a U.S. Air Force Major General—greeted them.

"Gentlemen, your State Department and Air Force leaders have asked a great favor from the Russian Federation. We have granted that favor—one of you will be transported to your destination in the greatest air craft ever built. Because of the apparent sensitivity of your mission, we have even agreed not to demand to know the destination. You may direct the pilot, *Polkóvnik "aviátsii"*, Leonid Andreivich Koronski, when you are airborne. Let me tell you this. This aircraft is every bit as secret as your mission, whatever that may be. It would do incalculable harm to Russian-American relations should any information about this aircraft be communicated outside those with an absolute need to know."

Both Salinger and Sheep Dog nodded their full understanding and agreement.

"Then, let us get you situated."

The general gave an almost unnoticeable signal with his left hand, and two enlisted men—one Russian, and one American—moved out of the shadows and indicated for Sheep Dog to follow. He turned and gave a small wave to

Salinger, turned back and walked to a small fenced off area next to the air-craft's entryway. He had never seen such an aircraft before. It was something from StarWars.

Ed Salinger left with the two armed guards who had escorted him to the hangar. As Sheep Dog stood in the small enclosure, he was frisked for weapons and ordered to change into full flight gear. His clothing—including the disguise mask—was carefully placed into a flight bag and hoisted into the rear of the plane. Sheep Dog stood uncomfortably by as the enlisted men readied the air-craft. They gave a thumbs-up signal; and a tall, powerful looking Russian officer emerged from the shadows and walked up to Sheep Dog and extended his hand.

"I am VVS Colonel Koronski, sir. I am at your service. I presume you are not familiar with the aircraft. Your people told me that you were expecting to be taken in a U.S. F-22 Raptor. However—for two reasons—that would not be fitting. First of all, the Raptor has only one seat; and the Sukoi PAK FA—at least this particular experimental model—has two. As a matter of fact, there have been only three units produced; and only this one has two seats. Secondly, your mission is of such importance—we are informed—that only this best airplane in the world would do."

He gave a wide, toothy smile—dotted with stainless steel caps—an acknowl-edgement of his boyish enthusiasm. Sheep Dog laughed briefly to cement the bond of pride among warriors.

"I really do not exaggerate, my American friend. This is what should be called a sixth generation Raptor, the only plane in the world able to compete with your magnificent F-22. Our Air Force modestly calls it our fifth genera-tion project. This is a T-51, an updated version of the prototype T-50. Your F-35 Lightening II has not yet been cleared to take to the skies, but may someday be a competitor. The PAK FA possesses advanced avionics, stealth capability, a ferry range of 4,000 to 5,500 km, and endurance of 3.3 hours. It is armed with the latest-generation air-to-air, air-to-surface, and air-to-ship missiles, and has two 30 mm cannons. Despite its fairly large size, its stealth capacity is the most advanced for any aircraft yet put into the sky. Under the direction of Deputy Defense Minister Vladimir Popovkin, the fighter has been under development since the early 1990s, and was only declared fully serviceable two years ago.

"Besides my obvious enthusiasm, there are things you need to know for the flight. First of all, the craft exerts 10-11 G with its rate of climb of 350 meters per second. It will be uncomfortable on take-off. More than one occu-pant has fainted; don't be embarrassed if you do. We will be traveling with a fairly light load. I have been ordered to fly at maximum speed which is in excess of 2100 kilometers per hour as is afforded by the completely updated engine, an AL-41F Turbo-Fan R. The R is for "Re-fitted"—at a final cost just to produce this one plane's engine of 150 million U.S. dollars and an overall engine project that cost 1.5 billion U.S. dollars. Such performance requires an immense amount of fuel; so, we will have to slow down twice to link up to in-air refueling. The deceleration and subsequent reacceleration will be temporarily quite uncomfortable. The auditory system is very advanced and most clear and useful. We will be able to converse with ease.

"Any questions?"

"No, sir. Just a couple of comments. First, I am tremendously impressed with the plane, and second, I can't tell you how grateful I am and my country is for what the VVS and you personally are doing. Thank you."

"We are comrades. I am at your service. Before we get aboard, you have to go through a brief escape and ejection training. Frankly, at the speeds we will be traveling, ejection would be like being blasted with a cannon and is unsurvivable. Nevertheless, comrade, it is protocol; and the VVS is nothing if not wedded to protocol."

CHAPTER TWENTY-NINE

The Sukoi PAK FA swept across the Gulf of Aden, over the port city of Aden, and streaked north nearly invisibly across the desert to Sana'a, the capital of Yemen. Both occupants surveyed the rapidly passing city and both saw two significant fires burning in the heart of it, one in the southwest and the other in the northeast. Colonel Koronski brought up his on-board GPS which showed a clear map of the city.

"If I am not mistaken, my friend, the more easterly fire is coming from your embassy. I'm sorry."

"That might complicate matters," Sheep Dog said sourly.

The swift bird passed over the well-lit busy Sana'a International Airport with its full complement of aircraft from the Airlines of Ta, EgyptAir, Air Emirates, Ethiopian Airlines, Air Etihad, Gulf Air, Luftansa, Middle East Ai, Qatar Airways, Royal Jordania, Turkish Airways, and Yemenia. Colonel Koronski slowed as much as possible, consulted his GPS manually, and assured himself of the computer setting. Moments later they made one pass over a very small local airport at Bar al Hazm which had only three small private craft on the runway. The main flight path was obviously too short for the high speed PAK FA, and Sheep Dog began to get nervous. The Russian aviator, however, was calm as the proverbial summer's morn. The PAK FA streaked out to the east, made a wide arced turn and rocketed down towards the ground on a parallel to—but a short distance north of—the well-lighted main public runway. The invisible parallel runway became lighted only a minute before touch-down. Sheep Dog felt his bowels begin to loosen as he watched the altimeter fall to zero at the moment the lights illuminated the strip. The plane was going 300 miles an hour when the wheels hit the tarmac. The Sheep Dog clenched his eyes shut.

The landing was perfectly smooth, and even in that desert at night, the landing corridor was sufficient.

"Airstrip is compliments of your CIA, comrade. Welcome to Yemen," Colonel Koronski said holding back his amusement at the Sheep Dog's discomfiture.

"Nice flight," the passenger said when he could gain control of his voice. "Routine."

Both men laughed—at the Colonel's mastery of understatement and with relief.

Sheep Dog said, "There is a phrase in Arabic that is appropriate for our arrival—'Al hamdulillah'."

"Ah, yes, 'thanks be to God'."

"And thanks be to you, comrade pilot. I understand that your orders are not to leave the plane, but to return immediately."

"То Родина-мать [*Rodina-mat*'], my friend. To the real world."

"To the Mother Homeland," Sheep Dog acknowledged. "Good-bye then."

Sheep Dog and a short, heavy-set man who had appeared out of the darkness unloaded Sheep Dog's gear from the aircraft and onto a small pick-up truck without a word being spoken. The colonel stood in the cockpit exit and shook Sheep Dog's hand, turned back into the plane, taxied around the tarmac, and accelerated off as Sheep Dog and the man from the ground drove away towards the southwest from the obscure airstrip. The roar of the great AL-41F Turbo-Fan R engine was deafening and final.

In the dim light of the dashboard, Sheep Dog noted that the driver had red hair. He spoke first.

"You're the Sheep Dog, I presume."

"Yes. And I presume you're Dustin?"

"Call me Dusty. That was my dad's idea of a joke when he saw that he had just hatched a red-headed son. We'll meet him at a safe house in Sana'a. Maybe you saw the fires in the center of the city as you flew over."

"We did. The pilot brought up his GPS and said it was our embassy."

"Yeah, that's right. The other fire is in the Old Sana'a Suq in Bab al-Yaman. We've been hearing for the past several days about some big plans by al Qaeda. I guess we now know what those plans were."

The road out of the small airport to the main highway south was execrable, and it took an hour and a half to navigate their way through the main suburban city of Al Jiraf to a small group of low beige mud-brick buildings west, just outside the population center of the main city called Rohm as Sufla.

"Home crap home," Dusty said. "Or more accurately, 'crap home away from home'. We used to have a place two doors from the embassy. It's gone now."

Sheep Dog and Dusty got out of the truck and carried his gear into the middle of three nondescript and unlit buildings that stood a little apart from the few other virtually identical buildings that constituted the town. After a few moments, a brilliant flashlight snapped on temporarily blinding the two men.

"Hands where I can see them," came a man's harsh voice.

As the effects of the dazzling light subsided, Sheep Dog made out a figure in full Arab dress holding a combat shot gun. He waited for the man to continue since the desert apparition certainly had the commanding position. Sheep Dog began calculating his chances of overpowering the Arab and Dusty. Sheep Dog looked at his situation and recalled Damon Runyon's quote, 'I came to the conclusion long ago that all life is *six to five against*'. Sheep Dog thought his odds worse than that, tensed, waited, and held still.

"What do you think, Dusty?" the Arab asked.

"He's okay, dad. He just got off the most fantastic plane you ever saw. I don't think either of us is worth somebody sending a Russian super jet with a colonel as a pilot just to snuff us out."

"Turn on the lights," the Arab ordered.

The room illuminated fully, and Sheep Dog noted that the windows had opaque black curtains; the man had a very menacing weapon; and he was not an Arab.

"My arms are getting tired. Can I let them hang by my sides?"

"Sure, go ahead."

Now the man's voice was now more affable. He removed his Arabic costume and dropped it to the floor and walked up to Sheep Dog and shook his hand.

"Sorry about the gun. Can't be too careful."

"I understand," Sheep Dog said quietly.

He scrutinized the man, obviously the father of Dusty. He was of medium height and powerfully built with arms like large hickory branches. Although he was rotund, there did not appear to be anything wasted on fat. He had military cut, short-cropped graying hair and looked to be about the same age as the Sheep Dog. For all of his serious demeanor, he had a pleasant, even handsome, and fetching face. Sheep Dog was drawn to him. He needed someone to trust, and he guessed that Dastrup would have to be the one. He waited for the man to speak.

"I'm Neal, Neal Dastrup," the former Arab said, "I'm the resident Company agent here in lovely tropical Yemen. You've met Dusty. He's my son and a good man. Right now, we don't have an office. It used to be in the front part of the embassy, which is now a pile of rubble. However, we have a back-up communications system here, and can operate fairly decently. To come to the point, we think we know where the perps are right now, or at least where they'll be this afternoon. In the meantime we can take care of one of the two missions you have been assigned this morning. That would be the elimination of Faizah Batool al-Faisal, the pesky Saudi lady physician who the Yemeni National Security Agency is holding and is at their wits' end to know what to do with. They don't want to anger big Saudi Arabia; so, they don't dare question her. They can't ship her away; nobody will have her; and, finally, the U.S. can't be seen to have treated her unpleasantly. After all, she is some sort of Saudi princess and all. I am under the strictest orders from The Company to be certain that there is never any connection between the agency and the girl. So…enter you."

"I read the particulars during my flight."

"We can't take you to where she's being held, but we can get you to a Yemeni transport service that can. You'll have to lie a little, I'm afraid."

The Sheep Dog just smiled.

"Your cover is that you're an oil company geologist for some company from Iceland. Let's see…"

He fumbled through a manila folder for a moment.

"Yeah, here we are. You are one Svein Magnus Thorsteinsson; you're oldern dirt, and you work for Royal Dutch Shell of Iceland. I have your passport and professional papers—they got here before the bombing. I don't think anybody but the transport guy will ever ask to see them. We have a customs entry stamp on the passport; so, you shouldn't have any problem exiting so long as you match the picture of the old geezer on the passport."

"That's part of the gear I brought. Incidentally, the stuff is all marked as belonging to Royal Dutch Shell. The gun case is labeled, *Fragile, Geological Instruments*. I can't imagine that fooling anyone, but who knows. I can be persuasive if the need arises."

"*I can just bet*," Neal thought after giving the Sheep Dog a visual once over.

The three men took advantage of the enveloping darkness and drove the truck and Sheep Dog's gear to a small hotel in the market district of a small town in southwestern Sana'a Governate about thirty kilometers southwest of the center of Sana'a, called Da'ir. The area was a sparsely populated flat desert region well outside the main population centers.

The Dastrups helped Sheep Dog get his gear into the Ruhm al 'Ulya Hotel lobby.

"The hotel is one of four little accommodations in a small chain owned by a friend of ours," Neal said.

The two CIA agents shook his hand and gave him a note containing the address of a local transport company. The front door was unlocked, and no one was about; so, he sat there in the dark for morning's light. The muezzin's call to first prayer, the *Fair*, came just as it had since the days of The Prophet. Sheep Dog pictured in his mind's eye that the light was barely enough to see a single hair. He was able to get a better look around the small hotel's seedy waiting room. On the wall behind the reservations desk hung a cork-board for announcements, all in English since the majority of Yemenis and essentially all tourists used the world's dominant language. He noted the currency conversions:

1 US dollar to 212.26 Yemeni rials (YRL)
1 Euro to 286 YRLs
1 Pound Sterling to 326 YRLs
1 US dollar to 3.75 Saudi Arabian Riyals (SAR)
1 Euro to 5 SARs
1 Pound Sterling to 6 SARs

The Company had provided the Sheep Dog with sufficient quantities of all of those currencies; so, he was confident that he could find transportation for his mission even if the prices were exorbitant. He stepped out onto the dusty street and dragged his large bags and sat on them to wait for a taxi or even a private vehicle to take him to the transport company that the Dastrups had recommended. Shortly, he was able to hail a taxi which was no more than a battered pick-up truck with an Arabic logo—جبل النبي شعيب— emblazoned on the driver's side door that Sheep Dog could not read. The driver turned out to be the proprietor and sole employee of Jabal an-Nabi Shu'ayb Mountain Transport Service who had not had a paying fare for days. As it turns out, that was the only service available in the town. The driver was obsequious and eager to take the well-healed, well-dressed, old man into the mountains; so, he could drill core samples for his petroleum company; so he said. He did not evince the slightest evidence of suspicion regarding the Sheep Dog's peculiarly shaped equipment.

"*Sabah al Khayr, Ismi* Mohammed Abdullah Selah. *Sh'nnu ismak?*"

"*Sabah al Khayr, Ismi* Svein Magnus Thorsteinsson," Sheep Dog replied in the best response he could muster from his brief study of common Arabic phrases he had worked to memorize on the incoming flight. "*Mutaasif*, Mr. Selah, *ma kan tkellemichi Arbia. Tkellem Inglisia?*"

"Oh, forgive me, kind sir, by the grace of Allah, the Merciful, I have learned English. We can easily talk in that dialect," Selah said, eyes down lest the European stranger think him immodest.

Sheep Dog had gotten used to haggling during his military years in Southeast Asia and afterwards while doing business throughout the rest of Asia. It was tedious for him, but he realized that it was a necessary and expected cultural courtesy and a way to establish that the buyer was not a rube unaware of how to protect himself. He had been prepared for the inevitable need for cash by The Company providing an envelope with large amounts of Yemeni Rials, Saudi Riyals, and Euros.

"How much will you charge me per day for two days transportation?"

"My friend, I would prefer to have that unpleasant subject dealt with at the end of our journey; so, we can travel as friends."

"Ah, in a perfect world, how I would also like to deal only as friends; but, alas, my company insists that all business transactions be conducted with the strictest accounting; and I must pay you up front. It is policy."

"Certainly you cannot offend the great leaders of your company."

He thought for a long moment, seeming to suffer a bit over the very necessity of having to charge.

"Shall we say 15,000 rials per day, my friend?"

Sheep Dog did a quick calculation-$75.

"That would be more than my company would allow, I am afraid. Perhaps 7,000 would be more appropriate."

Selah seemed to be genuinely hurt by such an insulting counter offer. After all, this was among friends, no?

"I have a family, and we are not rich people. We have debts incurred from the operation of this humble business. I suppose I could reduce our regular rate a bit...for a friend. Let me see...perhaps 11,000 would be reasonable."

"Since I really must be getting on with my business, and much as I would like to continue with our very pleasant chat, I can perhaps go as high as 9,000."

Selah looked Sheep Dog over, and considered whether or not he had reached his limit. Selah knew he would make a profit if he settled for seventy-five hundred, but this wealthy European appeared likely to be able to go at least a little higher.

"In order to secure the necessities for my family, I am afraid that I can lower my fee to 10,000, but that will have to be the limit of my generosity, I'm afraid."

Sheep Dog could feel the wasting minutes racing by. He did have to get going, and Uncle Sam had deep enough pockets to pay triple what the man asked originally. Still, there was the matter of face. He had to try once more.

"I will offer you 8,500. That, my friend, is as much as I can possibly afford and is adequate for expenses, your time and work, and some profit. We cannot be guilty of trading in usury, can we now?"

Selah hated to have his religion used as a weapon against him, but the man had him there. The look in the intense brown eyes of the older European convinced that it was futile to hold out for more.

"Well, my friend, why not. I can work again. I do not have to make all of my living from one man who is obviously astute and one who—in addition—understands the religion. Let us shake on a deal at 8,500 YRLs."

It was done. The two men spat on the palms of their hands and shook. Whatever else Mohammed Selah was; he was product of millennia of participation in the custom of the sanctity of keeping his word and honoring a bargain. Sheep Dog intended to give him a handsome bonus when they returned to Da'ir. Their handshake was a solemn sealing of a sacred bargain. The terms of the deal would not be mentioned between honorable men. It was not done.

Mohammed Abdullah Selah's truck proved to be a far more reliable vehicle for Sheep Dog's purposes than it appeared. The talkative transporter was happy to have someone to practice his considerably flawed English upon and kept up a voluble stream of one-sided conversation going the entire trip. He did not seem to mind that Sheep Dog responded only laconically and infrequently.

The roads were paved all the way to Jabal an-Nabi Shu'ayb Mountain but rutted and worn with time and heat. Sheep Dog's bones were beginning to ache. The truck had no air-conditioning, and the two men were sweating in the 40° C heat. Selah's body and clothes odors were wearing on Sheep Dog's Western sensitivities, a fact he took considerable pains to avoid letting his loquacious little driver know. They drove through a little burg which Selah named Baril and passed a rectangular block monument of some sort made of cinder blocks painted with peeling white wash with a painting of a falcon with its wings spread wide in a predatory dive on one side. The otherwise featureless structure stood slanch-wise at a 40 degree angle.

"That is al-Saqr, the falcon," Selah said as if that was something that should be meaningful to his Western client.

Sheep Dog grunted his appreciation.

Shortly further on at the foot of the mountain, they turned into a small grove of ancient olive trees to relieve themselves. It was cooler there, and the trees gave some shade. It had been a wet year, by central highlands standards, and a good year for crops. There were a few well tended vegetable gardens around the olive orchard, and the presence of some green was a pleasant contrast to the harsh beige and browns of the otherwise nearly plant free wasteland.

"We are about to ascend into a holy place," Selah told the Sheep Dog. "It is the mountain of the prophet Shu'ayb."

Sheep Dog decided not to seek further details about the august prophet; so, Selah let it go.

"It is the highest peak in all of Yemen…in all of the Arabian peninsula…3,660 meters tall," the driver said with pride.

"It is an impressive mountain, my friend," Sheep Dog said, mentally comparing it to his mountains in Colorado and suppressing a derisive smile.

They each drank a liter of bottled water and shared a *shawarma* which came out of a greasy paper bag. It was good and filling—layers of lamb and chicken that had been roasted by Selah's wife on a vertical spit. Selah produced a delicious *asabeeh* pastry—lady fingers made of rolled filo pastry stuffed with pistachios, pinenuts and honey as the *piece de resistance*.

"*Shukran*," Sheep Dog said in genuine appreciation, aware that his pronunciation of the word for 'thanks' probably came across as very westernized. "That was a truly delicious lunch. I will buy us and all of your family a fine meal in Da'ir when we get back."

The two men set out again and wound up a road that curved its way to the top of the rock strewn dirt mountain. They passed a stagnant green-water reservoir about half way up, and Sheep Dog made a mental note of its location and distance from the top and bottom. The mountain top held a fortress looking set of irregular large grey-beige mud-brick multistory buildings. There were no signs indicating shops or hotels or services; so, Sheep Dog concluded that they were more likely than not apartment houses. He studied his GPS and gave Selah directions to a poorly maintained rutted dirt road near the crest of the mountain behind the apartment houses.

"Stop here, please," Sheep Dog ordered. "Wait for me at the bottom of the hill by the reservoir. I may be quite a while looking for the right kind of rocks; so, be patient. I will make it worth your while."

"Yes, يﺪﻨﻓأ [*Effendi*]," *Selah said dropping into the formal Arabic use of the word denoting* a nobility title meaning a lord or master. "*Masha'Allah*," Selah went on, hoping that Allah would not will a wait past the time for evening prayers. He always liked to be home for Maghrib—the sunset prayer—and especially on this day.

Sheep Dog, now feeling uncomfortably hot in his disguise climbed the hundred yards to the crest of the mountain behind the multi-story mud brick edifices carrying his sniper rifle, took out his binoculars, and surveyed the valley below. There was a medium sized but apparently well-built house of the same mud-brick construction as most of the other buildings in the country sitting in a level area mid-valley. The road to the house was of a construction quality far beyond what one would expect for such a remote and unimposing structure. The other unusual feature of the property was the high—obviously electrified—elk fence with guard towers at each corner. The periphery of the house and the fence were patrolled by about fifty Yemeni soldiers, all heavily armed and apparently diligent. The court yard in front of the house had a small decorative tiled fountain for ease of washing for the five daily prayers; otherwise, the grounds were smooth and bare.

Sheep Dog noted the distance to the center of the yard in front of the main door with his range finder—748 meters. He set his sniper rifle on its bipod and drew the uncomfortably warm ghillie cloak over him. At a distance of even a few yards, he was, for all practical purposes, invisible. The information Ed Salinger had given him described the daily routine of the place. The lone prisoner in the house had been recorded as having a rigid schedule of outdoor appearances. She was allowed out for thirty minutes just after sunup and for thirty to forty-five minutes at noon. The CIA surveillance reports indicated that the noon appearance was invariable. The day was clear, and the sand shimmered in the heat. The sun was vicious. Sheep Dog was sweating as if he had been drenched by a garden hose.

As predicted, Faizah Batool al-Faisal walked out of the front door on the stroke of noon. It surprised the Sheep Dog to see her bare-headed and in a modest, but nonetheless Western style dress. Through the spotting scope, even at that distance, he could see that she was a beautiful, svelte, raven-haired young woman. She moved with grace. She did a series of stretches then walked briskly back and forth as her keepers watched appreciatively. She did not appear to pay them any heed, looking straight forward as if they did not exist.

Sheep Dog wiped the copious sweat from his brow and away from his tired eyes as the young woman began to slow down. When she took a seat on the edge of the fountain, he brought his eye to the eyepiece of the telescopic lens and fixed her head dead center in the reticle. He mentally computed the distance and windage. She seemed lost in thought and was as still as a statue, her attractive face turned away from the broiling sun.

Sheep Dog took three slow deep breaths. With his final exhalation, he slowly squeezed the trigger. The sound was no louder than if he had massed a hearty expectoration. Through the scope, he saw the woman's head explode in a burst of blood and fragments as dramatically as if he had just blown up a water melon. He retracted the sniper rifle in under the ghillie cloak, waited, and watched. The courtyard exploded into chaos. Guards looked all around the perimeter of the grounds in a futilely narrow search. Only the occasional set of eyes turned to the crest of the mountain where the Sheep Dog lay. Trucks began to buzz up and down the road. When the chaos reached maximum, Sheep Dog slowly crawled backwards until he could feel the declining edge of the mountain he had climbed three hours earlier. It was a slow and very uncomfortable process. When the valley floor was no longer in his line of sight, he hurriedly marched down the hill to where Selah sat sleeping in the hot truck cab.

"I have completed my work here," Sheep Dog said to the groggy driver. "Let's move on to our second destination."

Selah was still half asleep, and it was evident that he had heard nothing. The area on this side of the mountain top remained as tranquil as it had been when they first arrived. Sheep Dog pressed the driver to hurry, ostensibly to meet a fictitious deadline. He frequently, and as surreptitiously as possible, checked the rear view mirror to see if they were being followed. The route to their next destination, Ad Dummam, fortunately avoided all heavy population centers in the Sana'a Governate; and the activity generated by the assassination of Faizah Batool al-Faisal was concentrated north and easterly towards Sana'a. Ironically, al Qaeda and Saudi intelligence operatives and Yemeni security forces all suspected each other and all frantically made centripetal movements towards the city center. Sheep Dog and Selah traveled north and west to the drab little city of Ad Dummam then took the west road out into the flat, dry, farmlands of what was once North Yemen. No one paid them the slightest attention as they traveled out past the last houses.

Sheep Dog checked the satellite photographs against what he was seeing and followed his GPS coordinates to a point in the road where the GPS direction pointer demanded a turn to the left—south. That presented some difficulty since there was no road. Off in the shimmering dry distance, across a patchwork of dry stubble fields was a single house with one small outbuilding. It was 1515, and the meeting of the terrorists was slated to begin in forty-five minutes according to the information supplied to him by the CIA spies and analysts. There was no activity at the L shaped house, in the flat plains around it, or along the roadways. The western road was empty except for the Jabal an-Nabi Shu'ayb Mountain Transport Service pick-up truck and its occupants.

Sheep Dog had Selah park on the roadside for a few moments while he puzzled. He made up his mind.

"Friend Selah, I will get out here and take my equipment. Go to the city and wait by the fire station. We saw it on the way in. I will likely be two or maybe three hours; I can't be sure. I will catch up with you in time for evening prayers. I am counting on you."

"Of course, *effendi*, I will not fail you. May the peace of Allah, the Merciful, go with you."

"And with you."

Sheep Dog lifted his heavy bags out of the truck bed and watched until the little pick-up disappeared from view. Then, with one last look in all directions to be sure he was not being observed, he trotted off the road and into a dry stream bed lined with a sparse but useful line of scraggly trees. The stream bed was sandy; but the sand was packed hard; and Sheep Dog was able to make good time, covering the approximately one mile distance in twenty minutes. He had plenty of time to set up his watch site. He found a large, old, dead tree whose dry gnarled roots overhung the river bank. With a little easy digging in the loose sand, he made himself a hidey hole. His place was secure from any but the most scrupulous searchers, and he was able to see the entrance to the house very well. It was ten to four, and Sheep Dog was tense and ready.

He was beginning to develop a low grade anxiety that the terrorists would not show up, that they had been warned, or that the activity generated by the search for the assassin of Faizah Batool al-Faisal had scared them all off. His anxiety lasted only a couple of minutes. From the distance—from three distances—he heard the rhythmical whump-whump of helicopter engines and rotor blades. As they came steadily closer, he was sure that his information was correct. This was the place, and this was the time. His heart and respiratory rates began to climb, and he reverted to his training to calm down.

In all, five helicopters touched down in front of the house. The occupants of the Yemen Air Force helicopters—thirty-five of them—alighted and the principle players, all dressed in formal kaftans and thobes, moved swiftly into the house without superfluous chatter. A dozen guards fanned out around the house and began making regular walking inspections. Sheep Dog could see their faces. They were all tense, serious looking, and obviously well-trained and well-armed young men. None of them smoked or spoke to the others. They were all business. So was Sheep Dog.

He got out his AA-12 Combat shot gun and loaded 15 rounds each of special Frag-12 18.5 mm fin-stabilized HE, HEAP, and sensor fused HEAB airburst fragmentation shells—that were designed to detonate in mid-air—into the circular magazine, added several incendiary grenades, and made sure he was locked and ready. He set the shotgun on the edge of the dead river bank under the tangled roots; so, it would be readily available to him. He checked the position of his throwing knives, silenced Taurus 809B ambidextrous 9 mm, and his combat fighting knife, then slithered out of his hidey hole and up into the shadow of two bent trees. He flicked the 3 position safety to off and made sure the decocker was in the correct alignment.

A guard left his assigned surveillance circuit and came to a tree in front of Sheep Dog to take a leak. He died with his throat cut and a gurgling sound that carried no more than a few feet. A pair of guards walked the same circuit going in opposite directions and each man was dropped by a throwing knife that imbedded in his exposed throat. Sheep Dog crawled over to the men and dragged them under the trees. The way was now clear for him to stand among the trees looking at the front door of the house and not be seen for a few minutes, which was all he needed. He could hear the soft murmur of voices wafting from the door and the windows which were open to alleviate some of the oppressive desert heat.

Inside, Hamza Ali Saleh al Dhayani, the prime suspect in the September 17, 2008 suicide attack on the U.S. Embassy in Yemen sat in the seat of prominence at the head of a long, beautifully polished cherry-wood conference table. Around the table were freedom fighters from Saudi Arabia [Abdulkhaleq Abdel-Karim al-Wahishi and Saeed Shuaib ud-Din—al Qaeda top and second leaders in the kingdom], Yemen [Zacharias el-Faisal, Sheik Abdullah Moussaouie, and Imam Shuaib Mahmoud ud-Din, all hand picked leaders operating under al Dhayani], Iran [Mahdi Ali al-Dabbagy, Muhammad

Amin-Rashti ("Baba") from Rasht, and Alaeddin Baktiari, Hamas commander in Gaza, and a fiery assassin and teacher of suicide bombers, Fatima Khoshjamal], Somalia [Ali Hassan Nasser], and Jordan [Abu Musab Judeh and Mohammed al-Zarqawi, brother of the chief lieutenant of Usama bin Laden], and their lieutenants and executive officers—twenty-three in all. Prayers and praises for the Allah, the All-Wise, All-Powerful, and All-Merciful and for his Prophet, may Allah's praise ever be upon him, had been given; but it was not yet time to get down to the planning of jihad attacks for which they had gathered from far and wide in the Muslim world.

They sipped thick bitter coffee from Egyptian demitasses as they shuffled their papers. It was the privilege of the leader and caller of the meeting, Hamza Ali Saleh al Dhayani, to open the speaking, and he took his time collecting his thoughts.

Sheep Dog stood erect and aimed the shotgun. He tensed himself, put the firing mechanism on automatic, and squeezed the trigger. Explosion, fire, and death leapt from the weapon's hot barrel. Sheep Dog coolly moved the point of the barrel from the door to each window and back again. Occasionally he deviated to take out a hapless guard who was foolish enough or brave enough to show himself to do his duty. Those men evaporated. The building began to collapse from the weakening of the superstructure caused by the HE rounds and became a total fireball from the incendiary shells. A head rolled out of the front door and spun around on the concrete driveway. No more guards appeared.

Sheep Dog turned his gun on the five helicopters sitting north of the house and destroyed them all in a minute of devastating fire. The barrel of the AA-12 was glowing red and smoking but continued to fire with incredible accuracy. The noise was deafening; the smoke suffocating; and the heat unbearable. Sheep Dog backed up and moved north to protect himself from it. Two guards ran screaming as they burned from flames that had jumped out of windows. Sheep Dog mercifully dispatched them with his Taurus. He ran around the house in search of any survivors and found only one man, who was hiding behind the privy. Sheep Dog killed him with a Mozambique trio of 9 mm shots—two in the chest and one in the head. Seeing no more combatants, he stopped shooting. The only sound now came from the crackling of the flames and the crumbling of damaged walls and roof.

For a moment, he was spell bound by what he had done and what he was seeing. He had made 35 or so people not only be dead but essentially disappear and had reduced to ruin a building as effectively as an earthquake. It was awesome. He was too excited, too revved up to have moral qualms or misgivings about what he had done. He returned to his operational mind set and concentrated on getting out of that place as fast as possible. He was thirsty—very, very thirsty—and his mind now fixated on getting something to drink as soon as possible.

He hurriedly gathered his gear into his cases and set off at a steady hard lope along the dry stream bed reversing the route by which he had arrived. At intervals along the way, he took a look over the banks of the dry stream to see if emergency crews, police, or military units were on the way; but he was able to run all the way to the western road without seeing anyone and was confident that no one saw him. The return trip took less than 15 minutes. Now, he had only to get himself to the fire station in Ad Dummam and Selah's truck; and then he would have water.

He moved as quickly as his stamina would allow down the long road into Ad Dummam. His luck was holding; no vehicles were in sight and, as yet, no air traffic. He saw farmers dressed in beige colored woolen *salwar kameez* over rubber sandals and sleeveless jerkins, despite the oppressive heat. *Salwar* are loose pajama-like trousers. The legs are wide at the top, and narrow at the ankle. The *kameez* is a long shirt or tunic. The side seams [known as the *chaak*], left open below the waist-line, give the wearer greater freedom of movement for farming and fighting. The men worked with donkeys or tractors in their fields and the occasional woman or young child was occupied with outdoor work, but he did not attract their attention.

He was comforted by the fact that he was not seeing any electrical or phone lines. About half way in, he saw a set of about twenty farm houses around which were clustered farm vehicles and old trucks. He looked around carefully—saw no one—then made a bee-line for the nearest old truck. His luck was holding. He was weakening from dehydration, but the vintage truck's key was in the ignition. It started, sputtered, and jerked off down the path to the main road. Its maximum speed was no more than twenty miles per hour; but he was elated that he remained safe; and water was no more than ten or fifteen minutes away.

CHAPTER THIRTY

As he pulled into the town square of Ad Dummam, Sheep Dog edged down in the seat of the old truck. Two police cars rolled out of the police station followed by the town's only fire truck. Overhead, an army heli-copter was heading west.

"*Well, it has hit the fan,*" Sheep Dog said to himself.

He need not have worried about being seen since all interest by security forces was now obviously on points west; and besides, the windshield of the truck was so coated with dust and grease that someone with curiosity would have had to press his nose against the glass to see the occupant of the cab. He was parked directly in front of the fire station which emptied of occupants during the next five minutes. Sheep Dog looked around the entire square for Selah or his truck and could not see other. It was not like the little truck driver to be surreptitious, since there was no good reason for him to suspect Sheep Dog of being anything except who he appeared to be—an elderly European geologist.

The wait became annoying after fifteen minutes. Sheep Dog scrutinized the side streets as far as he could see. No Selah. After thirty minutes of anxious waiting, he decided to venture out. He checked his 9 mm to be sure it was fully loaded and accessible. He chambered a round, opened the door of the truck and got out, looking in every direction—even up at the second story windows. Seeing nothing of concern, he took a casual walk around a four block area, the only portion of the town that was on a gridiron plan. He counted five cars parked on the sides of the streets and side walks, but no Selah and no Jabal an-Nabi Shu'ayb Mountain Transport Service truck. He passed two restaurants and half a dozen street vendors, but Selah was not taking a lunch break with any of them.

Sheep Dog waited a full hour before making the inevitable conclusion that he had been abandoned. The issue now for him was whether he had been seriously betrayed. He decided that it was beyond mere probability that he had, and he formulated a plan as he returned to the farm truck and drove out of town as fast as the decrepit old farm vehicle could go. It was well for him that he had not waited even five minutes longer, because security forces moved in from the east and began cordoning off the town. Several police and military vehicles passed him on their way in but paid him no mind. It did not occur to any minion of the law that a vehicle puttering along at thirty miles per hour could harbor a terrorist band.

Once out of the vicinity of Ad Dummam, the nerve-wrackingly ponderous pace of his getaway truck wore on his nerves to the point that Sheep Dog had to find something better. He passed a truck stop where more than a dozen semis were parked while their drivers availed themselves of the chance to nap through the most oppressively hot two hours of the day. All of the trucks were left running, a requirement of the trucking companies to save diesel fuel which was expended in large amounts with restarting, and because the poorly maintained trucks often would not restart until they cooled down for several hours.

Sheep Dog parked in a far corner of the ill-tended parking lot among a cluster of oil drums, overflowing trash cans, and four semis which were polluting the atmosphere with a collective dispersal of vaporized diesel fuel and smoke. He left his old farm truck and zigzagged through the trucks to the line of vehicles nearest the main road. He selected the newest and most powerful looking truck and unobtrusively walked up to the cab steps. He climbed up and quickly took a peek inside. The driver was unconscious. His snoring rattled the half open driver's side window. The man had a tranquil expression of complete rest. Sheep Dog clipped him on the back of his bent neck with a hard side fist, and the driver gained the opportunity for a much extended nap. He was still alive, and his neck did not make any excessive movements as Sheep Dog moved him over to the passenger side of the seat. He checked the tool box behind the seat, found some duct tape, and bound the driver's wrists and ankles, and gagged the simple Arab citizen, who was not aware that his sleep was now a real unconsciousness. Sheep Dog taped over the man's eyes.

Confident that the sleeping driver was not a threat, Sheep Dog looked all around and saw no one in the parking lot. A few men sat relaxing on the stoop of the convenience store and on a pair of benches on either side of door leading inside. He reached over and removed the driver's turban and placed it on his own head. After a hurried trip back to the farm truck to fetch his gear, Sheep Dog pushed the driver well down into the seat, and put the truck into gear. He jerked the truck a few times as he began his exit from the parking lot, but no one seemed to pay him any mind. In five minutes, he was on his way to Da'ir at seventy miles per hour.

Da'ir was even smaller than Rohm as Sufla. Everyone knew everyone else. Families were large—the Yemeni birth rate is one of the largest in the world—and they were intertwined. An offhand conversation, a telephone call to a friend who has a friend, a religious confession to an imam who numbers in his flock one with ties to al Qaeda, and attention leads to the Sheep Dog. And the Sheep Dog now wondered about Selah's ties. He had left his fare alone in the blistering heat and had driven back to his home and hearth. And his telephone?

Sheep Dog drove through the town, past the Ruhm al 'Ulya Hotel and stopped half a block from the Jabal an-Nabi Shu'ayb Mountain Transport Service office. The sun was within a quarter of an hour of setting, and the streets contained only a few people scurrying home from work. Cooking fires were being lilt, and the day was winding to a close. The town was preparing to go back to sleep.

He tried the office door. It was not locked. He took one last look around then slipped into the waiting room. Selah's inner office door was open. Sheep Dog could hear the whir of the ceiling fan, the shuffling of papers…and the dialing of the old European Sultan rotary phone Sheep Dog had seen as he and Selah haggled over the cost of the trip to the mountain.

He took three long, extremely rapid steps into the office. The stricken look on Selah's ashen face answered all of Sheep Dog's lingering questions. He pulled out the black Taurus from the rear waistband of his pants. Selah's mouth opened.

"Eff…Eff…*Effendi*! This is…"

Sheep Dog put three rounds in the T Zone of Mohammed Abdullah Selah's face. The man fell face forward on his desk without another sound. Sheep Dog made a sharp about-face and left the inner office, the waiting room, and the town of Da'ir in less than three minutes. He was as innocuous as a puff of smoke as he did so. Driving the semi, he was one of Hedy Lamarick's invisible people, there but unseen.

CHAPTER THIRTY-ONE

Sheep Dog checked into the Sheraton Sana'a Hotel on Nashwah Al-Himyarst mainly because he wanted to be within walking distance of the American Embassy. He wanted to see the damage to America first-hand. The embassy was a short walk to the north and east of the hotel. He checked in wearing the full disguise that made him Svein Magnus Thorsteinsson. He called room service and asked to have his suit cleaned in time to be able to attend the lecture by Dr. Fahd Ayman al-Wuhayshi from the Faculty of Science of the University of Sana'a entitled "Is Darwinism Still Viable in the Twenty-First Century?"

He took a long muscle easing hot shower and a nap which brought him back to full function. When he was dry and dressed, he called Neal Dastrup on his secure line to find out the flight arrangements for his flight back to the states. It was to be late the next evening. He ordered a steak dinner with all the trimmings from room service and a nice bottle of merlot, of which he drank half and went back to bed.

The following morning, he got up early and walked to the embassy. He was shocked and dismayed by the extent of the destruction. The front half of the main building lay in a pile of blocks in a huge crater where the front steps had once been. The handsome façade was gone; the tenderly maintained plants on the porch were gone; only marine guards were left to patrol the gutted building. A few marchers paraded along the street occasionally shouting Arabic slogans which Sheep Dog did not understand, but could catch the drift. Placards read, "Death to the Great Satan", "Yankee Go Home", "Imperialist Pigs", and "Allah Protect the Freedom Fighters", "Our

Al Qaeda Forever!", all in clearly printed English and all manned by young people who were obviously university students.

Sheep Dog caught a gypsy taxi and spoke to the driver, "*Sabáh al-Kháyr.*"

"*As-salám aláykum, Sabáh al-Kháyr.*"

"*Waláykum as-salám. Mutaásif, ma kan tkellemichi Arbia. Tkellem Inglisia?*"

"But of, course kind sir. I speak English. Many people in Yemen do, you will be pleased to know. There is no need to be sorry. It is most pleasing that you have made an effort to speak the language of Allah and the *Qur'an.*"

Sheep Dog laughed and said, "*Shukran.* You have now heard all the Arabic I know."

"Where to?"

"A little sightseeing. First I'd like see the Old Sana'a Suq in Bab al-Yaman. I would like to start in al-Fulayhi Quarter and then see all around the Suq. I wish to hire your services for the entire day."

"I will be happy to be at your service. But you know that the bread market was the sight of an insurgent attack but a few days ago, *Effendi.* Perhaps another area of our city?"

"Thank you, my new friend, but no, I very much wish to see the old suq and the damage that was done there."

"That is a common enough reason for the adventurous tourist. I will let you know a small secret. I have been into the Suq and have not personally seen a great deal of destruction in the major corridors and alleys. I personally believe it is not so bad as the authorities suggest but serves as a good tool to use against the al Qaeda in the government crack-down."

"And what would be a fair price for such a day-long tour?"

There followed a lengthy bargaining process wherein Sheep Dog learned the driver's name—Bahman Ali Rumi—and that the man's last name was the same as the famous Persian poet, that he was Shi'ite in a country that was half Shi'ite. He learned more about Bahman's financial woes in carrying for his family of three wives and sixteen children than he wanted to know, and more about government corruption, inefficiency, and the need to expand Islam than he cared to know. Finally, the two men arrived at a price of 7,000 YRLs, more than Sheep Dog thought was appropriate, but he had met his match in Bahman and wore out from the haggling.

It was a pleasant sunny day with the sky free of clouds and pollution. The taxi lacked air conditioning—no surprise—and the automobile's windows were left down to let in the cacophonous noise, pungent odors, and the rhythms of the city. The new town was sprawling and monotonous with nothing to be said for it as a tourist destination; but the old town was vibrant, varied, compelling, and worth preserving. Sheep Dog enjoyed the bustle of the al-Fulayhi Quarter—a residential section—but it did not seem worth a stop.

The shops of the Baba-Yaman Suq area itself—however—were well worth parking the cab in a series of courtyards known to Bahman and paid for by Sheep Dog. The two men ambled along narrow winding tiled alleys, none of which could support a motorized vehicle except a motorcycle. Their stops took them to an assortment of separate suqs set aside for a wide variety of goods and services: tin, gold, silver, meat, poultry, bread, pottery, wicker and basket ware, jewelry, spice and perfume which cast off vapors so pungent that Sheep Dog had a sneezing fit. Other shops purveyed plastic ware, copper, and clothing. The goods were displayed in cloth bags, wicker and plastic baskets, on open tables, and hanging from racks. At each shop they met good-natured banter and importuning. Money changers were scattered throughout the many suqs. The men and women who made the currency transactions were multilingual and multiethnic, able to slide through ten or even twelve languages with a facility that astonished and amused Sheep Dog.

They stopped for lunch from a street vendor in the Bread Suq, which showed evidence of the recent bombing, but makeshift repairs covered much of the damage, and crews had worked feverishly to return the Suq—as much as possible—to a state of Islamic cleanliness. Sheep Dog took time to appreciate the slender, tall, irregular, mud brick buildings with their assortment of round, square, rectangular, and arched windows topped and often covered by a white lattice-work. The top portion of the walls of all of the buildings carried white decorations that were in harmony with the window dressings. Unlike the new city, Old Sana'a had a captivating charm and clean streets.

There was a kind of linguistic music floating along the alleys and streets and in and out of the shops. Sheep Dog gradually came to appreciate that he was hearing rapidly spoken classical Arabic of the *Qur'an* and the academics intermingled with the multiple dialects, regional nuances, local idioms, and colorful accents spoken by the more than 700 million adherents to the faith. Even those speakers would require a talented local translator to understand and to be understood. The language—like the exotic suq itself—was flowery and over drawn, full of evocative imagery, flattery, and exaggeration. He knew he would never be able to speak Arabic fluently, let alone like a native. There was too much simile, metaphor, and inferential meaning, too much subtlety and hedging about a subject without openly speaking one's mind, and too many meanings for a Westerner to cope with. For Sheep Dog, it would have to remain the music of the streets.

During their languid lunch of Moroccan and Yemeni food influenced by Southern Europe—olives and olive oil, assorted fresh fruits, and tomatoes; the French—pastries, light fish dishes and heavy sauces; Americans—hamburgers made of goat meat and lamb; and Moroccan proper—spicy sausages called *merquez*, lamb and liver kebabs, and *kefka*, a minced lamb molded into small cakes served with a pepper sauce. For dessert, they shared baklava served with Turkish coffee thick enough that a small spoon could stand in it.

Completely surfeited, Sheep Dog languidly observed the colors and sounds of life passing by him and gained an appreciation for the slow pace of Arabic life and the pleasant smiling faces that swirled by. Donkeys drank at ceramic barrels dotted along the alleys between suqs and in the aisles of the various suqs. Old men gossiped on the stoops of buildings. Gaggles of women—some in full cover, some in Western dress—chattered and laughed as they walked along enjoying life. Uniformed school children—like troupes of performers—marched gaily along behind their teachers. It was a scene from a hundred or even a thousand or more years of history; and despite all of its bloody history, life was good there, at least at that pleasant moment in time.

The first stop of the afternoon was the Old Sana'a Palace Hotel. Sheep Dog and Bahman wandered about the handsome ornate reception hall of the grand old hotel; then, avoiding the rickety open-cage elevator, they climbed the stairs to the top floor and walked out onto the roof top patio, found themselves surrounded with a desert scene of palm trees, potted plants, a spa and an azure swimming pool, and gained a dramatic panoramic view of the Old City. They looked down on the minaret of the Tin Suq mosque, the Street of a Thousand Lights, the hotel's own handsome gardens which were an oasis of green in a desert of beige, the grand walled Moutana Ali Mosque, and a large square facing a gated entrance into a series of suqs. The square was packed with people picking at the tables in a flea market that had been held on the same day of the week for over 1600 years, pre-dating the advent of The Prophet. In the far distance, Sheep Dog and Bahman could just make out the huge open city cemetery.

Then, as they surveyed the placid scene below—like two gigantic claps of thunder—simultaneous explosions erupted from the open square below hurling body parts and debris in every direction, and causing a major desecration in the sacred cemetery. The on-lookers on the roof top of the hotel were stunned into a horrified silence.

CHAPTER THIRTY-TWO

Bahman Ali Rumi was frightened, and he was not in good aerobic condition. He trailed behind Sheep Dog who was moving towards the smoke and noise, not away. That was crazy. The European had to be crazy.

"Wrong way, *Effendi*," he yelled.

Sheep Dog looked back to indicate that he had heard the driver, but he ran on towards the square. When Bahman caught up with him, the man was standing stock still looking at a scene of carnage beyond anything Bahman had ever even fantasized in his worst nightmares.

He moved up behind Sheep Dog and vomited. The center of the square—or more precisely, where the center of the square had been—was now a crater with tiled edges. It was like looking into the maw of a volcano spewing flames and smoke, and the acrid, nauseating smell of burned flesh. Body parts were strewn about the edges of the square, on the sidewalks, and plastered on the brick walls of partially destroyed buildings. Glass shards, flea market goods, pieces of tables and chairs, and garbage that had until very recently been the best fare the nearby restaurants could provide, lay in kaleidoscopic disarray.

Sheep Dog stared intently at a woman in a torn and bloody blue burqa. Her covering was askew, almost shredded off her body. The jilbab body covering was missing a section so that her legs, previously unseen by anyone, even her husband, were bared. The hijab lay in the dirt behind her, and the nigab lay over a child which appeared to be about two years old. The child had been eviscerated, and the mother was trying to cover the little belly with her veil. The obscenity of that tableau was not lost on either Sheep Dog or Bahman. The head scarf lay under the arm of a boy who appeared no more than seven.

For Bahman, it was spell binding and dreadful. For Sheep Dog it was Donna and Camille and Genevieve and Daniel. It was what he had not seen in reality when his family was murdered, but it was what he saw in his frequent nightmares. Something inside of him snapped. His face became a mask of hatred.

A woman wailed something in Arabic that stood out over the keening of several women seeing their family members dead and dismembered.

"What is she saying?" he asked Bahman.

The frightened Arab had never seen such a frightening specter of a face on a man before. If anything, he was more frightened of Sheep Dog than he was of the Stygian scene spread out before him. At least the dead were no threat.

"Ah...*Effendi*...she, aah, she says that 'It is the Saudis. They came here and brought Shaytaan, the Whisperer and his evil Jinns. They did this. They did this.'"

"Ask her what she means."

Bahman would rather have eaten broken glass. He balked.

"Ask her. I will give you 2000 YRLs right now if you will be quick about it."

The promise of more money overcame his qualms. He gently asked the woman why she had said that about the Saudis. She told him that she had seen two bearded rich men dressed in expensive white silk thobes and beautiful kaffiyehs escorting a poor young man wearing a robe and turban of a mountain clansman and a suicide vest. The young man stood in the center of the square, and the Saudis left. When they were out of sight, the young man pulled something on his vest, and Shaytaan's fire burst out of hell.

Sheep Dog nodded his understanding—his profound understanding.

Ambulance and mortuary crews and police began streaming in. The scene was all too familiar and commonplace to them. The ambulance crews began treating the walking wounded; the severely wounded were all dead. The mortuary crews produced shrouds for the corpses and the dismembered body parts. For all their self protective hardened firewall exterior to yet another disaster 'facilitated' by members of their own religion who took a different view about the sanctity of innocent life, these men—something akin to the Sheep Dogs of William J. Bennett's analogy—were eminently compassionate. They gently—even reverently—wrapped the bodies and the parts in white linen, the color of mourning. A young woman police sergeant wrapped her arms around a grief-stricken keening young mother and extracted a mutilated baby from the mother's protective arms. The mother collapsed onto the dirt.

A husband—obviously in shock, bloody and battered—aimlessly carried his wife in a meandering circuit of the edges of the smoking pit until a mortuary technician stopped him. Sheep Dog watched the horror grow on the man's face as he came to the full realization that his wife was dead. The technician gently persuaded the stricken man to relinquish his hold on the only thing he had of value in his meager life and laid her carefully on the ground. He closed the woman's staring eyes and folded her arms across her chest before signaling to a co-worker to fetch a shroud. A battle hardened soldier put an arm around the man's shoulders and lead him away.

Sheep Dog moved into the square and began helping with the wounded and dead as best he could. He placed a shroud on a child, carried a woman to a waiting ambulance only to find out from the doctor that she was already dead, and became a stretcher bearer for a another dozen corpses. Aside from three critically wounded men, he did not see another survivor. He had paid no heed to himself until the police officer in charge indicated that the work was done and that he should go back to his friend, who continually beckoned to him. His hands were soaked with a thick crust of blood, and he reeked from the coppery smell of fresh blood. He had trouble recognizing his hands as his own. He fought to prevent visual hallucinations of his own family from intruding into his psyche as he backed away. He was only partially successful.

A cordon of soldiers and police began to move the on-lookers away from the square, including Sheep Dog and Bahman. Yellow crime scene tape was wrapped around the makeshift morgue as the few survivors were carried out of further harm's way in ambulances and carts. There were pitifully few of them. The dead—wrapped in their final white linen—were placed gently but like so much cord wood into flat bed trailers in serried rows. Most of them were destined for a mass grave since there was no practical way to achieve identification before the mandatory Islamic practice of 24 hours of mourning and then burial within that same day.

Bahman pulled on Sheep Dog's arm.

"*Effendi*, we must go. It is not good for men to see such things. We must not stay. The Jinns are here, and we will be next. I can hear them whispering even now."

Sheep Dog could hear them, too.

Sheep Dog had an ice cold shower as soon as he got back to his hotel suite. He scrubbed himself until his skin was raw but could not shake the sense that he was still dirty, that he still carried the blood of those people on his hands.

In the marrow of his bones, he had the conviction that he must do something to even the scales.

When he was sure that he was in complete control of himself, Sheep Dog telephoned Neal Dastrup at the number the CIA agent in charge in Sana'a had given him.

"This the man from the Russian plane," he said.

"What?"

"Meet me at my room ASAP."

There was a pause while Dastrup said a few unkindnesses to his son, the least of which was "who does he think he is?"

Sheep Dog read his mind.

"Bring the orders you got regarding what you are to do for my purposes here. Bring 50K in mixed currencies and all the info you have for the country up north."

"You know—my active friend—it would be better for you to come here. I'll send the red son. Don't leave anything behind."

"10-4," Sheep Dog said and put the receiver back on its hook.

He packed swiftly then trotted down four flights of stairs to the main reception area. There he bought a copy of the *Yemen Times*. His cursory glance revealed three stories that interested him. The front page headline article covered the bombing in the Old Sana'a square and suggested broadly that Saudi mercenaries at least were involved or were the direct instigators. The article more tentatively hinted at the possibility that Saudi General Intelligence Directorate—the *Al Mukhabarat Al A'amah*—may have been behind the attack that killed 213 innocent Yemenis.

Below the fold in two columns which carried over to the second page was an article about the assassination of Faizah Batool al-Faisal while in Yemeni Army custody. Her relationship to a prominent Saudi princely family and her known association with al Qaeda Yemen was documented at length. The paper put forward the opinion that she had been assassinated by AQY because she knew too much. Again, the article hinted at a Saudi connection.

On page three an investigative reporter told of an attack by opposing forces—unnamed—on a farm house in the small city of Ad Dummam which had resulted in an unknown number of people being killed. The reporter was of the opinion that a substantial force of attackers had likely been involved in the attack based on the extent of the damage seen by investigators. The reporter went on to say that the terrorist attack occurred in broad daylight but with no known witnesses. Several names of prominent local and foreign terrorist agents were mentioned as having possibly perished, but none were confirmed. The report indicated that further investigations by the *Times* and governmental agencies were underway.

Sheep Dog obtained a large manila envelope and placed the article in it without any explanatory cover information. He addressed it to Karin Petersdatter in Reykjavik, a postal drop specified in his original orders, which was operated under an agreement between the U.S. National Intelligence Service and the *Greiningardeild Ríjuslögreglustjóra* [*GRLS*—Iceland National Security Agency] and the *Greiningardeild Varnarmálastofnunar Íslands* [*BVMSÍ*—Military Intelligence]. He overpaid the concierge to send it out by first mail in the morning. He paid his bill in cash and bribed the desk clerk to delete any reference to his having been a guest at the Sheraton.

He was waiting in the lobby when Dusty walked in twenty minutes later. They carried his two bags to the old truck they were using then drove rapidly to Rohm as Sulfa in the dark.

Neal Dastrup greeted Sheep Dog coolly, "What's this all about? You are about to leave my zone of responsibility tomorrow night. What kind of bug do you have in your bonnet?"

"I have had a busy day," Sheep Dog said.

"Now that's a real understatement. You apparently have been a one-man war machine since we left you."

"That might well be my job. Your job is to cancel the plane reservations you previously made for me to leave Yemen and to provide me with everything I need operationally—for a new operation. Here's what I need. First, $50,000 in cash in U.S. dollars and Saudi riyals. Second, I need to get to Riyadh as fast as is possible."

Neal raised a quizzical eyebrow.

"Third, I need you to keep quiet about me. Quiet as the grave, if you get my drift. No reports, no loose lips, no little memos to anyone I might encounter on my way to that city, and no 'wink, wink, nod, nod' to anyone ever that I might have been here. Read your orders. Do you need any clarification about how serious a fella I might be?"

Sheep Dog had decided during their earlier telephone conversation that he did not need friends; he needed compliance; and Neal and Dusty were tools toward that end. He could not afford emotional tiesl; and he could not afford loose ends, even if the loose ends were these two good men who had served him well thus far.

"Hey, no. We're on the same side. You don't need to get testy."

"I appreciate what you've done already, but I can't have anyone...any-one... suggesting my presence anywhere. You never saw me; you never heard of me; you have no idea what anyone is talking about if they suggest that the U.S.A. or I was ever involved. I have mentioned it before, but I am not a forgiving person."

There was a decided chill in the relationship of the three Company agents now. Dastrup decided to keep matters strictly professional. He was frankly scared of the man.

"What else?"

"You drive me to the Arabian border, and you arrange for a clandestine plane ride into Hatred's Kingdom tomorrow morning. You get hold of your nice fellow agents—the secret kind—in Riyadh to smooth the way for me. They need to ready a cover story that gets me into and around in the country swiftly. I don't have time to tarry. The reason for that will be evident in my next order. I need precise information on the exact whereabouts of Dr. al-Faisal's puppeteers and the controllers of any and all of the agents that work the Yemen terrorist pipeline. Pay whatever must be paid; extort, torture, or call in markers; but get me that working information, *tout de suite*. I guarantee that your hand, my hand, their hands, and the Company's hands will never be identifiable. That's what I'll do for you. Oh, and another thing I'll do for you is to disappear. I will not pass this way again...at least this go-around."

"We're glad for some good news at least," Dastrup said, his eyes set in a hard staring contest with Sheep Dog, "but those are tall orders."

Sheep Dog said nothing more. The assassin's remarkable hazel eyes with flecks of luminescent green looked back with that penetrating gleam that chilled men's insides. Dastrup blinked first.

CHAPTER THIRTY-THREE

The three men left Sana'a and drove west on the major and well paved highway to the west coast at Al-Hudaydah where they stopped to get diesel for the embassy Mercedes and to stretch their legs. They quaffed several cups of thick, black, and bitter coffee to keep them alert then drove hard along the coast through northern Yemen without encountering any road blocks, traffic, or problems with the road conditions until they came to Wadi Mawi.

"We've got about a hundred kilometers to Harad where we'll have to watch for the hard left turn towards Maydi which will put us within spitting distance of the border. We have to keep our eyes open from here on out. This is Indian country. There were reports of bandido activity as recently as last night. Lock and load, gentlemen," Neal said.

Sheep Dog and Dusty checked the weapons Neal had provided; each man had an air-cooled, light-weight, magazine-fed M16A2 5.56 mm rifle; and every weapon was taken off safety and its selector lever was locked in the automatic position. There was palpable tension in the car. No one spoke.

A little further on, Neal slowed quickly to a crawl.

"Something up ahead," he said in a hoarse whisper.

"Maybe a wreck. They've got a road block," Dusty said straining to get a better look.

"No. Military," Sheep Dog said. "Turn off the lights and stop by those three trees on the right."

Neal coasted to a stop. The activity at the road block did not change. They waited for five minutes.

"Whadda you think?" Neal turned to the back seat and asked Sheep Dog. "Doesn't look copasetic to me."

"Me neither," Sheep Dog said calmly. "Let's get out and have a quiet little look. Bring three extra magazines of ammo each. This can turn out to be a real contest; and if a single shot gets fired, not a one of them can get out of there alive."

Neal muttered to himself that this was exactly that he had been trying to avoid during his entire career; and now, thanks to this Sheep Dog character, he was about to get himself and his boy into a real mess that was likely to earn them an unwanted black star on the wall of the CIA Building in Langley. He was of half a mind to shoot Sheep Dog in the back, get in the car, turn around, and head back to Sana'a. He could just deny he had ever seen the man.

"Let's go." Sheep Dog's voice was insistent.

Neal and Dusty turned to look over their shoulders and saw Sheep Dog standing at the ready behind them. He seemed to be holding the end of his M-16 a bit too directly at them. Neal pushed the idea of causing harm to the assassin out of his mind—way out of his mind. He was more scared of him than he was of the bunch of unknowns up in front of them. They walked along almost silently on the paved highway. It was cool and clear. The crescent moon and myriads of stars shown brightly with a view unpolluted by city lights or clouds.

Fifty yards from the road block, Neal turned and brought Dusty with him to face Sheep Dog.

"This is no Yemeni police, military, or security force road block. These are bandits."

Sheep Dog scrutinized the men milling around the two truck road blockade. He counted seven or eight, maybe more. They had not seen the three Americans and were casual and careless. Several were smoking; one was relieving himself with his back to Sheep Dog, Neal, and Dusty; and two of the men were apparently having an argument.

"What do you want to do?" Dusty asked.

"Follow me," Sheep Dog ordered.

Dusty looked over at Neal who nodded reluctant assent.

Sheep Dog took a throwing knife out of his chest band scabbard and hurled it into the now relieved bandit's back. It struck home in the upper third of the left side. The man whirled about. A black fountain of blood erupted from his open mouth as he stood with a brief quaver facing his attackers. Then, he fell face forward onto the asphalt. Sheep Dog moved swiftly and silently forward to where the bandit had been standing and administered a *coup de grace*. He paused for a fraction of a minute, then stepped into the light formed by the trucks making up the road block. He began firing at once raking a half arc of chest high bullets from left to right and back again. Neal and Dusty took places on either side of Sheep Dog and added their automatic fire to his. Acrid gun smoke and the smell of fresh blood assaulted their nostrils. Thirteen men in front of them were beyond caring.

"Get them out of the road and move the trucks off enough to let us drive through," Sheep Dog ordered. "I'll get the shell casings."

The three men hurriedly went to their tasks. Sheep Dog picked up every piece of brass casing he could find. He made multiple crisscross passes before he was satisfied. He filled his pockets with the brass and turned to help with the removal of the bodies. The road was covered an inch deep in blood, and it proved impossible not to get their shoes in it. In less than five minutes since Sheep Dog opened fire, the bodies and the trucks were out of the way; and every bit of evidence that Americans had been there was removed, at least the best they could do in the circumstances.

They raced back to the Mercedes, removed their shoes, and drove quickly to the bloody area of road where Neal slowed down to avoid splashing blood on the sides of the car. Once past the bandit's road block and death site, they roared away to Harad.

"There's the sign to Maydi," Dusty called out barely in time for his father to make a wide, nearly two-wheel turn.

They crossed a small stream, and Neal stopped long enough for them to wash their shoes. A quick inspection of the car indicated that there was no blood on the body that would be likely to attract attention. The city of Maydi was asleep, and the drive to the border was uneventful. Sheep Dog's nerves were on full alert. A kilometer from the border, they stopped and hid the guns behind a rock wall near an ancient well where the Dastrups could retrieve them on the way back to Sana'a the next day.

At the border with Saudi Arabia, a very sleepy young sergeant gave a cursory look at the passports of the three men, asked their destination in the kingdom and their purpose for coming there. Neal had taken the precaution of placing a thousand riyals in his passport to encourage enthusiastic approval by the custom's official. The young man was satisfied that they were just going into the nearby coastal border town of Jizan for business, smiled, and passed them through. He was a thousand riyals richer and fell back to sleep in ten minutes. The border station did not see three people pass through at night in a month, and he did not give them another thought.

The city of 100,000 was quiet as dawn started to manifest itself. Jizan is the new name of the ancient capital of the Jizan Province in the far south-west of Saudi Arabia. The city is situated on the Red Sea coast and serves a large agricultural hinterland. It is famous for its high-quality production of tropical fruits including mango, figs, and papaya. The three Americans stopped at a road side fruit stand and helped themselves to a bagful of the fruits from the laden tables as the owners—Arabs and Africans who were at once Sunnis and Shi'ites, Somalis and Eritreans—snored peacefully on their blankets on the sandy ground.

"Nice and ecumenical, isn't it?" Neal mentioned as they drove away towards the small airport where he had arranged for a clandestine flight to take Sheep Dog into the heart of the Kingdom of Saudi Arabia right after first prayers.

CHAPTER THIRTY-FOUR

The light was now such that a man could see a single hair. The airport muezzin called the faithful to the first *Salah* of the day, the *Fair*. While the workmen scattered around the hangers knelt on their prayer rugs and said their orisens, a small jet landed on the runway opposite to where Neal had parked the Mercedes. Two private propeller planes landed closer by, but Neal held up a hand to keep his companions in their seats.

"Here it comes," Neal said, checking the luminescent dial on his digital chronometer.

A small twin engine cargo jet approached the runway. Neal blinked the car's lights on and off twice. The plane circled the airport once and settled onto the runway seventy-five yards from the car. Neal gunned the powerful Mercedes engine into action and sped across the tarmac and stopped beneath the pilot side hatch door. The door opened and a set of steps unfolded out onto the tarmac.

"Out," Neal ordered.

The three men moved out of the car with alacrity. Sheep Dog took his Beretta 9 mm out of his waist band holster and chambered a round. He mounted the steps two at a time and burst inside moving his weapon swiftly from side to side. He could see the pilot in the cockpit illuminated by the instrument lights. His eyes were already adjusted to the dim early morning light, and he could see enough to convince himself that the pilot was alone on the plane.

"Clear," he said, looking back at the Dastrups. "Get the stuff on board."

"Yessir!" Dusty muttered crisply, but not loud enough for the killer to hear.

Sheep Dog helped push the bags containing the tools of his trade into the otherwise empty cavernous cargo bay.

"Thanks," he said tersely to the Dastrups.

"Our pleasure," Neal said through clenched lips and motioned for Dusty to follow him out of the plane.

They were on their way out of the airport before Sheep Dog made his way to the front of the plane and spoke to the pilot.

Dusty said, "I have met the devil, and I didn't like it. Maybe it's time for me to get into another line of work before I get too old. Or, maybe before I lose the chance to get old."

"Maybe," said his father. "Maybe."

"Hello," Sheep Dog said to the pilot, a uniformed U.S. Air Force major with short cropped blond hair and a hard face.

"Welcome aboard. I have no idea who you are; but whoever you are and whatever your mission is, must be mighty important. You are the first civilian; or at least I presume civilian, to set foot on this new beauty."

Major Donaldsen, voluble from the start of the flight to the finish, told him all about the unusual new plane, the territory over which they were flying, and about his trepidations about flying a spook. Sheep Dog's attention turned on when the major finally explained where they were going.

"This is the Advanced Composite Cargo Aircraft—ACCA—for short, hot off the test flight schedule. The first test flight of the ACCA was June the second, 2009, and these babies were certified for use only last winter. It was built at the U.S. Air Force Plant 42—the Air Force Research Laboratory and Lockheed Martin's famous 'Skunk Works'—in Palmdale, California. Us Air Force types call that nonexistent place the 'Spook Works', no offense intended here. The ACCA is a modified Dornier 328J aircraft. The fuselage aft of the crew station and the vertical tail were removed and replaced with completely new structural designs made of advanced composite materials fabricated using out-of-auto-clave curing. Pretty different, even a might strange. Let's hope it holds together."

"Yeah," Sheep Dog said, "let's."

"We're going straight through to Taif Air Base—strictly speaking it should be Al Ta'if, but we Westerners can't seem to manage the glottal stop. It's located in the central foothills of the western mountains of the kingdom. Its altitude of 4,800 feet gives Taif one of the most pleasant climates in the Kingdom, something you'll come to appreciate once you go down altitude to almost anyplace else in the country. Temperatures are comparable to Phoenix, where I come from, but without the high heat of summer. It does cool down at night and in the winter. I hope you get to spend some time in Taif; it's a good city, not too intense about the Wahhabism and jihad and all that stuff. Oh, yeah, the women have to dress like ghosts; but that's the custom every-place. I've found the locals to be pretty decent, really."

"Am I expected?"

"Yes, but only by one or two folks with a need to know. I'm not cleared to have any information about what happens once you get to the base. I'm just the taxi driver. All I can say is there won't be any flight log for this trip. It never happened."

Major Donaldsen now focused all of his attention on landing with the base in sight tucked in among the mountains. Once on the ground, he helped Sheep Dog get his gear out of the cargo bay and onto the tarmac. The pilot left him standing there alone and moved the plane well away down the runway to its hangar. Sheep Dog sat on the larger of his bags and waited.

He fidgeted for less than five minutes until he saw a jeep moving rapidly across the tarmac towards him. The driver hopped out of the seat and walked up to greet Sheep Dog. He was dressed in olive drab BDUs; and conspicu-ously, was not wearing any insignias denoting rank or even branch of service.

"You're the Sheep Dog, I presume?" he said.

"Yes."

"I'm the base G-2. You're to come with me."

They loaded Sheep Dog's bags in the back and sped away to a Quonset hut building that, like the G-2's uniform, had no sign or other designation of its purpose.

"This's my office," the officer told him.

"What'll I call you?" Sheep Dog said to the head of intelligence for the base.

"Probably, just 'G-2'. I need to have some sort of name to call you. I don't suppose it is a great idea to keep bandying about your cover name."

"Right. I'm John Smith."

The men smiled. Both of them had been John Smith more than once.

"The Company man in Yemen told me that you have open-ended orders from the grand poobahs for pretty much anything you want, and we don't get to ask questions. I trust him, and will get something official in a couple of days. We won't let that stand in your way. I gather that your mission is not only on the full Q-T, but it's urgent. Everything here is politically sensitive; so, I take it for granted that you aren't an official representative of Uncle Sugar."

"You have everything correct."

"So, how can I be of service, John?"

"First off, I need to know the whereabouts of the co-conspirators of a prin-cess, Faizah Batool al-Faisal."

"The guy in Yemen already told me that. Us spooks in the Kingdom know all about her friends and the pipeline into Yemen. We have been hamstrung in our efforts to do anything about them, though. They are beaucoup politically sensitive; so, they get away with murder, quite literally. I can go you one better than you might have hoped. The Society for Preservation of the Faith—as they are so grandly known—meets every Thursday morning before the start of the Holy Days. They have a world-class catered feast for brunch, then close their doors and meet in absolute and holy secrecy. I don't know what you have in mind; and frankly, I don't even want to know; but I can get you up close and personal to the venue; then you are on your own."

"Not quite that easy, my friend. I need access to the catering crew. I presume they have uniforms and security badges. I'll need both."

The G-2 looked seriously perplexed.

"I really don't think that's possible. Oh, we can come up with a uniform. Our tailors can make you a perfect replica, but the security badge is another thing altogether. Those things will be keyed to a thumb print and have a photo ID. Every worker has been thoroughly vetted and is well known. Believe me, if we could get a security badge, we would have been in there well before now."

"Okay, get me the uniform, I'll have to take care of the rest."

"I'll get that done; but I have to warn you, my friend, you will not be able to bring any kind of weapon into the hotel—they meet in the pent house suite of the Al Faisaliah Hotel. The servers are all hand picked from the hotel's new 24 hour butler service, and the food and drink is imported from all over the world. They get frisked two or three times a shift."

Sheep Dog pondered his dilemma for a minute.

"All right. I'll need an expensive dark suit, shoes, shirt, tie, the works. That will get me in at least. I'll have to be inventive. I have a plan cooking in my head; so, here are a few more things I'll need that shouldn't be too hard to round up. Get me two throwaway cell phones—one for you and one for me and several micro SIM cards to allow quick changes for variety."

A SIM is a Subscriber Identity Module.

"I want you to print me some calling cards on paper that is manufactured in Yemen. This is how I want the cards to read."

He handed the G-2 a rough sketch which caused the man's eyebrows to elevate in a wordless question.

"There's more. Get me reservations—first class from Jeddah to New York on the red eye—for three days from now. Make sure that I can put my two special bags on board that special flight with diplomatic tags; so, they don't get inspected. I know that'll be tough, but it's important. Have the tickets made out in the name of Pedro Martine-Rodriguez. I just happen to have a Belgian passport in that name. You can think of that as the real me. Also, get me visas for both Rodriguez and Thorsteinsson. Some lower echelon— but bright young go-getter—needs to meet me and get me through security without a hassle. I don't really want the CIA to be involved. Let's tell the guy to meet me in front of the American Airlines ticket counter ninety minutes before flight departure on whatever airline you come up with. Can you do all of that stuff in a day, even a long day?"

"Sure, my people love a challenge. This isn't all that difficult, really."

"Good. I wish I could get you some professional kudos, but both us need to stay well back in the shadows if we're going to survive."

"And you can't have the slightest link to us here or to the U.S. If you get caught, it will go very hard for you. You'd better be prepared to hold your U.S. identity in some compartment of your brain way down deep. They are experts at finding out what they want to know."

"So I hear. And what makes you so sure that I'm an American?"

"Touché."

Sheep Dog got a taxi into the city of Al Ta'if the next day to pass some time meandering around while G-2's people were getting his clothing and other requests taken care of. Al Ta'if is located in the Western Sector of Saudi Arabia, near the summit of the Hejaz mountain range. It is situated 1700 meters above the Red Sea, between granite hills rising from the eastern slope of the Hejaz and the Asir—the "escarpment" leading to the large coastal city of Jeddah 150 kilometers to the west. The location of Al Ta'if is at the point where routes from the south intersect those from east and west; and its proximity to Makkah [Mecca], its hilly terrain, its green landscape, and favorable climate are the main reasons for the city's historical importance.

Al Ta'if is an old city, which was once used as the summer capital of the Kingdom, and is still very traditional in its views and way of life. The city is relatively small, but Sheep Dog noted that most of the essentials of life could be purchased in the local suqs. The main suq—which is considered the most authentic in the Hejaz—was a warren of alleyways lined with shops almost exactly like the one in Sana'a. Sheep Dog found carpets, tents, traditional embroidered dresses, hand-crafted jewelry, spices, Bedouin handicrafts, and a few hundred more things critical to the life of an Arab that he did not need but were interesting to see and smell. Anything else he might want, the suq owners told him could be found in Jeddah—located on the Red Sea—which is only a two-hour drive away on a good highway.

In the afternoon, he spent a pleasant three hours forty kilometers east of Al Ta'if in Wadi Layyah watching the bedouin people conduct camel races hosted by the Saudi National Guard from the base every July and August. The Saudis—especially the National Guard—loved to bet on the races; so, Sheep Dog parted with almost a thousand riyals he brought with him from Yemen. He melted into the crowd of nationals and tourists comfortably and without arousing interest in himself—invisible in plain sight a la Hedy. The dramatic views afforded him in the hill station along with walks to see the views, the variety of flora and fauna, and the cool crisp climate, made the hill station an attractive treat and a place where he could be alone.

That evening, G-2 introduced him to the G-3 in the unmarked Quonset hut with a story that everyone involved knew was a phony, but it did give Sheep Dog a place to hang out that was inconspicuous for his final day on base. The G-3's family was away visiting their family in the States; so, Sheep Dog had the run of his house and was able to get out and about in the base personnel compound. The G-3 was more than happy to stay well away from his house for the next couple of days. He was especially happy not to have to involve his wife and talkative children.

All assigned USAF personnel and their dependents reside at "Al-Gaim" Compound. The compound contains approximately 200 Westerners working for companies such as McDonnell Douglas, Pratt & Whitney, and Shell. In his reconnoitering about the compound, Sheep Dog found that housing was comparable to western standards and consisted of two, three, and four bedroom homes, all fully furnished and carpeted to give a look and feel of anywhere in American suburbia. All of the homes for enlisted, officer, and civilian families came completely equipped with color TV, microwave, dishwasher, washer and dryer, dishes, silverware, glasses, and 110V American standard electricity, an accommodation that cost the Air Force a small fortune. Sheep Dog saw that the compound had a four lane bowling alley, Olympic sized swimming pool, closed circuit TV [6 channels], softball field, racquetball, tennis, and basketball courts.

Al-Gaim is located about twenty minutes from the USMTM [The United States Military Training Mission to the Kingdom of Saudi Arabia] offices. The USMTM Advisory Detachment is responsible for providing advisors for key flag officers who oversee regional Royal Saudi Land Forces [RSLF] and Royal Saudi Air Forces [RSAF]. Sheep Dog saw almost everything in the compound to keep himself busy and exercising and to prevent the development of agitated boredom during the day he had to spend. However, he scrupulously avoided going anywhere near the USMTM offices.

He learned that Western food stuffs are obtained—by order—through the U.S. Military commissary in Riyadh and delivered weekly by Saudi trucking companies. That arrangement ensured that local supermarkets in the compound have a good selection of products and that they are readily available. Al-Gaim residents and their dependents may also use the dining hall and the snack bar located on the compound. Medical care is provided through the Al-Gaim dispensary and by the Al-Hada Hospital and Rehabilitation Center—a Saudi military hospital staffed mostly by Westerners)—and compound residents have an ambulance service to get them to the Prince Sultan Hospital. Sheep Dog hatched a plan to catch a ride into Riyadh with one or the other of the food or medical services transports.

Very early on the third day Sheep Dog spent in Al Ta'if, G-2 caught up with him and gave him the items he had requested.

"I've arranged transport by a USMTM truck," the intelligence officer for the command said.

Sheep Dog told him about his desire to be even more inconspicuous and to ride in with a food delivery truck. G-2 liked the idea, and made a call to the commissary; and transportation arrangements were easily completed. Sheep Dog asked that he be picked up at the snack bar, shook G-2's hand; and the two men parted without further conversation. G-2 was glad he was dealing with a professional and that he did not have to be involved any further. He might receive one call on the throwaway cell phone, and that was the extent of his fears for the future with this eerie man.

Sheep Dog sat down in the master bathroom of the base administrator, G-3's, house and made himself look like an Arab using his own make up and black hair dye, and with a few touches borrowed from the lady of the house's supply. He was pleased with the result; at 0800, he was standing in the shade of a tented picnic table in front of the snack bar dressed incongruously in a very expensive Italian suit when the Kingdom Delivery System truck pulled up.

The handsome young Arab driver greeted him in Arabic, and, finding Sheep Dog uncommunicative, turned on his truck radio to listen to Western hip-hop music and drove the quiet man and his baggage into the city's prestigious business and residential area—Olaya, which afforded easy access to the Diplomatic Quarter, ministries, government offices, shopping and business centers—and, more importantly, to the Al Faisaliah Center.

CHAPTER THIRTY-FIVE

After the Kingdom Delivery System driver let him off at the Al Faisaliah Center, Sheep Dog caught a taxi to the Tulip Inn Olaya House, a second rate hotel with poor ratings. The driver helped him lift his bags onto a luggage carriage. Sheep Dog tipped him well—but not too well—and wheeled the carriage into the busy lobby. He stepped up to the reservations desk.

"May I help you, sir?" the bored desk clerk asked in English.

"Yes, please. I would like a room for the week."

"Do you have a reservation, sir?"

"I'm sorry, no."

"Regrettably, we are full. Perhaps if you would check back in the afternoon…"

"That would be fine. May I check my luggage until that time? I will come back around three."

He was directed to the luggage room and checked in his two large bags. From one of them, he removed a small brief case containing the materials he needed for the remainder of his planned morning activities, obtained a voucher for his bags, tipped the porter, and left the hotel. He walked briskly out onto Al Olaya Street, turned south and walked the three short city blocks to Al Ameria Street and turned left. He made the jog onto Al Aminyah Street, which was dominated by the magnificent Al Faisaliah Rosewood Hotel. Limousines filled the entrance portico, and a stream of very well dressed people moved in and out of the hotel with their assistants and retainers. They were obviously from all over the civilized world—a veritable United Nations satellite in the Middle-East—and positively emanated the glow of money and power.

The time was only 10:30, which gave him time to do a necessary reconnoitering of the hotel. He first checked himself. He was dressed comparably to the rest of the well-heeled guests. Then, he focused entirely on the task at hand, viz. how to get into the penthouse meeting room before the meal was finished. He scanned the huge column-free banquet and meeting facilities to locate a concentration of liveried members of the butler service. He saw heightened activity, carts entering and leaving, and major-domos issuing orders in the second floor area of banquet halls and kitchens.

Sheep Dog climbed the flight of marble stairs and casually walked down the bustling hallway looking as if he belonged. He found what he was looking for, the room where assignments were being handed out. He then took the express elevator to the pent house and made himself into one of the invisible people, which, in that hotel, were the men in Hugo Boss and Armani suits. What he saw was perplexing. Entrance into the pent house banquet room was obtained only by a thumb print, just as G-2 had warned him. The security badges worn by the employees seemed only to be of interest if a worker was challenged. Quite obviously, Sheep Dog did not have the right thumb print; but after his tour of inspection, he did have an idea.

He returned to the second floor carrying his brief case and walked into the men's room. He stood patiently at the urinal watching carefully as a few men moved in and out to relieve themselves. It took fifteen minutes before he found himself alone with a man who looked acceptably similar to himself in his Arab disguise and was nearly his same height and weight. He watched the man and the entrance door and tensed himself. The other man was similar in build to Sheep Dog, but more than a little softer. He was dressed in the livery of the butler service, which could not have suited Sheep Dog's needs better.

He walked over and stood by the man as they both washed their hands. The butler turned his back on Sheep Dog and began a step towards the door. Sheep Dog caught the back of the butler's neck with a sudden very violent knife-hand karate chop which felled him as effectively as if the weapon had been an ax. Sheep Dog swiftly dragged the man's inert body into the men's room work closet where he broke his neck. He stripped the corpse of its livery and white gloves and took off his own clothes and replaced them with the livery. He carefully folded his suit, shirt, and tie into as tight a pack as possible and forced them into his brief case. He had to stand on the case to force the lock clasp to connect. Then, he removed several arm loads of paper and cloth toweling trash from the wheeled container. He cut of the man's right thumb then hoisted his victim up and into the trash bin, and replaced the trash on top of him. He wrapped the severed thumb in plastic torn from the roll of waste can bags sitting on one of the work room shelves and slid it into his pocket.

He walked out of the men's room and into the general hubbub of the working hallway wearing the butler's livery, gloves, and ID badge. He was one of the invisible work figures and attracted no more attention than did any of the other employees. On his first inspection of the area and its activity, he had noted a pantry shelf lined with gallon sized glass bottles of nonalcoholic fruit juice imported from Albania. He strode into the pantry and poured a few drops of the deep burgundy colored juice onto the palm of his hand. It was a little bitter and cloyingly sweet. That suited his purposes perfectly. He walked back into the hubbub and found a line of food carts ready to be taken up to the pent house for distribution to the august guests. The major-domo was gathering his butlers into a line to take them. Sheep Dog took the first one in the line and moved it quickly into the unoccupied pantry.

He removed the food and put it into the trash bin. He filled a dozen empty crystal water pitchers with the viscous fruit juice, added a generous helping of purple/blue crystals from his baggies of Furadon, mixed them well, and put them on the cart. He opened the pantry door and took a quick look into the hall. The line of butlers was marching in lock-step down the hallway to the elevators with the major-domo in the lead. Sheep Dog moved into last place and followed them to the bank of elevators, waited his turn, and went up to the pent house floor.

The butlers were streaming into the banquet hall, each one stopping long enough to press his thumb print against the sensor. In the busy rush, the muscular security men could give only a cursory look at IDs before passing each butler into the main room. Time was of the essence. It was nearly 11:30, and the food had to be on the table in front of every important guest by the stroke of 11:45 when the opening toast would be drunk.

Sheep Dog surreptitiously exposed the end of his victim's severed thumb from the opening of the baggie and pressed it on the sensor. The door opened. As Sheep Dog moved the cart through the door, the major-domo demanded:

"Where have you been, lout!? You have fifteen minutes to fill every glass, or you will be working in the laundry room, understand?"

He was speaking English, because the butlers came from so many different countries and cultures that it was necessary to use American English as the lingua franca. Sheep Dog lowered his eyes and his head obsequiously— nodded his understanding—and hurried into the room. His task was— indeed—daunting. There were twelve regular circular tables of ten men each and a rectangular head table for twelve men. Women were not allowed in the room or even on the pent house floor.

Sheep Dog moved quickly and efficiently. The table settings were elegant with white damask table cloths and napkins. Gold plates and utensils, three on each side of the impeccably clean plates, and three Waterford English goblets of varying size constituted the place settings. Fresh orchids from Indonesia stood in single flower vases by each setting and a huge bouquet of flowers from the Spice Islands sat in an Orrefors Swedish crystal vase in the center. Sheep Dog puzzled briefly over the choice of which goblet to use for the punch and decided on the one furthest to the left. He began to pour half a glassful for each man.

At the second table, in his hurry, he let a droplet of the heavy dark juice splash on the back of one man's hand. The man glanced at the drop on his left hand with such repugnance, that it was as if Sheep Dog had spat on him. Sheep Dog—the butler—quickly dabbed away the drop; and the imperious Arab snapped away his hand and snarled some invective in Arabic. Sheep Dog was angry; here was a man who used that hand instead of toilet paper, and he was upset at a drop of sterile fruit punch soiling it. He drove away any thought of showing his displeasure on his face and hurried on to the next seat and the next table and the next. He finished at 11:44, and he was sweating.

He moved his cart with its empty crystal pitchers quickly and quietly to the door. As the guard passed another butler out, Sheep Dog laid a calling card discretely among the cards sitting on the small round cloth covered table placed at the entrance door for that purpose. His card was printed on the finest polished card-stock paper manufactured in Yemen. It had a simple message:

Anwar al-Awlaki

The Arabic is "Al Qaeda", and the English printed name is that of the generally accepted leader of Al Qaeda in Yemen.

As Sheep Dog pushed his cart the rest of the way out through the door, Abdel-Karim al-Wahishi, leader of al Qaeda in Saudi Arabia, flicked the nail of his third finger on his right hand against the edge of his delicate crystal goblet sending a melodious chime resonating through the hall.

"*La ilaha illa Allah*, Brothers, *Mohammadun Rasulu Allah*, bless his name forever. Let us toast to the success of our enterprise with the pure juice of the grape that comes as a gift from those of our compatriots in jihad in Albania."

He lifted his goblet and downed the entirety of the sweet aperitif in single swallow. Each of the other 135 men, including the security agents, followed his lead, chorused his praise of Allah and his Prophet, and quaffed their fruit drink to the last drop.

He pointed his goblet and smiled at Afshar Ali Montazeri, Supreme Leader of Hezbollah, who had flown in that morning from Tehran to attend the large ecumenical gathering. He, and the director of Hamas in Palestine, were both seated in places of honor at the head table. Both honorees gave a self-effacing little head nod to acknowledge having been singled out.

"Brothers," al-Wahishi, said simply.

It was the first time a Shi'ite had ever been in the same room as the al Qaeda Sunnis. The Arab upon whose hand Sheep Dog had spilled the drop of juice gave a look of complete disdain at the interlopers from Iran.

He muttered to his seat mate, "Dogs. Sub-human *kaffirs*."

CHAPTER THIRTY-SIX

Sheep Dog moved quickly but without drawing attention to himself. He knew that he was on borrowed time, but was unsure of exactly how long it would take for the Furadon poison to bring on symptoms. He had put enough into the grape juice for a glassful to kill four or five people, but maybe most of the targets had not drunk it down. He found himself alone on the second floor for the moment. All hotel kitchen and wait staff activity had shifted to the subbasement where a factory like process of cleaning dish ware and utensils was in full swing.

He pushed his cart into the pantry, removed all of the tainted pitchers and hosed them out quickly and lined them up on shelves. With any luck, they could possibly dry in place and not be noticed until the next banquet. He knew the body was still in the trash can, and would shortly be discovered which would start a dragnet after him. There were several dozen trash bags piled up in the hallway outside the pantry door. He tested them and found that they were segregated into bags of heavy wet garbage and lighter dry trash. It seemed to be worth a try; so, he lugged the heavy sack of corpse and paper trash into the hall and set it under a pile of heavy garbage bags. Now he was panting with the exertion and keenly aware of the passing time and mounting danger.

He walked calmly to the exit stairway and tentatively opened it and peered in. No one was there; his luck was holding. He ran down to the basement which opened into a lower garage. He found a rest room and dashed inside to change back into his starched white shirt, Armani-like suit, and Hugo Boss tie. The clothes were wrinkled, but passable. It did not matter; they would have to do. He jammed the butler suit and white gloves into the brief case, opened the heavy metal door into the garage, and walked briskly across the pavement towards the exit. He passed several people exiting from their cars and a few going the same way as him towards al Aminyah Street.

He reversed his route back towards the Tulip Inn Olaya Hotel and shortly encountered his first impediment in the form of a street crowd filling the sidewalk and Al Ameria Street. A folkloric dance troupe had been brought into the Al Faisaliah Center by the hotel. Although he was in no mood to be entertained, he recognized that he was witnessing one of Saudi Arabia's most compelling folk rituals—Al Ardha—the country's national dance. This sword dance is based on ancient Bedouin traditions which pre-date the very existence of the nation itself. Sheep Dog was trapped in a crowd of tourists and city dwellers and found himself having to edge his way through sets of drummers beating out a rhythm and a poet chanting verses while a dozen sword-carrying men danced shoulder to shoulder even moving out around him and leaving him caught in the middle temporarily. A street commentator called out information to his tourist group from Germany who had gotten off a huge Al-Sherif air-conditioned bus to view the spectacle.

Despite his sense of ever pressing haste, Sheep Dog had to hear about Al-sihba folk music from the Hejaz, Mecca, Medina, and Jeddah, that this kind of dance and song incorporated the sound of the mizmar—an oboe-like woodwind instrument in the performance of the mizmar dance. As Sheep Dog slowly threaded through the crowd—whose numbers were diminishing at the periphery—he heard the throb of the drums important and native to the Samri, a popular traditional form of music and dance in which poetry is sung. The performers had been flown in from the Eastern Region of Saudi Arabia for the week. His ears were assaulted by the music of the Arabian oud—a pear-shaped, stringed instrument commonly used in Middle-Eastern music. It is considered to be the predecessor of the western lute, distinguished primarily by its lack of frets—drums. The musical number included a screeching singer. In addition to the unpleasant auditory stimulus, Sheep Dog's sense of smell was assaulted by the pungent aroma of oud perfume that permeated the gathering; and his sense of well-being by men waving swords and bamboo canes which came uncomfortably close to him as he began to worm his way out of the crowd. He cleared his last hurdle by literally making a running jump over two rows of men seated on their knees and swaying to the odd tempo of the Arabian rhythms.

The dispersal of the crowds which helped Sheep Dog make progress was being facilitated by the arrival of the *mutaween*—religious police—which are numerous in ultra-conservative Riyadh. Known by locals in their very private conversations as the "Dead Center of the Kingdom", Riyadh is the most straight-laced of the Kingdom's big cities owing to the great local power of Wahhabism, the most stringent, most intolerant, and harshest sect in Islam. With most forms of entertainment banned, few sights of interest and a brutal climate, Riyadh is a business-only destination by determined design; but it is also the best place in the Kingdom to watch at arms length the continuing collision of tribal Wahhabi conservatism—manned in the streets by the *mutaween*—grappling with modern technology and Western influences. The *mutaween* moving into the crowd took a dim view of the festival in progress.

He was back out on Al Olaya Street finally. It seemed like he had been stuck in a human quicksand for hours; but in reality, it had only been about twenty minutes. There was no indication of police action behind or in front of him, except for the *mutaween* thugs. Aside from them, he sensed no threatening presence. Now, he made rapid progress up the street to the Tulip Hotel.

Once inside the lobby, he took a deep inhalation and calmed himself. He was going to be his own worst enemy if he did not stop looking so harried and nervous. He closed his eyes and tried to think of the towering La Plata Mountains of his native Colorado, a place where he always found peace. Under better control now, he walked calmly to the door leading to the subbasement where he found an overfull dumpster ready to be hauled away. He dug into it enough to be able to bury the butler's suit and white gloves, ID badge, and severed thumb. Now back in full control of his keen senses, Sheep Dog went back to the lobby, turned left to the luggage room, and presented the cards for his two bags to the woman behind the shelf of the half door of the room.

She was not the same worker who had taken his bags that morning.

"Do you see them, sir?" she asked.

She spoke with a mild lisp, and that, coupled with the face covering veil that was perfectly in concert with the Islamic principle of modesty—hijab—made it difficult to understand her. Sheep Dog strained to make out what she was saying. He pointed to his two large bags. She seemed not to be particularly inclined to help; so, he pushed open the half door and fetched them himself. She was perfectly content to have him do her work, and was positively overjoyed when he gave her a somewhat excessive tip.

"Do you need help getting your bags to the reservation desk, sir?"

"No, thank you, I can manage."

She paid him no mind as he left her, turned right into the lobby; and, avoiding the gaze of the reservation desk attendants, he made his way swiftly out onto Al Olaya Street in front of the hotel. Shortly, a white taxi cab driven by a Pakistani wearing a ghutra—a plain white square made of finer cotton held in place by a cord coil—pulled to the curb in front of him. Sheep Dog knew to keep safe by only getting into a metered cab; and further, he knew that the only likelihood of getting a driver who spoke decent English was to find an Indian or Pakistani.

"Where to, sir?" the cabbie asked with the typical Indian sub-continent lilt to his accent.

"King Khalid International Domestic Terminal," Sheep Dog said, leaning into the passenger side window to inspect the meter. "How much?"

He and the driver discussed the meter and off-meter price, and after a bit of good-natured haggling agreed on an acceptable fee for the 35 kilometer, 30 minute, ride north. As they discussed the price, Sheep Dog observed two burly and angry *mutaween* beating a woman with short billy clubs. She was middle-aged, a suicide blond, and was wearing a low-cut casual blouse that exposed her technologically enhanced bosoms, a decidedly foolish thing to do in Riyadh. The *mutaween* were screaming at her in Arabic, which she obviously did not understand, and had reduced her to a tear-sodden shadow of her former self as her aging husband stood helplessly by.

"Do not look at them, kind sir. Best not to get involved or even to show an interest. Take it from one who knows."

Sheep Dog knew better than to call interest to himself and was relieved when they pulled out into traffic. The route took them through the bustling city with a series of hair-raisingly daring maneuvers executed with the voluble driver all the while providing a travelogue, history lesson, and social commentary as if he were talking to himself. Sheep Dog relaxed as he listened to the impassioned soliloquy while they weaved in and out between cars, trucks, busses, motor scooters, and inattentive pedestrians. From Olaya Road the cabbie careened onto Al Arouba Road, then out onto the teeming King Fahd Highway.

The educational part of the excursion came in rapid staccato bursts which amused Sheep Dog, and he did not mind not having to respond the entire trip.

"Kind sir, let me tell you about Saudi Arabia, which is, of course, officially the Kingdom of Saudi Arabia. Did you know that it is an African country and both the largest and the richest country of the Middle-East? That is why I am here. There is no work in my poor country. I come from Lahore as do many of my countrymen to be abused by the haughty Saudis."

He laughed at his bit of irony.

"The Kingdom is also known as 'The Land of the Two Holy Mosques'. I am sure even you as a Westerner have heard of Mecca and Medina, the two holiest places in all of Islam. I have made the Hajj, just last February; so, you could call me Haji Hakimullah Farooq, but that would be too complicated. Just call me Haki." Scarcely taking a breath, Haki went on, "The two mosques are the Masjid al-Haram and Masjid Al-Nabawi, but surely you already know that. Forgive me for even suggesting that you could be ignorant, kind sir.

"Less than two percent of the kingdom's total area can be watered and made fertile for crops. Were it not for oil, the Bedu would still reign here, and there would be no need for the likes of me. The country can't run without imported workers like me, the Filipinos, and the Turks. For one thing, there are a lot of stupids here. That is because they produce Mongoloids and have lots of other mental illnesses coming from the extraordinarily high rate of cousin marrying cousin here. This is forbidden in my country. And you know, there are 7,000 useless princes who do nothing but suck up the money that Allah and the land gives the people. Maybe not so many, but they are all lazy and arrogant. It is an awful place to live as a foreigner. It is my sad lot to have to find work in this accursed place."

"What is so bad about it?" Sheep Dog hazarded an interruption to the stream of conscious conversation coming from Haki.

"Ah, I am glad you asked. The list is endless, but I would not want to bore you."

A mini-bus swerved in front of the cab, and Haki rolled down the window and hurled invectives at the offender which were met with the world's universal one-finger signal of disrespect."

"Tourists!" Haki spat.

"Now, where was I. Ah, yes. I am going to tell you secrets about this bad place. You must promise not to tell anyone that it was I, Haki, who has told you these things. First of all, the legal system here prescribes capital punishment like beheading—you know the cuttings off of the heads—and what they call corporal punishings like even the cuttings off of hands and feet for crimes as bad as murder and rape of an important girl, and even for such much more minor things like robbery. You know there are many poor ones here who sometimes have to become robbers to live. The amputations are also for drug smuggling, adultery in women, and for the kind of thing between men that the *Qur'an* forbids. The rich ones don't seem to get such bad punishments. Unfairness is everywhere.

"But, even for us poor ones, the courts can be less severe. They have punishments, such as canings and floggings, for less serious crimes—what they call against public morality like that woman we saw back there and such as drunkenness. The *mutaween* can even come into a man's home and arrest him for drunkenness. I'd like to see the day that they went into a prince's palace and arrested him."

He spat.

"But," he went on, "there are good things in the system like we have in my country. Murder, accidental killing and hurting someone's body can be handled by punishment from the victim's family. Like us, retribution may be sought in kind or through blood money. It is like our country where the blood money necessary for just a woman's accidental death, or that of a Christian male, a person of the Book, but not a true believer is half as much as that for a Muslim male. All others, like the polytheists—Hindus, Buddhists, Sikhs, and Shi'ites—are valued at 1/16th of a person. What I hate here, is that guest worker noncitizens—even Muslims—are not worth as much as a mere woman. The main reason for this is that—according to the Sharia—men are rightly expected to be providers for their families and therefore are expected to earn more money in their lifetimes. The blood money from a man would be expected to sustain his family, for at least a short time and maybe for life. Honor killings—to protect the honor of the family—are, of course not punished as severely as actual murder. Everyone knows that this is only right."

"How about slavery?" Sheep Dog spoke up for the second and last time.

"That is an anomaly of this unfair place. No other country that I know about has slavery. Oh, they abolished it officially in the sixties, I think it was, but it still goes on. Just ask any Filipina or innocent Turkish girl. They'll tell you about being raped, and starved, and beaten, and forced to work, and worst, not getting paid. Of course, they won't dare say anything until they get out of this accursed country. They don't even count as persons in the legal system. Those girls are about the only people worse off than me here. And I forgot to mention a thing that could be very important for a foreigner such as yourself. Work visas were introduced for external workers in 2004, and a lot of us get flogged for little paper-work mistakes. Even such a one as you could get a flogging if your visa isn't just perfect. Be careful about that very important piece of paper, my friend. I can't even remember a lot of laws that carry such harsh punishments. You're fortunate to be leaving. It would be wonderful to be a Westerner such as yourself. America is heaven, you know. I have a sister in New York, two brothers in Los Angeles, and an uncle who makes Cadillacs in Detroit. They are rich and important. Nobody cares what mosque they go to. I am going there someday when I can get enough money to pay all of the fees. America. It's the real heaven, if you want my opinion."

Haki had to take a breath and to turn all of his attention to driving the final leg of the trip. He got into a line of cabs pulling up to the International terminal of the airport.

"I need the Domestic terminal," Sheep Dog said.

"No worries," Haki said, "that's what they say in Australia. You can take the Travelator connection to the Domestic terminal. This is the quickest way. I like to stop here; so, my friends can get a SkyCab to take their luggage over to their plane. That way, their bags don't get x-rayed or held up while those thieves in security go through them. That's good, no?"

"That's good, yes."

Sheep Dog thanked Haki and gave him a 500 riyal tip which caused the Pakistani to break into an apparently permanent grin and a flurry of kow-tows. Haki toted his bags to the SkyCab porter and gave him explicit and copious instructions about how such a one as this European should be treated. That cost Sheep Dog another 500, but the peace of mind was worth it.

CHAPTER THIRTY-SEVEN

S heep Dog went into a rest room to check his disguise. He was confident that he would pass as the Tunisian Arab, Taoufik Ben Brik, whose picture appeared on one of the passports and visas the Ta'if G-2 had prepared for him. The documents appeared to be in perfect order. He got on the Travelator and got to the Domestic Terminal with time to spare.

He checked in with Saudi Air and confirmed his flight on the civilian 66 seat EMJ 2 engine jet to Jeddah's King Abdulaziz International Airport.

With that out of the way, Sheep Dog realized that he was hungry. He found a food shop in one of the lavishly appointed concourse food courts. He scanned the al la carte selections and ordered a mixed plate with tastes of fresh lamb, shawarma, falafel, and *ful medames,* which is an ancient Egyptian dish with origins that reach back to the time of the pharaohs. This simple dish of slow-simmered ground brown Egyptian fava beans is seasoned with olive oil, lemon juice, garlic and spices. *Khobz* [Arabic unleavened bread] which is eaten with almost all Saudi meals, came with the plate.

"Would you like tea, sir?" the server asked.

"Please."

She gave him a steaming, strong black brew with a mixed herbal flavoring Sheep Dog could not identify and did not much like.

His flight to Jeddah was flawless; the 500 miles passed in an hour and a half which he spent sleeping. He took the Travelator to the International Terminal and found a rest room. He locked a toilet booth and with the use of a small mirror and some make-up and wig magic, he went in as Taoufik Ben Brik from Bizerte, Tunisia and came out as Pedro Martine-Rodriguez from Bruges, Belgium. With ninety minutes before his flight was scheduled to leave, he went to a small café across from the security area behind the American Airlines ticket counters and found himself an obscure booth.

Fifteen minutes later, two young American menobviously American men, who looked like they had just graduated from BYUwheeled his two bags on a cart to the end of the line waiting to go through security. Sheep Dog watched for a few minutes, and, seeing no one that caused him concern, sauntered casually up to the men.

"*Buenas noches,*" he said, emphasizing the lisping s's of Castilian Spanish.

"Are you in the sheep business, sir?"

"I am. Any problem with my bags?"

"Nope. See the diplomatic tags? Your stuff has diplomatic immunity, and so do you. Here's an identification tag. You need to wear it around your neck until you clear customs in the U.S. You need this picture ID card for you wallet."

Sheep Dog took the ID cards and thanked the men.

"Finally, here's your tickets. You're straight through to New York on United. It's the red eye; but the flights are usually not full; so, you can stretch out and get some sleep. My boss gave me this Ambien for you if you want. I love the stuff for those long transoceanic flights."

Sheep Dog accepted the pill gladly. He had built up a considerable sleep debt, and the flight should help get him back to full function. He followed the two short haired young men to the separate flight crew and diplomatic security line. They talked briefly to the security agents, and Pedro Martine-Rodriguez and his bags whisked through without a glitch. He sat calmly in the waiting area until his flight was called then boarded promptly when the first zone for seating was called. He staked out a window seat on a three seat row towards the middle of the plane and took his pill.

The take-off and cruising was scarcely noted by Sheep Dog, and he slept a full eight hours before his bladder forced him to move. He returned and slept another two hours before awakening for the day. The woman seated in the row in front of him yawned and stretched. She got up and moved around a little, then stopped at his row.

"Would you mind some company? I just can't read another word, and I'm getting a little stir crazy."

"Sure," Sheep Dog said, "glad to have someone to talk to. Tell me about yourself?"

She found that truly refreshing. She reckoned that it was the first time in her adult life that a man had actually wanted to hear about her.

"I don't want to offend; but I'm from Texas; and I can't tell you how glad I am to get out of Hatred's Kingdom. I just read the book, by the way; are you familiar with it?"

"Can't say that I am."

"I'm done with it. You can have my copy."

She handed him the book, *Hatred's Kingdom, How Saudi Arabia Supports the New Global Terrorism*, by former Ambassador to the United Nations, Dore Gold.

"Thanks, I'll read it. But, go ahead, tell me your story."

Once she got started, an emotional out pouring took place.

"I'm Madeleine Danousky, and I do business analyses for a consortium of U.S. and European oil companies. The corporation wanted me to go to Saudi Arabia because they needed what I do. First off—when I applied for a visa—I was told that I could not travel alone in the Kingdom. It made me mad, but I already knew that. So, I went through all of the hoops to get a male companion to be with me all the time, to drive, and to be able to talk to the loonies that stop you everyplace. I had to get one of the Saudi oil guys we do business with to sponsor me to make sure I didn't go around exposing myself or raping poor little innocent Saudi men…give me a break!

"I figured I could put up with it all, get in and get out. Was I in for an education! We landed in Riyadh and took an airport taxi into town to the Al Faisaliah Hotel. On the way into town, I read in the newspaper that they had just beheaded a guy for being a witch. This is the twenty-first century! A witch! I got out before my male companion, who is a nice guy but useless in business and about as much protection as my aunt Gertrude. This nasty little *mutaween*—that's the religious police—creep walked up behind me and whacked my ankle with a little club. Big deal, my ankle was showing. It still hurts. He made a hard grab on my butt, and the hotel doorman yelled at me not to fight back or to protest, or they would arrest me. That set the stage. Later, when I got to the foreigner's compound at the oil station, a couple of women there told me that one of the most common reasons for women to be in prison in that hell-hole of a country is because they were raped. That's it. Because *they* were raped!

"Men can marry girls younger than one year of age. Under Sharia law, they can lawfully consummate the marriage with a nine year old. That's to protect the girls. Supporters of a law to ban child brides were declared to be apostates under the Sharia. Some progressives got a bill prepared to raise the marriageable age to 17; it was sent back to parliament where it was declared unIslamic!

More than a quarter of all marriages involve girls under the age of fifteen; that's so the girl can be shaped into an obedient wife, bear more children, and be kept away from temptation. What crap! It's every bit as much about the money; poor fathers sell their daughters; so, the dirty old rich men can have little girl virgins to deflower. The Arab men I talked to kept telling me about how peaceful the religion is, how protective it is of women and girls who, are considered so feeble minded that they can't do business, drive a car, or handle their own sexuality. This nine year old business is just one of the 'protections'. In the Kingdom, the accusation of rape requires four witnesses. How often do you think four witnesses see a rape.

The foreign working girls haven't got a chance. If they get raped, the only thing they can hope for is to be able to get out of the country as fast as they can; and that is not all that easy. Make an accusation, and you are more likely to do prison time than the rapist. And that is as if those poor neglected men can't get enough sex. Any man can have four wives and even one temporary wife for a year if he wants. It's heaven for men, apparently. In the tribal areas a woman can be murdered just for leaving home without permission, let alone for speaking to an unapproved man. They don't admit it, but they still practice female genital mutilation out there in the hinterlands. Most of the poor little girls die because of the filthy conditions and failure to control hemorrhage when the mutilations are done. Their mothers take them to the butchers and hold them down. You learn a lot if you listen to women. They suffer, and they pour out their hearts to a sympathetic listener.

"When I was not crying over the women and girls, I was being furious over the obstructions the men put up to interfere with my getting my job done. My MBA wasn't enough. They had to have the approval of the kid who had to come with me. He didn't know the oil business from apple butter. It was a terrible waste of time. In the end, the *dumbkopfs* just couldn't bring themselves to conclude a deal with a woman.

"They are horrible bigots. I saw a bunch of Saudi National Guardsmen cut up a little group of Shi'ite pilgrims with their swords. It seems that the Saudis made it illegal to celebrate the main Shi'ite holy day, the one called Ashurah, which is a *day* of deep mourning for the death of one of their saints or something which occurs on the 10th of Muharram. That's some month on their old inaccurate calendar. That's the day when all those crazy people go around whipping themselves. Anyway, I saw. I mean—*I saw myself*—that they killed some of those poor fools. That was it for me. I called the consortium and got myself out of there as fast as transportation could make it happen.

"Now, I am going to eat a ton of bacon and have pork roast dinners with wine every day for a month, drive my car across the U.S. all by myself, and prance around half naked if I want to. This is the best day of my life so far. I am out of Saudi Arabia."

Sheep Dog had had his fill of the Muslim world as well, and enjoyed a sort of vicarious catharsis listening to the angry woman ventilate. The two seat mates went on to less agitating subjects, and having her talking to him helped to pass the time. He did not like to admit it, but it had been comforting to listen to a woman pour out her heart to him. He was having trouble remembering the last time that Rosie had held him in the spell of one of her impassioned soliloquies. He wondered if he had allowed the woman he had loved—and still did—to get all of her feelings out as he had for this stranger.

CHAPTER THIRTY-EIGHT

August

D uring his first week back in the States, Hunter took a complete break from his life's work as an assassin and became a totally absorbed businessman. He made a trip from Denver to the Rifle Post Office box to check on his banking status. He found that he had on record seven months of pay—including an add-on for hazardous duty—and nothing had been spent. He established a new account on-line with Commercial Federal in Denver and then went home to make some changes. When he was done, he had created accounts in the Altajir Bank in the Sigma Building, Hospital Road, in Grand Cayman—the Cayman Islands being the 5th largest banking system in the world—in the Port Vila Copra Development Bank in Vanuatu—the most secretive and protective bank in the world in the country which has more than 100 exempted banks registered, making it the leading offshore banking centre in the Eastern hemisphere—in two Hawaiian banks—American Savings Bank and Central Pacific Bank—both small and rather obscure Honolulu business institutions, and in the Bank of Guam on Montgomery Street in San Francisco—all without talking to another human being. Each of the foreign banks had very liberal taxation laws and the maximum off-shore banking secrecy.

He then sat at his computer and transferred his Post Box Navy funds, and a million dollars from his long-standing old account with the Commercial Federal Bank in Denver to Grand Cayman with electronic instructions to move the funds first on to Vanuatu, then to Hawaii, then to San Francisco.

He used different names at each bank, and for the Bank of Guam in San Francisco, he had the account listed as belonging to The Heiden Enterprises Corporation. If one were to spend the time to plow through the extensively interwoven layers of holding companies, the final layer would reveal the only officer to be David Pepperdine, a man whose required photographic identification was strikingly similar to that of Hunter Caulfield. As he went through the machinations of obscuring the locations of his money, Hunter felt paranoid, but his time as Sheep Dog had altered his psyche. He determined to make himself as nearly invisible and obscure as he could.

Furthermore, he determined that his transmogrification into the character of the secretive Sheep Dog would occupy his mind to the point of making him useless—even a detriment—to his legitimate company. He decided to extricate himself from his past affairs of business altogether. He kept his personal credit cards with the Western Rockies Federal Credit Union in Rifle for convenience and never exceeded the $10,000 credit limit. Beyond that, he began the process of disappearing from the public and social record.

He had little to do with anyone he knew during his visit back in the states except for making an appointment with Conrad Devlin—who still had the title of COO of the Starbright Corporation—but who was now in complete charge of Hunter's company for all intents and purposes. When he met Devlin in his old office in the Starbright Building in downtown Denver, he came right to the point.

"Conrad, I have taken stock of my situation since my family was murdered. I have not been able to get over it enough to carry on my responsibilities as the CEO of the corporation."

"Time will let you heal, Hunter. Give it a chance. We can work around your absence for a little longer."

"No, Conrad, I have made up my mind. My life is inalterably changed, and I just can't bring myself to concentrate on the business. It isn't fair to Starbright or to you. I know the company is doing well and can afford to cash me out. I want to take my stock options now and turn the chairmanship officially over to you. I am going to spend some quality time in retirement and do some writing. I have wanted to do that for some time, and I'm going to arrange to enter Oxford, if they'll have me, and do research towards getting a PhD in molecular genetics. Sounds nuts, I know, but I need to do something completely different and to have full freedom to do it without the interference of business obligations."

"So, you're going to become a hermit?"

"Not at all. I am just going to immerse myself into the world of academia. We've been friends for a long time. I want you to wish me well, and help me get on my way."

"You're serious."

"I am, Conrad. I want you to be able to take the company wherever it needs to go without dragging me along as an anchor."

He got out of his chair behind the desk and said to the COO, "I'm done. I have the papers filled out requesting the board to release me and to appoint you. It's time for you to take the seat of authority officially. Come around to this side of the desk and see if the chair fits."

They shook hands, smiled in amusement at the little changing-of-the-guard ceremony, and Conrad settled into the chair.

"Fits you well, my friend. Don't screw it up."

Over the next two days, the change was finalized, and Hunter received $245 million from his stock options. He distributed the money to his new set of banks and instructed stock and commodities brokers recommended to him by each of his new banks to make conservative investments under half a dozen different names. Hunter himself retained only three-quarters of a million dollars in checking and savings accounts in his own name in the Commercial Federal Bank in Denver and an identical sum in the American Savings Bank in Honolulu.

To complete his transition, he put his Denver house up for sale at a price that could not be passed up by any bargain hunting house buyer. He entrusted the entire transaction to his real estate broker who made the sale in less than a week. With the proceeds, Hunter paid cash for a small house offered from a short sale by a bank in Bell Gardens, California that he found on the internet. The rest of the money from the sale of his house in Denver, he donated to the Mormon Church humanitarian department because he was convinced by his late son's descriptions that the church did the best work for the least cost; and no one profited from his donation except the poor around the world who were served by the church.

On his tenth day in the United States—as he did every day—Hunter checked his special encrypted e-mail account and found a message for the first time since he returned. He entered the decryption key under his desk and read, BUSINESS CONFERENCE AT THE RED OFFICE ON THE FIFTEENTH AT TEN. That obscure message told Hunter that he should sit in the lobby of the Salt Lake City Marriott Hotel on the tenth of September at 1500 hours. He was to carry a red package so that he could be identified.

No reply was expected or sent. He had sixteen days to get his affairs in order before the meeting.

Hunter flew to Los Angeles under his own name, ran up some restaurant bills, bought a Spartan houseful of cheap furniture for his new house, and established utility and telephone hook-ups with payments by his own credit card and future billing to be made by automatic withdrawals. He was the proud owner of a rundown home on a rundown street in a rundown neighborhood. He took every step to ensure that his name was thoroughly connected to 1856 Bell Gardens Drive, Bell Gardens, California. All transactions were conducted by telephone and on-line. No person ever saw his face or would be able to tie an identifiable person to the name of the owner and bill payer.

He then flew to Salt Lake City on Southwest using the photo ID of one of his bagful of CIA aliases and got a room in the Grand America Hotel at 555 South Main Street for one night under still another alias. The next day—the tenth—he took a cab to Temple Square to pass as a tourist in the famous Mormon Church historical site located near to the Marriot. He walked around the beautiful grounds for an hour, then made his way to the Red Rock Brewing Company for a late lunch where he paid cash. He walked from the small restaurant back to the Salt Lake Marriott. Along the way, he stopped in a store and bought a straw Panama hat with a bright red hat band. He arrived at the Salt Lake Marriott City Center Hotel on 220 South State Street twenty minutes early and found a comfortable leather chair in the lobby from which he had a view of the whole large room. He slouched the hat down over his brow and pretended to be asleep.

Twenty-five minutes later—with one eye open—he saw a familiar figure saunter through the main entrance of the hotel and walk casually to the newspaper and magazine shop across the lobby from where he was sitting. Hunter looked all around the room to see if there were other agents, but could not see anyone suspicious. At fifteen past the hour, he got up and circled the room past the shop and walked on towards the hallway leading to the elevators and conference rooms.

He became aware of a man's foot falls behind him, and he tensed slightly.

"Pardon me," Oliver Prentiss said as Hunter stood facing the elevators, "Do you know how to get to Red Rock Gardens at the University of Utah?"

Hunter looked around, and seeing no one else, said, "Sorry, I don't."

He did not look at Oliver's face.

Very softly, Oliver said, "Ride up with me. I have a room where we can talk without being noticed."

They entered the elevator and did not speak to each other. Hunter followed Oliver to his room, then they spoke.

Chapter Thirty-Eight

"I take it you've had a busy few months, my friend," Oliver said.

"Did you get the newspaper reports from Yemen?"

"I did. I can add a bit to what is known about that. The Yemenis have admitted that Dr. al-Faisal was assassinated and have rounded up three local al-Qaeda suspects to take the blame. All three admitted during questioning that they killed her to prevent her from betraying the cause of jihad. The Saudis are furious, but only with the Yemenis so far. Nobody has suggested that any U.S. person or organization was involved. The removal of the leaders at their meeting has not been handled quite so openly. Officially, there was a fire, and several citizens were killed. Identification of the bodies has not been made as of this time because of the intensity of the fire. The situation is under investigation. Our man in Sana'a tells us that the locals told him privately that something like thirty high ranking al-Qaeda operatives were in the fire. Whatever, al Qaeda in Yemen is in a world of hurt.

"You obviously covered your tracks well. We haven't a scintilla of evidence that anything happened that could involve us. We have records of a few Europeans coming and going from the Aden airport during that period, but none of them fit your description.

"There is one other thing that might interest you. Seems that there was some kind of mishap in Riyadh around that time. Nothing has made it into the media; and the local gendarmes are not forthcoming with any information; but apparently more than a hundred important Saudi dignitaries and some visitors from Iran and Palestine got food poisoning and died within a day of a big banquet in the Al Faisaliah Hotel. I don't suppose you would be knowing anything about anything like that would you, Hunter?"

Hunter said nothing. Several awkward minutes passed.

"No, Oliver said, "I don't suppose you do. I am confident that you know that the soil of the Kingdom is sacrosanct. We don't conduct operations there, and this occurrence will just serve as a reminder that we leave them strictly alone, no matter what we may privately think they are doing. The Saudi ambassador sought our help to see if we could find out anything and to run some toxicology. Since all of the victims were buried within twenty-four hours of their demise as is the Islamic custom, and the very efficient hotel cleaned all of the dishware within two hours of the incident; the FBI has very little to go on except for a calling card with a well-known al Qaeda name on it, the significance of which is obscure.

He showed Hunter a copy.

القاعدة

Anwar al-Awlaki

"Mean anything to you?"

"He's the putative leader of al Qaeda in Yemen so far as I know. Otherwise, I don't know anything much about him. Maybe he thought the Saudis set up a hit on in Yemen against the Saudi and Yemeni al Qaeda agents. Who knows?"

Oliver sat quietly for a moment a reply forming in his brain. He thought better of it and continued his previous thought.

"The Saudis, for some reason, found it necessary to question the president and Secretary Southem about the possibility that The Company might have been somehow involved. The president and secretary were troubled that the ambassador should even feel a need to ask, but were able to deny any connection adamantly. I have to say that such a fortuitous occurrence has not caused any great dismay around my patch, but any future accidents or coincidences would cause the secretary of State to demand an intense investigation. The DCIA wouldn't like that. I don't think you and I would like to have that happen, eh, Hunter?"

"I'm sure not. Let's hope that no coincidences take place that could falsely suggest our involvement."

He said it with a perfectly straight face.

"Well, we're both busy. I have here a folder with seven assignments. You can take it with you, but I don't have to remind you, I'm sure, that no one but you can ever see the contents of the folder."

Hunter nodded.

Oliver took the next hour to flesh out the material in the folders to explain why the items in the folder were on the cancellation list.

CHAPTER THIRTY-NINE

October

Rob McCreary sat comfortably at his desk in the Teamster's Hall of Local 723 of the Borough Employee's Union of the International Brotherhood of Teamsters. It was quarter past one; and he was still full from a large dinner, compliments of NYC. He was installed only two weeks earlier as the eighth president of the local, and was the first African-American to hold the reins of a Teamster Local in New York. He was responsible for 28,551 New York teamsters, a responsibility that had been a long time in coming. McCreary had worked in one position or another for the union for the past forty-two years.

He had been effective, very persuasive, and able to get along with the rank and file and the five families of New York, who were as much a part of the union infrastructure as the series of Jimmy Hoffas who had served as presidents of the union. He knew every facet of union life and business. More importantly, he was well aware of where all of the skeletons were hidden and knew that his union pals knew that he knew. The most current general president of the nationwide union, James Riddle Hoffa IV, had presided at McCreary's installation as president and had given the new president of the local an effusive fifteen minute introduction to the members of the local and the new board who had already known the man for decades. It was a moment that McCreary still savored as he sat in his chair.

McCreary had just moved over from his office at 447 West 18th Street from the old Citywide division headquarters and was still in the process of settling in. He wished his dad was still alive to see how far the son of a courthouse janitor had come. He had just finished a speech to the New York City Labor Council in which he castigated Wal-Mart for letting America down by lowering wages, forcing good paying American jobs overseas, and cutting costs with total disregard for the values that have made this nation great. Wal-Mart, McCreary said, needlessly exploits illegal immigrants and women, breaks child labor laws, and forces workers to work in an unsafe environment. He knew he had established himself with his forceful and emotional presentation; and he was satisfied with himself. It was a good public start. He had received a standing ovation from the largely Democrat council, and had received personal congratulations from every member of the council and from the mayor, himself.

However, all was not roses. Sitting across from him was a brutish looking Italian in a $1,200 suit, a $200 tie, and $800 shoes. Guido "Crazy" Castellani, held the title of Supervisor of Employees in City Housing, a position which paid him three-quarters of a million dollars a year and for which he did nothing but convey messages from his real superiors and receive a check. For McCreary, the ever-present shadow of Cosa Nostra that lingered behind the scenes of the union had always been a major thorn in his side. Over his forty-seven years as a teamster and forty-two as a union boss at one level or another, McCreary had come to an uncomfortable, but safe accommodation with the Diportello Family. He had seen six different *Capo di tutti capi*s come and go along with their underbosses. Crazy was just the latest. But Crazy was the worst. He had taken the Local into an area that McCreary could not condone and wondered if he could live with. Underboss Crazy Castellani had come once again to siphon off funds from the local's pension funds. McCreary hated him, and was beginning to hate himself for having to give in.

"Hey, paisan, congrats on the new digs. Don Forenzi sends his regards. Here's a little token of his esteem."

He nearly choked at using the word for countryman or brother to this schwartzer.

Crazy handed McCreary an unmarked envelope. McCreary did not open it, but told the underboss thanks and waited for the man to get down to the real business of the afternoon.

Crazy was not offended by the rudeness of McCreary's silence. You couldn't expect better from them.

He said, "Look, my friend, our deal is done. The stuff is all in the Braiden Building on 23rd, and some of the family'er gonna have a meet with the rag heads on the week end. They are bringin' in a boat load of clean cash for the goods, and they are even gonna have some union guys do the hauling to the docks. The stevedores'll put it on their boat; and that's the last of it for us and them, unless they wanna do another sweetheart deal. They got money runnin' outta their ears, and we got connections. It's good business. You keep the faith, *paisan*; and we'll all die rich."

McCreary was not all that enthusiastic about dying rich. He'd seen too many teamsters fly too close to the Cosa Nostra flame to retain any adolescent illusions—like Jimmy Hoffa, the first—to take just one glaring example. He had had this dumped on him by his predecessor, Lucas Broadman, who had all but run his office from the capo's restaurant by the City of New York PS 130 on Baxter and Mulberry in Little Italy. Way too cozy for McCreary. It was one of those "step into my parlor said the spider to the fly" kinds of deals. However, he, himself, and accepted three envelopes from the underboss, and had personally let the gangsters use the vacant building. He could hardly extricate himself at this point just because his patriotism was affronted by helping those al Qaeda A-rabs get more guns and ammo to kill Americans. Oh, they said it was for the Taliban in Pakistan, as if that made any difference; and none of the arms would be used against Americans. Sure. McCreary was disgusted with himself, but not enough to turn down the money, and certainly not enough to get on either the Teamster's or the Diportello's black list. Besides, it was not like he was going to be shooting any American soldiers himself.

Castellani helped himself to one of McCreary's congratulatory cigars, lit it up, and blue a cloud of aromatic blue smoke into the union leader's face. He pushed his chair back on its back legs and let out a self-satisfied sigh of contentment.

"Hey, *paisan*, lighten up. Not to worry; we got it all under control. There's not a soul outsidda us and a few guys from the outfit that I trust, that knows a thing. Relax a bit. Think about all that nice money. It's easy street. Trouble? Fagetaboutit."

McCreary did not have time to think about it. A black man wearing a union jacket and a black wool cap walked into the office without knocking.

McCreary started to say, "Hey, buddy…" but he only got out the "hey".

Eleven 9 mm bullets spat out of a silenced handgun and perforated the union leader and mafia capo's chests before either could react in any meaningful way to the shooter's presence. The killer took two steps forward and fired one more round into the space between the mafia boss's eyes, then took two more and administered an identical coup de grâce to McCreary.

The assassin placed a calling card and a printed invoice on McCreary's desk.

He quietly said, "I don't like folks who supply terrorists," and walked briskly out of the office.

At 1420, NYPD sergeant Alphonse Ivory Mathews called in his report to dispatch. The best he could determine from the only witness willing to talk was that a lone gunman, an African-American male, had walked into the Olivieri Men's Club on Baxter Street and mowed down every person in the place with a machine gun. As far as he could tell, "Crazy" Castellani, the Diportello number one capo's entire crew had been wiped out in less than half a minute. Castellani didn't seem to have been the club. He did not add that it looked like the old Valentine's Day massacre in Chicago. He did say that it had every appearance of being a gang hit, and dispatch needed to get the word out that they were probably going to see a lot more gang violence in the next few days. When he hung up, among the debris, he found one thing that seemed out of place, a calling card with what looked like Arab writing:

Anwar al-Awlaki

Sergeant Matthews had no idea what to make of it. He'd leave that to the crime scene investigation unit. He was going to have his hands full dealing with the mafia wanna-bees that he was going to visit as soon as the CSIU got there.

CHAPTER FORTY

O f Brooklyn Heights—considered to be part of Boyle Heights, Los Angeles—it was once said that "all roads lead to Brooklyn Heights". Before that, when the area still belonged to Mexico, all roads led to the same area, then known as Paredon Blanco [White Bluffs]. The neighborhood sits on the east side of downtown L.A. bordered on the west by the Los Angeles River; Indiana Street on the east; Mission Road and Valley Boulevard on the north; and 1st Street on the south. The heights—once a district peopled by the rich—lies on the east bank of the river and comprises the bluffs for which the district is named. The muddy land below was called simply, "The Flats" and was occupied by the poor.

The massive East Los Angeles Interchange is located in Boyle Heights allowing access to the Golden State (I-5), Hollywood (The 101), Pomona (SR 60), the San Bernardino (I-10), the Santa Ana (I-5), and the Santa Monica (I-10) freeways. The Arts District is on the north; the Business District is on the west; the community of Commerce is on the Southeast; and to the east lies the sprawling largely Latino city of East L.A.

The area has always been a crossroads that attracted new immigrants. In its time, the citizens of the area were predominately Mexicans, then came waves of Russians, Yugoslavs, and Japanese, all escaping their impoverished and turmoil ridden homelands. Each people and their respective cultures were displaced by the next more dominant group. African Americans gave way to a vibrant and energetic Jewish community, unable to compete with the wealth of the Jews. The Japanese were removed to the Manzanar concentration camp during World War II and never came back. Theirs' and the Jews' abandoned stately homes were occupied for a time by African Americans, but they could not withstand the powerful influx of Mexican immigrants, including some Mexican-American citizens and some illegals. The Mexicans took over the abandoned mansions and filled them with multiple large families.

Towards the latter part of the Twentieth Century, the diversity of the area dwindled to almost nil. Now, more than 97% of the people living in Brooklyn Heights are Latinos. There are a few Korean groceries, but otherwise all of the businesses are Latino owned. Brooklyn Avenue—for which the area is named—became officially Cesar E. Chavez Avenue in 1994. The Breed Street Shul, which opened in 1923 at 247 North Breed Street, was one of the oldest synagogues on the West Coast. It lost its sizable and supportive congregation and closed in 1996. The building was ravaged with time and vandalism and became ramshackle and an eyesore.

Into the vacuum left by the Russians, Yugoslavs, Japanese, blacks, and Jews, poured more Latinos, almost all from Mexico. Most of them were hard working large families who brought in their own vibrant culture and added to the excitement that is California. Along with them, however, came crime and then—for the most part—neighborhood domination by brutal Latino gangs. The most brutal of them all is MS-13—Mara Salvatrucha—which originated in the barrios of California and later spread to Central America, Canada, and the rest of the United States.

The criminal organization is one of the largest in the Western Hemisphere with over 50,000 active members and is the most violent of all gangs in North and South America It attracts attention of law enforcement for its criminal activities including auto theft, carjacking, home invasion, felonious and aggravated assault, assault on law enforcement officials, drive-by shootings, neighborhood intimidation and terrorism, contract killing, and murder. Since its inception, the gang has been under the scrutiny of the FBI, ICE, ATF, and every level of state and federal law enforcement. In recent years, the CIA, NSA, the State Department, and Homeland security have become very interested in the drug smuggling and sales and arms trafficking activities of MS-13.

National and international raids have been conducted against the gang with thousands of arrests, but gang membership and wealth continue to increase despite all efforts. One reason for the growth is the fear on the part of law enforcement to enter areas dominated by the gang with anything less than a small army. In the United States, such law enforcement activities are roundly denounced by Latino and left-wing activists as racial profiling and therefore are political quicksand for any elected official to sponsor or even to condone. The costs of combating gangs—and especially MS-13—are prohibitive both in financial terms and political fallout. Either out of fear or because of favoring the empowerment of Latinos represented by the profound respect the gang commands, citizen cooperation with law enforcement is infrequent, patchy, and diluted. Accusations of racial profiling accompany and hamper all regular law enforcement and frustrate the aims of law and order.

The second of Sheep Dog's seven new assignments was directed at taking another route to discourage MS-13 activities. Although he was afforded assistance of almost any type, his assignment required that anything done in the field be by him alone. The reason for engaging Sheep Dog's services had little to do with carjacking, murder, or larceny and everything to do with a CD recording of a conversation that was included in the file he received:

October 9. NSA Intercept. Top Secret. Copies limited to POTUS, Secretary of State, Directors CIA, NSA, ATF, FBI, INTERPOL.

"Respect, Domingo. Thank you for taking my call. I assure you this is a secure line."

"That ees good, Zia. When and where?"

"I like your way of doing business, my friend. You come right to the point. I take it you have the ordinance in a secure place and ready to be transported to the port of our choice."

"We do. You got the money?"

"Yes. We have the equivalent of $50 million U.S. dollars in bearer bonds in five banks ready for you upon delivery of the weapons."

"Let's do eet. The sooner thee better."

"Truck everything so it will arrive in PONO at three a.m. on the 14th. Our man will be at pier 18 standing in front of a freighter called the *Chilean Sea Merchant* flying a Panamanian flag. He will give you the bank names and account numbers then."

"That better happen, Zia. We got our necks stuck way out. We'll get prison for ten lifetimes if some cop opens the back doors of our two semis and finds a shipment of new SAMs, grenade launchers, mortars, machine guns, armored troop carriers, digital guided missiles, and half a dozen Scud missiles. Our last shipment and the payment went just fine. Don't think about messing weeth us. We don have no sense of humor, an we don' forgeeve."

"Nor do we. That's why our business arrangement goes so well. We have mutual respect, and neither of us has any love for the Zionist Entity that runs America."

An explanatory note accompanied the CD. "Zia is Ayatollah Zia Muhammad Ali Kader, number two in Hezbollah. Voice identification techniques proved that Domingo is Juan Domingo Gonzalez-Buester, a member of the ruling council of Mara Salvatrucha, commonly known as MS or MS-13, a particularly vicious Latino gang. Domingo lives in Brooklyn Heights, Los Angeles at 1411 Malebar Street. It is imperative that the shipment described in the communication not leave CONUS or even get to the Port of New Orleans. Full caution is expected."

Sheep Dog stole a beat-up fifteen year old Ford and reconnoitered the address on the night of October 11. The information he was given was not strictly accurate. There were two residences side by side, the third and fourth houses on the east side of the street. The street at night was devoid of traffic; Sheep Dog presumed that no stranger would dare to come into the neighborhood. He knew he did not need to fear meeting a stray LAPD patrol unit. The houses were made of stone imported from outside the area, and had once been mansions. The remnants of once well manicured lawns, shrubbery, and fountains were now relics of history. Nearly a dozen cars were parked on the street, on the sidewalks, and on the lawns. At each house, two guards sat on the front stoops smoking and drinking beer, obviously bored with their task since no one ever had the temerity to enter the neighborhood. Their AK-47s lay at their feet among empty bottles of Dos Equis beer. Otherwise, Sheep Dog saw no one from the neighborhood on the street. All of the houses were well lit and had the blue-white images of operating televisions showing through curtained or shuttered windows. Every window and door on every house in the entire section of the city was barred.

Sheep Dog wore black from head to toe including his leather gloved hands and a full face black silk cover. He was wearing night vision glasses. He parked two streets away on Folsom Street and walked in the shadows to Malabar Street carrying a large satchel. He was armed with his throwing knives, a combat knife, his 9 mm silenced hand gun, a set of garrotes, and flash-bang grenades. He had decided against carrying more or heavier weaponry to allow for better mobility.

It was midnight. Most of the houses were dark including two across the street and two located next to the MS-13 houses on the same side of the street. As he crouched in the shadows of a large, but now skeletal Jacaranda tree, a black Jaguar XJ pulled up onto the lawn of the southern most house. The driver was bare chested and was covered with characteristic MS-13 tattoos, including one that arched across his chest with the words "Mara Salvatrucha" emblazoned in a handsome decorative script. He flashed the "devil's head" hand sign—or "click", as the gang members would put it—formed by extending his tatooed index and little fingers and bending his the middle and ring fingers to tuck with the thumb which formed an 'M' as he displayed the click upside down to each of the guards. They responded with a desultory backhand wave, and the newcomer entered the house where a wild and noisy party was in progress.

Sheep Dog gave the area a few minutes to settle back down. He placed his satchel beside the tree, then he walked slowly and silently in the shadows of the house keeping close to the walls. A guard stepped off the stoop and stood two feet from Sheep Dog to relieve himself against the wall. Apparently that was considered more courteous than watering the sidewalk or the ruined lawn. He zipped his fly and turned to go back to his guard post where the second guard lay sprawled out in a drunken sleep. Sheep Dog moved like a silent and unseen lightening strike and whipped a garrote around the man's neck. He was small and wiry; and, lifted off his feet by the strangling wire, he was no match for Sheep Dog. The assassin took a few painful kicks on his shins, but the guard's struggles were brief and without sound other than his agonal attempts to breathe. Sheep Dog crept onto the stoop and dispatched the second guard with a hard swipe of his razor sharp combat knife across the man's trachea and both carotid arteries. The man never knew what killed him.

Sheep Dog crawled on his abdomen across the lots to the second house. He determined that he would not be able to get close enough to kill the men sitting on the stoop because they were alert and arguing, and he did not think he could move across the last ten feet of ground without arousing an alarm. He moved slowly into the dim light coming from the house. He planted his feet in the FBI shooter's position and took careful aim as soon as he could see both men at the same time. He half squeezed the trigger, and the laser sight put a red dot on the first man's temple and squeezed the second half of the necessary pressure. A soft splut sound came from the gun and a sound on a par of a surprised exhalation came from the man as he died. Two tenths of a second later, the second guard met the exact same fate.

Sheep Dog swiftly slid the four bodies off the two porches and into the scraggly bushes on the sides; so, they would not attract immediate attention should anyone step out of either house. He ran back to his satchel and removed a coil of det cord, plastique, and a set of fuses. He moved swiftly and warily around each house setting the charges and linking them with the fuses. On each fuse, he placed a digital detector keyed to the disposable cell phone's number he was carrying. The entire operation took no more than five minutes.

Sheep Dog dropped a calling card and an envelope onto the driver's seat of a customized Ford convertible, which he noted was a "low-rider" that stood two inches above the pavement. The vehicle was painted crabapple red with yellow lightening strips across its doors and was undoubtedly further customized by installing an hydraulic system that could raise the car to the legal height minimums if they were stopped by the police. The hydraulic system almost certainly allowed the car to bounce up and down the streets of L.A.

The card was simple and printed on fine linen paper manufactured in Beirut. It read:

Ayatollah Zia Muhammad Ali Kader
Hizbullah Central Press Office
Baabda, Beirut
Lebanon

The envelope contained a bill of lading and a contract for loading "heavy machinery" signed by the Ayatollah, Juan Domingo Gonzalez-Buestar, for the Gonzalez Long Haul Cartage company, and the Port of New Orleans Dock Workers and Stevedore's Union secretary.

He trotted back to his car as fast as he could and still remain in the shadows. He drove down Folsom Street to North Breed and turned left to East Cesar Chavez Avenue before turning on his lights. He drove as fast as he dared without attracting a police cruiser onto the interchange. He followed the signs and turned south onto the I-5 Golden State Freeway headed to San Diego, and Tijuana before he dialed the number on his cell phone. The response was a ball of fire and an explosion that was audible even out on the freeway.

CHAPTER FORTY-ONE

S heep Dog drove through San Diego south to San Ysidro on the I-5 which was—at that point, named the San Diego Freeway where he checked into the Travelodge on East San Ysidro Boulevard, paid cash for a one day stay, and occupied the room for an hour while he disguised himself as the Mexican trucker, Rodrigo Pancho Vila Dominguez. Satisfied with his transformation, he left the motel through its rear entry. In the parking lot he found a large decrepit old pick-up truck with Mexican license plates. The truck bed was loaded with boxes of Gerber Baby Food. He removed six boxes and loaded his two bags into their places and replaced enough of the boxes to cover his bags. He threw the left over boxes into the dumpster then folded the tarp over the load and got into the cab. Under the driver's seat, he found a manila envelope which contained a Mexican passport and all of the documents necessary for a Mexican citizen to cross the U.S./Mexican border to return to his native country and city of Tijuana. The CIA covert documents division had outdone itself in the preparation of completely genuine papers. The lone exception to the authenticity of the documents was that the possessor of the documents was entirely fabricated.

The San Ysidro border station is located a mere twenty miles south of downtown San Diego. The U.S.-Mexico border has the highest number of both legal and illegal crossings of any land border in the world except for the Canada-U.S. border. The San Ysidro border station—the gateway to Tijuana, State of Baja California—is the world's busiest port of entry. Seven lanes of traffic enter and exit the border station; and on the day Sheep Dog crossed over, there was a two hour wait—which was about par for most days. Thousands of American citizens cross the border every day for business or vacationing or to return to their expatriate homes on Rosarita Beach and points south. Nearly as many Mexican citizens return from the U.S. to Mexico after shopping, vacationing, visiting relatives, or doing business. Sheep Dog was one of the latter.

When his turn came, he spoke halting English to the customs agent. The agent politely asked if he would prefer to use Spanish, but Sheep Dog shyly told the lady that he was trying to practice his English. She smiled and told him that was a good idea. She was tired; it was nearing the end of her shift on her sixth day work-week. 40,000 vehicles enter the United States from Mexico every day. Every year millions of people pass through the border station in the opposite direction. She had a right to be tired and to hasten the process whenever she could.

When directed to do so, Sheep Dog presented his well-worn Mexican passport which contained so many entrance and exit stamps that an additional five pages had been added to accommodate the busy passport. The name on the passport was Rodrigo Pancho Vila Dominguez, occupation—trucker. The customs agent scrutinized his visa which entitled him to travel more than twenty-five miles from the border. The detail conscious CIA preparers had stapled the receipt from the U.S. Embassy in Mexico D.F. for $100 to the visa. The agent next checked Rodrigo's Form I-94 Arrival and Departure Record, known to the Mexicans as the "Permiso".

Attached to the Permiso was the receipt for $6 obtained at the San Ysidro Port of Entry Office four months previously and the exact conditions of the travel record: Rodrigo was permitted to travel for longer than 30 days but not longer than six months before being required to renew the Permiso. The Permiso authorized the trucker to travel beyond the more common 25 mile limit. It was properly signed by a Port of Entry officer. Had the officer examining Rodrigo's papers cared to investigate, she would have found that the officer's name, badge number, and signature were genuine—the latter compliments of the Company forgers. The agent smiled and pronounced his papers to be in order. He passed through Mexican customs in short order—all of his papers having been certified at the U.S. end—and drove out onto Mexico Highway 1 to Tijuana.

It was four o'clock in the afternoon—the hottest part of the day—when Sheep Dog drove down Avenida Revolucion. He observed the people walking the street hawking their doilies, serapes, sombreros, guitars, jewelry, crude and colorful paintings, candies, and pastry, and the well-kept and brightly painted stores and street stalls of all sizes and shapes. The city had no zoning or building laws so far as Sheep Dog could tell. He had a laugh at the street stall advertising the "Tijuana Zebra", a donkey painted with stripes and surrounded by gaudy products, signs, and displays. The "Zebra" had been there since 1940, or so the entrepreneurial owner's sign said. On the Avenida, there were fruit and vegetable sellers, and flower stalls selling brilliantly colored flowers—Sheep Dog's favorite kind, the plastic ones that did not require watering and weeding. Unlike American tourists—because he was obviously indigenous to the city—he was not beset by persistent Tijuana shopkeepers, who knew that none of their countrymen would be interested in their wares.

From his CIA briefing papers he knew to drive to a quieter spot—the Arts and Crafts Market—which is not marked on most Tijuana tourist maps. It is located two blocks from Avenida Revolucion at Avenida Negrete and Calle Secunda. He was sweating, and he was thirsty and hungry; so, he bought an iced Negra Modelo beer and a fish taco and took a brief power nap in the shade of one of the stalls. When he awakened, his attention returned to the street scene: beggars—most of them children—harassed the gringo tourists and made them scurry, and sweet, cherubic, brown young girls in brilliant skirts, blouses, and bare feet were expertly picking the tourists' pockets.

With time to kill he walked to the Jai Alai Fronton Palace—one of Mexico's oldest venues—at Avenida Revolucion at Calle Octavia, 7 blocks from the arch. He was confident that his beat-up truck would not attract the attention of thieves; so, he spent a relaxing late afternoon and evening in the Palace's shade and watched the boringly repetitive games. It was dark when he left the building.

He drove east out of town towards the Rocial del Bosque area using the detailed Google map provided by his Company minders. He stopped from time to time to consult the map as he weaved his way along the Paseo del Bosque, then to the Priv. Los Alamos, and to the north-south Calle Del Rio. He turned immediately onto Calle Del Roble and drove to the end of the road and parked in front of the last of a long block of attached apartment buildings. There were few people on the street at that hour, and he was confident that no one paid him any attention. He took another sleep, this time for four hours.

Now, the night was deep and dark. There were no street lights in that poor neighborhood. The Sheep Dog took his two bags off the truck bed and selected defensive weapons—his throwing knives, combat knife, sound suppressed 9 mm Beretta, a cross bow, and night vision goggles. He picked up a carrying case the size of a lady's handbag and slung it over his shoulder. His parking place abutted the unpopulated desert to the west, and Sheep Dog walked around the corner to the left and cautiously made his way over the rough terrain to the next street over, Calle Del Romerillo. On Del Romerillo, the scene was different from that on any of the other streets in Rocial del Bosque.

There were scores of cars in front of the last apartment parked with no attempt at accommodation of other people who lived in the neighborhood. The walls of the three story apartment building were covered with gang signs, with the words, "MS-13", "MARA SALVATRUCHA", and the "Devil's Horns" hand sign and, more esthetically, artistic renditions of a horned demon. This was the Tijuana home base of MS-13, and the gang obviously considered itself to be above the law since it took no pains to conceal its location or activities. It was another one of those places where the police did not patrol, and the neighbors seldom left their homes.

Unlike the MS-13 house on Malebar Street in Brooklyn Heights, this apartment building at four o'clock in the morning was dark and silent except for the occasional outcry of a baby. There were no guards; the arrogant apartment dwellers felt no need for security beyond the terrifying intimidation they exerted over the people of the neighborhood, the local police, and the federales. These gangsters were a new breed of criminals in Mexico. Although the gang got its start in Los Angeles in the 1980s, most of them were now Salvadorans—the descendants of Salvadoran guerrillas—the source of most of the gang's early manpower—men used to killing without a moment's hesitation and for the slightest motive. The most common belief about the etymology of the gang's name is that *Mara* refers to the Spanish slang term for gang, and *Salvatrucha* refers to the Salvadoran guerrillas. The youngest killer-gangster in the building was thirteen, and he could count thirteen notches on his gun handleone for each year of his lifelike the fabled American bandit, Billy the Kid. The oldest man in the house was thirty-four. Longevity was not a common characteristic of the gang members. Almost every person in the apartments, except for three babies, was intoxicated with alcohol or one or another illicit pharmaceutical.

Sheep Dog silently padded his way across the dirt ground behind the building. Seeing no one, he tried the door and found it unlocked. He slid into the room and surveyed it with his night vision goggles. It was full of overflowing trash cans. The stench was almost overpowering. The floor was slick with grease and the remains of rotten vegetables and fruit. The cans were filled with diapers, liquor bottles, and wrappers from junk food. The gangsterslike most of the Mexicans around themwere addicted to packaged fast food. Most of the containers were greasy from McDonald's hamburgers and French fries, which outlet appeared to provide the food staples of preference by far.

He silently reconnoitered the house floor by floor. On the second floor, in the first apartment at the head of the stairs, he heard a baby cry a few times. From most of the apartments, he could hear deep loud snoring. Apparently the occupants were enjoying the well-earned sleep after a long, hard day's work—intimidation, rape, plunder, murder, and pillaging are fatiguing. Sheep Dog closed every door and every window he found. He tried several doors and carefully peered inside. Not a single apartment had an open window. Latinos have a fear of letting in the cold night air. There in Rocial del Bosque, the night time temperature had to be in excess of 95ºs; but apparently, the occupants were comfortable because the air was very dry.

Having assured himself that all doors and windows were sealed, Sheep Dog went down to the first floor and began his night's work. He selected the main room, a cluttered open area that could possibly have been termed a parlor had it ever had a woman's touch. He opened his satchel, put on white cotton gloves, cleared an eight foot square space, and covered it with aluminum foil. He then opened four bottles of Fumitoxin aluminum phosphide tablets packaged in resealable aluminum flasks, 500/flask, and enclosed in cardboard cases—tablets which produce phosphine gas.

The gas was the principle poison gas during World War I and thereafter banned by the Geneva Convention. The tablets originated in a Pestcon Systems chemistry lab as a colorless solid which was prepared cheaply and sold as a grey-green-yellow powder—due to impurities—formed into tablets. One tablet releases one gram of phosphine gas, enough to produce 25 ppm of phosphine gas in a volume of 1000 cu. ft. of space. Phosphine gas has an odor like carbide, garlic, or decaying fish, and even the miniscule amount of dust from the opened flask assaulted Sheep Dog's nostrils. He hurriedly spread about 60 tablets per square foot taking care to avoid contact between individual tablets.

He now worked with maximum speed to limit his own exposure. The tablets react with moisture from air, water, acids or other liquids to release phosphine gas. The chemical reaction is AIP (aluminum phosphide) $+3H_2O \rightarrow Al(OH)_3 + PH_3$. Sheep Dog found two humidifiers and a fan to activate the process and spread it into the air. He did not turn the machines on for the moment.

Sheep Dog washed his hands thoroughly in the fetid bathroom then rushed upstairs to the apartment where he had heard the baby cry out. He opened the apartment door, gun in hand; he need not have bothered. A naked man and woman lay with limbs akimbo on their sweated bed. Two children—one a girl of about a year of age, and a boy that looked to be two—lay naked on a filthy, fecal soiled mattress. Sheep Dog stood over the babies, took out a flask and poured just enough chloroform to moisten a handkerchief and put the anesthetic cloth over the children's faces. When he was sure they were fully unconscious but still breathing, he picked them up and rushed them down the stairs and ran to a car parked on the street. He put the children gently down on the rear seat and, on the front seat, left the same calling card and receipt as he had left in the gaudy low-rider in Brooklyn Heights the night before.

He dashed back to the house, all of his senses operating at maximum adrenalin warp speed, and placed a pan of water in front of the fan and turned on the fan and the humidifiers. He took a moment to evaluate his work while holding his breath then turned and ran out of the building and back to his truck.

CHAPTER FORTY-TWO

Before Sheep Dog reached his destination at noon the next day, every person in the MS-13 apartment building was dead. Usually, death from Fumitoxin rodent poison takes hours or even days to work in humans, but the huge excess of poison he spread on the aluminum sheets that wafted as deadly phosphine gas spread throughout the tightly closed apartment building rapidly produced dizziness, cyanosis, unconsciousness, severe pulmonary edema, and a suffocating death. When the bodies were discovered by gang members coming in the next day, all of the bodies were bloated; a frothy red foam was drying around their mouths; and they had soaked their beds with bloody urine, victims of their own overarching arrogance and the wrath of their great account keeper, the Sheep Dog.

Sheep Dog drove out of the city on Benito Juarez Highway well to the east until he turned north onto Presidente Lazaro Cardenas road in Tecate. He parked his truck in a back alley and abandoned it. He carried his bags two blocks north to Tecate Industrial Road and found the caretaker's shack on the east side of the wide expanse of concrete roadway and loading ramps with lines of semi-trailer trucks parked in neat rows. The shack was tucked between two tall cypress trees behind six over filled Dempsey Dumpsters. No one appeared to be anywhere around, but his instructions and directions had been explicit. This was the right place.

He found an obscure piece of shade behind a stack of plastic bags of trash and drifted off to sleep. Nearly four hours later, the sound of voices coming from the vicinity of the caretaker's shack alerted him to the presence of people and danger. He became instantly alert and felt for the reassurance of the handle of his knife in its belt scabbard. He left his bags by the trash bags and walked warily towards the voices.

"*Buenas tardes, señor,*" he said to a thin light skinned Latino with the Cassius face wearing a yellow guayabera decorated with white lace work.

"*Qué tal, Viejo?*"

Sheep Dog switched to English. He had taken an instant and instinctive dislike to the man. Maybe it was his greased-down pompadour, or maybe it was the intentional display of a Bowie knife hanging from his belt.

The coyote shifted into his second language smoothly. "Jou the man that the federales tol' me to take over?"

"Um-hmmh."

"Jou steel gottu pay. I don' take notheeng but cash—American cash. Jou got that?"

"How much?"

"Two thousand."

"More like three hundred."

The human trafficker gave Sheep Dog a hard look.

"Jou keedin' me, man? Jou really think I'm gonna haggle like one of those Tijuana street punks?"

"What's your real price. Let's get on with it."

"I won' take jou for anythin' less than a thou'. Thass it."

Sheep Dog fought with himself. He so wanted to smash that smirk off the man's face. The coyote spat a black gob of chewing tobacco through a missing front tooth. Some of the spittle landed on Sheep Dog's shoe. His jaw tightened.

"I have two bags that go with me."

"No jou don'. Bags hold us back, can' run from the *Migran.*"

"I can run from the border patrol. I can run faster, and I can run longer than you can or they can. The bags go."

The coyote did not like the look in the man's cruel eyes. That look was not a put-on like his sometimes was. This was born in him—*generado del Diablo*!

"Jou pay an extra thou', eets hokay."

"500, and no more crap from you, *amigo.*" Sheep Dog drew out the "*aamiigo*" so that the disrespect was palpable.

The coyote shrugged and accepted five crisp 100 dollar notes. He stuffed the money into his shirt pocket, then gave a sharp dog whistle. Seven frightened people peered out of the door of the caretaker's shack and moved tentatively out into the open.

"Les get going," the coyote snapped. "*Vamos!*"

Sheep Dog hefted his two precious bags and fell in behind the coyote in front of the line of timid and obedient would-be illegal border crossers. He had time to scrutinize them. Aside from one elderly man dressed in peasant attire that would make him a classical poster of a *campesino*, there were six members of one family. At least, Sheep Dog presumed that they were one family: a man who was affectionate with and protective of a pretty young woman, three young girlsnone of whom was more than ninewho clung to their mother's skirts, and a teenage boy and girl, who might have been cousins of the rest. The little snake of followers moved along in near absolute silence. The investment made by the family, Sheep Dog later learned, had been exorbitant—$1,200 per person up front in Mexico and another $300 if and when they reached the other side of the border.

The U.S.Mexico border region is currently experiencing unparalleled trade and exchange as cross-border flows of goods and people continue to reach new highs. The U.S. border economy thrives on the daily influx of tourists, shoppers, workers and immigrants from Mexico. Approximately 700,000 Mexicans cross legally into the United States every day to shop and work, returning at night to their homes in Mexico.

A much smaller number of border crossers enter illegally. Illegal immigrants represent only about 0.5 percent of total south to north border crossings. Still, the continuous flow of illegal aliens—upwards of 500,000 each year—over the past 35 years has contributed to an illegal immigrant population estimated at between 7 million and 20 million people—about 60 percent of them from Mexico.

Because the poverty in Mexico is so pervasive—owing in large part to governmental corruption—and U.S. border patrol vigilance is so high, illegal immigrants tend to hire smugglers—human traffickers, known as "coyotes"—and there has been a steady increase in coyote prices over time. Migrants are more likely to hire coyotes when they perceive a higher chance of apprehension were they to attempt a crossing on their own. If coyotes are more in demand or if risks increase—as is the case when criminal penalties on smuggling are increased—use of coyotes and prices rise.

There are more evils in the system. For U.S. law enforcement, there is drug smuggling and the movement of violent criminals crossing the border to join up with gangs like MS-13 and unfortunates who are pushed to emigrate illegally into the United States. U.S. law enforcement personnel have become somewhat more inclined to engaged in shoot-outs more quickly for their own safety; and coyotes care only for money and have been knownall too oftento cheat the emigrants out of their money, rape the girls, leave the emigrants in the desert no-mans land between Hermosillo State and San Diego County to perish of heat and thirst, and even to murder them outright somewhere out there in the desert.

The constant threat of encountering U.S. Border Patrol agents or even Mexican Federales is a severe strain on the emigrants who stand to lose their investment and be forced to return to their meager poverty ridden lives in Mexico and points south. Ever since the 1844 Treaty of Guadalupe Hidalgo which established the U.S./Mexico border, the efforts to secure the southern border of the United States have escalated. At the time of the Sheep Dog's crossing, the border was guarded by more than seventeen thousand border patrol agents. However, they only have effective control of less than 700 miles of the 1,954 miles of total border. Border Patrol activity is concentrated around big border cities such as San Diego which do have extensive border fencing. As a consequence, the flow of illegal immigrants is diverted into rural mountainous and desert areas, or more recently through cross-border tunnels, leading to several hundred migrant deaths along the Mexico-U.S. border each year.

Sheep Dog was well aware of all of that and did not want to become an accidental casualty in the ongoing border war. He did not let down his guard for a second. He was prepared for a truck ride or a long walk into the desert, but was astonished when the little troupe had advanced less than 100 yards before the coyote signaled a stop. Sheep Dog fingered his knife.

"Thees is eet."

"*This is what*," Sheep Dog thought.

Sensing the bemusement in his little following, the coyote laughed softly but heartily.

"I love thees part. Thees is where we cross."

Despite the darkness, Sheep Dog could easily make out the outlines of the forbidding border fence.

"Jou there, big one, *ayudame* with thees cover."

He was kneeling in a six foot square flat area surrounded by the trees Sheep Dog had noted to the north as he had reconnoitered the Tecate industrial area when it was still light out. The coyote was working a pry-bar along the edges of the vegetation covered piece of desert among the trees.

"Here, jou use this bar, gringo," he said and handed Sheep Dog a crow-bar that he produced from nowhere.

Sheep Dog thought it was an ingenious hiding spot for a tunnel opening, and he had to hand it to the resourcefulness of the coyotes as they made their fortunes in the human trafficking business. He set to work. Shortly, the two men had the edge of a trap door in view; and they heaved it up until it stood by itself. Sheep Dog peered into a well-made maw of a tunnel. It was as black as a mine shaft below.

"*Vengan*," the coyote called down into the tunnel.

At his command, three men clamored out onto the floor of the desert. They were as fine looking a set of pirates as ever raped a captive, scuttled a ship, and cut a throat. The four outlaws gave each other a quick hug and surreptitiously flashed the devil's head hand sign, unseen by anyone but Sheep Dog. He set himself.

On their way out, the three fellow conspirators had switched on a light which illuminated a sloping passageway that was as well engineered and lined with support beams and concrete walls, ceiling, and floor. The tunnel had a row of naked light bulbs that lit the entire distance across the border, Sheep Dog presumed.

The coyote pushed the young husband into the tunnel opening.

"Catch jour whelps," he whispered loudly and pushed the little ones down into the opening.

The father had barely enough time to catch each of them. The old campesino jumped down of his own volition. The pretty young wife was crying softly from fear. The teenagers stood at the margin of the tunnel paralyzed with fear.

"Now, jou, beeg one. Jump!"

He pushed on Sheep Dog's back. Sheep Dog had assumed a very stable karate stance, and the coyote's push was as if the man was trying to knock over a tree.

"I stay until she goes, and I come in behind you."

"She don' go until we get a little piece of her, jou *entiendes, amigo?*"

"Yo *entiendo*, but it's not going to happen. We paid you good money to cross, and cross we will. Leave her alone and get back to business."

The coyote and the three pirates laughed—evil, arrogant laughs. One looked directly into Sheep Dog's face, stretched out a dirty hand and ripped open the girl's blouse exposing her. Her eldest daughter, watching from the pit, let out a yelp. Her father put his had over her mouth. He had seen this exact scene before, and it was not unexpected. The teenagers covered their faces; they had seen this and worse in their short years of life; but they did not want to see any more than they had to.

The coyote's hand now held a switch blade that had come from a lanyard hanging down his back. He swept the knife with lightening speed across Sheep Dog's belly from the victim's left to right. Sheep Dog's muscle and brainstem reflexes were one fraction of lightening faster. The cruel tip of the razor-like blade nicked a line through his Mexican shirt and drew blood in a fifteen inch line. Sheep Dog turned sideways, and when the coyote swept the switch blade back across, Sheep Dog met the man's forearm with his own and whipped it backwards around the knife wielding arm and bent the arm over backwards. The coyote let out a pained cry; the three pirates ceased their unwanted dalliance with the young mother; and they advanced at Sheep Dog in leaps.

He shoved the coyote and his broken arm into the oncoming attackers. They tumbled against each other giving Sheep Dog a precious few seconds. He used them well. He brought out his own knife, a weapon three times the size of the coyote's and cut the man's throat. He stepped quickly to the side and planted a well-practiced foot in one pirate's face bringing him down. He knifed the second pirate directly between his carotid artery and trachea transecting both. The third pirate made a pirouette and forced his legs to take two running steps towards the industrial area of Mexican Tecate. Sheep Dog leaped across the bodies at his feet and in three steps was on the pirate's back and had his arms locked on the man's neck in a *mata leão* choke. He was unconscious in a matter of seconds. As the pirate slumped, Sheep Dog broke his neck. He had not broken a sweat.

The young woman was crying hysterically. Her husband and children were sobbing in sheer terror. Each of them expected the devil himself to return, and they waited in misery to die. Sheep Dog walked up the girl and put his arms gently around her.

"*Estas segura, señora. No tengas miedo.*"

She had no choice but to believe him. He had not hurt her or tried to force her. She began to feel safe, and she was able to obey his command not to be afraid after a minute. Sheep Dog wiped away her tears, pulled a shirt from his bag, and covered her nakedness. He took her by the hand and helped her negotiate the slope into the well-lit tunnel. The teenagers walked behind the woman who was effectively their mother. Her husband and children embraced her as fervently as if she had come back from the dead. Their tears were now silent ones of joy.

Sheep Dog pulled the four corpses in behind him, brought the trap door down behind them and followed the mother down into the transverse portion of the tunnel. The Mexicans made a point of not looking back. There was not enough room to stand erect even for the smaller adults, but the walking would be nothing but a little uncomfortable.

"*Hablan Ingles, amigos?*" he asked.

To his surprise, the old man responded in very clear, scarcely accented English, "I do. I can be of service because I have been this way before. Those *bandidos* always stole my money before. You are a man of respect."

He gave a little bow to show his respect. The members of the little family all kissed Sheep Dog's hand as if he were a cardinal. He waved them off, giving each a warm smile. Everyone relaxed.

The eight emigrants walked briskly through the tunnel following the campesino. It was almost 200 yards to the far end. They cautiously opened the tunnel trap door and peered out long enough to ascertain that there were no *migrans* lurking.

The campesino beamed at each of his new friends and said, "Welcome to the *Estados Unidos.*"

CHAPTER FORTY-THREE

Los Estados Unidos! America!, Tecate, San Diego County, California, the United States of America! Sheep Dog looked like Rodrigo Pancho Vila Dominguez, but he felt like Hunter Caulfield, American, and it felt good. He knew that he and the rest of his now rather dependent friends had very little time to savor the moment. The grandeur of the feeling was equally intense for each individual, but for different reasons. The task now was to find a way to get north without the border patrol catching up with them.

The coyote had spoken of a truck; so, they spread out for a hundred yards each and began to search, a search greatly hampered by the starless darkness. Smoke from the city had so polluted the air that the moon and stars could not be seen. They could hear but not see a helicopter passing overhead. The young father found the vehicle first and hastened to round up the conspiratorial immigrants.

The teenage niece, Maria Innocenta del Coronado, said carefully to her aunt as they climbed into the covered bed of the truck, *"Él hombre es viejo, pero él es un hombre muy peligroso."*

"Si, Maria, pero nosotros continuamos a vivir por que él es <u>nuestro</u> hombre peligroso."

The campesino said quietly enough that all of his compatriots would listen, "It is a mistake to pick a fight with an old man. If he is too old to fight, he will just kill you."

Sheep Dog hurried the Mexicans into the truck. He and the campesino jumped into the cab, and Sheep Dog hot-wired the ignition. The old engine sputtered a couple of times then started. He had to gun the old engine continually to keep it running. The gears ground, and Sheep Dog had to double-clutch to get into gear. Finally—frustrated and nervous—he got the cumbersome old vehicle in motion. They entered U.S. Highway 188, less than 100 yards north of the border station, which was located about 100 yards inside U.S. territory. Sheep Dog left the lights off until they were a mile from the station. It was so dark that he had to drive with extreme caution and very slowly. When he thought the risk/benefit ratio favored turning on the lights and gaining momentum, he took a deep breath and switched the headlights on, first using the parking lights; after a mile, he turned the headlights on at the dim setting. He still could only see about 50 yards ahead of him, and progress was too slow. Five miles out of Tecate, he turned the light switch to bright.

As soon as he did, a black border patrol helicopter swept down on the highway in front of the truck, and a black SUV pulled up behind the truck. Sheep Dog and the campesino were startled, and the Mexicans in the truck bed were terrified. He had no choice but to stop.

A bull-horn on the SUV blared the message: "Get out of the truck," in both English and Spanish.

With great reluctance, all eight illegal immigrants climbed out and stood, heads down, avoiding the brilliant lights from the car and helicopter.

"Kneel on the ground."

They did. Sheep Dog carefully fingered his 9 mm automatic. He hated his position; but he could not be arrested, armed to the teeth as he was. He would have to kill a U.S. officer and that went against everything he cared about. Two border patrol officers—one male and one female—walked up to the huddled group of Mexicans, guns drawn.

"Hands behind your backs."

All of the illegals complied. Sheep Dog's gun was in the back of his waistband, and he kept his right hand on the handle under his overhanging shirt. He was at full battle-level alert status.

The officers split up, segregated the illegals by gender, and began putting plastic wrist restraints on them. They had the family's wrists all secured in five minutes. One of the officers signaled to the helicopter, and the pilot acknowledged and flew off. Both officers approached Sheep Dog and the campesino.

"Turn around," the male officer ordered.

The campesino appeared to be complying when suddenly and with agility and speed that Sheep Dog would never have imagined possible leaped to his feet and ran east into the pitch blackness of the desert. The female officer shouted for him to stop. When he failed to comply, she fired her .45 into the air and took off after the elderly Mexican at full speed. Sheep Dog took advantage of the momentary distraction and threw himself at the burly male officer. The officer was startled, but had presence of mind enough to get off a shot at Sheep Dog.

A searing pain exploded in Sheep Dog's left deltoid. His adrenalin was at maximum input, and the injury only spurred him to move even faster. The officer's second round went awry as Sheep Dog zig-zagged towards him. Before he could get off a third shot, Sheep Dog's hammer fist connected with the point of the border patrolman's jaw lifting the man off his feet. He crumpled in a heap at Sheep Dog's feet unconscious.

The rest of the Mexicans—the young family—scattered into the darkness to the west of the highway as soon as Sheep Dog attacked the officer. They did not make a sound, and nothing could be seen of them. It would take hours—if not days—to round them up, even hampered as they were by their wrist restraints.

Sheep Dog ignored the pain and growing stiffness in his left shoulder. He hurriedly removed the officer's gun and radio, put plastic restraints on the man's wrists and ankles, and forced his mind to decide whether to go after the border patrolwoman to buy himself more time or to take the SUV and make a mad dash north up 188. His adrenalin had begun to subside; so, he could think more clearly. He decided that he would get nowhere by running; it would only be a matter of time until he was caught, no matter how fast he drove. The border patrol officer's radio could move faster than anything he could do.

The woman settled the question for him. She came running back towards the two parked vehicles as soon as she heard the two shots fired. She was in such a hurry to protect her fellow officer that she was heedless of the noise she made as she tore through the brush and kicked over rocks. Sheep Dog rolled into the shadows at the side of the SUV and lay in wait for her. She foolishly burst into the glare of the SUV's headlights and was momentarily blinded. Sheep Dog hurled himself at her knocking her down like a football blocker. She fired one shot harmlessly before Sheep Dog's right fist connected with her left temple. She was stunned, but not unconscious.

Sheep Dog wrested away her weapon. She struggled feebly; but Sheep Dog was considerably stronger, even using his only good upper limb.

He pointed the gun at her face and said, "Stop struggling. I won't hurt you unless you force me to. Your partner is unconscious, but he's alive and will be all right. Put your hands behind you. You know the drill."

She considered her options. The probability of escape or of overpowering this criminal were between slim and none. Maybe he wouldn't kill her. She gave him a poisonous look but slowly put her hands behind her back. Sheep

Dog secured her ankles and wrists with her own map black handcuffs he removed from her belt and divested her of her weapon and radio. He took a hurried look in the patrol SUV and found a box of tools that included in its contents a roll of duct tape. He covered the mouths and eyes of both officers and dragged them off into the dark desert about twenty yards, one to the east and one to the west of the highway. He then got in the old truck and drove it off through the rough desert terrain 50 yards to the east and abandoned it about fifty yards further down the highway in a clump of Joshua trees. He was feeling nauseated from the pain and the absence of the protective adrenalin and cortisone rush he had developed during the fight and flight portion of the last five minutes. He dragged his bags out of the truck and painfully lugged them back to the border patrol SUV.

The vehicle's engine was still running, and the headlights were on. He struggled to throw the bags into the rear compartment. Even opening the hatch back caused a jarring pain in his throbbing shoulder. He ran to the driver's side, got in and drove away at 120 miles per hour, burning away the miles between himself and the crime scene. He knew that it would be only a matter of an hour or so before a state wide man hunt would be launched in earnest for him. He was able to roar past Potrero and Dulzura without seeing any evidence of police activity. Outside Dulzura, he drove into the rear parking area of an all-hours Exxon truck stop and got out of the car. He was dizzy and felt as if he might faint as he stood on the asphalt trying to regain his equilibrium.

He found what he was looking for. There was a Toyota Prius Hybrid parked next to the rear entrance into the truck stop. He moved the SUV and parked next to the Prius. He looked around, and seeing no signs of lifeopened the front door of the car. The keys were in the ignition. That was the first piece of luck he had had since the border patrol had stopped him. He knew that he would not get far looking like he did. He had to get the bleeding stopped or at least hidden; he had to become an obvious American; and he had to do it in a hurry. He made his decision. He took out his hand gun and opened the door of the truck stop. There was no one in the hallway. To his left was a neat storeroom, and to his right were the rest rooms. He went back to the SUV and transferred one of his bags to the rear seat of the Prius. He was sweating profusely.

He carried the second bag into the truck stop's men's room and as quickly as he could, tore off his bloody clothes. He stripped all the way down and surveyed the damage. He was covered with blood, but the bullet had passed through and through without hitting bone or nerves. Blood was slowly seeping without pulsatile spurting; so, he was pretty sure that no major artery had been hit. He would live; he probably would not get infected; and the blood would probably stop on its own fairly soon. He ran water in the sink and used up all the paper towels in the room to clean himself up and to pack over the holes in his shoulder. The bleeding had slowed to a trickle and; as he stood there, did not seep through the makeshift paper bandage. He tore apart his Mexican shirt and painfully knotted a clumsy bandage around the wad of paper. He scrubbed the makeup off his face and thoroughly rinsed his hair and slicked it back with a comb. He donned a Polo shirt, a clean, starched pair of khaki cargo pants, and a pair of slip-on deck shoes. Again, he surveyed himself and made sure that he was no longer Rodrigo Pancho Vila Dominguez and pronounced what he saw as acceptably yuppie—not great, but acceptable. He took two plastic garbage bags and stuffed his bloody disguise clothes and the paper trash inside them.

He opened the men's room door and peered out into the hallway. No one was in the hallway, and the sleepy all-night attendant was helping a customer lug a couple of cases of Coors Lite to the check-out counter. Neither man paid any attention to the area where Sheep Dog was located. He quietly gathered up his belongings and slipped out into the dimly lit rear parking area. He loaded the trash bags and duffel bag into the rear seat. He had the presence of mind—in fact, having cleaned himself up, was feeling better—to move the old truck across the parking area, beyond the rear gasoline and diesel pumps, and left it behind the long rows of Dempsey Dumpsters and fuel drums. He raced back to the attendant's Prius and drove away, leaving the headlights off until he was two miles north and on his way to La Mesa.

It was still extremely dark out although he was now passing lighted buildings and businesses. He held his speed at 100 miles an hour as long as he dared. He passed through Jamul and Rancho San Diego, then decided that he could not risk attracting a traffic patrolman and slowed down to the speed limit which made him feel like he could get out of the Prius and run along the side. He stopped at an all night diner and switched cars. This time he had to settle for an old Ford which he could hot-wire. The newer computerized cars were the bane of the existence of car thieves since they could not be hot-wired with any chance of success. He dumped the border patrol officers' guns and radios in the restaurant's garbage cans.

He did not stop again until he was in the heart of San Diego and felt a modicum of safety. He was sick, tired—dead tired—too nauseated to eat although he knew he had to; and his mouth was parched dry. He had to get something to eat and had to have sleep. He was well aware of his age and his limitations. Hollywood action heroes can fight dozens of villains for days on end without food, rest, or taking a leak; but Sheep Dog was all too aware that he was not a Hollywood or any other kind of hero. He had to get out of the car and get horizontal.

He found a run down small motel—the Love Nest—which catered to patrons and their companions seeking a place to stay. The Love Nest offered rooms by the hour, and Sheep Dog paid for three of them, cash in advance. His signing in as John Smith did not cause a reaction from the bored wino who worked the night shift. Half of his guests were named John Smith.

Once in the dingy room, Sheep Dog took stock. There was a little blood on his shirt, but not enough to draw immediate attention. He looked haggard, but like a haggard American WASP. He drank a large draught of water from the bathroom faucet and almost immediately perked up. He set the bedside alarm for two and a half hours later and laid down to sleep the sleep of the just.

It was light out—early morning—when he heard the alarm; at first its significance did not register. He was able to wake up in a few minutes, enough to wash out his mouth and to down another good slug of water. He watered down his hair and slicked it back again and moved out of the room's door. The door and the motel itself badly needed a paint job, and the parking lot was strewn with potholes. The clientele did not relish recognition of their existence much less conversation. It had been the perfect choice. He asked the new attendant where the Greyhound station was located and with pointing, gesturing, map drawing, and some contradictory verbal descriptions, Sheep Dog was confident he could find it. He was feeling much better now; the sick feeling was gone, but the shoulder pain had increased exponentially.

He bought a one way bus ticket to Salt Lake City and helped the driver load his bags into the belly-bin bus cargo area. He left the Ford where he parked it and got aboard. He fell asleep as soon as the monotonous rhythm of the 55 mph bus sounds provided the white-noise so conducive to sleep by babies and wounded killers.

CHAPTER FORTY-FOUR

December

The morning was beautiful. Outside the warmth and inviting ambience of the world-class lodge, the sky was a cloudless azure; the mountainsides, trees, and vehicles were covered with a heavy raiment of white velvet. It was freezing, and the brave souls who had to go out for one reason or another watched their exhalations create small, short-lived jet streams. Guests entering the lobby of Deer Valley Resort Snow Park Lodge stamped their feet and clapped their hands to get the blood flowing again. An air of conviviality and the expectation of being ostentatiously pampered was the order of the day, as it was for all days in the splendor of the resort. It was the place where the rich, the famous, and the aficionado met for the sheer joy of skiing down manicured hillsides on the world's best snow.

Sheik Abu Bakr bin al-Wattab, his third wife of four, and their seven young children observed the *Fair* at the correct hour because he had instructed the desk clerk with some fervor that he must be awakened five minutes before first light. That had required the young woman to consult with the climatologist/weather reporter from the Salt Lake City CBS affiliate, KSL, for information precise enough to suit the needs of the strictly observant Saudi dignitary. Fatima and the children had been half asleep during morning prayers and had quickly resumed their slumbers as soon as it was over. The Sheik dressed in his handsome Spider ski ensemble, made sure he had his card-key to avoid having to awaken the family when he returned to the suite, and walked down the six flights of stairs to the Snow Park Restaurant for breakfast.

The sheik was a tall darkly handsome man with long black hair, a slightly aquiline nose, and prominent cheek bones. His dress, manner, and interactions with everyone he met set him apart as a patrician, and a man of wealth, education, and power. He was all of that and more. Sheik al-Wattab came from the line of one of two paramount families in Saudi Arabia. The Wattabs and the Sauds established the nation together, and the Wattabs controlled Allah's religion and the nation's justice system now as they had always done. The Sheik controlled several of the most powerful Islamic charities in the world, a combined enterprise that generated and expended hundreds of millions of dollars a year. In his world, Sheik al-Wattab's word was law.

Everything about his brief stay at Snow Park Lodge had been perfect thus far. It was nothing less than what he had expected—what he always expected. He had been amused for a moment while checking in when an Italian lout had first bumped the man next to him at the reservations desk and knocked his several card keys to the floor, and then had bounced off the rather annoyed man and into him, knocking his card keys and wallet to the floor as well. One had to be indulgent in America. The country attracts the great unwashed like no other. The Italian had at least been polite enough to pick up his cards and to hand them to him with a sincere apology. Al-Wattab had been in a relaxed and forgiving mood and paid the lout no real heed.

Sheik al-Wattab did not notice that same Italian sitting on the balcony above him as he breakfasted. The Sheik had the mind of a computer when he concentrated on his responsibilities for the charities. He was lost in concentration about them as he enjoyed his fresh fruit compote, eggs Benedict, and freshly squeezed grapefruit juice. He delicately removed the watermelon from the compote because the Prophet, may his name be blessed forever, had not received from Allah information about watermelon; and the fruit was not mentioned in the *Holy Qur'an*.

He tallied rows of numbers in his mind. His most recent success had been to renegotiate the long standing memorandum of understanding between UNICEF and his International Islamic Relief Organization (IIRO)—a Saudi charity of massive scope—which keeps branches in more than 20 countries and has over 100 offices worldwide. The memorandum solidified the team effort between the United Nations and al-Wattab's domestic Saudi branch to promote the rights, health, equality, and education of children in the Kingdom. He had to smile at the naiveté of the UNICEF governing board and their lack of requiring even the most rudimentary accounting. Had they done so, they would have readily observed that well over 80% of the U.N.'s contribution went to serve the needs of jihad around the world. The IIRO's branches in the Philippines and Indonesia—for which the sheik served as CEO—had been responsible for the deaths of hundreds of kaffirs and servants of the Great Satan throughout East Asia. The IIRO proudly financed the lives of the families of the martyrs from the Philippines, Indonesia, Yemen, Palestine, Syria, Libya, and England, to mention only a few. He counted as a friend Usama bin Laden's brother-in-law, Muhammad Jamal Khalifah, who founded the Philippine branch and directly served al-Qaeda.

Sheep Dog, with his ebony black hair slicked back and his olive complexioned skin glowing from his recent shave and application of Roger & Gallet Extra-Vielle Cologne that had come to him from Oliver Prentiss—directly from Rome—was dressed in the latest Sombrio ski fashion adorned with the image of Alberto Tombo. He watched his target from his vantage point in the balcony above the sheik. He rubbed his left shoulder unconsciously. It still bothered him some, but had healed almost completely. He was well aware from his briefing from the ADCIA of the fact that the U.S. Treasury Department designated the IIRO's branches in the Philippines and Indonesia as terrorist entities for funding and supporting terrorist groups.

He was also aware of the sheik's involvement in several other so-called charity entities—The Afghan Support Committee [ASC], a non-governmental organization established by Usama bin Laden; the Revival of Islamic Heritage Society [RIHS]; the Aid Organization of the Ulema [AOU] based in Pakistan and successor organization to Al Rashid Trust; the Al Akhtar Trust, Elkhart Trust; the Azmat-e-Pakistan Trust; and the United Composite Islamic Fund, managed by the Usama bin Laden Fund Managers Limited [UBLFM], to name only a portion—with the same motives and accomplishments. It had not been lost on Assistant Director Prentiss that the charities had been largely considered off-limits or were regarded as untouchables by the United States and its allies because of being too politically sensitive. Since governmental diplomatic and law enforcement had been generally rather ineffective in preventing the dispersal of funds for terrorists, it had become Sheep Dog's assignment to create mischief.

The ski lifts were due to open in fifteen minutes. The sheik left his name and room information as the payment chit for the waiter and strode purposefully out of the restaurant and up the stairs to make his final preparations for an unfettered ski outing. He promised himself that he would not think about business. It looked to be a perfect day.

Sheep Dog's room was two doors away from the al-Wattab's, and he followed the sheik at a discrete distance to ensure himself that the sheik was indeed on his way to the slopes. He lingered in the hallway long enough to have the sheik pass him going in the opposite direction towards the lower level of the lodge where he would have an employee carry his skis and poles to the Wasatch Express gondola from the complimentary overnight storage room for the ride to the top of 9,400 foot high Bald Mountain.

Sheep Dog was a decent skier but was not in the same league as Sheik al-Wattab. The American agent followed the Arab billionaire only long enough to observe the man schuss down the black star Ruins of Pompey run and into the trees. Sheep Dog took the somewhat less hazardous double-blue square Tycoon trail. At intervals, he caught a glimpse of the sheik—who skied like an Olympic athlete—and contented himself to know the general whereabouts of his quarry. Shortly before noon, he sidled up behind the sheik as he walked arm-in-arm with a woman not his wife into Cushing's Cabin restaurant atop 9,100 foot Flagstaff Mountain that stood majestically to the west of Bald Mountain.

Deer Valley was once the calving grounds and over-wintering shelter for a resident herd of about 300 deer, hence the name. The deer were almost all gone now, but their valley was still surpassingly beautiful, especially when covered with an eight foot deep snow cover. The fir and pine trees were frosted, and their branches were weighted down by the snow. Utah snow has 11% water content rendering it dry and soft, "the best snow on earth" as the advertising brochures touted. The sheik and his new-found friend and Sheep Dog alike found great pleasure in the opportunity to take in the view. Sheep Dog would have been more content with the pleasant bit of esthetics lying before him had he not an important professional purpose for being there.

The sheik enjoyed a leisurely day skiing with the woman, a blond entertainer named Sheri Van Wagoner. She held out the promise of an evening's entertainment; and this evening, his family had reservations for a Broadway performance—The Nutcracker Suite—at the Pioneer Theater in the University of Utah complex. The great day was looking like it would turn out to have a culmination in a great evening. The two nascent lovers were oblivious to Sheep Dog as they worked their way down the mountain on a series of ski runs, taking advantage of the necessary chair-lift rides for some kissing and fondling. He was never close to them, but he never let them completely out of his sight.

The lifts were due to close in three-quarters of an hour; so, Sheep Dog left the loving pair on the mountain and skied rapidly back to base. He checked his skis, poles, and boots into the overnight storage area, tipped the attendant, and moved quickly to his room. There, he changed into a jet black outfit and carried his aluminum brief case with him to the door of the al-Wattab's room. He knocked softly. There was no answer; so, he knocked again, this time more vigorously.

When he satisfied himself that the family was out, he took his key to the al-Wattab quarters, inserted it and walked in as if he had paid for the place. He had acquired the key by a bit of slight-of-hand. The previous day when he and the sheik and his family were checking in, he bumped a flustered German gentleman and knocked his key cards to the floor. He substituted one of his extra cards for one of the German's. Then, he ricocheted off the German and into the sheik, knocking his card keys to the floor. He deftly switched the German's card for one of the sheik's leaving each of them with one key that would not work and him with a card that would admit him to the sheik's inner sanctum without risk or bother.

He looked all around the room. The desk in the anteroom between the bedrooms was cluttered with an open account book, a fat wallet, a Toshiba lap-top, a Blackberry, and a small black note book, all carelessly left in the open. The closet door containing the hotel's small security safe was ajar. The beds were made to navy precision, but expensive clothes were strewn about on the floors along with toys, left-over trays of food scraps, and empty cans of soft drinks. Sheep Dog decided on the master bed room as his place of rendezvous with his quarry, put his face cover in place, took out his 9 mm, and sat patiently on the bed.

Half an hour later, he heard the latch on the entry door click and became instantly on full alert. The voices of a man and an eager young woman carried into the rooms. Sheep Dog stood stock still behind the bed room door and listened to the rustling of clothing and the woman's excited giggling. Ever the gentleman, the sheik allowed the now naked woman to enter the bed room before him. Sheep Dog held his ground.

The girl was totally unaware of Sheep Dog's presence, and Sheik Abu Bakr bin al-Wattab was caught by complete surprise by a hard rabbit punch on the back of his neck that toppled him forward to the floor at the foot of the bed. The woman opened her mouth to scream, and was knocked out by a sharp blow to the point of her chin. Sheep Dog swiftly bound the naked pair's wrists and ankles with duct tape and covered their mouths and eyes so that they would have no good idea what was happening, and they could not cry out.

He removed his black leather gloves and put on two pairs of latex surgical gloves. Only then did he open the locked section of his aluminum case and drew out a syringe and a vial. He drew up a slightly viscous clear liquid, the conotoxin tetradoxin—TTX, for short—the powerful paralytic sodium channel blocker neurotoxin prepared for his use by Dr. Heinz Bühler-Rothe. He flexed both of their legs apart. He then placed approximately a teaspoonful of the deadly fluid on a small gauze bandage and rubbed it thoroughly into the skin of their upper thighs adjacent to their pudendae where no one would be at all likely to investigate. He was briefly saddened by having to include the beautiful young woman in his assassination, but it could not be helped. She was collateral damage.

They were dead in five minutes. Neither had been aware of what was happening and; being unconscious beforehand, they suffocated from the neurotoxin quite comfortably; or so it appeared to Sheep Dog. He removed the duct tape and cleaned their skin with acetone from his case. He washed the acetone residue thoroughly from the skin where the duct tape had been, leaving no trace. Then, he tucked the pair nicely together under the covers. He checked his watch and decided that he had time.

He moved into the anteroom and picked up the notebook. There were a series of numbers in rows with corresponding Arabic words. Sheep Dog decided that they were account numbers and identification codes. He tried out his hypothesis on the computer, and was rewarded for his efforts with a cornucopia of information about a list of corporations, trust funds, stock and bond accounts, and personal banking data. He checked his watch again. The family would not be back for hours, and there was no reason for room service to disturb him.

He methodically arranged transfers of all funds from each account to his own personal accounts. It was a dizzying job trying to keep track of all of the sheik's account numbers and codes and those of his own. It took over an hour to complete the transfers and to deplete all of the terrorist funds under Sheik al-Wattab's control. Sheep Dog was now richer by over a billion dollars; and it would take a forensic computer expert and a team of forensic accountants months to unravel what he had done; if, in fact, anyone were to be that curious. The United States would not be aware that the funds had been diverted, and the terrorist Islamic charities would not have any desire to call attention to themselves by launching such a cyber search. In an act of rather infantile malice and greed, Sheep Dog tried a number from the little black book and found that it opened the room safe. He placed a card in the bottom of the safe under a stack of cash:

Ayatollah Zia Muhammad Ali Kader
Hizbullah Central Press Office
Baabda, Beirut, Lebanon

Rummaging through the al-Wattab family's prized possessions, he found their cell phones and hurriedly copied down the names and telephone numbers. He went through their identification documents, and he purloined the sheik's. The man did not look so different from him, and the IDs could prove useful one day in the future. You never knew.

CHAPTER FORTY-FIVE

On the twenty-third of December, Scotsman Dr. Angus McFarland, accompanied the IAEA inspection team to Iran. He replaced an American, Donald Edward Hutchison, PhD, who had become unable to travel due to a recently contracted mysterious illness. The twenty person team was required to fly Iran Air on an Iran Air Fokker 100 EP-IDA with Iran military pilots after their Lufthansa flight arrived from Frankfort in the IATA-Imam Khomeini *International Airport.* Their flight landed at the military's Esfahan Shahid Beheshti International Airport, a one level building with limited services that was rather grandiloquently titled. A new terminal was under construction—ostensibly to accommodate international passengers—but the desultory pace of the construction suggested that Esfahan was not likely to become a tourist or a business Mecca any time soon. The officials and scientists were met by a delegation of Revolutionary Guards officers and three nuclear scientists, hand-picked by President Mahmoud Sofrekheneh himself. The tight control of their movements from the get-go did not bode well for the inspection tour.

Ibrahim ibn Sharif al-Tezari, head of U.N. International Atomic Energy Agency delegation, announced directly upon arrival that the delegation wished to be taken immediately to the Zirconium Production Plant [ZPP] which produces the necessary ingredients and alloys for nuclear reactors. The Revolutionary Guard colonel—and part owner of the Esfahan facility—was taken aback by the unexpected request. The facility had been left off the itinerary purposely, and the Guards presumed that the inspectors would want to focus on The Uranium Conversion Facility where yellowcake is converted to uranium hexa-fluoride. The UCF had been tidied up considerably in honor of the inspection.

"No sir, our agreement was for you to see the UCF, and perhaps later the waste storage facility," the stone-faced colonel stated with finality.

"That is unacceptable Colonel Kutchemeshgi, you know that perfectly well. We have come all the way from Germany, and we did not come to waste our time. We will see the UCF in our own time, as agreed by President Sofrekheneh. We demand to be taken to the ZPP now."

This was a classical Iranian stand-off; neither of the men was about to budge. Ibn Sharif al-Tezari was not surprised by the refusal, and knew that in all likelihood, he would not prevail. However, he wanted the refusal to be clearly established. One of the team members was filming the entire transaction as was permitted in the lengthy agreement that Sofrekheneh and ibn Sharif al-Tezari had signed in Paris the week before.

A Revolutionary Guard sergeant yanked the camera out of the team photographer's hands.

"That is a clear violation of the agreement. Do you intend to comply with any aspect of the agreement for inspection, Colonel?"

Stone face looked at the IAEA director with complete disdain.

"I will have to consult my superiors about your irregular requests. It will take some time, I am sure."

"We do not have a great deal of time. Our arrangement included no impediments by your side. Either take us to the ZPP or take us to see the two reactors and all of the centrifuges at Bushehr."

The colonel had difficulty containing his distaste for this Sunni that had betrayed Islam by joining with the kaffirs to undermine work of Allah under the colonel's control. He had no intention of giving in or taking responsibility for throwing up road-blocks.

"No," he said flatly.

"Then, Colonel, we require a no-nonsense statement by your superiors that you refuse to honor your commitments."

That was enough for Colonel Kutchemeshgi; "Who are you, a kaffir, and all of your Great Shaytaan lackeys—people of the left hand—to make demands on the soil of the Islamic State?"

The insults were meant to sting and were meant to be intolerable. It was a tribute to al Tezari's vaunted patience that he did not show any reaction. That further greatly annoyed Kutchemeshgi.

Al-Tezari said quietly and firmly, "We can certainly agree on one thing. You need to talk to your superiors. We will wait for two days, and two days only, and we will wait in Tehran."

The Revolutionary Guards colonel turned his back on al-Tezari to add further insult. With a backhanded flick of his wrist he gestured to the Air Fokker pilot to get the vermin out of his jurisdiction.

The plane made the trip with silence on the part of the guests of the Islamic Republic. They all knew better than to make any comment that could be construed as being critical of the regime. They also all knew that their every word was being monitored and recorded.

When they touched down at Mehrabad, an obsequious diplomat in an English morning coat right out of central casting met them and was effusive in his welcome and apologies for the unforeseen delays.

"*Inshallah*," he said more than once.

God's will or not, Angus McFarland—the Sheep Dog—had to control himself not to gag.

"I am Mohammed," the very minor diplomat told the delegation of inspectors, "we have arranged for you to attend a lecture by our foremost educator, the chairman of Nuclear Development of Iran, Professor Ayatollah Alaeddin Muhammad Khamenei of the Department of Islamic Studies at Tehran University. It is a singular honor for you members of the foreign delegation. You may realize that the Ayatollah is the nephew of our esteemed Supreme Leader, may Allah bless and keep him. President Sofrekheneh, himself, has said that you will benefit greatly from this opportunity to have an in-depth look into our religion and our nation—his very words. You will be required to wear black tie, I think is your term for tuxedos."

The sweeping adulation expressed by the minor bureaucrat, the intimate association of secular government, the military, the higher educational system, and the omnipresent and omniscient ecclesiastical authority informed the delegation—as it was meant to do—that they were likely to receive a hardline approach. The Sheep Dog presumed that they were going to be sent packing without having accomplished anything and that this would be his only opportunity to come into contact with his target.

Ibn Sharif al-Tezari shrugged in defeat.

"Take us to our hotel, Mohammed."

Mohammed fetched limousines for the delegation, and they were whisked through the teeming streets to northern Tehran to the "best five-star hotel in Tehran" as Mohammed modestly described it. It was obvious to the entire delegation that their drivers were military men who made no real pretense of being otherwise. Their weapons were worn openly. Everyone was more than happy to be dropped off at the Azadi Grand Hotel on Chamran and Evin Cross Road Expressway, a place with which they were all too familiar from previous unproductive inspection tours.

Prior to leaving Frankfort, al-Tezari had briefed the man he knew as Angus McFarland, "I'm afraid that you will have to change your expectations when you travel to Tehran with us. The fact of the matter is that the hotels in Iran are not that popular with foreigners because you can't get what you get in the hotels all around the world—big things like casinos, discos, fancy restaurants—or little things like a comfortable room. What you do get by going first class is barely an average room in a building that resembles a Hilton Express Hotel in the States. In many rooms, there is a TV but no HBO or other movie channels. Usually, if you do luck out and get a TV, there are only six local channels in Persian, and, if you are really lucky, you might get the BBC or CNN.

"Interestingly, there is wireless internet but the speed is no more than a dial up and it's filtered, and I do mean filtered. When the government doesn't like what's going on in the country or in the world—or just doesn't like the foreign guests—the internet is more likely than not to slow down to an unusable speed and conk out entirely. You won't like the bathroom. Expect it to be small and sparsely fitted out—no hot tub, shampoo, or soap; and if you forget to bring your own towel, you can make do or do without. I doubted that you would know that; so, I took the liberty of buying you a couple."

He neglected to mention that the toilets did not work, and Sheep Dog had to find that out later as he prepared for dinner. The hotel provided a small bowl of water atop a handsome rectangle column tiled with sayings from the *Qur'an*. Since there was no toilet paper, Sheep Dog presumed that his left hand was supposed to do. He performed his ablutions and wiped with one of the thin towels provided by his leader, Ibrahim ibn Sharif al-Tezari, carefully folding it so that it could be used a second time should the occasion arise.

The German Embassy had been authorized by the American ambassador—in a quid pro quo gesture on the part of each ambassador—to divulge to the IAEA director the fact that not everything was quite as it appeared to be with Angus McFarland; and it was best not to inquire overmuch. The favor of taking on Dr. McFarland—whom the German ambassador admitted did not know a thing about nuclear physics or anything related to the production of nuclear energy—had "another purpose for being in the Islamic Republic" was to be repaid with a future marker for a share of German satellite intel. The

Americans—in turn—would similarly reward the Germans. Ibn al-Tezari rather hoped that McFarland's purpose was intended to bring harm to the arrogant and dangerous Iranians; but, of course, he never suggested such an opinion aloud.

They were curtly informed by the inhospitable assistant manager of the Grand Azadi that the delegation was to present itself decked out in full black tie regalia at the stroke of 1830. They would be then taken to the Revolutionary Guards instructional auditorium at Tehran University where they would be privileged to hear a lecture from the great Professor Ayatollah Alaeddin Muhammad Khamenei.

"You will then be returned to the Grand Azadi and retire for the night," the officious Persian said.

"Let's get some dinner," ibn al-Tezari said. "The food is the least bad thing about the hotel."

He said it loud enough that the assistant manager could not help but hear.

The dinner was not all that bad, in fact. The floor was clean—unlike the carpet in Sheep Dog's room—and the table linens were spotless. They were not given a choice from a menu; but rather, the waiters brought in ample servings of *Sabzi Polow*, a dill rice dish, followed by a delicious dried fruit soup made from soaked red beans browned in olive oil and lamb stock, mixed with cubed boneless lamb, lentils, julienne beets, and minced onion and spiced with turmeric, cardamom, cumin, black pepper, and salt. The mixture was boiled, then a mixture of chopped dried fruit including apricots, prunes, pears, peaches in light lemon juice was added. The dish was served garnished with parsley and lemon wedges. The next course was *Kabab-e Ozungorun*-sturgeon kebab, and *dolme-ye Barg-e Mo*—stuffed vine leaves. Dessert was *Shollehzard*-saffron rice pudding. The meal was the best thing that had happened all day and lifted the mood of the thoroughly dispirited U.N. Nuclear Radiation Inspection Committee. Sheep Dog was able to order a small bottle of Johnnie Walker Black from room service which is illegal for Iranians, but perfectly all right—albeit very expensive—for visiting kaffirs.

Despite an acceptable breakfast of eggs, bacon, a rasher of wheat toast, and corn flakes, the general mood of the Europeans sagged again as they dutifully boarded the Revolutionary Guard chauffeured limousines at 6:30 As a minor gesture of defiance, the members of the committee all left off their ties and buttoned the top buttons of their collars, a timid mockery of the vain refusal of the Iranians to wear full Western attire. The Iranians viewed the

Europeans' dress as the opposite: a gesture of respect for their chutzpah for defying Western customs, a product of the glorious Islamic Revolution.

The IAEA inspection team and their minders formed an armed convoy from the Azadi to Tehran University. The team was divided up into four separate limousines, each protected by a dour pair of Revolutionary Guardsman from the security branch. The silence of a funeral cortege reigned as the four huge seven seater black Russian Zils—20 feet long and weighing nearly four tons—moved through the streets of Tehran. Cars, trucks, motor bikes, and pedestrians alike gave way quickly to one of the ultimate symbols of Soviet power and now of the commanding presence of the Islamic State. The limos were comfortable, unlike anything in the Azadi Hotel. Sheep Dog settled into the beige velvet seat and had a short power nap.

The particular Zil in which Sheep Dog and the rest of his group were traveling was a famous model 41052 assembled by hand. To underscore the dominance of the Revolutionary Guards over the IAEA team—and indeed, the entire Middle-East region—this model was custom fitted with armor plate which was bullet and grenade resistant. It had cost the Islamic Republic of Iran a million dollars, and its intimidation factor was worth every penny to them.

The University of Tehran—"the mother university of Iran"—is the oldest and largest university in Iran. It was officially inaugurated in 1934. Its library is the largest in the country. The limos pulled up to the front steps of the administration building on Enghelab Avenue near the middle of the central Pardis campus—the oldest and the best known of the campuses of the sprawling university complex. The IAEA delegation was swiftly ushered out and marched up the stairs to a reception lobby by prodding Revolutionary Guards, who made no effort to disguise their contempt for the Westerners.

Sheep Dog was aware of the history of the roadways he had just traversed as the cortege entered the Pardis campus. He was not very well versed in the glorious ancient history of Persia, but he well remembered its key roles in the political events of recent history. It was in front of the same gates of this school that the Sheep Dog had just passed that the army of Mohammad Reza Pahlavi—the Shah of Iran—opened fire on dissident students, killing many and further triggering the 1979 revolution of Iran. It was there and 20 years later—back in July 1999—that a much smaller number of dissident students confronted police.

Currently, at the university, the leaders of the country deliver some of their most potent speeches often on Friday during prayers. Since the 1979 Islamic Revolution, the main campus of the university and its surrounding streets have been the site for Tehran's Friday prayers to emphasize the direct and complete linkages between the government of the Islamic Republic of Iran, the Supreme Leader of the nation, a powerful grand ayatollah, and Allah, himself.

Six goose stepping soldiers led the appropriately intimidated IAEA delegation into the third largest of the building's many classroom auditoriums. They were ushered to their seats; guards took their places around the room, and conspicuously by the entrances; and the room fell into a hush. Sheep Dog made sure that he sat in an aisle seat.

The disquieting hush endured for thirty minutes until a side door admitted two guards, then the republic's foremost educator and the chairman of Nuclear Development of Iran, Professor Ayatollah Alaeddin Muhammad Khamenei of the Department of Islamic Studies at Tehran University. He walked briskly to the podium and stood impassively surveying the audience until there was silence in the room. He was surprisingly small, a diminutive bespectacled man dressed in the ultra conservative black suit and tieless white shirt worn by every senior official Sheep Dog had thus far seen during his stay in the republic. He had a peaked face, strikingly white skin, and a shock of jet black hair that was decades younger than his seamed face. His voice was high-pitched, and his English was unaccented Harvard American.

"Good morning, ladies and gentlemen," he began.

There was slight murmur of acknowledgement.

"Welcome to the delegation from the International Atomic Energy Agency. I intend that this communication to you by me and from the government of the Islamic Republic of Iran will prove to be instructive. I suggest that you pay close attention. I will not take questions."

Al Tezari looked at Sheep Dog and cautiously rolled his eyes. Sheep Dog gave a scarcely perceptible negative shake of his head.

"My lecture will be as follows: First, I will give you an overview of Islam, then of the Islamic Republic of Iran. We will then take a ten minute break. Second, I will present the world as seen from the eyes of Iranians. That will lead me into my third segment, wherein I will set you straight as to the provocations of the Zionist Entity and of its master, the Great Satan."

Professor Khamenei looked down upon his audience with a glare that challenged anyone to defy him. There were no takers. The members of the captive audience sat in a silence that would have befitted a spectator in the Soviet show trials of the 1930s.

He continued, "Lastly, after our second break of ten minutes, I will instruct you on the peaceful nuclear program embarked upon by the peace loving

Islamic people of Iran. The lecture will conclude; you will be taken back to your hotel; and you will depart on the Air France flight to Paris which leaves at 1600 hours on the dot."

Al Tezari stirred uncomfortably in his seat itching to protest but knowing that it was futile. He and the delegation already had their answer. There would be no real inspection, and he would not be party to a visit to a Potemkin village.

"Now that we understand each other, I shall begin. Islam is the one religion of the One God. All others are subservient at best and opponents at worst. It has ever been so since the day of the Prophet, may Allah bless him and his posterity forever."

Professor Khamenei gave a sweeping laudatory history of his religion, its five pillars, its accomplishments, its historical opponents, its golden age, and the pivotal role played by the Shia.

"Next, I shall enlighten you about the glorious Islamic Revolution of 1979. There was much affection in the West for Mohammed Reza Shah, the brutal dictator who founded a dynasty on the backs of the Iranian people and had the temerity to challenge the Ayatollahs and the faithful in Iran. Despite the economic growth in the nation and the apparent prosperity, that which was so greatly beloved in the West, there was a great deal of opposition to the would-be shah particularly for his unIslamic use of the secret police—the Savak—to control and subjugate the Iranian people and to westernize and to dilute the true religion of Allah. Civil war approached with the opposition lead by the genius Ayatollah Ruhollah Khomenini—a grandfather of seventy—who had the iron will of one of Mohammed's rightly guided *Khalifat Rasul Allah*, the political successors to the messenger of God, may all bless his holy name. Grand Ayatollah Khomenini is surely the *Mahdi*, the Guided One whose life fulfilled the prophecy; and he has heralded the coming of the day, *Yawm al-Qiyamah*, the Day of the Resurrection, the Day of the Standing."

Khamenei paused, too caught up in emotion to continue.

A shiver passed quietly through the now enthralled audience. It was like hearing Hitler's oration at Nuremburg. The Sheep Dog pondered his problem. He was stuck in the auditorium listening to the rantings of a madman, a man who was informing a select group of people determined to save the world from nuclear holocaust that the holocaust was in preparation. At least, that was what Sheep Dog was hearing. Professor Khamenei was sweating; the volume of his voice had increased by several decibels; and the pitch by an octave.

The professor shuddered briefly and went on. He told of Khomeini's exile, his triumphal return, "the beginning of the Iranian revolution". He told of the despised Shapour Baktiar, the shah's appointed prime minister and his ouster.

"The cur went into hiding. The accursed French kept him from Islamic justice. They will pay dearly."

Sheep Dog said silently to himself, "*and the supporters of the shah were ruthlessly hunted down and murdered. Khomeini's reign of terror made him one of the greatest mass murderers in history. Present company possibly excepted,*" which gave the assassin a small smile.

Professor Khamenei told of the powerful choice of the people to make the Grand Ayatollah the supreme spiritual leader—*Valy-e-Faqih*—of the overwhelming demand for the Islamic code of behavior, of the unanimous acceptance of the new regulations of dress for women and their return to the proper place in the home, and in glowing terms told of the great moment when the Muslims of Iran shamed and humbled the Great Satan.

"On November 4, 1979, right thinking Iranian Islamic students stormed the accursed embassy of the Great Satan, taking 66 people as hostages. 440 days later, the humbled Americans on January 20, 1981 agreed to the release of the hostages. The American president, Carter, a weak and ineffectual puppet of the Jews, conceded to transfer money and to export military equipment to Iran. And this paper tiger nation now demands that Iran cease from production of nuclear energy for peaceful purposes. Who is this decaying entity which demands that inspections on Iranian sovereign territory by kaffirs be permitted? The Great Satan will, in the end, concede again."

Sheep Dog's attention had wandered and returned to focus again only when the professor got around to the point of nuclear energy. He had to restrain himself from snorting out loud at the mention of "peaceful purposes".

"Seyyed *Ali* Khamenei succeeded *Ayatollah* Khomeini after his death. I am most honored to be the humble nephew of the new *Valy-e-Faqih*."

He paused for effect. The Iranians in the audience broke into enthusiastic applause. Khamenei bowed his head in humility.

Sheep Dog felt like sticking his finger down his throat and having a good puke.

Professor Khamenei stopped after that sentence, turned away from his podium and strode purposefully out of the side exit.

A university functionary announced, "You may all take a rest for ten minutes, no more."

There was a mass exodus from the stifling room with relief on the faces of the IAEA delegation but almost no conversation. Sheep Dog watched them head to the lavatories and the handsome stone floors of the auditorium's lobby. He had observed the direction of exit of the professor and calculated that he knew a private area in the rear of the building where he could collect his thoughts in preparation for another fascinating chapter in Iran's history. He wandered through three hallways before he found the glass doors that lead to a terrace paved with concrete tiles. There were three long rectangular flower beds with tall shrubs obscuring his view of the outside edge of the terrace.

Sheep Dog casually made his way forward, appearing to anyone who cared to notice, that he was fascinated with the horticulture. He was aware that there were two uniformed guards who did notice and did seem to care, but they did nothing to interfere with his ramblings. He put on a diffident expression, kept his hands in plain sight, and moved slowly and casually towards the professor, who was leaning on the low guard rail of the terrace.

"Hello, professor, I wanted to compliment you on the thoroughness of your presentation. I found it most informative," Sheep Dog said softly and with his eyes on his shoes.

Ayatollah Khamenei was annoyed, mainly because an interloper had invaded the privacy of his inhalation of a third cigarette. His choice—not surprisingly—was the Iranian Bahman and 57 brand which was produced by the state monopoly. The bright red pack featured the Farsi language on the pack front and English on the back side. Bahman is the eleventh month of the Iranian year. The number "57" represents the Iranian year 1357—1979 on the Gregorian calendar. The obsequiousness of the approach from a Westerner assuaged his pique, and he deigned to speak to the foreign kaffir.

"I am glad that you did. It is not often that we have a chance to speak candidly to outsiders, and it is even less common for such an outsider to understand and to appreciate our position. May I ask your name?"

"Angus McFarland...from Scotland."

"I have visited Edinburgh frequently in the course of my work and of my training. Are you from there?"

"Yes, sir. I received my training there...my PhD from the university."

"I was educated in the U.S., at Yale undergrad, and Harvard for my first PhD, and then Oxford for my second."

"That is impressive. I am impressed that you could be accepted at not one, but two prestigious American universities. I am more impressed that you were then able to matriculate at Oxford. That would have required a most impressive record. And not one, but two PhDs. That *is* remarkable. Finally, you are not only a nuclear physicist, but also a renowned Islamic scholar in a country full of major religious scholars. It is a privilege to be able to learn from you, professor."

"I prefer Ayatollah, but thank you for your kind words. I hope your stay in Iran has been a pleasant one. Now, however, we must get back to the lecture."

The next segment of the lecture was a lengthy listing of all of the perfidy of the Zionist Entity—hundreds of unprovoked attacks, causing the wars between the Entity and its peace loving Muslim neighbors, and not least for betraying The Prophet, may his name be blessed.

"The most grievous of the attacks, the most unconscionable, were those by the Israeli Air Defense. To name but a few: the unprovoked and unwarranted attack on June 7, 1981 to destroy the Iraqi nuclear facilities of Osiraq; then on October 1 1985, the Israeli air force carried out bombing of the Palestine Liberation Organization headquarters in Tunis; after that the Israeli Air Force took an extensive part in IDF operations during the righteous al-Aqsa intifada, which was no more than a protest against the desecration of the Final Mosque. This outrage included targeted murders of peace-loving Palestinian leaders, most notably Salah Shakhade, Mahmoud Abu-Hunud, Abu Ali Mustafa, Ahmed Yassin, and Abed al-Aziz Rantissi. There was considerable collateral damage—the death and maiming of innocent civilians, in truth—in that nefarious raid. I could go on, but a fairly complete listing of the terrorism instituted and perpetuated by the Israeli murderers is being handed out to you. Keep it as a reminder of the truth."

The professor took a swallow of water from a Bedu gourd.

"I need hardly say that the Islamic Republic of Iran will most vigorously oppose any incursions or attacks from the Zionist Entity. Let the Entity and its puppet master be informed on this day and hour that we will not sit idly by and be injured or destroyed. Iran is not a paper tiger. Do not underestimate our will or our power. While our nuclear research and preparations are peaceful in nature right now, further provocations—including the unwarranted so-called U.N. sanctions—will not be tolerated without more vigorous preparations or without a vigorous response."

Ayatollah Khamenei continued his oration—which was now a bombastic peroration—until the break. As he had done earlier, the professor swiftly exited the lecture hall without announcement.

Again, Sheep Dog made his way apart from the other members of the IAEA delegation and onto the rear terrace. Again he wheedled his way to where the Ayatollah was standing in a personal cloud of cigarette smoke. He stood near to the man, but did not initiate conversation.

"Angus McFarland, are you offended by my remarks in there?"

"No, sir. You have every right to make your protest. I am sure that you know that most of intelligent and educated Europeans favor the Palestinians and their protectors in the great debate that is taking place. Few of us agree with the fact that the State of Israel was carved out of Muslim territory at such great hardship to the displaced. And—certainly—we do not condone Israel's militant actions. For that matter, most Europeans do not condone the actions of America since World War II."

"Pardon me, Dr. McFarland. The very word "Israel" causes offense. I am sure you did not intentionally wish to offend me, but please in future refer to that area as the "Zionist Entity"."

"Of course, professor. It was thoughtless of me."

The two men talked about world politics, the place of Iran in that world, the decline of the West, and the moral decay seen outside the world of Islam. Sheep Dog was surprised and impressed to learn that the professor was completely up to date and an enthusiastic fan of World Cup Football. Sheep Dog was interested, but deferred to the professor's expertise on that area of sport. Once Khamenei was able to divert his attention away from his dogmatisms, he proved to be affable, well informed, and interesting. They had a two-way conversation that did not get into politics, religion, or nuclear energy; and when it was time to return to the class room, they had advanced to a rather personable acquaintanceship.

Sheep Dog left the professor and re-took his aisle seat in the auditorium. The audience was tired and bored, and strongly desiring to get the harangue over with. The IAEA delegation had already admitted defeat and was anxious to get back to Europe and spread the gloom.

Professor Ayatollah Khamenei stood at the podium and collected his notes for a technical presentation.

"Now, we shall consider the subject that many of you have come for—Iran's peaceful nuclear policy. As you well know, weapons grade uranium requires an 80% concentration, and I am here to inform you that the Iran Nuclear Development project has succeeded in achieving just over 10%. Even if we wanted to do so, we do not have the capability to make weapons. We do have sufficient low-grade uranium to begin plans for peaceful nuclear reactor operation, and will go on line in two months time. In addition, we do have self-defense short, medium, and long range missiles capable of neutralizing our enemies even without placing nuclear warheads on them. So, it must be readily apparent even to the most resistant among you that Iran is capable of defending itself against any and all attacks, and will not develop, import, or consider utilizing nuclear weapons. We demand protection by all peace loving nations from the hegemonist Zionist Entity."

He seemed to be tiring, took a large swallow of water, and cleared his throat.

"Let me present the technical details, the material you can take back to your United Nations superiors. Hopefully, we can put this nonsense about Iran having nuclear weapons or other WMDs to a final rest."

Khamenei spent another hour with a PowerPoint program describing in fully technical terms what Iran had done, what it envisioned, and what was expected from the United Nations. The calculus was over Sheep Dog's head, and the subject was of minor interest to him, because he was convinced that it was nothing more than a web of lies. He tuned out the speaker and caught forty winks while still sitting upright.

The lecture concluded at long last, and Professor Khamenei exited promptly. The audience slowly began to leave the auditorium and to gather in the lobby. No one paid any attention to the Sheep Dog as he prepared to go to work.

CHAPTER FORTY-SIX

S heep Dog walked briskly into the now empty hallway at the left of the auditorium and quickly made his way to the rear of the building. He fingered his weapon, feeling vulnerable because he had not been able to bring in a gun or a knife. For the first part of his operation, he would have to be the weapon.

This time as he sauntered out onto the terrace, the guard on the left was not there, and the guard on the right paid him little heed since he had talked to the Ayatollah twice already that morning. The guard turned away from Sheep Dog and leaned out over the right protective rail to enjoy a Bistoon cigarette. He took a deep drag, held it, and was about to exhale, when Sheep Dog silently stepped up behind him, took hold of his chin and occiput and broke his neck. The guard was dead before he could cry out, even before he could register contact or pain. Sheep Dog quickly looked around to see if he had generated any on-lookers. Satisfied that he had not, he lifted the large man up and over the guard rail. The corpse landed with scarcely a sound on the pavement of the garbage collection area below. It lay hidden among a large pile of black garbage bags. The uniformed corpse was altogether camouflaged lying there among similar colored plastic bags.

This time when Sheep Dog looked at the terrace, he saw the professor occupying his usual place and enjoying his usual Bahman and 57. He was experiencing a rather severe bout of smoker's cough and paid no attention to Sheep Dog. The guard on the left had returned from what Sheep Dog presumed had been a head call and was standing bored and sleepy in his assigned place.

Sheep Dog moved slowly and deliberately along the face of the building, keeping in the shadows as much as possible. The guard turned away from him to spit over the guard rail, and Sheep Dog took advantage of the momentary inattention to dart behind the large plant bed. The dwarf junipers stood over six feet tall, and ground cover and flowers obscured the guard's view of the Sheep Dog as he moved swiftly to the end of the bed. This put him three feet away from the guard, and he maintained a statue-like immobility and silence as he watched for the guard to afford him another opportunity.

The Revolutionary Guard sergeant pulled out a pack of Bahman and 57's and lit up. He took a large drag on the cigarette and exhaled a pungent fog of aromatic smoke that covered his face. Sheep Dog covered the three foot distance between him and the guard and swept a rigid palm under the man's chin with all of the force he could muster. The man's head cocked back in sudden and extreme extension. The sound of bones snapping was audible for several feet around. Sheep Dog caught the guard's body before it could hit the ground, and stood holding it as he checked to see if the professor had heard the bones breaking. Apparently, he had not. Sheep Dog dragged the lifeless body to the edge of the railing and surveyed the ground below. Directly beneath them sat two cars. The noise of the corpse landing on one or the other of them would be too much. Sheep Dog moved the corpse to the very back of the railing where there was nothing but concrete below and hoisted it up and over the edge. The body struck the ground with a satisfyingly muted thump. The assassin turned his full attention back to the professor.

As he had done on two previous encounters that morning, Sheep Dog—in the innocent appearing guise of Dr. Angus McFarland, liberal European scientist—sauntered at a leisurely pace up to his new-found friend and congratulated him on the success of his lecture that morning.

"You must be tired, Ayatollah. It is a strain, I think, to give such a long and complicated lecture. The mathematics alone exact a considerable amount of energy."

"I take it you are speaking from experience, doctor."

Sheep Dog leaned in towards the Ayatollah to be able to hear him better. He grasped the plastic syringe and unsheathed the needle, carefully avoiding contact with the sharp point. He started to speak as the Ayatollah exhaled a puff of delicious smoke.

"Fine way to relax."

He drove the two inch long needle into the buttocks of the Ayatollah and depressed the plunger fully injecting 10 ccs of succinyl choline deep intramuscularly. He knew his victim would not be able to cry out or to retaliate;

so, Sheep Dog stood stock still against the Ayatollah to catch him as soon as the neuromuscular paralytic drug took its full effect.

Sheep Dog had underestimated the diminutive fighter he had just attacked. To his great surprise and terrible chagrin, the Ayatollah whipped a razor knife across the Sheep Dog's belly opening a ten inch gash through his epidermis and dermis. As the drug took its full effect, and the Ayatollah collapsed, blood gushed from Sheep Dog's wound.

Fighting off the shock of the unexpected attack, Sheep Dog dropped the Ayatollah to the concrete tiles of the terrace and tore off his coat to staunch the bleeding from his abdominal wall incision. The Ayatollah lay inert on the floor looking at Sheep Dog with motionless but knowing eyes. He was well aware that he was dying, a horrible suffocating death, and he was powerless to prevent it. However—as he lay dying—he was pleased that, even in his extremis, he had killed his despicable assassin and now he would meet The Prophet, bless him, and his 72 *virgins*, 72 wives, and everlasting happiness. As his consciousness began to dim, his last thoughts were on the *Qur'an*, sura 56, verses 12-39, which he had committed to memory in his diligent youth: "They shall recline on jeweled couches face to face, and there shall wait on them immortal youths with bowls and ewers and a cup of purest wine (that will neither pain their heads nor take away their reason); with fruits of their own choice and flesh of fowls that they relish. And theirs shall be the dark-eyed houris, chaste as hidden pearls: a guerdon for their deeds...We created the houris and made them virgins, loving companions for those on the right hand..." He could not think all of the verses as the darkness closed in, and his soul took flight.

Sheep Dog had to take flight as well. He had to have clothes that were not blood soaked, and the Ayatollah's were four sizes to small for him. It could not be helped. His first priority had to be to hide the body. He took a moment to place a card in the front pocket of the man's pants.

Anwar al-Awlaki

He lifted the small corpse up and threw it over the side. It landed directly behind a large old university dump truck. Sheep Dog was aware that no one would be likely to enter the rear area of the university building until after the weekend; so, the obvious evidence of his morning's work would not be detected until he was out of the country. Now he contemplated the not-so-simple set of tasks before him; so, he could get out of the country.

Of immediate concern was the fact that his abdominal wound had begun to bleed briskly again. He tore off his shirt and rolled it into a long tight bandage and pressed it into the wound. The pain was excruciating, and Sheep Dog felt himself beginning to pass out. He bit his lip hard, and slowly the feeling of faintness began to subside. He hastily removed his belt and wrapped it around the bandage in the wound and tightened it to the point that he had some trouble breathing. The bleeding stopped.

He had seen a fire escape on the rear of the terrace where he had thrown the second guard's body over the side. He ran to it, holding his belly and the syringe in one hand. He climbed down the side of the building clumsily because of having only one hand to hold on with and for balance. At the bottom, he turned the guard's corpse over. He had been dead before he fell; so, there was almost no blood on his uniform. Sheep Dog set down his GlobalStar satellite phone and removed his own remaining clothing, stripped the guard's body as fast as he could and found that all of the clothing fit fairly well except for the boots which were too small. He would have to brazen it out with his own patent leather opera slippers. He threw his clothing and the syringe and needle into the bottom of the Dempsey Dumpster, and, for good measure, struggled to hoist the inert body up and then into the dumpster.

He picked up the sat phone and dialed in the emergency number he had been given for use in a last resort emergency.

"Embassy of the United Kingdom, how may I direct your call?"

"This is my code number—19-8-5-5-16-4-15-7 + 01-22. Got that?"

Sheep Dog could hear the sounds of typing on a computer keyboard.

"Yes, sir. I am at your service."

"Get me code name Phillip, directive E2, ID code SIS114631."

"It may take a moment. Please hold."

The moment seemed like an hour, but eventually a clip British accent came on the line.

"Phillip, here. What is the nature of your problem?"

"Medical emergency. Abdominal slashing. Bleeding under control, but I require immediate emergency suturing. I have a serious deadline."

"What is your 20?"

Sheep Dog gave the officer his location.

"We'll have a station car there in less than three minutes. How shall we recognize you?"

"I am in a guard's uniform. Six feet tall, about 200 pound Caucasian, salt and pepper hair, scar on my face."

"Right-O. Be there in a jiffy. I can arrange care as I travel."

A black Range Rover pulled up beside him five minutes later. After a quick inspection by both parties, a burly SAS master sergeant assisted him into the back seat.

"Best if you stay down, sir," the driver, a corporal, said.

SAS Major Donald Henderson-Gruel, military attaché and resident U.K. intelligence officer, spoke to Sheep Dog as they pulled away from the university without turning to look at him.

"We're heading up Manuchehn Street then we'll take a hard right and go north east on Shariati to Kaj and turn right. Hang on, it'll be a twisty and bumpy ride. Hospital is on the corner of Kaj and Padegan e-Vali-ye-Asr Street. There we'll meet Professor Doctor Hossein Masoud abu-Boroujerdi. He's one of ours and an ardent supporter of Mir Hossein Mousavi. I'm sure you're aware that Mousavi is the politician looking to a future Iran which is progressive and has a measure of law, justice and freedom. The good doctor is taking a terrible risk, and we expect the Cousins to reward him accordingly."

"I have sufficient money with me to satisfy the man," Sheep Dog said. "Just hurry."

"The doctor is a general surgeon, a professor of medicine at Tehran University of Medical Science. That is right next door to where you were standing."

"Sounds good," Sheep Dog said.

The driver drove quickly down through the long parking lot next to the Amir Alami Hospital and turned into an alleyway between two large sections of the hospital. A doctor in a starched white lab coat was waiting. The Range Rover pulled to a stop, and the two SAS men helped Sheep Dog out. The doctor gave him a once over look and directed them to hurry into his clinic.

"Are you in good health, young man?" Dr. abu-Boroujerdi asked.

"Except for my wound, I'm fine. No allergies, drug sensitivities, or chronic diseases."

Dr. abu-Boroujerdi quickly removed Sheep Dog's make-shift bandage.

"This will require general anesthetic; no one could tolerate the pain of suturing such a wound. Unfortunately, I do not have access to such anesthetic in my clinic. We would have to move to the operating room, and there would be a lot of explaining to do."

"No general, doctor. Do what you have to do. And do it quickly. Time is of the essence."

Dr. abu-Boroujerdi shrugged. Doubt clouded his face.

"You're sure?" he asked kindly.

"Yes. Let's get started."

Sheep Dog stripped naked. Before the procedure started, he asked the SAS major to get him a tuxedo and shirt, no tie. Major Donald Henderson-Gruel gave him a quizzical look, but immediately got on his cell phone and called the U.K. Embassy.

"We'll have a fine bib and tucker for you before you are all sutured up."

"Thanks."

"Just part of The Firm's service for the Cousins."

The procedure was horrifyingly painful from the initial cleansing of the wound with normal saline and Betadine to the two-layer closure. Sheep Dog briefly fainted twice, but he controlled his need to cry out. His skin had a cadaverous hue when the doctor finished. Dr. abu-Boroujerdi shook his head, reluctant to release his patient in such condition.

It took two tries before Sheep Dog could get to his feet and begin some halting steps. He took a bundle of 500,000r Iran Central Bank notes—about $50.50 USD each and handed them to the doctor. The huge denomination notes, and even 1,000,000r notes are treated the same as cash in Iran, whose currency is worthless outside its borders. The amount he gave the doctor amounted to just over $2,000 USD, a huge sum in the Iranian economy for the work of half an hour. Dr. abu-Boroujerdi was grateful.

"You won't be needing to discuss this case, doctor," Major Henderson-Gruel said pointedly.

"It would be more than my life is worth," the doctor said; and there was no doubt about his sincerity.

"Now, we have to get you back to your hotel, my friend," the major said as soon as they were out of earshot of the doctor.

Sheep Dog looked spiffy in his new bib and tucker, although he remained pale. The driver drove out of Amir Alami Hospital and reversed the directions from which they had come. He pulled over to the curb on Manuchehn Street three blocks from the Azadi Grand Hotel.

"Think you can make it from here? It wouldn't do for a U.K. spook wagon to deliver you to the front entrance, I don't think."

"I can make it. I don't have much time."

It was quarter to one, and Sheep Dog knew that he would have to worm his way back into the hotel, collect his bags, and be ready to travel in less than half an hour. He controlled his facial expressions to keep away any indication of pain, and began his deliberate stroll to the hotel. There was little activity outside the entrance except for the four Zil limousines that were waiting to transport the delegation back to IATA-Imam Khomeini *International Airport.*

Inside the lobby, there was no one except for three overly modest young women reservation desk attendants. Sheep Dog walked nonchalantly to the elevator and punched the four. No hitches thus far.

He got out of the elevator and almost walked into Ibrahim ibn Sharif al-Tezari, the delegation head.

"We were wondering where you were, Dr. McFarland, did you come back with the rest of us in the limos?"

"That was the only ride possible, Dr. al-Tezari. I got off at the lobby and took a left while the rest of you went straight ahead to your rooms. I got to take in a little of the local color on a bit of a stroll. Nice, after the stuffy auditorium. When do we depart this desert paradise?"

Al-Tezari gave Sheep Dog a little smile of agreement.

"Twenty past," he said, "And I've always thought the only difference between the moon and these deserts is that the moon is monotonous grey, and the deserts are monotonous brown."

"I'll be in the lobby with bells on," Sheep Dog said jovially, masking the grimace he wanted to make.

He left the director and hurried to his room. He jammed his belongings into his suitcase—the delegation had only been permitted one personal bag each—cleaned every surface in the room thoroughly to be sure that he left no fingerprints or DNA behind—and made his way with the rest of the delegation to the lobby.

At 1320, they were loaded into the Zils again, and the limo drivers sped off towards the airport.

Steven Croyle, the British member of the IAEA leaned over to Sheep Dog as they moved along and said, "Well, chap, I have a wee bit of good news after this debacle. A little something to warm the cockles of your heart. Actually, two things. First, Sofrekheneh has been forced to devalue the rial yet again. Nasty break. And, as if that were not enough, you may be interested to learn that the Zils—the ultimate symbol of Soviet power—are about to disappear from the streets of Russia. Going belly-up, I hear, after 60 years. Seems the Krauts and the Cousins have a better business model."

Sheep Dog gave the smiling Brit a thumbs-up.

Airport security was its usual stringent self, but nothing out of the usual. Sheep Dog figured that the bodies had not yet been discovered. However, he did not relax or even take a deep breath until the Air France flight to Paris lifted off the runway and left Iranian air space.

CHAPTER FORTY-SEVEN

S heep Dog made himself scarce for two weeks in the South of France for R&R to allow his wound to heal. Dr. abu-Boroujerdi had done well. There was no infection, and minimal pain once his wound had been sutured closed. He was weak for the first few days, and started his own rehabilitation on a "start low and go slow" basis. He took the opportunity to study his remaining quarries. The next man on his list was Abdel Said Badr; his name was underlined in red.

TOP SECRET
EYES ONLY SHEEP DOG

Source of report: Need to know basis only
Date of report: Need to know basis only

Abdel Said Badr is a missionary, a *tabligh*, trained in madrassas in Gaza and Kandahar. He received his formal *Qur'anic* education there and his more serious training in the Tarnak Farm training camp of al Qaeda, a 100 acre compound in the Afghanistan desert three miles from the Kandahar airport. The *wali*—UBL—actually lived there with one of his wives while Abdel was there, and it was the defining moment of his life to be able "to see and hear the greatest man since The Prophet, may Allah bless him and make his name revered". The main compound was encircled by a ten foot high crude mud-brick wall. Inside were eighty small two-story mud structures; Abdel shared a room with fourteen other men, but whatever lack of privacy or inconveniences there might have been were nothing compared to the fact that Usama—the *wali*—lived in the very next house. Security there was integral with the terrain—miles of open brush and sand desert that allowed a few lookouts to see any approaching threat from even afar off. Abdel was given the assignment to guard the drainage ditch near the wall on the airport side of the compound, a task he pursued with a singleness of purpose that both captured the attention of and amused the holy leader.

Abdel Said Badr's first assignment after leaving Tarnak Farm was to coordinate the traffic of heroin from Southern Afghanistan to the hideouts of UBL in northwestern Pakistan. He was aided by the men of the Ahmedzai Wazir tribe and made fast friends with many of them, as much as the fiercely xenophobic and independent tribesmen would allow. Funds were drying up from the usual Saudi Arabian sources due to the difficulties imposed by the "illegal invasion by the Americans". Badr was an integral part of the network that provided Usama bin Laden and his followers with $24,000,000 a year in heroin and enabled the "Savior of Islam" to continue his vital planning and work.

Afghanistan produces the vast majority of the world's illicit opium, the raw ingredient in heroin, and more than a million and a half Afghanis depend on opium farming, and therefore, on Usama bin Laden, for their livelihood. The entire industry which cycles around farmers, traffickers, and freedom fighters totals more than two and a third billion dollars a year. Usama, himself, had personally laid his large hand on Badr's shoulder and, in his soft voice, called the young missionary "one of God's best". It was the highlight of the pious twenty-one year olds life to date, and his faith was intensely enlivened. Abdel Said Badr, blessed by the man whom he considered to be next in importance after The Prophet, himself, "may Allah's blessings be upon His Messenger", was the servant of the cause to the death if needs be.

Abdel is an energetic, vivacious person with a quick smile and an equally quick readiness to help. His full face beard is reddish brown and unruly like his hair. He looks more like a wild Scotsman in from the distant hills than a Muslim of fifteen generations heritage. He is modest and retiring by nature despite his outward friendliness. He has never complained, and he worked tirelessly to help his fellow freedom fighters to maintain their morale during the dark times. He is too small, has too high a voice, and his manners are too unsure and almost effeminate to be a leader, we presume, but his quick wit and native intelligence—coupled with his fanatical willingness to obey the leaders of his religion at every level—make him the ideal follower.

UBL and select members of the Council of the Leaders of Islam recognized the young man's intrepidity, cleverness, and dedication to the cause, without being heedlessly reckless, which were all qualities desired in a follower. It was an added bonus that Badr speaks passable English and could even pass for an Englishman with a little quality hair makeover. Usama allowed Badr to be promoted and to leave his vital role in the Islamic freedom fighter-heroin linkage and to take a role as a missionary or *tabligh* for the religion and for al Qaeda. The "Savior of Islam" made the assignment, and Abdel was transferred to Pemba, Tanzania.

Funding for Abdel's work comes from al Qaeda—originating in Saudi Arabia, Kuwait, and Pakistan. The money makes a circuitous but efficient journey to the freedom fighters. A Liechtenstein based corporation called Galp International Trading Establishment, which is a wholly owned subsidiary of Portugal's principal oil company, employs a law firm called Asat Trust. That trust is the financier of al-Qaeda through links to Al Taqwa, a group of financial entities all over the world controlled by the Muslim Brotherhood. The United States and United Nations designate Asat Trust as an al Qaeda financier.

With the freedom afforded by his al Qaeda funding, Abdel Said Badr moves freely about Tanzania speaking in a myriad of small mosques around the Zanzibar archipelago. He is sometimes invited by the older imams, but more often those men are suspicious of him and of the other *tabligh* who volunteer to spend forty days of each year preaching. Like the others, Badr wears traditional Pakistani clothing—a simple turban and tunic. He never fails to perform his five daily *namaz* prayers. After speaking in the mosques to the faithful, Badr meets with the young men, always in deep secrecy for fear of arrest by the police. Wahhabi charities provide faxed textbooks extolling an extremist fundamentalism which Badr conveys to the earnest young faithful by lamplight deep in the night. The endemic and recalcitrant poverty of East Africa produces a growing body of men who feel disenfranchised and are fertile soil for Badr's recruitment. He is known to take pride in getting the desperate youngsters to join al Qaeda and made arrangements for them to be sent to schools in Pakistan and Afghanistan. By day the boys memorize and recite the *Qur'an*, and by night they learn by rote the Palestinian side of the Israeli/Palestinian conflict. They learn in secret to reject the gentle and pacifist brand of Islam, Sufism, which is popular in Zanzibar. They eventually learn to be killers, and for his part in that, Abdel Said Badr has earned a name for himself among the "men of the list". Al Qaeda began in 1988 as the list of *mujahedeen*—one who wages jihad—fighting in Afghanistan. The name means "the list" or "the base".

Badr's young men went to Afghanistan and to Iraq to fight and to become *shahids*—martyrs—and East Africa even now contributes almost twenty-five percent of the foreign fighters there. Madrassas for girls also turn out zealots ready to become martyrs, but Abdel Said Badr has sworn to live a life of celibacy and has forsworn all contact with women. He is an intense young man, and is to this day acknowledged to be the most effective recruiter for jihad in all of Islam. He answers only to UBL and to UBL's number three, Musab Sarayrah Abdulmutallab, who directs the world-wide recruiting effort. Abdulmutallab has a bottomless purse so far as the Company can find out.

Currently, Badr's disciples are known to foment rebellion, suicide and homicide terrorist bombers and assassins, and to head the crime syndicate of al Qaeda in the region surrounding Tanzania. Despite the region being among the poorest per capita in the world, Badr's outlaws have been able to terrorize and to plunder the economies of Tanzania and its border nations: Kenya and Uganda to the north, Rwanda, Burundi, and the Democratic Republic of the Congo to the west, and Zambia, Malawi, and Mozambique to the south. An estimated $100 million is extorted from these countries every year and sent to supply the treasury of al Qaeda.

The accompanying photograph is the only one known to exist of Badr, and may not be particularly useful since it was taken several years ago. It could not be enhanced better than what you have here.

DISPOSITION: Terminate with maximum prejudice. Must be accomplished before 1 March. CAUTION: Abdel Said Badr is to be considered most dangerous. He commands the adulation and fanatical obedience of well over 1,000 adherents, any one of which would be willing to die for the man or to kill for him.

Sheep Dog arrived in the Julius Nyerere International Airport in the Indian Ocean coastal city of Dar es Salaam—capital of Tanzania—in central East Africa on 15 January. He and his two bags were met by the CIA Chief of Station, Glen Gabler, and were taken to a safe house overlooking the ocean. Neither man spoke until they were ensconced in the house.

"Welcome to the United Republic of Tanzania," Gabler said.

"Thank you. Do you have what I need?"

"I know where the man is, and I can get you close to him; but if you think you can take him out, or capture him, or kidnap him, you are just a dead man with a grandiose idea."

"Again, thank you. If you know where he is now, I want to go there *now*."

Gabler shrugged, "Your funeral."

"Maybe. First I'll need some less conspicuous clothes, say those of a donkey-cart teamster. While you obtain that, I'll get into disguise."

Sheep Dog took an hour. When he was done, he looked every bit a Tanzanian—more like a turbaned Indian pirate than a peasant teamster; perhaps, and that contributed to his authenticity.

Sheep Dog walked out of the back door of the house and came around to the front. He knocked on the door carrying a crude cardboard sign that read: DEAF AND LAME, PLEASE HELP. A marine infantry lieutenant answered the door.

"Ah *Effendi*, I must see the master of the house. I have an urgent message from an American man who met me in the bazaar and paid me to bring the message to one called Gabler."

"Give it to me. I'll see to it that "Gabler" gets it," the lieutenant said brusquely.

"Only to Gabler," the beggar insisted.

The peasant was adamant, even belligerent; and finally, the lieutenant sighed and brought the man into the entryway.

"Wait here," he told him.

"Yes, *Effendi*."

The chief of station walked behind the marine officer and confronted the beggar.

"So how much do you want?"

"Ah, *Effendi*, you do not give me respect."

There was a prolonged silence. After a few uncomfortable moments, the beggar sheepishly said, "Perhaps two dollah American would be fair."

Gabler smiled smugly. He was an old hand, and he had been through this several hundred times. He handed the beggar one dollar and glared at him."

"May the blessings of Allah, the merciful be upon you, *Effendi*."

"Now, what has my dollar bought me?"

"Only a question."

"What!?"

"The question is: How is it that you are unable to recognize a fellow countryman?"

Gabler was bemused at first, then he took a harder look at the beggar; then he took an even harder look. The man's eyes were a striking hazel with flecks of luminescent green, and they held his attention. He reached out and clasped the man's upper arm. It was as hard and sinewy as a healthy tree branch, not the arm of a chronically undernourished beggar.

"Who are you?"

"You must answer my question first," Sheep Dog said losing his Tanzanian pirate accent and showing a smile of perfectly straight bright white teeth that could only have been made in America.

"You are the visitor. You stood in my office not an hour and a half ago."

"Good job, Agent Gabler. Do I pass muster?"

"I'll say. You have made it one step. I hope you are as good as you seem to be. You won't survive the day unless you are."

Gabler and the marine lieutenant drove Sheep Dog and his two bags inland north from Dar-es-Salaam about 50 miles on a rutted red mud track.

"This is as far as we are allowed to go, my friend. There be monsters beyond. This is Indian country. You take care."

"I will."

"Look, I'd like to be able to help, but I am under strict orders not to do anything more. Whoever or whatever you are, I don't want to know. I regret to inform you that there is no electronic or telephonic transmission out here. You're on your own. God speed, man. Watch your back."

Sheep Dog gave the two men a small salute and hopped out of the jeep. The sergeant handed him his bags, then the jeep worked its way to face the opposite direction with some difficulty. By the time the two men could look back to see where their passenger had gone, he was out of sight.

He walked through the arid landscape lugging his bags during the remainder of the day, enduring the heat and annoying insects. He felt safer well away from the road, such as it was. It was approaching dusk when he came into the village. He took note of the center of activity in the town and made his way in that direction.

From early afternoon, Abdel Said Badr assisted in an eye clinic in the tiny African village, so small that neither the village nor the surrounding area warranted names on the map. Abdel participated in the treatment of patients with old, stone hard cataracts. Only the area witch doctor had any medical knowledge, and he had long experience and was much sought after. While Abdel pinioned the arms of the patient, the witch doctor gave a well practiced one knuckle punch on the blind eyes. Frequently, the calcified lens of the eye would be dislodged, and the patient returned to possession of a distorted and shrunken vision of the world, but it was better than blindness with milky lenses. The witch doctor's terse rationale was that "one is better than zero". Of course there were many failures, *masha'allah*. There was no time to treat women.

Sheep Dog hovered in the background of the clinic tent unnoticed and watched Badr at his work with the last few patients. When Badr left the clinic and walked wearily to the mosque, Sheep Dog and his bags followed. Two frightening, very black, and very heavily armed Tanzanian men walked immediately behind Badr, and another two cleared the way in front of him. The obvious guards sat in the back row of the mosque, and Sheep Dog found a place on a prayer mat between two men who did not look appreciably better than him while Badr gave a stirring, but non-inflammatory lesson on Islamic cleanliness. The young man passionately described how The Prophet, May God shine his mercy upon his Messenger, plucked his armpit and pubic hair and bathed twice a day.

The four guards kept themselves in the shadows as much as possible. When *Maghrib*—the sunset prayer—was done, the guards—and behind them deep in the developing gloaming, Sheep Dog—followed Badr as he made his way in the dark to his rendezvous with prospective recruits in the secluded jungle. He observed the skillful way the young missionary cajoled and motivated the boys to join in the struggle. When the last of the young men who were being recruited had faded back into the tangled thicket, two strangers were brought to Badr by the guards. They greeted them as a brother.

"*Masaa el-kheir, akh, Salam alekum.*"

Badr replied in kind, "*Wa alekum es salam.*"

"We come from the Leader of the Council and would have words with you."

"I am honored. Speak."

"We are the new couriers."

He handed Badr a sealed envelope.

"We come directly from the *wali.*"

"I see that. I will have the money for you tomorrow. Bring a sturdy truck and meet me at the Christian church at the stroke of noon. Be prepared to do real work."

"That kind of work for Allah and the jihad, we will willingly do."

In fact, they were positively excited at the prospect of lugging crates of currency onto the *wali's* truck. Anything would be better than the boredom of guard duty or the terror of partisan combat in the desert or the jungle—their usual lot.

Sheep Dog made a decision. He silently followed the two strangers to their truck which was parked a mile away from the village. When they started up the engine, he hitched a ride in the back, hiding himself and his two bags among the truck's boxes and covered himself and them with a tarp. After *Isha'a*—the night prayer—he was hungry enough and felt safe enough to venture out to find some food and water. He was parched and achingly tired. It was a starless dark night, and he had to feel and smell his way to the mess tent. All around him he could hear men snoring, the sounds of men playing cards, and the murmurs of the devout as they read the *Qur'an* aloud. Each man was absorbed in his own pursuits, and no one paid the least attention to Sheep Dog as he padded softly into the mess tent. He swiped a hind quarter of a lamb, a round loaf of coarse Bedouin bread, and four plastic gallon containers of water and took them back to his hiding place in the truck. The food and water were restorative, and he was better able to tolerate the oppressive desert heat. He even fell asleep.

As first light began to be noticeable, there was a sound of padding feet. The freedom fighters were heading to their prayer rugs for the *Fajr*. Again, Sheep Dog could hear the murmuring of prayer. To maintain security, these devout bandits could not afford the luxury of a muezzin or of a strong-voiced preacher. They made do with ritual and a few quotes from the *Qur'an*. Sheep Dog remained in his supine position in the truck bed until he heard the men marching off to breakfast. He slipped out of the truck and hid behind a clump of scrub bush, planning to join the men as they loaded up for the day's planned work.

There were over two hundred jihadists milling about taking down the camp and loading trucks. Sheep Dog counted on the anonymity of similar dress, similar clothing, similar weaponry, hoods, and hats. Sheep Dog found a stockpile of bullet belts and crossed two over his chest. He wore his large K-bar knife in a leather scabbard on his belt and melded into the Brownian movement of the crowd. He attached himself to a line of men passing boxes of food and ammunition from one man to the next to load them onto trucks. He feigned deafness and mutism, and since he was a good worker and did not bring attention to himself, soon no one attempted conversation.

The troops mounted the backs of troop carriers, pick-ups, and three decrepit rusting school buses. There was a train of thick dust as the convoy moved out. All of the men wrapped cloths around their faces, and then Sheep Dog did not look at all out of place. All of them became beige sand men together. He sat in the back of a pick-up on his bags with nine other men, and no one evinced any more interest in his belongings than they did in him. They left their camp at 0900 and arrived in the nameless village with the incongruously immaculate white church facing the town square at 1115.

The jihadist soldiers clambored out their vehicles and sought out shady spots to rest and to stretch their cramped limbs. A few of them were sent to sentry duty. Sheep Dog unloaded his own bags and carried them to the shady side of a building that was once a store but was now empty and derelict. He made several other trips, collecting crates of ammunition for a submachine gun he dug out of a crate of them, still encased in creosote. He worked himself further and further away from the crowd as noon approached.

As promised, Abdel Said Badr was driven into the middle of the square bringing three other pick-ups along side his as he stopped. Badr was dressed in a bright blue flowing Bedu cloak which made him stand out from the olive drab and beige of the other men. Sheep Dog chalked it up to a small display of vanity—perhaps a fatal one. The leader of the bandit militia and Badr exchanged perfunctory greetings, hugs, and cheek kisses, then they separated and sent out two men from each camp to transfer the many boxes of money Badr had brought. The four pick-up loads fit comfortably into one of the militia's large trucks, and the work was efficient.

Sheep Dog stayed on the periphery and worked equally efficiently. He set his personal bags on a sand berm, then opened a crate marked *Grenades* and with a devil's head MS-13 mark that could have adorned an adobe wall in Tijuana. He pulled out handfuls of Stingball grenades and set them in small piles in strategic locations around the periphery of the square. When the transfer of the money boxes was complete, most of the soldiers and officers found cooler places inside the buildings emptied by the terrified citizens of the town and settled in for a siesta. Sheep Dog picked up two three gallon cans of gasoline and walked to the trucks pretending to top-off their tanks. He worked his way to the large truck holding the money and made a theatrical effort to look legitimately busy. He poured the gasoline on the tops of the cardboard boxes and ditched the cans. Anyone walking near the trucks would have noticed the smell of gasoline; but, fortunately for Sheep Dog, no one passed by.

He leaned a piece of corrugated metal siding against a dried up tree stump and climbed under it with his gear. It was like being in a reflector oven, and the sweat poured off him soaking his shirt and crotch. He bore it without movement or sound.

It was almost 1500 hours when the yawning, stretching, grumbling men reappeared in the center of the plaza. The trucks were all parked very close to one another, and a large crowd of something like 250 men and a third that many women gathered to mount up and get on to their next project of plunder, murder, and rape all in the name of Allah and for the cause of jihad.

Only then did Sheep Dog stir. He wriggled into his ghillie suit and slowly crawled on his abdomen into the position he had selected to be able to have a downhill field of fire. He had the AK-47 which he stole earlier along side him, and he brought his AA-12 Combat shot gun into position in front of him. A smoker carelessly tossed a glowing cigarette butt on the ground where Sheep Dog had spilled some of the gas he used to saturate the boxes of money, and a quick burst of fire erupted and spread up the truck's rear tire and closed in side. Men began shouting, and several ran for water. A large crowd of combatants gathered around to watch the fire, pushing and shoving until almost every person in the village packed together. There was little else in the way of entertainment in that part of Tanzania, it appeared.

Sheep Dog fired a series of bursts of three grenades, the first of which impacted the money boxes causing a tremendous explosion which filled the plaza with a deafening boom and a blanket of thick, black, choking smoke. Debris flew in all directions—body parts, truck parts, shreds of clothing, burning tires, and money. Lots and lots of burning money. Sheep Dog guessed that he had just blown up $10 million, maybe more. He kept his cool and waited until survivors or lucky ones began to appear. They walked around in a collective daze, all stunned by the blast and unable to launch a counterattack. Sheep Dog logged fifteen grenades into the closely packed groups of soldiers, and the effect was devastating. To the chaos of the scene came the addition of screams, shrieks of pain, and curses.

Finally, several shooters traced his shots back to him, and Sheep Dog scrambled away. He ran to his several caches of Stingball grenades and began throwing them. His enemies became fewer and more cautious. Sheep Dog kept on the move running from grenade pile to grenade pile producing ever more confusion, explosion, death, and mutilation. Several men ran screaming with their BDUs aflame. Wounded men limped or dragged themselves or companions away from the furnace blast in the center of the square. Sheep Dog picked of nearly 15 of them with his AK-47.

He was living on luck, and his luck ran out. Abdel Said Badr, conspicuous in blue, emerged from the carnage apparently unhurt and began rallying his troops. His men were battle hardened and undeterred by heavy incoming ordinance or casualties. They began a steady beat of machine gun fire at Sheep Dog keeping him on the move enough to prevent him from being able to bring the destruction of the AA-12 to bear to protect himself. He ran out of ammunition for his AK-47 and had to abandon it. He zigzagged around behind several buildings on the dead run until he came to an alleyway. He spotted a stairway leading to the flat roof, and he took the stairs three at a time. He fell over the top and onto the scorching silvery surface of the flat roof, burning the palms of his hands. He sprang to a crouch quickly enough to avoid serious burns and duck walked to the building's front edge and peered down onto the heads and backs of Badr and a dozen of his best men two stories below.

He inserted his second and last magazine of explosive and flammable loaded grenades into the AA-12 and opened a withering fire down on his tormentors. They disappeared in a blood mist and smoke screen. He could smell the cordite and the copper/iron smell of blood. When the air pollution cleared he could make out legs protruding from under a blue cloak. The Sheep Dog knew that he had been successful because the legs and cloak were headless.

His mission accomplished, Sheep Dog now had to escape. Ordinarily, he planned his route well in advance, but this had been a seat-of-the-pants thing from the start. He could see three intact trucks on the rise where he had been standing and firing at the congregation in the center of the plaza twenty minutes previously. He had not noticed them before, but they looked like at least temporary salvation. Hopefully, one of the trucks would be in good enough condition to get him to Dar-es-Salaam. There was one little problem, however. He had no good idea where the capital city was from his location. He did a little reckoning by the post-noon day position of the sun and decided that he was still north of the city, and he was pretty sure that he could tell which way was south. Not that he expected to see a road, but at least he had a plan and a direction.

He sucked in a deep breath and ran full out for the stairs and descended them as fast as he dared and out into the alleyway. No bullets. So far, so good. He turned and ran at full gallop down the alley and around the back of the building and did not stop until he reached the corner where he could see the trucks. He saw no one alive. There were half a dozen scorched corpses in his view, but no threats. And no bullets. So far, so good.

He moved slowly keeping close to the building now. He was fifty yards from the first truck. He was tired from carrying his bags for the better part of the last twenty-four hours, and he was breathing hard. And, as he paused, he was aware of his mouth being as dry as if he had been lying face up with his tongue lolling out in the middle of the *Ar-Rub'-al-Khali*. Worse, he was getting dizzy; and his thoughts were coming more slowly and with more difficulty.

He poked his head out around the corner of the building. No bullets. So far, so good. He took a few good breaths, tensed himself and raced out into the open. The high-pitched twang of an AK-47 on full automatic came from his right from behind a scrap pile that had been a truck in the forenoon. He bent low, zigzagged, dropped and rolled, and several of the Klimovsk 7.62 x .39 *rounds* kicked up dust pockets within a foot or two of him; but he was not hit. He had twenty yards to go to make cover. On impulse, he made a sudden hard right turn and headed obliquely in the direction of the shooter. He paused behind a smallish oil barrel which was rapidly turned into a sieve. It was most disconcerting to have bullets hitting his meager two-foot wide shield.

There was a pause in the staccato firing. Sheep Dog hoped the guy was reloading. He took a chance and ran as fast as he could move in the same direction he had been going. Ten yards from another burned out hulk, he made a front somersault followed by a side role, and he was three feet from safety. A bullet trail skipped along side him spraying dirt and rocks. The bullets passed so close to him that he could have reached a hand out and gotten it shot off. No bullets in him. So far, so good.

He threw himself the last three feet and was out of the line of sight of his tormentor and behind a bullet proof barrier. He worked to calm down and to think. Where was the guy? Had he stayed in the same place? Sheep Dog took a quick peek. He saw no one, and since no bullets came his way, he decided, optimistically, that no one had seen him. He readied his 9 mm and crawled along hugging the bare ruined metal of the one-time truck. He had to be within a few yards of where the shooter had been. Maybe the guy would be stupid enough to stay in place—thinking himself safe—or maybe he was even more optimistic than himself and presumed that he had killed his quarry.

He crawled silently and slowly over the rough and uncomfortable desert floor. To his total consternation, his last forward movement brought him face-to-face with a terrified boy. The child could not have been more than thirteen. The child was so stunned to see his enemy almost within kissing distance that he froze. Sheep Dog pointed his 9 mm at the boy's face. The boy threw down his rifle and put up his hands. Sheep Dog shot him between his eyes. Without a sound, the child slumped forward dead. Sheep Dog saw one notable thing about his victim other than his tender age. He was missing half of his left hand. The portion of the hand remaining had a crisp edge which was well healed. The little boy had been punished for some infraction by having the outer part of his hand chopped off with an axe or a machete. Sheep Dog had one more thing to hate about Islamic terrorists, and he no longer made a distinction in his mind between what the Muslims called their "extremists" and the rest of the "peace-loving" and friendly majority. He had mentally adopted the old Wild West idea that the only good Indian was a dead Indian. He just substituted the word 'Muslim' for 'Indian'.

He was still not at the truck and had about thirty-five yards of no-man's land to cross before he could get to transportation. How many unfriendlies were waiting unseen for him to venture out? He would just have to find out. He crawled over to the boy's body and expropriated his canteen and drank it down in a single long swallow. Thus fortified, he leaped up and ran helter-skelter across the open space.

No bullets. So far, so good. He was able to run up to the passenger door of the truck and was startled to hear its engine running. He took a quick look into the cab and saw a distinguished beturbaned older Arab man struggling with the pesky gears. He pointed his hand gun through the open window directly at the man's face and waited. The man—obviously a person of some importance by his wearing a clean dark thobe and Western eyeglasses—finally turned and looked in Sheep Dog's direction. He clasped his chest and let out a kind of squeak. Sheep Dog shouted for him to keep his hands in plain sight, and the man complied immediately.

The man's eyes riveted on Sheep Dog's finger as it began to squeeze the trigger.

"Don't shoot," the man shouted. "I am worth far more to you alive than dead."

"Convince me."

"First, I know how to get back to Dar es Salaam."

"*Maybe the man reads minds,*" Sheep Dog thought. "*I guess I just look like I'm lost.*"

"And…" he said.

"I am Musab Sarayrah Abdulmutallab."

Abdulmutallab paused to allow the import of his name to register with the gunman. The Indian man facing him did not seem to recognize who he was holding hostage.

"The number three officer in al Qaeda. The *wali* is the first among men; I am the recruiter; I am responsible for gathering the faithful to the jihad to bring about the *Yawm al-Qiyamah.*"

CHAPTER FORTY-EIGHT

Abdulmutallab sat stock still with both hands on the steering wheel. "Get out. Slowly. Keep your hands up and in plain sight."

"You don't need to kill me. I am an old man, and I know my time is up in al Qaeda. I presumed you came for me."

Sheep Dog shook his head.

"Do you know that we call you "The Shadow"?"

"No, and I don't care. I am going to frisk you?"

"Sorry, what does it mean, "frisk"?

"Search. Keep your hands up."

"I'm trying, but please move ahead. My arms are not what they used to be."

Sheep Dog stood inches in front of Abdulmutallab and pushed his gun barrel two inches into the man's soft abdomen, enough to make him grunt.

"I am going to put my hands everywhere on your body. I will ask you only one time. Do you have anything sharp? Any kind of weapon at all? If I get cut, even a tiny bit, you will meet your dark-eyed beauties a second later."

"I have a Shibriya."

"What is a Shibriya?"

"It is a Bedouin side dagger which in Jordan is locally known as Shibriya. All men carry it and it is very popular between the Bedouin tribes residing in Israel and in Jordan. The blade is short and double edged with an acute tip. It is extremely sharp. The scabbard is set with a belt loop at the rear side and hangs just to my right side, near my groin."

Sheep Dog lifted the hem of Abdulmutallab's thobe and located the wicked six inch re-curving blade with an almost pin point sharp tip. A man could get a clean shave with either side of the blade. The well worn blade was engraved with an Arabic inscription and dated to 1847. The grip was made of horn and the scabbard of wood, both covered with white metal and engraved in geometrical pattern. There was dried blood at the hilt of the blade and on the junction between the blade and the bolster and guard. The shallow blood groove had old blood in it, and a quick sniff gave off the coppery tang of blood. Sheep Dog could well imagine the close shave a kaffir or two had been given by this dagger.

"Anything else?"

"No."

"Strip off your clothes."

"Must I…the *Qur'an* tells the faithful…"

"I couldn't care less. This is not a debate, and I have no time. Strip or die."

The menace in those piercing pale eyes convinced Abdulmutallab that his life depended on violating the *Qur'an*. Allah would forgive him. He stripped to full nudity.

"Spread your legs."

Abdulmuttalab assumed the position, and Sheep Dog ran his hands over the wrinkled flabby naked body. It seemed superfluous, the man being naked, but Sheep Dog could not take even the slightest chance. He made Abdulmuttalab lie prone on the hot desert sand while he rummaged through his bag and found a latex glove. He inserted it into the Arab's rectum quickly and found nothing in the way of a weapon. He discarded the soiled glove.

"Put your clothes on except for your shoes. Remove the laces and hand them to me."

Abdulmuttalab gave his captor a quizzical look but complied with alacrity.

"Get in the truck—passenger side."

The Arab did as he was told. Sheep Dog put down his 9 mm, brought Abdullmuttalab's thumbs and great toes together and tied them very tightly together—thumb to thumb, and toe to toe.

"It hurts," Abdulmuttalab said with an imploring look.

"I know it does," Sheep Dog said, "if you are a good fellow for an hour, I will loosen them before they turn black and fall off."

Abdullmuttalab nodded his head, and thought, "*This is a real man; we could use a few like him, men who do not shrink from the unpleasant but can think.*"

He kept his thoughts to himself.

Sheep Dog made a quick detour to the next truck and left a calling card on the driver's side seat.

Ayatollah Zia Muhammad Ali Kader
Hizbullah Central Press Office
Baabda, Beirut, Lebanon

"*Another little seed of discontent between the Sunni and Shiite brothers,*" Sheep Dog whispered to himself.

He took his place in the driver's seat next to Abdulmuttalab and said, "We're off to the U.S. Embassy."

"Do you know where it is?"

"Only that it is most likely in Dar es Salaam."

"I want you to know that I mean you no harm, at least no harm that I am in a position to inflict. I know the way and will direct you, if you will permit me."

"Sure. Lead on MacDuff."

"Terror and Shakespeare in the same Indian. This day has certainly been one of surprises for me."

Abdulmuttalab pointed south. There was no road, and the terrain was rutted and seamed from rare torrential rains and eons of shifting sands. Sheep Dog supposed that he might well be being taken far into the desert where they would run out of gas and water, and they would both meet a bevy of dark-eyed angels before night fell. He held his peace for the time being and was rewarded with the truck coming onto a dirt track, perhaps even the one on which he had driven with Glen Gabler the day before.

Both men relaxed, and Sheep Dog backed away from his litany of threats. He was satisfied that he had made his point and decided to ride it out. It was an adventure, and he was an adventurer.

They approached the outskirts of the capital city after driving for two hours.

Abdulmuttalab said, "Before we get too far into the city, I would like some assurances from you. I don't suppose you are a man who takes bribes?"

"You are correct. Don't bother. I am a man who collects scalps. What assurances do you expect and at what cost?"

"I ask only that you spare my life and that you protect me from the hotheads we are likely to encounter at the embassy. I will make no trouble. I will freely give information, asking only for anonymity. No one needs to torture me. I do not plan to withhold anything. Perhaps your CIA can find me a nice seaside house in Florida?"

"I'm not in charge of much of anything, Abdulmuttalab; and I can't promise much of anything. But you have my word of honor that I will do all in my power to protect you so long as you are straight with me."

"Perhaps you could put in a good word to keep me out of Guantanamo Bay, Mr. Shadow?"

"I'll give it a shot."

Sheep Dog pulled to the side of the road and loosened the thumb and great toe ligatures. Abdulmuttalab gave a small sigh of relief and rubbed his throbbing digits.

"Thank you," he said.

"Now, let's get to the embassy before dark. I don't think either of us wants to be loitering around Dar es Salaam out of doors for any extended period of time."

"No, Mr. Shadow, we are sort of Siamese twins for the time being. Our safeties are closely intertwined."

Abdulmuttalab gave Sheep Dog good directions, avoiding areas of high crime and areas of high police presence. Using his captive's precise instructions Sheep Dog drove carefully along Old Bagamoyo Road in Kinondoni at Msasani Village. They passed the LDS church, Tanesco Electric Supply Co., Royal Plaza Shopping Complex, President's Hotel, and Anghiti Restaurant. The area was as up-scale as Century City in Los Angeles.

"This is it, 686," Abdulmuttalab said. "It used to be the site of the Old Cinema before the U.S. bought it. One thing to be said about the Americans, they certainly can make a better world with their limitless money when they try. By the way, I never asked before, are you an American?"

"Do I look like an American?"

"No, you look like a Somali pirate."

"I'll take that as a high compliment from you—takes one to know one."

Abdulmuttalab gave a short genuine laugh.

"I think we can pull over to the Chancery Building; it's right up ahead."

There was a heavy security barrier of squat concrete pillars and over-sized and over-armed marines.

"What's the other building?"

"It's the USAID building. Maybe it'll be less forbidding. I have only been in the compound a few times and then only to make plans to blow the place up. I trust that I will be more welcome and public this time."

The 22 acre compound had 10,000 trees—baobabs, a huge mango tree, and a Rain tree. It was beautiful and had an air of sophistication, security, and abundance meant to cow a detractor. Sheep Dog noted that his captive was a bit pale and had drawn lips. He was no longer talkative.

He stopped the truck thirty yards from the USAID Building main entrance. The building was impressive for both its size and beauty. The façade was an ascetically pleasing combination of indigenous Mazaras stone and Mningo hardwood.

Sheep Dog watched as a marine lance corporal walked from the entrance holding an M-16 directly at his face. It was disquieting. It was also disquieting that his disguise was so nearly perfect. In the truck cab sat an obvious Indian pirate and an equally obvious senior Arab terrorist. Things did not look good.

"Step out of the vehicle. Do it now," the gravel voice from the huge unsmiling black man with the machine gun said.

"No. Get Glen Gabler. You do it now."

"You give'n me orders, Mahatma? Get out!"

"Look, corporal, things are not what they seem. This is a Glen Gabler thing. You know who he is and what he does?"

"Nope. And I don't care. Get out, before I lose my cool."

Things were getting less cool by the second. The truck was now surrounded by a small army of big men in desert camo BDUs with glares on their faces and big guns in their hands.

"See my hands, corporal. I am no threat to you or to your place. We are well away from a building. If we had intended any harm, we would have done it before stopping in the middle of a concrete field. Please, get Gabler."

"Who is this Gabler, anyway? He work here?"

"Spook."

The corporal wavered.

"I hate spooks. They're not gentlemanly. I will go check. You will stay put, and your hands will remain hanging out of the windows of that truck. My guys are twitchy. Don't give them an excuse."

"No sir."

"I am not a sir. I work for a living. I'll be right back."

He moved double time to and then through the main door of the USAID building. He was gone for fifteen tense minutes. When he appeared through the door again, Glen Gabler was with him. Sheep Dog took a long slow inhalation and an even slower exhalation. Abdul-muttab looked across the cab seat at him, and Sheep Dog put his right thumb up, still keeping it outside the window in plain sight.

Gabler looked a good deal less genial than he had the first time he and Sheep Dog met. His scowl carried with his voice.

"Oh, it's the chameleon. I didn't expect to see you back so soon—or more accurately—ever. What is going on, pray tell?"

"How about you take the two of us safely into a top secret room somewhere in that cavernous building, and we have a serious classified chat. I am about to make your day. No…I am about to make your career. I would be deeply disturbed if one of these nice young men were to have an accident with his trigger. They all seem pretty nervous."

"Corporal, get a man on each side of the truck and open the doors at the same time," Gabler raised his voice, "the rest of you point your weapons at their heads. Anything hinky and you shoot them, but take care now and don't shoot the rest of us in the cross-fire."

The doors flew open, and Sheep Dog and the al Qaeda general were unceremoniously yanked out of the truck and onto the ground and handcuffed.

"Thanks," Sheep Dog said.

"No thanks necessary," Gabler said sarcastically. "We'll lighten up once we see your real selves under all that native garb and have a frank talk."

As they walked into the building, Sheep Dog spoke quietly to Gabler, "Glen, I can't have anyone—not even you—see me as I really am. I can't discuss my mission here, and there can't be any report on that. You got the directive. I know you did. You will be watch captain on Diego Garcia, if you screw this up."

Diego Garcia is a coral atoll in the Chagos Archipelago in the middle of the Indian Ocean located about 1,600 km—1,000 miles—south of the southern coast of India. The closest other countries to Diego Garcia are Sri Lanka and the Maldives, and they are a very long distance away by boat or plane. In the 1960s, the Chagos archipelago was secretly leased to the United Kingdom by Mauritius; its entire population was expelled; and a U.S. military base was established. The island is strategically important, only 37 miles long and 22 feet high, essentially free of females, devoid of meaningful activity outside of one's military occupation; and there is no place to go and nothing really to do but drink. The very name of Diego Garcia is synonymous with slow death for healthy young men.

Sheep Dog's point was not lost on Gabler. He left Abdulmuttalab under heavy guard in one room and took Sheep Dog into another. He shooed out the guards.

"This is a secure room," he said.

"Do you know who that guy in there is, Glen?" Sheep Dog asked Gabler sharply.

"Of course I do. The question is what is he doing here with you? What do you have to do with one of the two or three most wanted terrorists in the world?"

"Actually, almost nothing. I can't give you the details of how this came about; but he saw things that convinced him of the error of his ways today; and rather than have me blow his brains out onto the scorching sand, he agreed to be my prisoner."

"Just like that."

"Yep."

Sheep Dog could not suppress a smile.

Gabler shook his head. Sheep Dog envied Glen his handsome shock of snow-white hair and his ruggedly handsome, albeit overly tanned face. He was stout, but free of excess body fat—a no nonsense man who was used to dealing with the truth and had no patience for people who lied to him. Sheep Dog understood that.

"Well, let's say that there was a bit of a dust-up out there, and Abdulmuttalab had no other choice. I cannot be associated with his capture or in any other way. I cannot stay in your lovely country much longer, and I cannot be the subject of prying eyes or reports. I'll make a deal with you. No one will ever hear about my part in all of this, from either of us. You will get full credit for the man's capture and for all of the information he is going to spill. Instead of Diego Garcia, I see you looking out of a nice corner office at Langley towards the end of the year."

"You are full of it you know."

"I've got a couple of more requests."

Glen groaned theatrically.

"It's all for the cause. Look, I've had a good long trip and talk with this man. He hasn't by any means forsaken his religion with all of its vicious murderous intolerance, but he knows when the jig is up. He is willing to divulge just about everything, and you can be in charge of milking him for years. I'll tell you; I think you or anyone else would be outright nuts to ship this guy to Gitmo, or to torture him, or to expose him publicly. You have a perfect out: he died out there with a substantial number of his confreres. You can leave it at that. You know what he wants?"

"I'm sure you're gonna tell me."

"He wants a nice little anonymous house on the beach in Florida and to fade into oblivion. He is a dead man if the rest of his al Qaeda brothers find out about him. Put him in WitSec and monitor him constantly. You will know more about al Qaeda in the next three years than has been learned since anyone ever heard of Usama bin Laden and his list. Just picture this in the *New York Times*: Glen Gabler, senior officer of the Central Intelligence

Agency, is almost single-handedly responsible for locating and for the capture of Usama bin Laden. Think of being DCIA, maybe even a senator. The possibilities are limitless."

"Enough crap. I'll take good care of him. He won't lose his fingernails. I can't be sure about the little Florida bungalow, but I don't see him in prison either. Now, what do you want out of this?"

"In no particular order of priority, I want to get to a completely anonymous little hotel. I want to scrub this Indian paint off me; I want a steak and a beer; I want anonymity—I was never here. Finally, I want to be on a plane tomorrow night. How's that grab you?"

Gabler was no fool. He realized that, despite the jocularity, Sheep Dog was handing him a future with the Company he could not have dreamed of yesterday.

"I'll make it happen. We'll wait until the hullabaloo quiets down, then I will personally take you to the perfect place. Have a seat. I'll get our new VIPI guest settled, then I'll get you taken care of. And, thanks."

"You're welcome. By the way, what does VIPI mean?"

"Very Important Person Indeed."

Sheep Dog laughed, "That couldn't be more true."

Sheep Dog spent an uncomfortable hour waiting for the senior intelligence officer to return. He had entered the USAID Building dirty, hot, sweaty, and tired. And he knew that he stank. The marble floors under his feet were immaculate except for little tell-tale clumps of desert debris that dropped off him. Passers-by walked out around him to avoid the smell—and, like people everywhere—to avoid eye contact or having to communicate with a homeless person. Sheep Dog felt as out of place as the proverbial whore in church.

He fell asleep sitting up in his chair.

"Hey, 007, let's get up and get you to a bath."

It took a few seconds for Sheep Dog to wake up fully. Gabler escorted him through the back way to a waiting embassy Cadillac SUV. Some thoughtful person had spread a protective blanket over the back seat in anticipation of his occupancy.

"I have just the place for you, my friend," Gabler said as they moved smoothly out of the compound and out of the up-scale Msasani Village and Kinondoni section of the capital city. "it's private; it's cheap; no one who is anyone goes there; and it isn't far from the airport. Oh, and it's air conditioned."

"And running water and towels and electricity?"

"Most of the time," the CIA officer laughed. "I should let you know that you need to pay with Tanzanian Shillings. They'll overcharge you if you offer U.S. dollars, Euros, or pounds sterling. Do you have any TZSs?"

"I don't."

"I'm feeling generous. This'll be enough. It only costs twelve fifty a night American."

He passed back a wad of used shilling notes; at one USD to 1,348 TZSs The wad came to 140,000 TZSs, just over $100 USD. It was half an hour's drive from the embassy towards the Zanzibar Ferry Terminal and the air terminal. Gabler knew his way around. He pulled off on to Bandari Street and into the tiny parking lot of the unimposing Safari Hotel.

"Okay, James Bond, this is it. The Safari Hotel. Fifteen single rooms, twenty-five doubles, and three that are even air conditioned, God willing. You will be pleased to know that—since it is past two—you will have electricity. A decided amenity is the fact that all rooms are *en suite*, and the toilets work most of the time. There is a potential bit of difficulty, which is that many of the staff speak only Swahili; so, I'd better go in with you to get you settled without frustration. Unless you speak Swahili, that is?"

He gave a mildly questioning look at Sheep Dog who replied that his Swahili was rusty.

"The two national languages are English and Swahili, but this far away from civilization, you'll hear more of the latter than of the former. They do have the internet and an international call facility here, and both have a sterling reputation for reliability."

"By 'civilization', I take it you mean the embassy compound."

"Right on."

The two men went into the office and got Sheep Dog registered. Glen was right; no one spoke English that day. But he was wrong about there being air conditioning, at least not that day. "Electrical difficulties" they learned. Overall, the hotel was more like a hostel than a hotel or even a motel. Everything was more than a little worn and seedy and generally poorly kept. But it was certainly private. There was no evidence that there were other guests, and the friendly staff people were sparse in number.

Glen took his leave, and Sheep Dog took a cold shower. It was part of the "electrical difficulties". The toilet and the rest of the ceramics and the floor of the bathroom were unclean; so, Sheep Dog spent half an hour and the expenditure of one of his towels to bring it up to a level of safety if not quite sterility or esthetically pleasing. It took him an hour to scrub off the Indian pirate persona. He dressed in Western clothes for the first time in several days and felt more like himself again as he went down to the office to take advantage of the internet. He had only one e-mail message which was encoded. The decoded message read:

EYES ONLY TOP SECRET
PROCEED ASAP TO PARIS, L'ERMITAGE SACRE COUER HOTEL, RUE LAMARCK, MONTMARTE. RESERVATIONS IN THE NAME OF PIERRE GOTSCHALK. AWAIT FURTHER COMMUNICATION. ADCIA.

It had to be pretty important to warrant a direct, albeit encoded, message from Oliver Prentiss. Sheep Dog called Air France and made reservations for the next afternoon. He found the Parisian hotel on Google Earth and checked the reservations. He dug into his bag to be sure he still had the CIA forged Pierre Gotschalk, French citizen, passport; and he did. As he drifted off to a twelve hour sleep, he thought that he had an adventure awaiting him.

CHAPTER FORTY-NINE

EARLY JANUARY

Tel Aviv, Israel. OFFICE OF THE PRIME MINISTER, 0200
Present: PM, Commander-in-Chief IDF, Commander-in-Chief
IAF, Minister of State, Director Mossad, Ambassador to the
United States

"Please keep your seats, gentlemen," Prime Minister Ehud ben Cohen directed as he hurried into the War Room. "Any hint of a leak, Ari?"

"No, Prime Minister. So far as we can ascertain, we will have the advantage of complete surprise," the Mossad Director, Ari Maor bar-Lev, replied crisply

"Everything ready, Balfour? Michael?"

"We have been in preparation of Operation Endgame for six months. We are confident that nothing has been overlooked. The amount of fire power we are about to deliver will create complete shock and awe, complete destruction of the facilities, and minimal loss of life on either side. As the Americans say, you can't ever count out Murphy's Law; but we have taken every precaution we could imagine."

General Balfour Fürstenberg, Commander-in-Chief, IDF, spoke for himself and for Major General Michael Biram Edelstein, Commander-in-Chief, IAF. Their full confidence showed in their faces, and that gave the PM a brief sense of lessening of his tensions.

"Daniel, when will you get in touch with Jeremy Southern?"

"In exactly thirty minutes post launch, sir."

General ben Moises could hardly wait to break the news to the smug U.S. secretary of State.

"Are you sure they won't balk and feel like they have to inform the enemy?"

"Almost certain. But, as insurance, we will not communicate until the launch is beyond recall, and we will not inform Congress at all. If we were only dealing with Southem, I would have profound doubts. Storebridge is not nearly such a political correctness pettifogger. I think he will make a post raid bluster for appearances sake, but won't lift a finger to help them. It is in his country's interest just as it is in ours to put a stop to them. Remember Rabbi Hillal's famous quote?: *If I am not for myself, then who will be. If not now, when?* Storebridge will see it the same way, I'm sure. If we don't do it, the U.S. will eventually have to. Today, we take the onus off the president's back. Even the worst left-wingers in his country won't be able to blame him, and he is the consummate politician. He'll go for it."

"Anything else, gentlemen? Are we set?"

Every man in the room nodded his head in affirmation.

"Then may *Yahweh* bless our armed forces and our nation."

ZROA HaAVIR VEHAGALA—IAF (Air and Space Arm) Sed Dov Airbase, Tel Aviv, Israel, 0400.
15th Air Wing, 100th Squadron, "The Flying Camel Squadron", operating Beechcraft King Air, 135th Squadron, "The Kings of the Air Squadron", operating Beechcraft King Air and Beechcraft Bonanza

Over the past two weeks, the non-threatening Beechcraft planes had been lined up on the major runways for any spy on the ground or in the sky to see. The hangars had—during the same period—been filling with U.S. Lockheed Martin F-35A Lightening II stealth multi-role fighters. Throughout the world from Ta'if to Washington D.C. to Moscow, the best informed aviation experts were unanimously of the opinion that the world's most effective air plane was more than three years from active production. All of the experts were wrong. 75 of the incredible planes had arrived at Sed Dov under the greatest secrecy since the Manhattan Project. They were now being wheeled out onto the runways to take the place of the innocuous appearing Beechcraft. The last on-ground checks were completed by 0410. The flag men were in place.

Major Hadara Bodenheimer climbed into her F-35A cockpit and in the last minute before takeoff, re-read her orders. Her first role was protection of the bombers. Her second—and more critical mission—was to deposit four

AGM-88 HARM missiles [High-speed Anti-Radar Missiles] into Ardekan Nuclear Fuel Unit near Yazd, Iran where yellow cake uranium is processed before being sent on to the Uranium Conversion Facility [UCF] at Esfahan. At the UCF at Esfahanusing the yellow cake prepared in the Ardekana number of by-products including uranium hexofloride (UF_6), metallic uranium, and uranium oxide (UO_2) are produced. These are later used for uranium enrichment. Major Bodenheimer's mission was shared by three other F-35As. If they were able to drop their payloads successfully at Ardekan, and still have sufficient fuel to return to Tel Aviv; the four Israeli Air Force officers were ordered to assist in the destruction of the UCF on the way back.

The impenetrable blackness of the Middle-Eastern night was broken by the sudden lighting of the flight supervisors' hand held blaze orange torches. In unison, the supervisors waggled their torches; and the powerful engines of the Lockheed Martin F-35A Lightening II stealth fighters roared into life. Take-off began at 0425, and the last of the four jets left the runway at 0430, precisely on schedule.

Three IAF squadrons, the 150th, 199th, and 248th, based at Sdot Micha—responsible for Israel's surface-to-surface nuclear strike capability—had worked feverishly since the onset of darkness the night before on final preparations of their stockpile of 100 upgraded Jericho II missiles. The ordinance was originally intended for medium range targets to protect against retaliation from neighboring Islamic states. Beginning in 2008, Israel launched a program to extend the range of its existing Jericho II ground attack missiles to make them capable of sending a one ton nuclear payload 5,000 kilometers. The final upgrade resulted in the range of the missiles—now capable of being modified to carry nuclear warheads no heavier than 500 kg, to over 7,800 km—becoming, in effect, ICBMs. The Jericho IIs were fully loaded with the nuclear warheads and aimed with computerized precision at Damascus, Tunis, Cairo, Casablanca, Baghdad, Tehran, Esfahan, Tripoli, Amman, Riyadh, Ankara, Islamabad, Peshawar, Manama, Muscat, Doha, Kuwait City, and Abu Dhabi. The squadrons held their Jericho II missiles in full menacing readiness.

The preparations for their Jericho III missiles were substantially more aggressive. Jericho III ICBMs became operational in January, 2008 and are able to carry MIRVed warheads. The maximum range estimation of the IAF Jericho III ICBMs is 11,500 km carrying a payload of 1000-1300 kg, and their accuracy is surgically precise. Of the 100 Jericho IIIs at Sdot Micha, 50 were launched at Iranian based nuclear facilities in the first wave of attack at 0430.

From Tel Nof Air Force Base, 72 huge pilotless Aheron TP drone planes were put in the air at 0445. The drones can remain in the air for a full day and can easily fly as far as the Persian Gulf and the farthest reaches of Iran. The drones have a wingspan of 86 feet, making them the size of Boeing 737 passenger jets and are by far the largest unmanned aircraft in Israel's military. They were armed with JDAMs—Joint Direct Attack Munitions, GBU-31, 1000 pound laser-guided missiles. In addition, from Tel Nof, 76 Tel Nof Delilah anti-radiation attack drones were air-launched from Sikorsky helicopters with the purpose of finding radar sites when they lit up on the drone, allowing them to be found and destroyed. They have a range of 150 km [90 miles], and can destroy targets both on sea and on land. An autopilot onboard as well as an INS/GPS navigation system allows the missile to perform its mission autonomously; a data link enables intervention and target validation. The missiles were fitted for Operation Endgame with a variety of warheads that can be fitted to most aircraft. They can be fired from aircraft, helicopter, or ground launcher. Predominately, the missiles were placed on IAF Sikorsky helicopters to allow for maximum maneuverability. The Delilahs were among the first line of defense precautions to protect the Israeli motherland from counterattack.

The Aheron TP drones were directed towards military installations throughout Iran and at selected nuclear facilities including the uranium mines in Saghand—125 miles from Yazd—and the Natanz Uranium Enrichment Facility, a high security uranium enrichment facility using gas centrifuges, about 40 kilometers southeast of Kashan, about 150 kilometers north of Esfahan, and 280 kilometers south of Tehran. At Natanz hardened nuclear fuel pellets are produced and subsequently formed into nuclear rods. The two largest underground structures at Natanz have horizontal dimensions of about 190 meters by 170 meters, with a gross area of approximately 32,000 square meters each. The smaller structure, situated adjacent to both large structures, has a gross ground area of approximately 7,700 square meters. They are 25 meters underground and are roofed with 12 meters of reinforced concrete and 22 meters of packed fill dirt. The underground compartments hold more than 50,000 centrifuges.

Also high on the attack list were the Qom underground uranium enrichment facility at the Islamic Revolutionary Guard Corps base with its more than 3,000 nuclear centrifuges; the Lashkar Abad plant for isotope separation and laser enrichment; the waste storage facility at Esfahan; the Kalaye Electric Company where nuclear centrifuge components are made and tested; and the massive nuclear facility at Bushehr where two reactors are in actual production of the 80% pure weapons grade plutonium necessary for the production of WMDs.

The Bushehr reactors are fully operative and are in production of nearly half a ton of plutonium a year—enough to produce fifty atomic bombs. Israel's spy network estimated that thirty-two of the WMDs had already been stockpiled. The Atomic Energy Organization of Iran (the AEOI), with the generous contributions from the Russian Federation, accomplished the successful final steps leading to production in absolute secrecy and with an international bluff of Olympian proportions. The IAEA had been systematically prevented from getting an in-depth look into that plant. Israel, however, had incontrovertible evidence of Iran's accomplishment obtained two years previously from their own imagery satellites and more recently at the cost of the lives of three Mossad infiltrators.

0430 - Ramat David Air Base, Northern Israel: F-16C/D Squadrons 109 and 110.

The entirety of the two battle experienced squadrons lifted off for waves of sorties carrying, by the planned end of the attack, a total of 600 "bunker buster" 900 kilogram GBU-27 and 2,268 GBU-28 bombs capable of penetrating 2.4 meters and 6.0 meters of concrete respectively at even an oblique angle and another layer of earth 30 meters deep. Most of the pilots' work concentrated on the problem that for these bombs to penetrate their targeted Iranian facilities—known to be ultra-protected—they will have to strike the targets with absolute accuracy and at an optimal angle. The men and women of the squadrons knew full well the critical precision required of them and had complete trust in themselves and in the marvelous computer systems aboard their flying ships. A few of them also had faith in the divine protection of their mission by *Yahweh*, the one God.

There was considerable overlap in targets by the IAF, especially against Bushehr, which is located eleven miles south-east of the city of Bushehr, between the fishing villages of Halileh and Bandargeh along the Persian Gulf. Coordinated attacks were planned and executed using the Lockheed Martin F-35A Lightening II stealth fighters, the Aheron TP drones, and the Jericho III ICBMs. Regular IAF F-16A, F-16 C and D, F-15, and F-22 Raptor fighter squadrons launched 146 jets as protection for the bombing fleet. In all, by 0450, 612 of Israel's 886 air force planes were in the airspace over Iran—an armada of historical proportions. Even the Beechcraft planes were fitted with heavy machine guns and sent on patrol over the Golan Heights.

This strike dwarfed the combined previous strikes of Operation Opera which occurred on June 7, 1981—eight IAF F-16A fighters covered by six F-15A jets carried out a mission to destroy the Iraqi nuclear facilities of Osiraq; Operation Wooden Leg on October 1 1985, when, in response to a PLO terrorist attack which murdered three Israeli civilians in Cyprus, the Israeli Air Force carried out an attack on PLO Headquarters in Tunis, Tunisia by F-15 Eagles; Operation Orchard which destroyed the Syrian Kibar Nuclear Facility and its tons of North Korean supplied plutonium on September 6, 2007; and the targeted killings of Palestinian militant leaders during the al-Aqsa intifada. Every member of the IDF was put on full alert, even retired personnel, for the massive new strike, Operation Endgame.

0430: General ben Moises in Tel Aviv was connected to United States Secretary of State Jeremy Southem in his home in Georgetown, Virginia by secure telephone. Simultaneously, General Balfour Fürstenberg contacted his counterpart, General Lemuel Simons, Chairman of the Joint Chiefs of Staff of the United States and Secretary of Defense, Michael Chisholm on a conference line. Mossad Director, Ari Maor bar-Lev and DCIA Gerald Lang were put together on another secure line. Prime Minister Ehud ben Cohen awakened President Thomas Collingwood Storebridge in the White House residential quarters. The message for all had the same script:

"The Nation of Israel, and the combined Israeli Defense Forces have—within the hour—launched an all-out military attack on the nuclear weapons facilities of the Islamic Republic of Iran. Before noon today, it is anticipated that every portion of the nuclear capability of Iran will be destroyed. We request your forbearance, but not your help. At 0800 U.S. eastern daylight savings time, we will make an announcement to the world that the attack is entirely the effort of Israel, unaided by the United States or its allies. We will state the obvious—that the survival of our nation required the nullification of Iran's weapons of mass destruction which were directed at the annihilation of Israel. We are fully prepared to defend ourselves against the expected retaliatory efforts of Iran and any of its Muslim allies who consider taking the risk along side that terrorist regime."

The response was the same from every American contacted:

First there was stunned silence. Then, each man exclaimed, with minor variations, "Oh, God, what have you done?"

There followed an extended effort to assuage the wounded egos of the Americans and to assure them that the attacks were necessary.

The ambassador to the United States told the secretary of State, "Before you act in anger or in haste, Mr. Secretary, consider the fact that this problem of the nuclear capacity of Iran on a war footing has not just been aimed at Israel. For more than ten years, your country and—indeed—the United Nations has agonized over how to deal with the threat. You are well aware that your military has presented attack options to your past three presidents. Now, the threat has vaporized. You do not have to be the object of criticism in this affair. You are at liberty to make politically correct protestations against this "unprecedented military intervention by the Nation of Israel", and you can maintain your stance of neutrality in the United Nations and with the world's communications media."

Similar arguments were made to the other American officials and the responses were very much the same, and very much expected by the Israeli callers:

"This will be World War III! The rest of the Middle-East, probably Russia, and maybe even China, will intercede openly. The United States will be drawn into the conflict. We will have to make the terrible decision to defend Israel with our military might, a decision we have fortunately never had to make before. You have done irreparable harm to the United States, sir."

To which the scripted Israeli caller replied, "None of that will happen. No nation on earth really wanted the madmen in Iran to have nuclear weapons, much less to use them. They will bluster about Israel, but they will secretly heave a collective sigh of relief. We have studied the diplomatic fallout for months and are convinced that the Europeans lack the will to confront us militarily; the Russian Federation will respond with bombast and sanctions, but will stop short of war because of their fear of your country's military might; and China will protest but will not violate its long-standing policy of avoiding foreign military interventions when their own security is not threatened."

The phone lines were coated with frost when the calls were completed, but no threats were made by the United States or its counterparts. Consternation reigned in the halls of the White House, the Pentagon, and Congress; and the security status of America was elevated to red for the first time since the department of Homeland Security was established.

By 1130, every target had been hit; and Israeli follow-up footage was provided by their F-16A intelligence over-flights equipped with AN/ASD-83 wing pods, ISR pods for signal capture, and separate pods for photo reconnaissance. The Mossad's assets confirmed at least a 90% destruction of the nuclear facility targets without any very serious collateral damage. The Mossad estimated that there were very few civilian casualties.

Sleeping on his lumpy mattress in the Safari Hotel on Bandari Street in Dar es Salaam, Sheep Dog was totally unaware of the horrific military strike in Iran. Even if he had been sitting awake in his chair, he would not have known. The hotel did not have television service; the electricity was turned off at night; so, there was no radio. The newspapers would not have the news until late morning. Sheep Dog would likely have to wait to learn the headlines and the details until Glen Gabler drove him to the Julius Nyerere International Airport late in the afternoon.

THE PREDATORS AND THEIR PREY

CHAPTER FIFTY

White House Oval Office: Daily Briefing, 0630
**PRESENT: POTUS, SECRETARY OF STATE, SECRETARY OF
DEFENSE, CHAIRMAN JCS, SECRETARY OF HOMELAND
SECURITY, DCIA, DFBI, and AMBASSADOR TO ISRAEL**
(by speaker telephone)

"We might as well have had this meeting at 2:30. I haven't slept a
wink since Cohen called me. I presume you have been equally
afflicted with insomnia," the president said.

Everyone nodded agreement.

"Well, let's get to it. Give us the damages thus far Director Lang."

"Mr. President, gentlemen, what we know more than we did at 2:30 comes
largely from our own satellite photos and a set of excellent flyover passes with
more close up detail on the Iranian nuclear sites. In general, every one of them
that we know about has been seriously—probably irreparably—damaged.
Take a look at these sequential shots of the Natanz and Bushehr facilities."

A set of high-definition glossy color photos showed piles of dirt still
smoking, and a few tattered remnants of concrete blocks and steel girders at
each site. No building remained standing or even partially so.

"You remember how the Romans chafed and became frustrated after each
new attack and partial defeat by the Carthaginians? When the Romans finally
won the decisive Third Punic War, they marched in and leveled the city of
Carthage then salted the land over and around it. These pictures give me the

sense that this is what just happened to the cities of Iran," the DFBI, Sinclair Y. Thompson, said.

"Are they all like that?" President Storebridge asked.

"Pretty much."

"What retaliation has Iran made? How big a war do we have on our hands?"

"The Israelis appear to have been right, Mr. President. The Iranians have been silent."

"What do you all think that means?"

"They're biding their time before a massive nuclear strike on Israel—tit-for-tat," said the Secretary of Defense, Michael Chisholm gloomily, "and we'll be in it with both feet."

"I agree," said both Gerald Lang from the CIA and General Simons of the JCS.

"I plan to prepare for the worst and hope for the best. Nothing has happened, and I'll take no news as good news, at least temporarily," Jensen Dräger from Homeland Security said.

"Jeremy?"

"I might have some good news. The Swiss sent a message that Sofrekheneh himself wants to talk. He is flying in to meet with Kurt Haagensen, himself this evening. He wants you, Mr. President, me, Mr. Lang, and General Simons to be at the meeting. I haven't replied yet. What do you want me to do?"

"It sounds like Sofrekheneh is on the ropes. Maybe we can capitalize on what is probably a fleeting opportunity. Meeting with the U.N. Secretary-General as a buffer has to be a plus. Set it up. If there is nothing else, let's consider this meeting adjourned. Keep up the good work and keep me posted."

Office of the Secretary General of the United Nations, New York City, 2130.
PRESENT: SECRETARY-GENERAL, PRESIDENT OF THE UNITED STATES, PRESIDENT OF THE ISLAMIC REPUBLIC OF IRAN, MINISTER OF STATE FOR THE REPUBLIC OF IRAN, SECRETARY OF STATE OF THE UNITED STATES, THE DCIA OF THE UNITED STATES, CHAIRMAN OF THE JCS OF THE UNITED STATES

The delegations of the two countries sat across from each other at the long conference table. Secretary-General Haagensen sat at the head of the table. The table contained only small sets of paper and a glass of water in front of each participant and a carafe of ice water at each end of the gleaming table.

Mahmoud Sofrekheneh was wearing a scruffy pair of chinos and a tee shirt, an obvious show of disrespect for the rest of the men who were all in custom designed dark suits and expensive ties. He scowled, much to the amusement of the other men.

The secretary-general opened the meeting, "I will generally sit back and observe, only venturing a thought as the occasion is appropriate. Since President Sofrekheneh has come from such a distance—and the hour is getting late—why don't we have him speak first?"

Sofrekheneh gave an arrogant disdainful look at the other men then said, "We have been the subject of an unwarranted and vicious sneak attack by the Zionist Entity. Presumably the Jews were aided by American Jewry and the U.S. government."

He waved off President Storebridge as he started to protest.

"This is only the latest in a long series of provocations by the Zionists against Iran and the peace loving peoples of Islam. Before you is a partial listing of the crimes perpetrated by the Zionists. I will limit myself to pointing out a few of the most egregious."

President Sofrekheneh recited from memory Operation Opera, Operation Wooden Leg, Operation Orchard, the attacks on the intifada leaders, the murders of unconvicted alleged perpetrators of the "so-called Munich massacre", the explosion of a tourist bus carrying Iranian officials and peace-loving Hamas members outside of Damascus in December, 2003, the fiendish murder of Hezbollah top leader, Imad Mughniyah in February, 2008, the murder orchestrated by former Mossad Chief, Meir Dagan of Hamas leader Mahmoud al-Mabhouh in the Gulf City-State of Dubai in his room at the Al-Bustan Rotana Hotel on January 19, 2010 and cited the complicity of British, German, Austrian, and French operatives.

"And I neglected to mention the murder of Bulgarian journalist Georgi Markov who died in England in 1978. A Scotland Yard autopsy revealed— imbedded in his leg—a BB studded with tiny holes. It had been shot into Markov with an umbrella rigged as a pellet gun. The holes in the BB had been packed with ricin. Sofrekheneh's voice rose in volume and stridency as he said, "and it is perfectly well known that the Zionists were behind that murder of an innocent."

He took a breath and a long sip of water.

"You will see in the papers I have provided, all documented by VEVAK as you may know it, or the SAVAMA; more correctly—the *Sazman-e Ettela'at va Amniat-e Melli-e Iran*, our Ministry of Intelligence and National Securitya list of over a thousand murders, mass murders, grand thefts, tortures, and atrocities that have fallen on the peace-loving Muslim peoples at the hands of the Zionist Entity and its collaborators. This is corroborated by our sister service, Joint Intelligence X of the ISI."

Again, the U.S. president started to speak; but Sofrekheneh was still on his roll, and Storebridge held his peace again.

"We are also disturbed by a number of terroristic killings all over the world—nearly 500—that have occurred to some of our more prominent Muslim brethren and to innocent by-standers during the past year. We cannot definitely lay those killings at the feet of the Zionists, nor can we prove any complicity by the Great Satan in these crimes. Give us time; and we will. Minister Darzi, what is the fanciful name of the criminal who has done all of these acts of terrorism against our innocent people?"

Foreign Minister Ali Abu-Darzi spoke for the first time, "Yes, Mr. President, he has been called "The Shadow".

Gerald Lang could not take any more, "You're telling us that one man killed over 500 people—assassinated them—in places all over the world just in the past one year? 'The Shadow', oh, come now. Even you have to admit that your conclusion is pure fantasy. One man, indeed."

"You are correct on that point, Mr. Lang. We do not think it to be the work of just one man. It is a terrorist organization. You Christians and your pets— the Jews—are such hypocrites. You profess such outrage against Muslims for being terrorists, while you have an organization that rivals anything you have ever accused Muslims of doing."

"Mr. Secretary-General. I think it is my turn to speak," President Storebridge finally found an opening.

"Yes, President Sofrekheneh, I think that would be appropriate and fair."

Sofrekheneh pouted like a child, but yielded.

"I am not going to answer for any of the so-called crimes you have described. I am not at all sure that any or all of them ever occurred, and I don't care. What is it you want? I'll tell you what we want. There has been enough killing and destruction. You—yourself—have made that clear. We want the attack by the Israelis to remain what it is, an attack, and not to have it become a war. What would it take for you to listen to reason and to negotiate?"

Sofrekheneh made a change that—to anyone who was not familiar with him—would not have imagined could occur. He became a serious, crafty, sensible negotiator.

"Assuming you are serious," he said, "my country has certain demands. If you meet those demands, we will bear our sorrows and wounds and will not retaliate against the Zionist State. Our demands are as follows:

First: You will force the United Nations to cancel all sanctions against our country immediately. Our people are on severe fuel rationing which impedes our ability to move and to do business. We are unable to buy more, but our domestic demand has not reduced. The head of our National Distribution Oil Products Company has reported to me that consumption was steady despite a twenty percent cut in rations just since December. This is a non-negotiable priority.

Second: You will reign in your lap-dog, the Zionist Entity. You will guarantee that there will be no more attacks. They will respect our air space. They will not spy on us. They will not impede our ability to do business throughout the world.

Third: You will impose controls—and if necessary, sanctions—on the Zionist Entity to prevent incursions into Lebanon.

Fourth: You will impose controls on the Zionist Entity and whatever other terrorist organizations you control to cease and desist from covert action assassinations.

Fifth: You have treated me with disrespect when I brought up the idea of "The Shadow". While you may well use a different name—and even if you are not responsible—you will find out who this person or organization is, and terminate it. We will not believe in your sincerity unless and until you demonstrate a dead body. We will cooperate with you in any way you need to bring this terrorist to justice.

Sixth: You will pay us $6 billion U.S. immediately to cover our most pressing and serious losses, and you will pay us another $6 billion a year for ten years while we build a mountain over the radiation contaminated ground.

Seventh: You will unfreeze our assets being held illegally in your country. It is theft and kidnapping of our national treasure and pride, and it must stop.

Eighth: You will radically alter your policies aimed against the Islamic Republic of Iran and will restore our mutual relationship to full recognition—ambassadors, embassies, consulates, and the like. We will be granted diplomatic immunity, freedom to travel in and out of your country and around and about it without restrictions."

He stopped abruptly; "that is all," he said.

President Storebridge looked at the Iranian leader with something just short of astonishment. He mulled over what he had heard for a moment before he responded.

"President Sofrekheneh, what you have presented is at least a good first step in achieving better relations between our nations. It will take time and some political and diplomatic maneuvering to work out a mutually acceptable agreement on your requests. I will have my best people work on it and get back to you in a week—seven days. Is that satisfactory?"

"No, sir it is not. I will remain reluctantly in New York for twenty-four hours. If Minister Darzi and I have not heard a satisfactory reply from your side by then, I will make a simple telephone call and *Yawm al-Qiyamah [Arabic: The Day of Judgment—the Apocalypse]* will commence. Good day."

He and Darzi stood up peremptorily and stalked out of the room.

When they were gone, the Secretary General asked, "Do any of you think that it is possible to negotiate with the man or that if you achieve an agreement, that it will be honored?"

There were no affirmatives.

White House Oval Office: Conference, 1830
Present: POTUS, VPOTUS, SECRETARY OF STATE, SECRETARY OF DEFENSE, SECRETARY OF HOMELAND SECURITY, CHAIRMAN JCS, DFBI, DCIA, ADCIA

"We have an unprecedented conundrum before us, gentlemen," The president said. "You have all had the afternoon to prepare a response to the demands made by The president of the Islamic Republic of Iran. We will give the man a firm answer tomorrow morning; so, let me hear your recommendations. When you have all made your pitches, I will make a decision, and we will get it into formal language. Mr. Secretary of State?"

"Thank you Mr. President. Here is the proposal from State."

He passed out a single sheet of paper to each man seated around the room.

"We see no alternative but to acquiesce to most of Sofrekheneh's demands. Items 1 through 7 are unpalatable but are—in the last analysis—acceptable. It will take some spin doctoring to get the American public to accept the requirements. Politically, I think it may be a winner for us. We can come across as the broker of peace. Maybe there'll even be a Nobel Peace Prize in the future, Mr. President. It would certainly be deserved.

"What we cannot accept is item 8. Our place in the world would be severely compromised if we cave in and give recognition to this terrorist extortionist. What we at State propose is a gradual and minimalist process towards normalization, say over the next fifteen to twenty years. We have to broker the immediate peace or risk World War III, but we also have to consider the future. To accomplish that, one element of the agreement must be a firm commitment on the Islamic nations' part is to get the terrorist activity under control. We are giving up our most effective asset, and we need a quid pro quo."

"Thank you, Jeremy. Mr. Secretary of Defense?"

"We're okay with everything State has proposed. In this, we are the tool of enforcement and not policy. We can live with Sofrekheneh's demands, but we don't trust him to keep any of his promises. We would like to get the fleet into place, and the air force up to strength in Iraq and Afghanistan during these first tense weeks. Israel has pretty much exhausted its military resources and is highly vulnerable right now. As for item 8, it is about as distasteful as all of the rest, and Defense won't venture its opinion. That is up to the diplomats and politicians."

"Thank you, Michael. General Simons?"

"I have nothing to add to what Secretary Chisholm said. I would personally like to carpet bomb the Iranians back into the seventh century, but that doesn't seem likely to be the prevailing scenario here."

"I have much the same feelings, General, but we are all stuck with reality. Mr. Dräger?"

"Homeland Security is on full red alert and will remain so until all of this is settled. CIA and NSA have mobilized all of their assets for the effort, and Defense is on board with every state National Guard unit on full alert for the duration. From the strictly Homeland Security point of view, we reluctantly favor giving in to all of Iran's demands. Anything is better than a real war. Who knows where that could lead?"

"Thanks, Jensen. Any other thoughts from the FBI, Mr. Thompson?"

"Not really, sir. We are fully on board with Homeland Security. All of our special agents and other assets are operating with counterintelligence as first priority. If this goes on for any length of time, we will see a sharp upturn in crime in the country, but that can't be helped in view of the gravity of the present situation."

"We appreciate you help, as usual, Sinclair. Where is the CIA in all of this, Director Lang?"

"To be blunt, we hate it all; but, like everyone else in the room, we are onboard. There is area that we have glossed over that I would like to discuss, however. Items 3 and 4 are sticky for us. It is the Company's conclusion that our Sheep Dog program has been successful beyond our original expectations. We think that is why Sofrekheneh is making this demand. We have gotten them nervous, outright afraid. They call our program, "The Shadow", which indicates their superstitious natures coming out. That is exactly what we intended, and it is a winner. Why not just deny that we have anything to do with the assassinations and leave it at that?"

"Because it is a cheap thing to give up, Gerald," Jeremy Southem broke in. "Let's be candid. It is hardly a 'program'. We all pretty much know we are talking about one man who gets some good but anonymous help. We could just cancel the effort and bring the man home. The Iranians would see the cessation of mysterious and highly effective killings and know that we have honored our part of the bargain."

For the first time, the vice-president chimed in, "Hold on a minute. We created a monster. When things were going well, we liked our monster. Now, we have to look at this man as a soldier; and we have to recognize that—like any other soldier—he is expendable if it serves the greater good. Mr. President, I have to tell you, this man is a ticking time-bomb if he ever gets back to the U.S. and out of our control. Can you imagine him having a special on Fox News? I am quite certain that this administration would fall if he were to be allowed to tell what he knows. It is not out of the question that some of us in this room would go to prison. Picture Richard Nixon. Try and answer the inevitable question: 'Mr. President, what did you know and when did you know it?' You and I would be sitting there with egg on our faces and saying something lame like, 'I am not a crook'."

The president's countenance registered the impact of his V-P, Douglass Carter's, salient observation.

DCIA Lang responded, "This man *is* a soldier. It is against everything this country stands for to throw a man who has served honorably to the wolves. That said—from a practical point of view—he cannot be allowed to live. Let's face that fact. He knows where all of the skeletons are buried. He knows who did what and when, and he can tarnish the reputation of the United States of America irreparably if he gets angry and decides to do so. We could not watch him all of the time forever. If you elect to terminate the Sheep Dog program, he has to disappear without a trace."

"How about something like the WitSec program?" DFBI Thompson asked.

"You know as well as I do that WitSec doesn't change the basic character of criminals. They are their own worst enemies. The program has a pot full of failures to its credit. They are embarrassing, but a disgruntled Sheep Dog out there someplace who decides to rat would be a national catastrophe. We cannot leave that to chance. The CIA would be severely damaged, and we cannot afford that in a world full of external enemies," the DCIA argued.

"We are going to be adamant about not granting full recognition," Southem said, "so, we can't try and argue everything else down. Sheep Dog is the least valuable asset on the list. He'll have to go, as distasteful as it is to all of us."

The president called for a vote, item by item. After the discussion, the result was predictable; the first seven passed quickly, and item 8 was unanimously rejected.

Before adjournment, Gerald Lang turned to his ADCIA and said loudly enough for everyone in the room to here, "Oliver, you need to take care of this."

"But, Director, he's my friend. We go back a long ways. He trusts me."

"That's the very reason why you have to do it. Sheep Dog is not a man to go down easily. He will have to be lured and set up. It's nasty, but it comes with the territory of your office."

Oliver Prentiss thought about resigning. He thought about refusing. He thought about making an all out effort to shift the job to some one else. He thought about trying to persuade his superiors that Hunter Caulfield would keep his mouth shut for the rest of his life and keep the secrets.

However, what he said was, "I'll take care of it."

CHAPTER FIFTY-ONE

Glen Gabler drove Sheep Dog to the airport. They talked very little on the way, except that Gabler told the incredulous Sheep Dog about yesterday's attack by Israel. He gave Sheep Dog a sincere thanks for bringing Musab Sarayrah Abdulmutallab to him and letting him have all of the credit. It was an important coup—Gabler knew—and the chance of a lifetime.

"I owe you big time, buddy. If you ever need a friend, I'll be it."

"Thanks, Glen. You're a good man. Just keep fighting the good fight."

The Air France flight to Orly International Airport in Paris was pleasant and restful. The French still served meals on board, and in First Class, Sheep Dog dined like a prince. He caught a cab to Montmartre and had the driver let him out in front of the *Basilique Sacré-Coeur.* He walked the winding short block to his hotel, *L'Ermitage Sacre Couer*—an elegant hill-top mansion-turned-guesthouse on Rue Lamarck—and checked in. The hotel was a classy bed-and-breakfast place, and his room was located on the fifth floor with a "face the Basilica" view. The hotel offered a "face Paris" view as the only other alternative; but his room had already been booked by Oliver Prentiss; and Sheep Dog had no complaint.

All twelve of the rooms in the family-owned B&B were artistically-minded guestrooms. Each room was papered with English flower-print fabrics and furnished with handcrafted beds, armoires, tables, and cut glass lamps dating from the early 1900s. Each room had a slightly different décor; but all were designed to charm even the most finicky guest; and Sheep Dog felt at home in his. The guest-house's nod to the modern man—at least in Sheep Dog's room—was deep plush synthetic French-made wall-to-wall carpeting. The carpet was so soft that he made no sound as he crossed to set his bags on the luggage holder under the window. The room—like the hotel—was otherwise simple: No TV, no elevator, and no smoking. All rooms were equipped with standard tiled bathrooms, his with a blue and grey design of French countryside silhouettes. There was a narrow shower, i.e., a French shower, and even a bathtub—white, small, and with gold claw-feet holding it well off the floor that was clean to the point of sterility. His window—which provided a breath-taking vista centered on the Basilica of the Sacred Heart—opened onto a small terrace to which was attached one of the few outside fire escapes. Sheep Dog recognized Oliver's hand in providing him a security escape route. Like Sheep Dog, Oliver Prentiss was always on guard, and Sheep Dog appreciated the small touch of his friend's concern for him. It was good to be back in civilization—in the most civilized city on the planet.

He took a long nap, then showered, dressed, and took a small walking tour, mostly centered on the Basilica. It was a frosty day, and he was not dressed for it; so, he stopped by a small haberdashery and bought a very French looking heavy camel hair overcoat. Before taking the Basilica tour, he walked down the hill to Rue Cardinal Dubois and back. The walk was cold and invigorating since the Basilica is located on the highest point of Paris in Montmartre. Except in winter, the area was highlighted by emerald green lawns and beautiful trees and flowers. This was winter; the trees were bare ruined choirs looking at the Basilica; and the lawns were brown.

The drabness of the winter scene did not dampen Sheep Dog's enthusiasm for taking the tourist tour of the *Basilique Sacré-Coeur*. The beautiful edifice with its tall medieval dome is in the Romanesque-Byzantine architectural style, and has a relic that his guide bore solemn testimony was the very Sacred Heart—*Sacré-Coeur*—of Christ. Sheep Dog had no more faith in the Catholicism that held reverence for the sacred heart kept in a French church or an infallible pope than he did in the visions of Mohammed or Joseph Smith, or for the tale of Buddha walking on pond lily pads when he was seven days old. He did like the comfort, peace, and enthusiasm of the old docent; and he accepted the comfort and peace that true believers got from their religious traditions—with the exception of the violent intolerance of the Muslims. The cool darkness that pervaded the Basilica's interior was restful and soothing. He felt up-lifted and ready for whatever assignment seemed to be so important to his friend, Oliver.

CHAPTER FIFTY-TWO

In the aftermath, he hit the light switch and bathed his small room in *L'Ermitage Sacre Couer* with a shock of light. His chest was heaving from his exertions of the last few moments; his muscles ached; and he was confused at what had just happened and about the implications of the attack. His was an orderly mind and one that needed plausible answers. He knew he had been careful and was as certain as he could be that he had not been followed to the hotel. His brain cleared as his adrenaline rush subsided. He forced himself to think, to piece together everything that had just happened.

There was not that much to remember: He had been asleep—in that level of sleep below REM, beyond dreaming—benefiting from the deep levels of worry free restorative slumber. The hotel window behind its drawn drapes had suddenly crashed inward, and only with his finely toned reflexive instincts had he saved himself by throwing his sleep benumbed body over the edge of the bed away from the window as the bullets from a silencer-muffled 9 mm automatic stitched a trail up the length of the mattress where he had been outstretched less than a second or two before.

The shooter had come up the fire escape from the well lighted street five stories below intent on assassinating the sleeper—a wiry, late middle-aged agent code-named "Sheep Dog" who was making a small contribution to his country's security. In a former life—that man—had been a businessman named Hunter Caulfield. That life was now irretrievably in the past.

The slender, lithe, well trained professional killer, secure with the knowledge that the element of surprise was in the intruder's favor, had smashed the way into the hotel bed room that was as dark as the bottom of a mine shaft.

The shooter's young eyes had not adjusted to the blackness of the room as fast as Sheep Dog's reflexes had propelled him from the bed. The shooter had only a portion of a second to bemoan the fact that he had not been wearing night vision goggles.

The intruding killer moved with the speed of a leopard toward the side from which the sound of Sheep Dog's body landing on the carpeted floor had come. Sheep Dog balled himself up at the foot of the bed. The shooter whirled around the edge of the mattress and stumbled headlong over Sheep Dog's spring-coiled figure. Two more rounds pumped out of the silenced end of the gun as the would-be killer pitched toward the floor. Sheep Dog had three advantages now. The muzzle blast had momentarily blinded the shooter to the darkness in the room, and he was now badly off balance. And he was now in an equal battle with a consummate fighter and killer. Sheep Dog executed a smooth uncoiling to envelope the shooter's flailing legs. He lay prone on the intruder's back like a coiling anaconda inexorably squeezing the life out of its victim. He moved swiftly up the shooter's body and pinioned the intruder's gun arm before the shooter could turn back and fire. Two more shots spat out of the gun impotently into the side of the mattress.

Hunter and hunted locked in a death struggle. Sheep Dog knew that he had won when he realized how slightly built his attacker was. He lay on the intruder's back. Despite the attacker's violent struggles, Sheep Dog had been able to hook his feet around the attacker's shins and his right arm around the slim neck. He tucked his head against the side of the attacker's head and brought his left arm up to finish the slow death choke—the *mata leão*, [kill the lion]. Sheep dog had patiently squeezed with all his might. His breathing slowed down and became more nearly normal. The attacker's struggles waned as the *estrangulamento* robbed the blood supply, then the critical oxygen supply to the attacker's brain; and the struggles became feeble, then finally ceased. Sheep Dog released his compressing hold gradually and listened carefully to the attacker's breathing.

"*Buon dormo*," [sleep well] he had whispered soothingly, using the Portuguese of his Brazilian Jiu-Jitsu masters.

Wary that the attacker could have been playing possum, Sheep Dog had slowly begun to remove his arms from around the man's slim neck. His over-worked imagination heard soft regular breathing. But there was no reaction, no movement. Sheep Dog let go slowly and cautiously. There was no response, no counter-attack. He grabbed the attacker's chin roughly in one hand and his occiput in the other and lifted sharply upward. There was still no reaction.

Sheep Dog had then made a sudden violent lifting and twisting motion of a coup de grâce and heard the bones high and deep in the neck crack as loud as if he had broken a base-ball bat. The attacker's head canted at an impossible angle. Sheep Dog eased up on both hands and took the attacker's shoulders in his hands and shook violently. The thin muscular intruder's head moved independent of its body in a way that could only occur with a complete disconnection of the head and neck.

It was over. Less than fifteen seconds earlier Sheep Dog had been sound asleep. He became aware of his rapid cardiac rhythm pounding in his chest. It occurred to him that there could be others. He scooped his Sig-Sauer Glock 9 mm from under his pillow and moved silently to the broken window. He peered outside from the window's edge quickly and then moved back out of sight again. No one. He stepped hurriedly to the hotel room door and peered out through the peep hole in the hotel door. The limited view indicated no one in the hallway. He undid the two chain locks and the bolt lock as quietly as possible and flung open the door and scrutinized the poorly lit hallway holding his Glock in a two-handed FBI crouch swinging it side-to-side. The hallway was empty. He closed the door—bolt locked it again—and re-attached the two chain locks.

Sheep Dog flicked on the hotel's room lights and was momentarily dazzled, but moved swiftly to the side of the inert body of his would-be assailant. The slim figure was dressed in a one piece mat-black stretch nylon body suit, a thin Kevlar vest, a ski mask that showed only open dead eyes now, and black lace-up fighter's shoes with thick rubber soles. A black commando knife was attached to a heavy black web belt buckled tightly to the slender waist. Another, shorter, double-edged dagger was attached to the right ankle; and a sub-compact, semi-automatic 7 round magazine, .22 LR Beretta Bobcat in a concealed weapon holster was attached to the opposite ankle. He examined the larger handgun that had come too close to ending his life. It was a well-used 9 mm Belgian Fabrique National [FN] High Power contract manufactured pistol originally designed and made by Browning. The ID numbers had been expertly removed. Sheep Dog ejected the magazine and examined the bullets—VBR Belgium armor piercing projectile technology. He shivered a little.

"*Loaded for bear,*" Sheep Dog whispered to himself. "*Somebody was right serious.*"

His attacker was dead, and now Sheep Dog needed answers. Who knew about him? He did not believe in coincidences; this was no B&E gone wrong. Who wanted him dead? Specifically—and right now—who was after him? There were plenty of the compatriots of his own victims who would want him dead, but there was no reason to think that any of them—on their own—could have traced him to this country, to this hotel, during this night. He contemplated the answers and came up with a very disturbing train of thought.

He unsnapped and removed the attacker's Kevlar vest—a NATO Level IV Ballistic Vest with imbedded ceramic trauma plates—unzipped the sheath-like black suit and began to search the corpse thoroughly. His search produced two shocks. The first came immediately when he removed the ski mask from his victim's head. It was a woman—young, attractive, and blond.

The second came after he failed to find any identification in the pocketless clothing. He removed her shoes and tore out the insoles. There he found a photo identification card which shocked him with its familiarity. The name meant nothing to him, but the card had been issued by the Central Intelligence Agency of the United States of America. Sheep Dog numbly put the ID card on the room desk top reacting as if he had been struck a violent blow to the center of his sternum.

He was momentarily afraid that he would faint. He was a hunter who had become the hunted, and he was going to have to go dissect every event in his history with the Company to find his mistake. If he was going to survive, he could never make another one. He mentally kicked himself for not having the good sense to immobilize the attacker and to have extracted all the information she possessed that could have led to her masters. He had a highly honed skill set for extracting information from the reluctant, and it was useless to him now.

He took mental stock of his situation. His cover was blown. He had been betrayed. He was obligated to think the unthinkable. Only two people on earth knew his identity and his present location: John Smith I, AKA CIA Officer Edward Liam Salinger, and ADCIA Oliver Prentiss, his friend of thirty years. Sheep Dog took a moment to remember Salinger's parting warning to him about the fickle loyalty of the Company. Salinger did not seem to be a man with an overweening ambition, and he did not seem to be a man who would desert a brother-soldier in trouble. Oliver was nothing if not ambitious. He wanted nothing more than to occupy the director's office. Sheep Dog was pretty sure that the man would do almost anything short of selling-out his family—and maybe even that—for his career standing.

He hated the thought—it had been Oliver. He hated the implication—there was no safety net for him, no one to call. He once had Oliver, Ed Salinger, and for a while, Neal Dastrup, and Glen Gabler. Now, there was no one but himself. He had never felt so alone and unsafe.

CHAPTER FIFTY-THREE

Sheep Dog hurriedly moved his two bags out of his room and down the hall to the laundry chute and dropped them in. He kept only his Beretta 9 mm and knife, and his folder with money and passports. He had to travel light; his life depended on being able to move very quickly and without being hampered. He returned to the room and threw the dead assassin over his shoulder in a fire-man's carry and dumped her corpse down the chute as well. That might buy him some time.

He left the hotel through his window. It was still very dark below, and he could not be sure but that a Company vehicle was parked on Rue Lamarck waiting to help the assassin to escape. Without a second thought, he climbed up the fire escape instead of down and pulled himself onto the roof. He dashed across and looked down over "the Paris side" for another fire escape. It took five minutes to find it in the dark, and he descended it to the ground in less than two minutes. He could feel the clock clicking away his life and could almost feel the hot breath of pursuers.

He trotted along the side of the hotel until he could see out onto Rue Lamarck. His trepidations were confirmed. A large black SUV sat on the street between street lights in the only dim light available. Its engine was running, and two large men sat in the front seats smoking, thereby breaking one of the spook's or soldier's first rules while hiding. The hard, short cropped look of the two men convinced him that these were CIA agents. A moment of panic gripped him, but he shook it off. He had to in order to get away. Once those men figured out that the assassin had been too long, they would go up the fire escape to his room. Finding it empty, they would launch a manhunt throughout Paris, and he needed a head start.

Rue Maurice Utrillo was brilliantly lit; and Sheep Dog raced east on it then turned and ran alongside Rue Paul Albert, then Rue Feutrier putting as much distance as he could between himself and the hotel. He was now in a densely populated but sleeping residential neighborhood and was having difficulty orienting because the streets angled and turned without common sense planning. He followed Rue Feutrier until it made a sharp right turn to become Rue Muller. He found a garden that was heavy with foliage and lay down among the tall bushes to catch his breath and to think.

He allowed himself no more than five minutes of respite, then he walked to the back of the house in whose garden he had been resting and found a car. This was a low crime area, and the Peugeot's keys were in the ignition. He had caught a break. He drove out to the front and away from Montmartre as quickly as he could without attracting attention. He stopped only long enough to switch license plates before making a bee-line out of the capital and on towards Lyon. He traded cars twice in the 246 mile trip, and it was still quite dark when he pulled into the *Gare de Saint-Exupéry* TGV railway station near Lyon—which is directly attached to *Lyon-Saint Exupéry* Airport.

This was old stomping ground from his Viet Nam war days. He had made at least twenty trips to France during his ten year off-an-on tours of duty. He got rid of his last car and went into the men's room. He sorted out his passports and set aside thirty of them to keep and the other twenty-five that had come into his possession from CIA sources. They would have been a dead give away, and he knew that very soon a dragnet for him would include alerts on all of his CIA derived documents. He took the dangerous passports out the back door and onto the train waiting area. At this time of night, it was frequented by drug addicts, winos, and criminals, just the nice sort of people he was looking for.

He passed by several particularly nefarious appearing men and pretended to drop his now useless passports. He was not at all surprised to see on his way back down through the outdoor waiting area that there was no sign of his them. Having accomplished his aim, he went inside and downstairs to catch the tram to the airport. He selected another of his French passports, compliments of Ed Salinger's secret cache, and booked a seat on a Lufthansa to Ho Chi Minh City, Viet Nam, another of his old stomping grounds. He was confident for the moment that Stefan Danglois would be able to make himself safe from the hunt that he knew was going to be underway in a matter of minutes.

He was able to take off, and only a scant ten minutes before one of a fleet of black SUVs pulled into the airport and disgorged four men who began their search. They were part of a large contingent of FBI, ATF, and CIA agents dispatched to check every bus, train, and plane station in the country. The French had not yet been informed because the Company wanted the manhunt to be kept in-house and in-family for as long as possible. Their efforts were made more difficult because thirty passports in the hands of thirty criminals roaming about the streets and airways gave out alerts all over France and in most of the rest of the world. All of the interceptions of Sheep Dog's passports took valuable time and put more distance between him and the predators.

CHAPTER FIFTY-FOUR

Air France flight 2012 landed at Tan Son Nhat International Airport, Terminal 2—a new international terminal funded by the Japanese ODA—at 1515 local time. Sheep Dog was thoroughly familiar with the airport from his Viet Nam War years and ever since on regular flights on business. He continued to be impressed with the progressive changes that had been occurring ever since the communists took over Saigon—now Ho Chi Minh City. He knew that the airport would soon become used only for domestic passengers, since the new Long Thanh International Airport was nearly completed.

He bought copies of the *Saigon Times Weekly*—a newspaper that covered largely general business—the *Saigon Times Daily* and *Vietnam News*the two dailiesand the *Sai Gon Giai Phong* newspaper—which is an organ of the of Communist Party of Viet Nam in Ho Chi Minh City—and hailed a taxi. Out of nostalgia, he spoke Vietnamese to the driver, although the man could speak English, and had the cabbie take him to the new Hotel Continental on Tu Do Street—number 132 to 134—new since 1989. He knew the address by memory.

He booked a room under his identity as a French citizen, using French to converse with the receptionist. He arranged for a "Superior Room" which the receptionist assured him was equipped with air-conditioner, IDD phone, satellite T.V, fire-alarm system, electric water heater, bath-tub, mini-bar, hair dryer, coffee and tea making facilities, toilet kit, complementary fresh fruits and daily newspaper, and that "all Superior Rooms have a superior garden view".

He sat on the bed and read the papers, looking for news about himself. The *Weekly* came out that morning and did not have a mention of him. The two dailies carried the story of the world wide manhunt that had been launched for him on a back page but did not include a photograph and did not have his current identity. He was described as an international terrorist and as the murderer of a large number of important diplomats and statesmen and of law enforcement officials in several countries. He also learned that the Israeli attack on Iran's nuclear assets had not yet resulted in retaliatory military action. President Storebridge and Iranian President Sofrekheneh were described as being "in consultation".

At this date, Sheep Dog was used to the new Continental Hotel, but had fond memories and considerable amusement for the venerable old French hotel of his Viet Nam War experience. Gone was the 'Continental Shelf'—so-called—which was the verandah of the Continental Palace Hotel where guests drank and dined in wicker chairs and learned everything there was worth knowing in Saigon. It was so-named—the newspapermen in the city had said—because one was likely to find so many odd fish there. Back then, it was located on Rue Catinat on the north side of the square. The *Le Perroquet* [Parrot] nightclub and cabaret that had been in the hotel lobby were gone, replaced by brass and glass. He had enjoyed many—probably too many—nights and too many drinks there in those days. The old hotel had been a handsome building with an attractive colonial façade—built in 1880 and host to dignitaries of the world—but needing a fresh coat of paint. The new hotel was more modern, cleaner, and more commodious, but less interesting.

To clear his head and to consider his situation, he waited for a *xy clo* and was taken towards the Saigon River. He walked the last kilometer down the narrow Tu Do Street through the old French Colonial heart of Saigon and sat on a bench absorbing the sense and culture of the city. In days past—after the war, when he sat on the same bench—he would be beset by seedy looking businessmen, displaced diplomats, clerics, and academics who wanted to practice their English with him and were hungry for news from the outside world. Now, no one paid him any mind. The sophisticated urbanites of the new world order in Viet Nam largely knew English; and their concerns centered on business, politics, technology, and their own vibrant social lives.

He crystallized what he had been considering during the flight into Viet Nam. He determined to remain in the country for an extended period of time and to contact his old friends for help in getting established in business, at least temporarily. Back at the Continental, he called his old friend and PRUC comrade, Yee Pang Hung.

A maid's voice answered in Mandarin. Sheep Dog asked if they could speak Vietnamese, and she shifted languages smoothly.

"How may I be of service?"

"I wish to speak to Mr. Yee, please."

"May I ask who is calling?"

"Tell him it is his old American business friend from the Starbright Corporation."

"Would you please hold, while I fetch him?"

"Certainly."

In three minutes, Yee's familiar voice came on the line, "Hunter, is that you?"

"In the flesh."

"What is going on with you? How are you holding up? I read about you in the papers this morning."

"I'd like to talk to you about all of that, but not on the phone. Could we get together?"

Sheep Dog had been concerned that his Vietnamese would be rusty, but it came back sufficiently so that the two men could converse fluently in the melodic tonal language.

"Where are my manners, my old comrade? You must come to dinner. In case you had not noticed, this is the week before *Tet Nguyen Dan*. You must celebrate with me and my family. We would be honored to see you again."

"The honor would be mine."

They arranged for Sheep Dog—known to them only as Hunter—to come to the Yee house in Cholon that evening at the dinner hour. Knowing that it would be a joyous but rather formal affair, Sheep Dog went shopping for some decent clothes. He got in a shower and a nap before the start of Tet Eve's formal activities.

The city had come alive in the past twenty-four hours, although the plans and preparations had been underway for at least the past two weeks for this most important of all Vietnamese holidays. *Tet Nguyen Dan* [Feast of the First Morning] is the Vietnamese celebration of the Chinese lunar New Year. The exact solar calendar date varies from year to year, but it occurs in late January or early February on the day of the full moon between the winter solstice and the spring equinox. Each year is named for an auspicious animal in the Chinese Zodiac in a repetitive series of twelve. This was the year of the monkey. Sheep Dog would never forget that 1968—the year of the incredible Tet Offensive—had also been the year of the monkey. The festivities of the week before Tet last seven days preceded by a week long flower festival. Saigon and Cholon were still resplendent with fresh blooms. Partly from memory of previous Tets, and partly from what he was seeing in this modern era that was not so different from the war days, it was the most beautiful and vibrant city Sheep Dog had ever seen.

Every drab little corner was festooned with a kumquat tree—which symbolize the coming of money into the household—a bouquet of flowers, or a small colorful ancestral shrine. This was the Eve of Tet, a spontaneous outburst of exuberance and an intense celebration of commitment to family. Fireworks exploded in the square and along the river—enough firecrackers to thwart the devils and make the already nervous Sheep Dog flinch a little. Fireworks of all descriptions were being sold in shops and by vendors throughout the city. By the time Sheep Dog reached the corner of Phung Hung and Nguyen Trai streets in Cholon, the noise was deafening.

Rapid-fire explosions were drowned out be even louder ones. Fire tops whirled off the balconies of houses along the streets, whirling and spinning into the sky in a myriad of colors. Rockets and shooting stars were fired off the balconies at hapless pedestrians, creating a thick, enveloping haze, a situation that pleased the Sheep Dog in search of anonymity. *Xy clos*, motos, cars, trucks, pedestrians, even little children playing their games in the streets, weaved in an out of traffic avoiding the larger pots of gun powder that were being fired off at random. Joss sticks were available in bales. The large red sticks—written in Chinese—promised good luck and wealth for the New Year.

Regular business, bowing to the inevitable, had ground to a virtual halt two weeks ago. Shops that had existed to sell clothing, electronics, or vegetables now operated twenty-four hours a day to make the favorite lotus seed candy or bean curd cakes, to dispense colored paper, or to provide noise makers—clackers—not unlike those the PRUCs used to use when they were in the field to signal one another. Occasionally, Tet dragons weaved through the narrow streets.

In a matter of seconds after he boarded his taxi, the air around them exploded with the noise of ten thousand drums beating and a hundred thousand fireworks bursting to bring in the Year of the Monkey. It was deafening and joyous—French Mardi Gras, Hindu Deevali, and American Fourth of July all put together. The city erupted into a great party ushering in seven days of colorful, fragrant, boisterous, noisy, and exhausting activities.

The week prior to Tet, Vietnamese perform the first and one of most important ceremonies of the year. It is necessary for each family to send its own household Hearth God up to heaven to make its yearly report to the Jade Emperor. In order to ensure a good report and therefore the benevolence of the Jade Emperor for the upcoming year, it is necessary to please the Hearth God; so, it can depart with a happy report. The whole family joins in to clean the entire house from top to bottom, inside and outside. The octagonal mirrors located in strategic places to reflect away bad spirits are polished until they sparkle and gleam. Walls are scrubbed and white washed; rugs are taken up and cleaned; and most important of all, the family altar is meticulously cared for. The graves of the ancestors are scrupulously swept, washed, and painted if necessary. The *Cay Neu*—New Year's Pole, or Signal Tree—with its attached clay bells, is set up in the yard or in the house. Lime powdered bow and arrow replicas are mounted in strategic places to frighten away the evil spirits. The people—especially the older ones—don their traditional conical hats and chew betel nuts, something they may not do otherwise all year long.

On Tet Eve, every effort is expended to ingratiate the ancestors and to make them feel at home with the family. *Tat nien,* the ceremonial dinner in honor of departed ancestors, is prepared with the finest New Year's foods. The entire family, nuclear and extended, gathers for one great feast and wishes each other "*Chuc Mung Nam Moi*"; "*song lau tram tuoi*" [live up to 100 years]— the traditional New Year wish for longevity from children to grandparents. Everyone is one year older on Tet. Other wishes are "*an khang thinh vuong*" [security, good health, and prosperity], "*van su nhu y*" [may a myriad of things go according to your will], "*suc hoe doi dao*" [plenty of health], and "*cung hi phat tai*" [happy New Year] in Mandarin or "*gung hay fat choy*" in Cantonese, and "*tien vo nhu nuac*" [may money flow like water].

Fathers read their children's horoscopes—their *tu vi*—and tell the story of the Jade Emperor and the legend of Tao Quan. A guest is greatly honored to be invited to one of these exclusive and festive family occasions, and it was a mark of the affection the family had for Hunter Caulfield for all of his kindnesses through the difficult years after the war that made him a guest of honor—one of the family.

It took more than an hour for Sheep Dog and his cab driver to weave their way through teeming Cholon [Vietnamese-*Cho Lan*, or "big market"] the name of the Chinese districts 5 and 6 of Ho Chi Minh City—the former Saigon. It lies on the west bank of the Saigon River and dominates the western part of the city. On an ordinary day, Cholon is a thickly settled district rife with teahouses, pagodas, small businesses, winding narrow streets, and narrow houses. It is an industrial center with many rice mills and factories and a bustling commercial center, Cholon is a fascinating maze of temples, restaurants, jade ornaments, and medicine shops. Gone—however—are the brothels and opium dens of earlier days when Sheep Dog first came to Viet Nam—the land of rice baskets balancing on a central pole—an allusion to the geographical shape of the country. On this Tet Eve, Cholon had the greatest and densest concentration of human beings on the planet.

The astute and experienced cabbie found Yee's house located on an obscure and unnamed side alley off Hung Phú Street. Like most houses in Saigon, and especially in Cholon, it was very narrow—the reason for the narrowness being the fact that Vietnam taxes homes primarily based on the size of the footprint, not the total square feet. The telephone poles along the street sported wires of all sizes and directions of connection, most to adjacent homes. At first glance, the arrangement appeared only happenstance; but in truth, the pattern was a tribute to the resolute frugality of the people of Cholon in dealing with their need for electricity and with their government.

Like their neighbors, the Yees had put their hearts and souls into decorating with red and gold, peach branches, kumquats, and a large *Cay Neu,* which reminded Sheep Dog of a totem pole. Theirs was a tall bamboo shaft flying the family's emblem on a piece of cloth to prevent the demons from coming in to disturb the family during Tet Eve dinner. The driveway was lit with Chinese New Year's paper lanterns that cast a softening golden light on the surrounding trees and flowers.

The cabbie parked; and Sheep Dog paid him, thanked him profusely for the safe ride, and gave him a large tip. A tiny Chinese maid welcomed him; he was expected. The house was an attractive Chinese home on the outside, but elegant and dramatic on the inside. The floors, walls, and ceiling were of teak—the floor polished to a mirror finish as were the walls and ceiling intricately carved panels. There were ornamental lacquer-ware screens, duck and chicken egg shell paintings, photographs of ancestors with incense and small offerings of oranges and bananas in front of them. There was an ancestral shrine covered with gold name inscriptions. The maid showed him into the main sitting room to await the arrival of Yee Pang Hung, his wife, Noi, and their three grown children and fifteen grandchildren. Around the periphery of the room were arranged Ming porcelain stools and vases in the shape of elephants holding potted palms. The walls held elegant Chinese calligraphy scroll paintings. Jade figurines sat in wall niches.

Chapter Fifty-Four

The family greeted Sheep Dog effusively.

"Hung," Sheep Dog said, "it is so good of you to have me tonight of all nights. You are most kind."

"It is our great pleasure. Come, it is time for the feast to begin."

Sheep Dog and the family, including a large extended family that he did not know, took their seats at the elegant oriental hardwood communal table. There was one empty place at the table symbolic of the missing ancestors, and each member of the family gave a small respectful nod to the special place of honor as they walked past. The table was bare except for a large centerpiece of fresh cut tropical flowers. It was made of Chinese teak and was inlaid with a mother of pearl avian design. The chairs were of matching material and design. There was an antique hand knotted Chinese rug on the cherry wood parquet floor.

Servants—as quiet and unobtrusive as ghosts—entered the room and began to serve the appetizers: shrimp toast and small dishes of melon seeds and pine nuts, bowls of celestial soup, and scallions in peanut oil and soy sauce, spiced with cloves.

The appetizer dishes, bowls, and ceramic utensils were swiftly cleared away, and the servants brought in the main dishes: Five Flower Pork and Pork with Bitter Melon, Hand Pressed Duck, Drunken Chicken, Red Simmered Fish with Snow-Peas, and the *pièce de résistance*, Peking Duck, served with steaming cups of aromatic tea. Dessert was Almond Float and *Hung Pien*—Chrysanthemum tea sweetened with rock sugar. The table was cleared again and tiny porcelain glasses of amber colored *Shaoshing*—yellow wine—were distributed for a series of toasts to the family and for the New Year. The delicate vessels were decorated with a reverse swastika design for good luck. Strains of five tone Vietnamese music were played by the girls of the family on three stringed Chinese lutes, on *kin* flutes, and *dan thap luc* [sixteen stringed zithers].

The family separated by age and gender. Children went with nannies for sweets and games. Women retired to their section of the house for gossip, and the men all moved into a plush sitting room. Servants brought in bamboo pipes for the men who reclined on cushions. Sheep Dog elected only to watch, but noticed that Hung readily accepted his pipe. The pipes were two feet long, made of straight bamboo with brass or ivory at the ends. Two-thirds of the way down the shaft of the pipe was the bowl, darkened and polished by the long history and frequent kneading of the gum ball of opium on its convex surface.

The servants—this time, all women—dressed in brightly patterned Ao Dai and impeccably clean full white silk trousers, placed a needle into the small cavity of the bowl and released the opium then reversed the bowl to heat it over a small flame. The beads of opium bubbled and popped quietly as the men inhaled the pungent thick smoke. Conversa-ion waned as the men of the family became tranquil and sleepy. As the hour approached midnight, most of them were sound asleep from several pipes, some able to inhale a whole pipe in one breath; and the room was fragrant and dreamy with the narcotic smoke.

Before he fell asleep, Hung leaned over to Sheep Dog and said languidly, "My friend, we will talk tomorrow about your future."

It was the Vietnamese way not to mix business talk during a meal, and it would have been considered a gross impropriety for Sheep Dog to have brought up his problems or requests during any family meal, let alone the Tet Eve feast.

He had learned patience during his war-time stays and his subsequent visits to Viet Nam, and he would undoubtedly have to learn more. He found a small bed room, undressed and fell asleep promptly on the rattan mat on the floor. His belly was full; he was safe for now; and he was at peace. The future did not seem so uncertain or terrifying as it had during the long past night and the hectic day.

CHAPTER FIFTY-FIVE

The hectic events of the Eve of Tet were over; and the first day of Tet was—as usual—going to be quiet. It was a day for families to eat picnics in the cemetery and to have simple meals at home. It was a clean-up day after the high spirits of the night before. Sheep Dog awakened before anyone else in the house, stretched and dressed, and walked out into the court yard to listen to the distant sounds of the morning. He stepped through the Judas Gate in the side yard fence and watched the city wake up.

The day was slowly getting into motion. Here and there an occasional person was warming up with Tai Chi exercises. A pig merchant was carefully laying out the parts of a hog on his sidewalk table while his son carted away the entrails of the animal on his *xy clo*. The blood and water used to wash it away were still collected in eddying puddles around the man's stall. The ubiquitous rice merchants were now awake and could be heard calling out to passers by. Two shaven head bonzes in their gray-brown robes were walking slowly by with their empty rice bowls in one hand. Thus far, they were finding no givers. A wheel of a cart load of squealing and lamenting piglets was stuck in the crack between the board walk and the open sewer trench running alongside it. Carts overloaded with chickens, ducks, shop surplus, vegetables and fruits, and used clothing began to make their way out into the market day traffic.

A few children were still lighting firecrackers to ward off evil spirits and were lingering near the stalls of fireworks dealers hoping to be able to snatch up one of the displayed explosives. Before breakfast, Sheep Dog walked a short way up the street browsing at the stalls selling everything from bicycle parts, to condoms, to Vietnamese, American, and Russian cigarettes, to bottled water and packed rice balls. Sheep Dog bought a bottle of nongaseous Evian water and a few left over New Year's cookies and ate them with chips of dried mandarin peelings and licorice root. The street was lined with kumquat trees and further beautified by the numerous collections of apricot flowers, peach blossoms, and artificial flowers of all descriptions. The twenty-four hour flower markets were beginning to pick up business after the early morning lull.

Hung came out of his room and sat down with the family at the breakfast table. He had the servants bring a fruit bowl and American corn flakes with milk for his breakfast. They ate in silence. When the dishes were removed, Hung began the conversation.

"We should come right to the point, Hunter. What can I do for you? I owe you a great deal, but I also must protect my family."

"I do not ask for anything owed, Hung. And I will go to almost any lengths to avoid endangering you or your family. I need to hide in plain sight in Viet Nam. I have given a great deal of thought to what has to be done. My plan is to settle for a while in or around Hué. I need your help to get through the red tape; so, I can purchase a little land and a house. I will operate my part of a business largely from there. I am asking you to get in touch with the PRUCs still in Viet Nam and get them to take me on as a nonpublic partner in one or more of their businesses. I will use a false name, of course.

"I will make my presence worth any small risk anyone considers is present by investing substantial sums in the business. I will also promise to give $10 million to be distributed by your network to the PRUC wives and families left behind and abandoned by the United States. Would that be sufficient?"

"That would be more than generous. As you Americans are so fond of saying, it would be a win/win arrangement. Do you have objections to entering into a partnership with one of the tongs?"

"Tongs, no; but I would be very leery about starting up a close association with one of the major triads. I am already in a risky position, and I would hate to make it worse."

"I cannot promise that I can find a business that is free of criminal taint, but I can assure you that I will not steer you to anything that I would not invest my family's money in."

"Hung, I know you had a terrible time in the re-education camps and in paying off your debts to the state. I also know that you and your family have worked hard all these years. You have done very well for yourself. I would be less than honest if I didn't tell you that I suspect that you crossed several lines outside legal boundaries over the years. You are crafty and careful, and you appear to have covered yourself."

"The money you gave us made all the difference, Hunter. I speak for all of the PRUCs and their families in saying that. I know that you have been of help to all of them."

"You are my friends. I trusted you during the war, and you covered my back. I could not turn that same back on any of you."

"And we all trust you. You gave us money and help in getting some of our people out, and you asked for nothing. I will help you, and I will get the others to help. We will ask nothing in return either. You need help. That is enough for me. I believe we can make you disappear in Viet Nam while you prosper. Today, we will make our separate ways into the Cho Binh Tay Market to meet with the head of the Chou Yen Lee Family tong. Do you know where it is?"

"Of course. What time?"

"Two hours. Keep a low profile until then and watch around the market for police or security people. When you see me enter the market, follow at a distance. I will move quickly; so keep a good watch."

"I'll be careful."

Sheep Dog wondered what he had gotten himself into now. It had all the earmarks of joining up with Chinese bandits, but it was late in the day to be dainty or choosy. He arrived in the market area less than fifteen minutes later—more than an hour and a half early—and slowly sauntered through Cholon. He made himself into a tourist with short trips to see the seven sacred pagodas in Cholon: Thien Hau, Nghia An Hoi Quan, Tam Son Hoi Quan, Quan Am, Phuoc An Hoi Quan, Ha Chuong Hoi Quan, Ong Bon, the Giac Lam and Giac Vien Pagodas away from the main concentration of sacred buildings, Giac Vien, and Giac Lam, the oldest pagoda. He was very familiar with all of the pagodas, having hidden out in several of them during the murderous VC rampage during Tet, 1968.

He saw Hung enter Cho Binh Tay Market without looking back, and he moved double time to keep up. They passed several dozen small to tiny stalls hawking everything from hats to ladies dresses, to medicines, spices, bolts of gorgeous brilliantly colored silk, men's pants, cooking utensils, and hapless ducks, and chickens tied in piles infested with flies. Hung paused at the largest fruit-vendor's stall in the middle of the market and spoke briefly to a fat Han Chinese man in a fruit-smeared white apron. The main attraction of his stall was apparently rambutan—the unattractive but delicious so-called hairy lychee fruit. An oddity of that stall was that it also sold ladies' shoes and hand-made steel screen colanders as well. The Chinese vendor turned and walked away from Hung. He looked back at Sheep Dog and made a small sideways nod to follow. They followed in a circuitous route to avoid suspicion and walked into the front of a three story building that appeared to be an office building. The three met at the doors of the elevator. A sign over the doors stated that no person weighing over 146 pounds could enter, and a weight of 800 pounds was the total acceptable limit. The elevator was only six feet high. It would hardly have served in America.

None of the men spoke or acknowledged each other's presence. They rode the elevator to the third floor with Sheep Dog stooping and glad that there were no more than three floors. They followed the vendor to a door over which—in Unicode rendering of Vietnamese characters—read: "Chou Yen Lee Family Tong". They entered into a spacious, well-appointed office and sat in red and gold brocade easy chairs as they were directed. The three men sat quietly for a few minutes until an office side door opened, and two large Chinese men in suits preceded a thin, wiry Caucasian into the room. He was dressed in cotton cargo pants, a Philippine barong, and scuffed open-toed sandals. Sheep Dog was aware from the outset by the demeanor of the new man and all of those in the room, that he was in charge, an incongruous situation given that they were in the heart of the largest Chinatown in the world.

"Are you Hunter Caulfield, formerly seconded to the CIA's Phoenix Program?" the newcomer asked without preamble or greeting.

"Yes."

Sheep Dog felt uncomfortable and began to tense. He watched the eyes and hands of all of the men in the room constantly.

"You've aged some. Not as much as me, but I have led a dissolute life here in-country. I take it you don't recognize me. Tsk, tsk, I'm hurt."

Sheep Dog strained but could not put a name to the face and body. He was looking at a man of probably sixty-five, but who looked to be in his early eighties. He shook his head.

The newcomer laughed, revealing a mouthful of yellowed and carious teeth and periodontal disease.

"I'm Roger Ward. That ring a bell?"

"You can't be. You're dead!" Sheep Dog exclaimed.

Roger laughed heartily, "As Mark Twain said, 'the news of my death is premature'. I am very much alive, a fact that disturbs more than a few people.

However—and I stress the importance of the fact—the United States government considers me to be dead; and that is the best thing about my being alive."

"So, you stayed on here, is that it?"

"You got it. I deserted to Cholon in late '74 and ignored the amnesty offered by the State Department when the U.S. occupation ended in '75 along with a couple of hundred guys. I had too cushy of a life to leave here. Admittedly—it was a life of crime—but who is it that can be a judge? the Bible asks. Smuggling, gun, and drug running provided wealth, women, and influence; and I developed a loyal group of friends here in Cholon and throughout Asia. Our business interests webbed out to most of the developed world. We have done well enough to have gone legit almost entirely in the last ten years."

"So, you're the head of the Chou Yen Lee Family tong, I take it."

"In all humility, yes. It is what business law in the U.S. refers to as a 'fictitious name'." He smiled. "As a result of our efforts in several directions, we do maintain some valuable connections outside the strictly kosher world however. Hung tells me that you might have need of some help that would involve such connections."

"Apparently, I do."

"Well, Hunter, we read the papers. You seem to be standing in it up to your lower lip at the moment. That about right?"

"Yeah, I suppose so."

"Look, Hunter, you're among friends here. You and I gave it all we had in the Phoenix Program and were rewarded by being branded as something just short of criminals when the effort to democratize Viet Nam went south. You and I both know that it would have been imprudent of us—or of any of the PRUCs—to make our pasts known. I know you kept a low profile in that regard. I also know that you gave a lot of help to our comrades all over the place. We have a pretty tight organization, and we try to help each other when we can. We can give you a hand."

"Thanks, Roger."

Sheep Dog thanked his lucky stars that he and Roger had covered each others' backs several times during the tumultuous Viet Nam War era, and that they had been cordial if not actually friends. He was also glad that the man was still alive. He looked like he had one foot in the grave and the other on a banana peel, however.

Roger walked over to where Hunter was sitting and extended his hand. Sheep Dog stood, and the two men shook hands warmly.

"You look like you're still hale and hearty, Hunter. Must eat right and stay away from demon rum and nasty habits."

"I've tried. You look like maybe you've been having a little trouble in the health department."

"Liver cancer. My own fault. I got into meth. It was stupid—cost me my teeth, my strength, and is going to cost me my life in a year or two. I'm glad I was still around to help set you up."

"I'm sorry to hear that, Roger. Thanks for thinking of me."

Roger shrugged, an admission of his own culpability.

With that, the men began to discuss a plan for Sheep Dog. It was obvious that Hung and Roger had put considerable thought into the matter. Sheep Dog was to become a planter outside the ancient Vietnamese capital of Hué under a new French *nom de guerre*. His connections with the triads in Hong Kong would provide Roger with the means to get new and authentic documents for Sheep Dog. He and Hung had already contacted their legitimate associates in Hué and Hanoi to set in progress the purchase of land and of a partnership in the business.

"It'll take a bit of money, I'm afraid," Roger said. "the communist government here likes a bit of a bribe to hasten the process. Otherwise you would be an old decrepit man before all of their red tape was satisfied."

"I have a bit," Sheep Dog told him, "how much do you think?"

"All told, to keep everybody happy, and happy means quiet, about ten mil U.S."

He said it without a flinch as if he were estimating the cost of today's groceries.

"I can do that and better. I promised Hung a similar sum to be spread out among the families the PRUCs had to leave behind. I assume you and your people can make that happen. I've come into some money—the source of which I don't want to share with the public or any of several governments—and I want to use some of it to help the cause."

"We'll be glad to help. You'll have to trust us. There won't be much in the way of accounting."

"I trust you."

Sheep Dog did, although that trust was not entirely complete.

He would hedge his bets with Hung and Roger until he had collected evidence that his trust was justified. He retained the powerful self-protective feeling that he was not quite out of the woods yet.

CHAPTER FIFTY-SIX

Two Days after the Israeli attack on Iran's WMD Facilities Interagency Fugitive Operations Office, Brooklyn Court Street Federal Building.

U.S. Marshals, Frank Jefferys and Linc Goodworth fidgeted with their reports, with their uniforms, with lunch, with anything to cut the boredom. They had not had a takedown assignment for three days, and the idleness was wearing on the two action-junky law enforcement specialists. Frank watched the fax and teletype hoping for the tell-tale sounds of an incoming message. Linc stated that he could not, would not touch another drop of the crude oil that passed for coffee in the cluttered IFO office. He thought about cleaning up the clutter; but it seemed pointless; so, he let it go. It was a sign of desperation that he even thought about it.

Except for the clutter—the room was drab and dull—almost sterile. There were mandatory large photographs adorning the west wall of President Storebridge, Attorney General Gertrude Heimel, and USMS Director Colin McPherson. Haphazardly placed on the drab, but spotlessly clean brick walls, were New York City maps, most-wanted posters of federal fugitives from FBI, ATF, DEA, and United States Marshals' Service sources, computer printouts of crime statistics and current statuses of some the truly most wanted, large print copies of federal regulations, and two No Smoking signs. There was no graffiti, no jokes of any kind, no personal memorabilia, and no photographs other than those of the most senior U.S. government officials and service directors.

There were regulation steel lockers and gun cabinets lined up neatly against the walls all around the room. A soft drink dispenser sat on one wall, and a coffee maker and small folding table with cups on another. In the rear of the room was a windowless steel door that led to the holding cells. The room contained fifteen desks; each desk had an uncomfortable straight back steel chair. There was no privacy, no interview room, and no comfort.

The desks were regulation gun-metal grey and had all accumulated piles of paper—mostly unfinished reports—the bane of the existence of the officers and the secretaries, and a top of the line latest computer through which most of the information passed and most of the communications work got done. Unlike the offices of the USMS Bronx unit's squad room, everything was clean; there was no tobacco smell or pollution of the stale air in the stuffy room, and everything was painted on a regular basis.

The fax machine stood in the middle of the room for the convenience of all of the officers who had occasion to work in or pass through the office. Both Frank and Linc jumped when the fax machine came to life. They hurried over to watch the bulletin print out an IFN [Interagency Fugitive Notice].

MESSAGE BEGINS

Message Origin: United States Department of Justice

Date and time of Transmission: 17 January, 0921

Message Recipients: Lead and Communications responsibility—IFO (Interagency Fugitive Operations); USMS (All 94 offices), FBI, ATF, DEA, JTF-6, NCIC, VICAP, FLO, NYPD FAT SQUAD, INS, CIA, NSC, ALL STATE AND D.C. POLICE AND MAJOR CITY POLICE OFFICES, ALL FPUs and STATE PURSUIT UNITS.

Canada: CPIC, FIRS-Nationwide.

U.K.: Scotland Yard, U.K. wide Special Police Forces, SOCA-Serious Organized Crime Agency,

France: *Gendarmerie National, Police Nationale*

Russia: Federal Security Service (FSB), Ministry of Internal Affairs Militsiya, OMON: Russian—Отряд милиции особого назначения; *Otryad Militsii Osobogo Naznacheniya*, Special Purpose Police Unit (*OMOH*)

Subject: Hunter (NMN) Caulfield, Capt. USN, AD.

Criminal counts. Felony: CHAPTER 7—ASSAULT, paragraph 111, Assaulting, resisting, or impeding certain officers or employees, paragraph 115, Influencing, impeding, or retaliating against a Federal official by threatening or injuring a family member; CHAPTER 35—ESCAPE, paragraph 751; Prisoners in custody of institution or officer, paragraph 758, High speed flight from immigration checkpoint; CHAPTER 40—IMPORTATION, MANUFACTURE, DISTRIBUTION AND STORAGE OF EXPLOSIVE MATERIALS, paragraph 842, unlawful acts; CHAPTER 41—EXTORTION AND THREATS, paragraph 878, Threats and extortion against foreign officials, official guests, or internationally protected persons; CHAPTER 43—FALSE PERSONATION, paragraph 912, Officer or employee of the United States; CHAPTER 44—FIREARMS, paragraph 922. Unlawful acts, 926 A., Interstate transportation of firearms and 929, Use of restricted ammunition; CHAPTER 51—HOMICIDE, paragraph 1111, class A felony murder, 1112, manslaughter, and 1113, attempt to commit murder or manslaughter; 1116. Murder or manslaughter of foreign officials, official guests, or internationally protected persons; CHAPTER 55—KIDNAPPING, paragraph 1203, hostage taking; CHAPTER 75—PASSPORTS AND VISAS, paragraphs 1541, Issuance without authority, 1542, False statement in application and use of passport, 1543, Forgery or false use of passport, 1544, Misuse of passport, 1546, Fraud and misuse of visas, permits, and other documents; Chapter 113 B—TERRORISM, paragraph 2332b Acts of terrorism transcending national boundaries, 2332d Financial transactions, 2332f Bombings of places of public use, government facilities, public transportation systems, and infrastructure facilities

BOLO-See CIA internal communication US9164-CT 4779, 0107TWEP.

Description:
See BOLO

Comment: Fugitive is an expert marksman, martial artist, a master of disguises, and a pitiless killer capable of using multiple lethal methods.
He is presumed to be heavily armed and willing to resort to violence at any instance in which his freedom is threatened. He is extremely dangerous and should be approached only with a JTF-6 or police swat team equivalent. He will not hesitate to kill law enforcement officers or bystanders. Use of deadly force is approved unless the fugitive complies with lawful commands immediately.

Linc Goodworth waited until Frank Jefferys finished reading, then the senior Marshal said, "Ya know, I have been at this for eighteen years. I have never seen a CIA fugitive memo like this except for the ones put out on Ilich Ramírez Sánchez in 1975…"

"Who?"

"Before your time. Before mine actually. He was the famous killer/terrorist, Carlos, the Jackal."

"Oh yeah, I seen the movie."

"I just read about him. Anyway—as I was about to say—the other one was what they put out on bin Laden. Obama guaranteed his presidency by killing that terrorist. This guy must be one baad hombre. They've sent this "Be-On-the-Look-Out-for" to everybody in the world. They want him bad."

"It'd make a guy's career, wouldn't it Linc? You'd go from a GS-11 to the USMS HQ in Arlington, and I'd go from GS-8 to a GS-12 even at my tender age. I'd have a real shot at the director's chair one day."

"Dream on Frank; dream on. We have about as much chance of seeing this guy as we had of seeing bin Laden come in here and give himself up back in the day. Ya know, I don't want ever to get anywhere near this rattlesnake. I believe the spooks and the fibbies when they say this is a *muy malo hombre*."

"How about we pull up the BOLO?" Frank suggested, his curiosity and excitement piqued.

Linc messed with the computer for a minute and got into the file.

BOLO- CIA internal communication US9164-CT 4779, 0107TWEP.

From: Office of the DCIA

To. ALL OFFICERS

Subject Hunter Caulfield is an active duty naval officer seconded to Central Intelligence. He is a rogue agent who is responsible for several hundred killings, presumably as a contract agent for a foreign power. He was assigned to analysis duties with the Department of Agriculture on assignment in the NASS; the USDA's National Agricultural Statistics Service working on RSS—Rich Site Summary feeds. He was responsible for research and reporting activity on Web sites that contain article headlines, summaries, and links back to full-text articles on the Web. His specific interest was the FAS—Foreign Agricultural Service. Agency evidence indicates that he used the cover of his rather mundane analysis work to allow him to pursue his role as a professional assassin. He is known to have killed at least five federal agents.

Description:

DOB-07/30/1950

Blood Type- A+, DNA on file with DOD and CIA

Race-Caucasian. Light complexion

Hair-Dark brown and graying. Variable hair styles.

Height-6"2'

Weight-225 pounds

Build-Athletic, muscular, slim

Tattoos-None

Marks and Scars-Multiple over almost every part of his body, including knife and gunshot wound scars, burn scars. Long diagonal left facial scar. See included photos.

"Scary dude. He's been through the mill, looks like."

"Amen."

"Still, I'd like a shot at him."

"Your funeral."

Hunter stayed an extra day at the Continental, then, as instructed by Roger Ward, took a night flight on Viet Nam Airlines to Phú Bài Airport, south of Hué, the old imperial capital. He picked up a copy of the *Vietnam News* for 5,000 VND, a *Washington Post* printed in Hué with a major emphasis on Viet Nam for 6,000 dong, and that week's *Economist* for 10,000. The exchange rate for one Vietnamese dong that day was 19,150 VND to one USD. Sheep Dog had had only Euros since he arrived in France, and that day he was getting 26,400 VND to 1 Euro. It was mildly amusing to have to stuff so much cash into his sport coat pocket.

He found a waiting taxi and haggled over the price for the trip into central Hué to 52 Le Loi Street, the Huong Giang Hotel. They settled on a price of 191,000 VND which substantially diminished his load of paper. He skimmed the reading material on the way to the hotel and found that now his name appeared prominently along with his picture, but only on mid-back pages of the publications. The real news was about the Israeli attack. Full front page articles and photographs told of and showed the devastation wrought on the Iranian nuclear facilities. The Iranian foreign minister decried the attack as "barbaric"; the defense minister avowed that the Iranian military was only "biding its time" before launching an all-out retaliation, and the interior minister told of the massive reconstruction effort that would be required to bury all of the radioactive waste.

A Reuters reporter quoted the interior minister as saying, "We have received generous offers of financial aid from the United States, and the government of the Islamic Republic of Iran will consider the offer with caution. We welcome the overture, but the climate of mistrust between our two countries will have to improve before we can accept assistance."

Hunter left the publications on the back seat of the cab when he arrived at the hotel.

He had always been fond of the Huong Giang Hotel, named for the beautiful clean blue Perfume River on whose bank the hotel sat. The river was named for the pungent aroma it once had from upstream cinnamon factories. The hotel was modern and commodious. A call came in shortly after he had settled in. Nguyen Tran Ky, senior partner of the Chou Yen Lee Family tong in Hué, welcomed him to the imperial city and asked if he would care to meet him for dinner that evening.

The two men took their seats for dinner at the Song Huong Floating Restaurant on the perfume River between the Huong Giang Hotel and the old Clemenceau Bridge. They passed only polite dinner conversation until after coffee, then Mr. Nguyen got to the matters of importance.

He spoke French, "Monsieur Le Croix, you are quite evidently a man of substance and an old friend of the family. It is my honor and pleasure to welcome you to the city. I was busy yesterday and was successful in finding what I hope will be an appropriate location—private and comfortable—for you to live here, and I will be able to include you among the partners in our Hué Import-Export Enterprises. That should give you plenty of time and opportunity to travel if you wish. Also, I have taken the liberty of some minor editing in your history with the company. You will find that you have been a corporate officer for over a decade. Is such a…how shall we say… "creative historical revision" acceptable?"

Sheep Dog laughed and said, "Eminently."

"Good. Why don't we take a small motor trip out to your new estate and to the office tomorrow. If it suits you, we will be able to finalize formalities at the land office and get you into an office in our building."

"I would like to get over the financial transactions as soon as we can; so, we can begin working together."

"Most of that can also be taken care of at the office tomorrow."

The next day started as a beautiful sunny, but quite chilly, morning. Sheep Dog had coffee and toast in the restaurant and walked out to see the day. Shortly, a limo pulled up and Sheep Dog joined Nguyen Tran Ky in the rear seating area; and they left for a brief whirlwind tour of the city and east into the countryside beyond the last named thoroughfare, Duong Van An Street. Mr. Nguyen gave the driver a series of directions leading a complicated route around poorly maintained dirt roads. They stopped about ten kilometers east of the outermost reaches of the main city in a small grove of trees bordering a large expanse of open fields. Mr. Nguyen pointed to the east.

"The family owns this beautiful piece of land and is willing to sell it to you at a reasonable cost. We ask four million dollars. However, you must realize that the government does not allow foreigners to own property in the Democratic Republic of Viet Nam; but rather, you have to lease it for 99 years. Is that acceptable to you?"

"Yes."

"Good, then we need only sign the proper papers back at the office, and you will have a part of the country where you can reside in peace and safety. You may build, irrigate, fence, and enhance the property as you wish."

"Thank you for your courtesy and help, Mr. Nguyen. May I ask how many acres there are in the parcel?"

"Seventeen. You will find the survey markers easily. They are brilliant red with gold lettering, and there are a plethora of them."

"I'll walk it tomorrow."

They were then driven back to the tong's office at 612 Tran Quang Khai Street near Tu Do Stadium where Mr. Nguyen and three accountants explained the business of Hué Import-Export Enterprises, and Sheep Dog's role in the company. It was apparent that beyond his initial buy-in costs, little would be expected of him in the way of work. Mr. Nguyen made it clear; however, that, if he wanted to do so, he would be welcome to serve as a consultant and, in time, to work his way into an actual directorship role. That was fine with Sheep Dog. He went on-line and transferred $10 million to the treasurer of the company and another $10 million to the charity arm of Hué Import-Export Enterprises, called The Golden Helping Hands.

Mr. Nguyen bade Sheep Dog farewell and had him driven back to the Huong Giang Hotel. It was noon. In four hours, Sheep Dog had started a new, hopefully secure, life in the Democratic Republic of Viet Nam as the Frenchman, Jean-Luc Le Croix. He remained in the hotel another two nights before paying his bill—using his old credit card under the name of Stefan Danglois—then discarded all documents in that name.

CHAPTER FIFTY-SEVEN

The manhunt began in earnest as soon as the DOJ Memo was circulated. It was hampered by the conflict of interest imposed on the federal agencies by the presidential order shifting the major emphasis in all law enforcement to the problem of maintaining the red alert following the attack on Iran. That decision was proving to be immensely expensive, both in terms of financial cost, but also because of the intensive concentration of man hours to the tasks. The directors of the federal law enforcement agencies began to worry about the expense and the increasing general crime rates within a week of the imposition of the presidential order and began to complain after two weeks during which there was no increase in terrorism activity. Local and state law enforcement agencies were overwhelmed by the costs and the dramatic increase in crime that took place as soon as the order took effect andafter three weeksdemanded a reduction in the alert status. Reluctantly, President Storebridge backed down to orange status one month after the issuance of his order while still keeping a heavy emphasis by the intelligence assets on homeland security concerns.

The day the DOJ memo was circulated about Hunter Caulfield's murderous and terroristic activities—which made him the planet's public enemy number one—almost every officer not directly involved in protecting the United States from attack was assigned to the "Catch the Hunter" detail. The newspapers and magazines were flooded with information on the terrorist and the manhunt. The *America's Most Wanted* television show hosted by John Walsh, featured the "Catch the Hunter" fugitive apprehension issue twice in the first month.

Police stations and federal law enforcement offices held regular briefing sessions. Special units were established just to try and deal with the flood of sightings and reports of suspicious persons resembling Captain Caulfield. Confidential Informants were diverted from their usual activities as snitches about common criminal activities and onto the search. In an average year, the federal government pays out between $25 and $100 million to CIs. In the first month alone after the manhunt was inaugurated, the government paid out $14 million. 25,000 separate reports from the public had to be investigated the first month.

Law enforcement—faced with the twin emergencies of the homeland security issue and the "Catch the Hunter" issue—had to cancel vacations, pay for a significant amount of overtime, and to explain why the crime rate was increasing so dramatically to an increasingly unhappy American public. Much the same situation existed throughout the cooperating world beyond the United States. By the end of the first month, it was obvious that the compounding homeland security and manhunt activities were unproductive and unsustainable; and the agencies began to ratchet down their intensity and to return to more usual pursuits. The news media began to lose interest, concluding that the news cycle for both issues had run its course.

White House Oval Office: Conference, 1300
Present: POTUS, VPOTUS, SECRETARY OF STATE, SECRETARY OF DEFENSE, SECRETARY OF HOMELAND SECURITY, CHAIRMAN JCS, DFBI, DCIA, ADCIA, DUSMS, ATTORNEY GENERAL

"That was a fine lunch, Andrew," The president said to the steward after he and the other federal officials left the West Wing dining room.

They adjourned to the Oval Office for the status report meeting.

"First, the status of the intelligence related to the likelihood of the Iranians attacking Israel."

Secretary of Defense Michael Chisholm summed up the first five days after the attack succinctly, "So far so good. We have nothing to indicate that they have done anything more than to get their air force—what is left of it—ready for defensive measures. They are not—at present—on an attack readiness status."

The DCIA nodded his agreement.

"That can only be good news. Gerald, Jeremy, anything from the Israelis indicating that they have any further aggression planned?"

"No, Mr. President. PM Cohen, Foreign Minister Leibowitz, and General ben Moises all act chagrined and are emphatic that the attack was successful enough for them; and they have nothing further planned. I wouldn't go so far as to say that they are repentant, but I think they have had as much of the world's scorn as they can handle for the time being," the secretary of State answered.

"It goes without saying that we have to keep our surveillance up."

"We are not slacking off a bit, Mr. President," the DCIA said.

"Now, how about an update on the manhunt for the world's public enemy number one? Gentlemen, the marshal's service is represented by Director Colin McPherson; I'm sure you all know him. And we also have the DFBI Sinclair Thompson with us this afternoon. Let's hear from Mr. McPherson first. Colin?"

"Along with the FBI and everything the DOJ can provide, we have just about carpeted the world's law enforcement agencies, the news media, and John Q Public with information about Hunter Caulfield. We are keeping up a relentless drive to get the public—and especially, the snitches—to keep a sharp lookout. It's early yet, but he'll turn up. Nobody can escape a dragnet of this magnitude and intensity for long."

"It's a messy business. Let's hope it ends soon. I tell you, I dread the man's upcoming trial. What do you think the chances are of him allowing himself to be taken alive?"

"Slim to none, and I mean, very slim, Mr. President," Attorney General Gertrude Heimel answered. "I agree with Mr. McPherson that it will be over soon, and probably with a fatality."

"Couldn't happen to a nicer guy," McPherson said.

Sheep Dog walked south from the hotel on Le Loi Street to the Phú Xuán bridge across the Perfume River to the Citadel. He spent the morning wandering around the venerable old imperial capital buildings. He could not shake the bitter memories of having been there during the Battle of Tet, 1968. After a light lunch purchased from a street vendor, he hired a *xy clo* and took a leisurely sightseeing trip around Hué during the afternoon. His first stop was at the Thieves Market on Tran Thuc Nhan Street where he bought three Philippine Barongs for 191, 500 VND, then he had the driver take him to see the old imperial tombs

On the south side of the Huong Giang lay the modern city with its fifty year old university, the university library, and the refurbished French style Provincial Capitol building, the country club, the Cercle Sportif with its well manicured wide green lawns stretching along the river, the Hue' City Hospital at number 16 Le Loi Street, and a triangular shaped residential district. During the war, there had been the USN boat ramp directly across from the Citadel and the MACV compound, both long gone. The nation and the city had done a superb job to preserve the city's history; the outskirts of the south side contained seven imperial tombs, the most splendid being the Minh Man, Tu Duc, and Khai Dinh which were all Sheep Dog had time to explore during that single afternoon.

Over the next month, he worked on fleshing out his newest pseudo-identity as Jean-Luc Le Croix, importer/exporter and gentleman farmer. He kept out of the public's eye as he grew a Van Dyke beard. He looked very much the role of an expatriate French planter, and found his French to be improving with every day in the country. He secured a reputable builder on advice from the members of the tong and commenced building. It was far easier to get things moving than it had ever been in the states where he did not have the clout afforded by the tong.

He fell into a routine: up early for a run, followed by a hard contact workout at a martial arts studio that practiced a combination of two Vietnamese arts, *Tay Son Binh Dinh*, and *Tay Son Nhan*, which developed during the violent Tay Son Rebellion of 1771 to 1778. After several months in the studio and proving his bona fides as a martial artist, he was accepted enough to be able to introduce some elements of Krav Maqa, Brazilian Jiu Jitsu, and taekwondo, thus enabling him to learn some new skills and to hone his previous ones. Every day he spent an hour or two exploring Hué and its environs and some days ventured north to Hanoi or south to his old stomping grounds in Da Nang and as far as Hội An principle municipality. Afternoons were spent at the office and periodically at the wharf directing the loading of merchandise. He did not always check very closely on the contents of some boxes, usually the ones bound for Hong Kong.

Chapter Fifty-Seven

**3 Months after the Israeli Raid on Iran's WMD Facilities
Interagency Fugitive Operations Office, Brooklyn Court Street
Federal Building.**

USMS INTRA-AGENCY MEMO
MEMO BEGINS

Date and Time of Transmission: 12 March, 0800

Recipients: All Offices, All Marshals

See BOLO- CIA internal communication US9164-CT 4779, 0107TWEP

Subject: Hunter (NMN) Caulfield, Capt. USN/AD. Fugitive Warrant

World-wide fugitive apprehension effort has been extremely costly financially and in expenditure of man-hours. To date, tens of thousands of reported sightings of the fugitive have been investigated, thousands of interviews conducted, and hundreds of search warrants have been processed without useful results.

Conclusion and Recommendations: The fugitive has eluded capture to date and there are currently no definite indications of the location of the fugitive. One definite lead involved his use of an alias, Stefan Danglois, French national, who is known to have fled Paris following the murder of a U.S. federal agent, en route to Ho Chi Minh City, Viet Nam. There has been no record of the suspect having left Viet Nam; but a high-profile search of that Southeast Asian nation has not borne fruit; and it is the conclusion of the USMS, FBI, CIA and others involved in that search that the fugitive has eluded law enforcement and has left the Democratic Republic of Viet Nam to a location or locations unknown in an unlawful effort to avoid prosecution. There is agreement among services to limit further efforts at apprehension to a routine basis.

Marshals Linc Goodworth and Frank Jefferys read the message with the bored expressions of cops who had seen it all before.

Linc said, "Hate to tell ya, but I told ya so."

"You did, but it was exciting to think about being really involved for a month. So it's back to work-as-usual. I've got today's takedowns. You can read them in the car."

CHAPTER FIFTY-EIGHT

One Year After the Israeli Attack on Iran
White House Oval Office: Conference, 1345
Present: POTUS, VPOTUS, SECRETARY OF STATE, FULL
CABINET, ASSISTANT SECRETARY OF STATE, CHAIRMAN
JCS, DFBI, DCIA

The discussion had been underway through lunch, and now focused on Swiss Ambassador-at-Large, Jeremy LeFevre.

"I have probably said enough, already, Mr. President; but in conclusion, I would like to emphasize the significant change in attitude that we are seeing with the Iranians. They complain that you have not brought the head of the person they call "The Shadow"—who is likely to be the fugitive—Hunter Caulfield. However, they are satisfied that you have done all in your power to do so and have spared no expense. They express great satisfaction over how exactly you complied with the demands they presented a year ago; so, they would not have to "annihilate"—their words—the Zionist Entity. They note that terrorist attacks from all sides have declined dramatically."

"You asked for the meeting, Mr. LeFevre, what is it that they want now? They already got the sun and the moon; are they after the stars this time?"

"In a figurative manner of speaking, that is exactly what they want. They have gained great confidence since the sanctions were lifted, and they want a seat at the world's table. They pressed me to demand of you that relations between the United States and Iran be normalized within the year. They hinted at a "serious change" if the United States does not move along quickly to make that happen."

The president excused Ambassador-at-Large, LeFevre, with his thanks, then polled his cabinet. There was an hour's discussion, but no significant difference of opinion: everyone was coming around to be agreeable to *beginning* the normalization process. The president concurred and instructed Jeremy Southem to light a fire under the Department of State to get the job done in less than eleven months.

The DCIA raised a hand once the voting was complete, and the president had given his order.

"Mr. President, we are glossing over one important issue that impacts on—and may derail—the normalization process. I have heard some opinions around the belt-way that Hunter Caulfield is likely dead since he cannot be located. I doubt that emphatically. He is an incredibly resourceful man; but he'll have to resurface in a year or two, or make a mistake along the line and be imprisoned or executed. I'm afraid he's just lying in a hole waiting for us to get into serious public education to convince Americans that a normalization process is important to us. Then—I predict—he will resurface and cause great trouble for the process. He has to hate us and to want revenge."

"Once the announcement of the plan to take Iran off the terrorist list is completed, we can make Captain Caulfield an offer he can't refuse as the Godfather would say."

"I think we are going to have to find him and kill him," the DCIA said.

"Get on with it. No one in this room is opposed. You have a green light from me."

Sheep Dog stood at the Queen Elizabeth Hospital bedside of Roger Ward along with Yee Pang Hung, Nguyen Tran Ky, the three men who had become his best friends—if truth were told, his only friends. Roger was an emaciated shell of his former self, scarcely recognizable even by his closest associates. His skin was yellow to the point of being almost orange; the whites of his eyes were the color of a lemon. He was sweating profusely which made his cadaverous yellow-orange skin and yellow eyes something out of a horror movie. His abdomen was grotesquely bulging with ascites, and his doctors now only shrugged when asked about his condition, and shook their heads when asked

about what they could do next. He had a dreadful body and breath odor—
fetor hepaticus, the smell of fulminating liver failure—the smell of death.

Roger was gradually going into shock, beginning to die by large leaps as
opposed to the last three months when he was dying by inches. For a while he
had been on renal dialysis because his kidneys had failed. Finally, the doctors
gave it up because the suffering of the skeletal man far outweighed the benefit. Now—like hovering vultures—the three friends waited for Roger to die.

Sheep Dog had spent as much time with his friend as was possible during
the past four months which won him the admiration and trust of Hung and
Ky and the hard men of the Chou Yen Lee Family tong. It was no longer Mr.
Nguyen, but Ky; initial wariness had grown into mutual trust. That trust had
grown exponentially when Sheep Dog had agreed to accompany their mutual
friend to Hong Kong in the desperate final medical efforts.

Sheep Dog had been deeply concerned about his friend since he arrived in
Viet Nam—nearly a year and a half ago—and now he felt a deep emotional
pain. However—he was, as ever—the ultimate pragmatist. He thought that
the obviously impending death of Roger Ward put him in a less tenable position in Southeast Asia. During the last months, Roger had made sure that
Sheep Dog had the names, addresses, e-mail addresses, business addresses,
land-line, and mobile telephone numbers of everyone in the PRUC network.
He laboriously wrote out a short and up-to-date bio on all of the former CIA
men who had served with Roger and Sheep Dog in the Phoenix Program Viet
Cong interdiction effort. He even contacted as many as he could before his
illness rendered him incapable of real effort. In his final day of struggle, Roger
told him to get to the man they had both known as Anders Bergstrom—the
Viet Cong had known as *con mau trang khong-lo* [the white giant ghost]—
and was now known to a very few, very trusted friends, as Steffan Johannson,
citizen of Quesnel, British Columbia, Canada.

In the last weeks, while Roger lay dying in Queen Elizabeth Hospital,
Sheep Dog began final preparations to leave Viet Nam. His first goal was to
get to Canada with a quick stop in Moscow beforehand; and for that, he had
to have Canadian and Russian passports, a couple of the few that he had not
secured earlier. When Roger made one long last exhalation, the remaining
three friends had him cremated—as the dying man had requested—and his
ashes spread in the South China Sea off the Po Toi Islands. Hung went back
to Saigon to run the business.

Before Ky left for Hué, he took Sheep Dog to an obscure street in the New
Territories where he could get seriously authentic documents for a serious

price. They went by the MTR Island Line and Tseung Kwan O Line to the center of the new town [Chinese: *Jiangiun'ao Xin Shizhen*] and got off at Tseung Kwan O Station in the town center. The area had nothing but new buildings including skyscrapers—and further out—low rise apartments and shops on reclaimed land. They took a cab past huge green parks to the Tseung Kwan O Village at the northern tip of Junk Bay—or General's Bay as the locals knew it. The village looked out across Victoria Harbor to Hong Kong Island from which they had come. On the train—and at every stop—Ky was obsessively security conscious, constantly looking over his shoulder to be sure they were not followed. The location and identity of the forger they were about to see was sacrosanct for the tong.

The cab dropped them off on a neat two lane road paralleling a two lane bicycle and pedestrian road. When the taxi was out of sight, Ky led the way to a short line of new white stucco three story buildings with blue tile roofs. The lower floors contained various shops, and the upper two floors of the buildings were apartments. Ky and Sheep Dog entered a Chinese apothecary shop and pressed a button to summon the proprietor from a back work room.

Ky and the man exchanged knowing nods, and Ky said, "Mr. Chun, this is my friend and a member of the tong, Mr. Jean-Luc Le Croix. He lives near me in Hué. I would be very pleased if you would honor his wishes."

Mr. Chun bowed politely and said, "Mr. Le Croix, it is my pleasure and honor to serve you." He turned to Ky, "will you be staying?"

Ky told him no, that he had to get back to Viet Nam to take care of pressing business matters. Ky and Sheep Dog made their farewells, and promised to keep in touch; but both men knew that would be a dangerous thing to do and would only happen in the case of an emergency.

Sheep Dog followed Mr. Chun into the compounding lab of the apothecary shop with its tables laden with a dizzying assortment of roots, seeds, branches, horns, skins, and smells and walked to the back stairs. They climbed the short flights of steps to the third floor. Mr. Chun took out his ring of keys and opened the door with three separate keys for three separate locks. The door was far heavier than one would have expected for a residence apartment. On first glance, the room was a typical Chinese bachelor's apartment littered with dirty dishes, cast aside clothing on a few simple pieces of furniture, and a worn carpet. The sink was full of dishes, and a microwave was the only apparatus for cooking. The room smelled of garlic, sesame oil, soy sauce, and fried pork. What struck Sheep Dog was that the rear wall of the apartment was obviously too close to the front wall inside in comparison to the depth of the building as seen from the outside—thus truncating the room. Mr. Chun, and Sheep Dog never knew him by any other title—he was not a personable man—tapped on the left hand of a figure on an intricately carved hard wood panel. As in the movies, a heretofore invisible door opened in the wall.

Mr. Chun led Sheep Dog into a high-tech state-of-the-art photography and printing studio. There was a table with a comfortable chair and a large gem cutter's magnifying lens on an articulated arm. The lights on the table were intense. X-Acto knives, fine white cotton and brown latex surgeons' gloves, an assortment of fine-tipped pens, laminating sheets, vellum and bond paper, and neat boxes of blank identification cards and authentic appearing passport folders were set out on the table's surface. In the center of the room sat an island of sophisticated professional photoshop equipment including an Epson B11b178061 Perfection V750-m Pro Flatbed scanner, a Continuous Color, Nonstop Productivity Xerox 490/980 Continuous Feed Printing System, an HP Color LaserJet Enterprise CP4520 Printer; an Agfa offset separation digital three-color photo engraver computer-to-plate [CTP] unit; a Fujifilm FinalProof digital color Luxel FinalProof 5600 halftone proofer; a VGA Capture-VGA2USB Frame Grabber with a Super VGA screen; and a world-class Spectra Digital Camera.

"Sit here, please, Mr. Le Croix," Mr. Chun directed.

He took several front and side view photos and fed them into the computer. He and Sheep Dog examined the photos; they were professionally perfect and passport size. Mr. Chun supplied a bald pate disguise and beard and repeated the photographs. The difference in his natural face and the new ones was incredible. Mr. Chun then set to work to produce driver's licenses for the States of Utah, New Jersey, and Oklahoma and for the Provinces of British Columbia and Quebec, and drivers' licenses and passports for all three states and Canada. The materials with which he worked were genuine laminates, bought from corrupted agents of the state, provincial, and national offices at exorbitant prices. Cultivating such suppliers had been the product of four decades of Mr. Chun's professional life.

He sat at the table with the photos, his X-Acto knife, and aerosol glue and affixed the new photos on driver's licenses and passports he had pre-printed with all of the required information for individuals—dead children—with real current—parental—addresses taken from telephone books in the United States and Canada. Mr. Chun had rock-steady hands, and an intensity of focus that would have qualified him to be a currency plate engraver, precious gem cutter, or a brain surgeon had he ever been inclined to seek out legal employment. He took out a series of official stamps from a dozen countries and made entrance and exit date stamps on multiple pages for multiple dates that could not be distinguished from the real thing.

$40,000 U.S. changed hands, and Sheep Dog became Richard Decatur from Salt Lake City, Utah, Peter Alan Webster from Oklahoma City, Oklahoma, Hyrum Edgar Poindexter from Port Coquitlam, British Columbia, Douglas Conroy Weaver from Atlantic City, New Jersey, and Pierre DeNeuve from Quebec City, Quebec—at least on official and genuine documents. He was five very different men on those documents, and the disguises would be simple to contrive when the time came. Sheep Dog thanked Mr. Chun and back-tracked to Hong Kong. He called a cab from the apothecary office, took the train from the Tseung Kwan O Station on the line of the same name to the Island Line and then to the Airport Express Line all the way to the Hong Kong International Airport. Mr. Chun had provided him with the materials for the first disguise, and Sheep Dog became a balding, stoop-shouldered minor bureaucrat from Canada. He was able to get a stand-by seat for a non-stop flight on Aeroflot to Moscow for later that night.

CHAPTER FIFTY-NINE

Aeroflot 4217 landed ten hours later at its hub in Sheremetyevo International Airport 18 miles north-west of Moscow, and less than ten minutes taxi ride to Sheep Dog's destination in Russia—a destination he had traveled to six times previously in his life. He had only his carry-on bag and a large black shoulder bag. He had no weapons and did not expect to need any. He walked out to the first cab in the queue and leaned into the driver's open window.

He said to the cabbie, "You speak English?"

The cabbie shook his head. Sheep Dog turned and walked towards the second cab in the queue.

"Mebbe a leetle," the cabbie called after him.

"Good. How much to Khimki Center?"

"200 rubles."

This time Sheep Dog shook his head, "100," he said, and the taxi driver had no doubt that he meant it.

"How about 150," he whined. "I don make nothing with a 100."

"I'm busy. 110 is it. If you wait for me at my stop, I'll give you 200 for the return trip plus 50 for every half hour wait."

The cabbie looked puzzled. His English was not good enough for the fast talking American or what ever he was. He shrugged his shoulders and frowned.

Sheep Dog smiled and said simply, "You take me. You wait. I pay, *друг.*"

The cabbie nodded and said equally simply, "*отвечать.*"

Sheep Dog took the man's guttural answer for a 'yes', and the cabbie decided to take a chance that the man really meant, 'friend'.

The traffic was lighter than usual on the Leningradskoe Shosse—the M-10. They were at the Khimki-Tverosky district in ten minutes, and at the city center in fifteen. The driver insisted on taking Sheep Dog a bit out of the way to drive past the Alley of Heroes in Novolyzhinskoe cemetery near the center and insisted on telling him all about it and the government's decision to move the memorial. Sheep Dog directed him to the corner of Ulitsa Raskovy and Ulitsa Kalinina Roads and had him park around the corner on Kalinina.

Sheep Dog held up a handful of rubles and said, "Wait."

That was the kind of English the driver understood, and he enthusiastically nodded 'yes'.

Sheep Dog moved quickly back onto Raskovy and walked two grey buildings down and turned into the entry path. No sooner had he done so than two plug-uglies moved out of the entrance of the building. They both wore wife-beater shirts, and their arms, chests, and faces were heavily covered with Russian prison tattoos that announced to the world that they were *Russkaya mafiya*. The ex-cons referred to their survival tattoos as the Mark of Cain. One had a .45, and the other had an AK-47, and both barrels were aimed at Sheep Dog's chest. He already knew that he was in a *mafiya* enclave. For all practicality, several sections of Khimki belonged exclusively to rich *mafiyas*, and they were fully protected by men for whom murder came as easily as slopping down a bowl of borscht and a tumbler of turnip vodka.

"What are you doing here," the ugliest one demanded, his show of teeth revealing that he was a long-time meth user.

"English," Sheep Dog said, confident that the man spoke his language from the American expressions on a couple of his inkographs.

The thug repeated his question, this time in English. He brandished his hand gun with a feverish menace. He truly wanted Sheep Dog to do something; so, he could fire.

"Yuri Yurievich" Sheep Dog said saying the man he had come to see's given name and patronymic.

"Not one by thet name heer."

"I'm busy. Get me to him."

"Now you the boss?" he asked in guttural Russian.

The Kalashnikov wielder laughed heartily at his partner's fine joke.

Sheep Dog fixed his pale hazel eyes on the thugs. He moved slowly forward. The thug waggled his pistol at the stranger. He lifted it to a direct chest aim. Sheep Dog patted aside the man's gun hand as fast as a lightening bolt and bent his wrist backward so swiftly that the criminal did not see it happen, and was surprised when his wrist snapped, and fractured in a splintering spiral. Sheep Dog kept the screaming man in front of him as the other *mafiya* began bringing up the Kalashnikov up to fire. Sheep Dog dropped the first man, batted away the rifle barrel, and was behind the second man before he could register what had happened to him. Sheep Dog rendered him unconscious by sharply clapping his cupped palms over the man's ears.

He leaned down and took hold of the Kalashnikov by the barrel, swung in over his head, and slammed the stock down on the concrete with such force that the barrel and the handle parted ways. He tossed it aside and picked up the first thug's .45 and put it in his rear waist band. He stooped down so as to avoid injuring his back; it is always a good thing to lift properly, and took the skinny muling *mafiya* by the neck and lifted him to his feet.

"Now," he said, "we go to see Yuri Yurievich." knowing that he had just spoken a language the man understood.

The much chastened *mafiya* meekly walked ahead of the Sheep Dog. At the entrance to the apartment building, he spoke briefly to a cordon of six more guards giving sullen looks to Sheep Dog, but they parted to let him past. Someone took the young man with the broken wrist to a side room to deal with the fracture. The cordon closed behind him as Sheep Dog ascended the stairs. The building's exterior belied the interior. Outside was all grey drab Stalinist concrete, small windows, and harsh angles with little in the way of vegetation to add color or to offset the menace. Inside—however—even the stairways were attractive in the style of a wealthy czarist Russia that was now largely gone. The stair wells were brightly lit; the walls were papered with scenes of gold Cossack horsemen on a blue background. The stairs themselves had a blue veined white stone facing. Brightly polished mahogany railings helped the unsteady to mount the steep and narrow stairs all the way to the third floor.

The door to Yuri's quarters and world was open. The entire floor was one large room, and that room could have been one of the last czar's second homes. A thick plush red carpet lined the room wall-to-wall. The walls were red with gold accents provided by multiple different wall paper patterns. The furniture and draperies were thick, heavy antiques, any one of which cost more than most of the guards made in a quarter of a year. Yuri was seated on a high-backed black leather computer swivel chair, the only item of furniture in the room that was not in the czarist/Stalinist red motif. He continued to peck away at a computer—one of five—on his immense desk area as Sheep Dog walked in.

Without a glance at the men following Sheep Dog, he said, "Go away," and they went away.

Yuri Yurievich Chopiak was an interesting contrast to the rest of the men hovering around the Khimki apartments. He was fifteen years old, had long, clean, blond hair and was slender to the point of delicacy. He was dressed in trendy Los Angeles teen-ager garb complete with heather colored flip-flops. He had rings on every one of his long pianist's fingers, piercings in his ears, lower lip, and tongue; and he had no tattoos. The boy had never been to prison, a fact which set him apart from the lower rungs of life that surrounded him. Yuri was under the full protection of Iosif Zaslavsky who was every bit the equivalent of the Cosa Nostra *capo di tutti capi* in Sicily. Over the years two of Zaslavsky's underlings had made the mistake of considering the delicate boy to be a tasty morsel. Their ham-strung bodies left hanging from a bridge served as an indelible life's lesson to all successive *mafiya* who might have had such evil thoughts, and Yuri led a charmed life in the inner gangland circle.

It was not some sort of father-son or uncle-nephew love that protected the boy. Rather, he was an incredibly valuable asset. Yuri Yurievich Chopiak—a gutter-snipe in origin—was the world's most accomplished hacker—a genuine genius. He could go anywhere he wanted in the cyber world. A substantial segment of Hunter Caulfield's Starbright Corporation effort had been to thwart Yuri's activities. That effort was largely a failure, and it had been Hunter's brain-child to hire the boy rather than to fight him. Starbright paid Yuri a retainer fee of $500,000 a year not to do his work, at least not to do it against Starbright's clientswho were more often than not—agencies weremore often than notagencies of the United States federal government. Zaslavsky, one of Russia's remaining 1.5 million Jews, happily accepted the half million dollar stipend as a welcome addition to the gang's wealth, especially since they really did not need to hack into U.S. government agencies with any frequency; so, there was very little in the way of a down-side.

Hunter knew that Yuri was not above being a double-agent and double-dipper, and maybe, at times, a triple-agent; but for the most part had honored the bargain with Starbright Corporation. Hunter had made several trips to Khimki over the years to have a chat with his Russian asset, and on more than one occasion had paid the boy a little extra to do some expert hacking for him and his company. That was the reason for today's visit.

"Hello, Yuri," Sheep Dog said.

"Hello, Hunter," Yuri answered in his quiet teenager's voice, "what brings you out slumming?"

"I missed you."

"Sure you did. You've become quite the world celebrity. I keep up with the news, you know."

"Okay, Yuri, in actual fact, I have some business for you."

"I'm hurt. What do you want me to do?"

Hunter explained in detail and handed Yuri a photograph, two sheets of explanatory prose, and a throw away cell phone which was identical to one he carried.

"Don't do a thing until I get in touch."

"This sounds like more than my regular retainer. Given your international fame, am I to expect something from a source other than Starbright?"

"I have several parts of this assignment, Yuri; I have personal sources of funds; and I will pay you handsomely when the work is done. Depending on whether or not I have to do everything I have in mind I will pay you in excess of a million American."

Hunter Caulfield had never played the cabbie-to-client haggling game with Yuri and neither had failed to deliver on their end of bargains. Sheep Dog had no intention of changing that paradigm.

"You know me, Yuri, we have trust with each other."

In Yuri's precarious world, trust was an exceedingly rare commodity. His mind calculated the risk/benefit ratio and found in favor of Hunter. He had never had a reason to doubt before.

"Do we have a deal, my friend?" Sheep Dog asked pointedly.

"We do. Send the money through the usual channels. You will be able to check my work on your toy computer."

"I'll keep close tabs on it," Sheep Dog said. "You might have deduced from my little entrance performance, that I am not one to be trifled with."

"Um hmmh,"

In Yuri's sphere, there were very few men to be 'trifled with', and almost none who stayed alive were unwary. There old mafiyas, bold mafiyas, but almost no old, bold mafiyas. He supposed it was much the same with the people with whom Hunter Caulfield now worked and his former U.S. government employers.

Hunter shook Yuri's slim hand and left him to his work. He descended the stairway and left the building and apartment complex without interference. The cabbie was waiting patiently where Sheep Dog had left him and was keeping a precise record of the waiting time on a small grimy notebook he kept on the passenger side seat of his cab.

Sheep Dog had him go directly back to the Novotel Moscow Sheremetyevo Airport Hotel. This time they were driving in rush hour, and the fifteen minute trip took almost two hours. Had Sheep Dog had a flight to catch, he would have missed it. At the hotel entrance, he gave the patient and faithful cab driver 600 rubles, a gross overpayment.

"Tenk you much, tenk you very much."

"My друг, I have paid you well. I come back to Москва several times a year, and we may meet again. Forget you ever saw me; do you understand?"

"Yes, друг, even now I forget you."

Anyone who came and went in that part of Khimki Center unscathed was one worth forgetting.

CHAPTER SIXTY

Olivia Perez was busy scrubbing the kitchen tile and carrying on a one-sided, order driven conversation with her husband.

"Daniel, are you listening to me?"

"Yeah," Daniel said perfunctorily.

He was absorbed in a piece of work on his computer.

"I said, I want you to move the Grand Canyon to Iowa this afternoon."

"Yeah, wait'll I get done with this."

Olivia got up off her knees and marched over to the computer and pulled the plug.

"Hey, you'll wreck the thing. It cost three thousand bucks, if you recall?" Daniel yelped. "You made me lose everything I just wrote. Jeez!"

Daniel could not get angry with Olivia. She was his mainstay and life's love. But, she was exasperating at times. Lots of times.

"So, what's so important?"

He was inclined to swear; but the house rule—Olivia's rule—was no swearing; and Daniel obeyed that one to the letter as long as he was on their property.

"I have six honey-dos, dear," she said sweetly. "I have had these six honey-dos on my list for just about that many weeks. How about you make me real happy and do them today. You got plenty of time. For one day, the PRUC stuff can wait. The hearing isn't for three more weeks, and you know they'll just get another continuance. Take a break."

"How happy would it make you if I did those honey-dos, Livy?"

"It would make me happy."

"How happy?" he asked with his boyish grin.

"That happy," she said and rolled her eyes.

The door bell rang.

"You get it, Livy; I have to restart my computer."

Olivia sighed in resignation knowing the moment was past. He would be able to put it off again.

She pulled aside the curtain on the side window to get a peek at who was ringing the bell at this time of day. She saw an innocuous looking stoop-shouldered, ponchy, balding late middle-aged black man in a frumpy grey suit standing there fussing with a folder of papers. She opened the door.

"Good morning, Mrs. Perez. I hope I'm not disturbing, but I need to speak with Mr. Perez."

"What about? If you have something to sell, we don't need it. If you are collecting for a charity, we already gave. If you've got a bill for us, you came to the wrong house."

Sheep Dog laughed, "None of the above. I have a message for Mr. Perez."

"What's it about?"

"Please, ma'am, would you tell Mr. Perez that one of his old partners has come by with a message from Roger Ward in Viet Nam."

Just hearing the name—Viet Nam—gave her a small shiver. Nothing good ever came from anyone who mentioned that country directly in reference to her husband. She and Daniel had married soon after he came back from the war and had settled in this same Alhambra neighborhood. Then, it was a pleasant place with neat rows of houses, trees, lawns, and gardens. People left their doors unlocked, the keys in their car's ignitions, and their garage doors open.

She and Daniel raised six kids there, and he was able to heal the wounds from the time in the jungle. They weren't wounds you could see, and it had taken him over twenty-five years to let the infection of PTSD out bit by bit. She hated anything or anyone who brought it up again. Daniel was a changed man. Over the years with a normal wife, a normal family, a normal job, he had lost the jerky tension, the night terrors, and the habit of always looking back over his shoulder.

When the gangs began to move in, the citizens began to move out, but not Daniel and Olivia. When the houses and yards turned to graffiti and trash, Daniel's and Olivia's had remained clean, neat, regularly painted, and the yard trim and presentable. When the violence and drive-by shootings became the order of the day, Daniel Gonzalo-Perez's family, house, cars, and person stayed safe. That was because Daniel had established from the get-go that no one threatened his family or his place. She was not sure what had happened exactly, but after that day, she became aware that her husband was treated with deference, and his family with respect. More than one gang-banger had been overheard to say, "man, that one is nobody to mess with. *El no está un hombre; ese es El Diablo proprio."*

"Come in," she said with some reluctance.

Sheep Dog stepped just inside the entryway.

"Wait here."

She walked back into his office and said to Daniel, "There's one of them here to see you. Says he has a message from somebody named Roger Ward from Viet Nam. Daniel, be careful."

"I'm always careful, Livy, you know that."

She did; but still, it was her job to worry about her good man.

Daniel did not recognize the African-American standing in his doorway.

"I'm Daniel Perez."

He offered his hand.

"Who might you be?"

"Roger Ward called you a while back. Do you remember."

"Yeah."

"I'm the guy he talked about."

"I don't remember any black guys with the Program."

"There weren't any. This a bit of Hollywood. I'm Hunter Caulfield. That name ring a bell, Daniel?"

It certainly did, and even the voice had some familiarity.

"If you're Hunter Caulfield, you're in a heap of trouble, I understand. The cops seem to think you're a number one bad guy."

"That's me, Daniel. Mind if we come in and sit down. I just got off a long flight, and this disguise stuff is hot."

They sat in the old-fashioned parlor on furniture from central casting for a 1940s Argentine movie. It was cool, dimly lit, and comfortable. Olivia brought in some cherry lemonade. Sheep Dog took ten minutes to explain something about what he had been doing, and how The Company had turned against him and made him the hunted instead of the hunter.

"Imagine that," Daniel said bitterly

He like all of the other PRUCs could relate to what Sheep Dog was saying from their own experience. There was no love lost between The Company and the former PRUCs with the possible exception of Oliver Prentiss, who still worked for them.

Sheep Dog said, "I need to get in touch with Anders Bergstrom. I know him, but I don't know where he is. All Roger knew was that he lived somewhere up north and played it pretty secret about his life and whereabouts. He was sure you would know how to get in touch with him. And I will also need some help from you and the rest of the PRUCs that you trust."

"People not like Jean-Luc DuParrier, maybe?"

"Very much not like that one," Sheep Dog said, "Any idea where he is, Daniel?"

"Nope. I hear he got sent to Nicaragua and then found something nasty to do in the Congo. We don't send Christmas cards."

"Will you help me?"

"I will until I learn for a fact that you are the vicious murderer the *America's Most Wanted* show says you are, then I'll even help the fibbies. Swear to me, Hunter, that you aren't a cop killer."

"You have my sacred word, Daniel. None of that is true. I did things like we did back in the Phoenix Program, but I am nothing like what they say. I need to disappear—and not to be terminated with maximum prejudice as The Company wants."

"Like Anders Bergstrom. That still sticks in my craw."

"Like Anders Bergstrom."

"Okay, let's get on the horn. I can fix you up. You know you can't say anything about what you learn from me."

"You know I won't."

"Let's get you out of this mess; so, you won't have to wear that Al Jolsen get-up."

The call was made, and Bergstrom, or whatever his name was now, agreed to see Sheep Dog.

Sheep Dog already knew that Anders Bergstrom was now known as Steffan Johannson and that he lived in Canada, but not where in Canada before he met with Daniel Perez. He had already made flight reservations to go to Vancouver the next day, and now he knew what the rest of his itinerary had to be. He laboriously cut up the passport and driver's license that he had used coming back into the United States and spread the shreds around in different waste cans throughout the hotel. He scrubbed off the mahogany darkening of his skin, took off the partial baldness wig, then scratched his itchy scalp until he felt normal again. The next morning, he took out the last of his wigs and noses from his old case and made himself into Hyrum Edgar Poindexter from Port Coquitlam, British Columbia, a CA, who had been in the U.S. to take his International Uniform CPA Qualification Examination [IQEX]. He was good with numbers but nowhere the match of a Certified Accountant. If anyone challenged him, he planned to fake it.

The flight was pleasant; first class is always pleasant; and the arrival in Vancouver uneventful; technically, the International Airport is located on Sea Island in Richmond, British Columbia, about 7.5 miles from from downtown Vancouver. He went straight to the Hertz Rent-a-Car desk and arranged to rent a GMC Terrain SLE-1 All Wheel Drive small SUV. He did not tell the clerk where or how far he was going, nor did he ask for any directions. Those he obtained at a Borders Books store in the airport pre-security area.

It was only ten in the morning; so, he set out directly north on the first leg of his road trip to Quesnel, 396 miles north in the middle of British Columbia. First, he took the TransCanada Highway #1 to Hope, B.C. then connected to Highway #5 and on to the connection to Highway #97, the Caribou Highway—the major north-south route between Vancouver, the Yukon, and Alaska. He took a break at 100 Mile House. There he filled his tank and bought supplies for a picnic lunch in a small grocery store.

The South Caribou is a vast sparsely populated pine and aspen forest land with rolling hills, frequent rivers, emerald green/blue lakes, and waterfalls, one of the most beautiful places in the world. He walked up a trail to a nice spot in Centennial Park by Bridge Creek, ate part of his lunch, and enjoyed the peaceful vista of the grassy open valley dotted with lumbar mills, ranches, 1,700 hardy people, and surrounded by low, pine covered hills.

There were few vehicles on the road, and no one seemed to be paying any attention to him. He made a pit stop in Williams Lake which has nearly ten times the population of 100 Mile House, and there encountered police for the first time since he left Viet Nam and Hong Kong. He parked by Mirror Lake to admire the reflections of the low rolling pine covered hills and rocky escarpment on the glassy smooth water surface. An RCMP truck pulled up behind him, and the trooper got out and came over to the Sheep Dog's car.

"How are you, today, sir?" the trooper asked in a friendly, courteous way.

Sheep Dog was on full alert, dreading what he might have to do.

"Anything wrong, officer?"

"Nothing at the moment. I came over to give you a little heads-up. We've been having a rash of car-jackings and other crimes against tourists lately around Williams Lake; so, the RCMP is warning people to avoid stopping by the side of the road for a while. You may know that Williams Lake has the highest number of crimes per capita in B.C., and the number of case files per constable is well above the B.C. average. Take care, and enjoy the beauty of the Caribou."

Sheep Dog was sweating and made a concerted effort not to show his tension.

"Thanks, officer, I appreciate the heads-up. It seems out of character to have a crime wave up here in all of this gorgeous wilderness."

"We think so too. We don't want you to be another statistic. Have a safe trip."

He tipped the brim of his cap and went back to his truck and drove on ahead of Sheep Dog. Sheep Dog lingered for fifteen minutes to give the Mountie a little distance from him before driving on towards Quesnel. Just south of the city, he saw the sign Steffan Johannson had alerted him about announcing the route to the "Nazko First Nations Reserve No. 1-120 km" and the "Gateway to the Nuxalk Carrier Grease-Alexander Mackenzie Heritage Trail". He turned west and drove along the straight highway fringed on both sides by a dense coniferous forest. Even amidst all of that isolation, he drove the posted speed limit to avoid even the remotest chance of coming to the attention of the RCMP. He did anyway.

A Mountie car pulled him over. As with his earlier encounter, he tensed for battle.

The Mountie politely tipped the brim of his cap and said, "Sir, are you aware that a permit is required to enter this First Nation's Reserve?"

"No, officer, I'm not. I just wanted to scout the trail, then spend the night in Quesnel and get some gear for a good back-pack trip."

"No problem. We're happy to have you. But just take the time to turn around and go back into town and get the permit at the Indian Office. It's by Laboardais Park; you can't miss it."

"Sure. I didn't mean to offend," Sheep Dog said, aware of how touchy the Native American Indians were about their prerogatives and how closely Canada protected those special rights.

It was because of a collective national guilt-complex, an outgrowth of their abysmal treatment of the indigenous people in the past.

"Put the sticker on the upper right hand corner of your windshield, and we won't have to disturb you again."

"Thanks, officer. Have a good day, eh?" Sheep Dog said, putting a little col-loquial Canadian touch to his speech for good measure.

"And the same to you."

Sheep Dog went back to Quesnel and found the office. It was next to a huge sign advertising the game schedule for the "BCHL's Quesnel Millionaires Junior A Hockey Team".

The Indian Center was a neat, simple building which served for both business and as an information service for tourists interested in the Dakelh people who lived along the Nazko River. He paid a modest fee—using Canadian dollars—and drove back to the turn off.

This time he drove west about 75 miles, keeping a sharp eye out for the next turn Steffan had described. To his right he saw a narrow road that formed a T junction with the main paved road to Nazko. A small crude sign said, "To Johannson Ranch". He made the turn to the north and bounced along for a little over 100 miles where the road had a four-way intersection out there in the middle of nowhere. A weathered wood sign with pointers in all four directions indicated four different ranch roads. The Johannson Ranch pointer told Sheep Dog to continue straight ahead. The road became a rutted dirt track logging path that tested the all wheel drive of his GMC SUV and finally dead-ended abruptly at a thick patch of brush.

Sheep Dog got out and reexamined the directions that Steffan Johannson had given him, and he was absolutely certain that this was the correct place. Steffan—however—had not mentioned that the road ended in the middle of the bush hundreds of miles from any vestige of civilization. He nibbled on some lunch left-overs and pondered his predicament. Rather than get frustrated or angry, he lay down in the back seat and took a nap.

From his deep sleep, he became aware of eyes on him by some trick of a fugitive's psyche and became instantly awake. There were four pairs of eyes on him, and the eyes belonged to young, earnest, and menacing Asians. All of them had guns, and all of the guns were pointed at him. The first thing that occurred to him is that he had been led into a trap. He was going to have to kill four men in the next few minutes or be killed himself.

The apparent leader of the group of young men gestured to Sheep Dog to get out of the vehicle. He tensed himself, shook off the grogginess left over from the nap, and slowly and deliberately climbed out. The gun muzzles continued to menace him.

The leader said, "Get down on your knees and lock your fingers behind your head."

Sheep Dog was not inclined to get on his knees for anyone, but pretended to start to obey. He spun around and knocked the barrel of the leader's M-16 away from where it was pointing at him. As he started to spin back around to take out the next gun in a desperate effort to create confusion and to gain the upper hand, he felt three then a fourth rifle muzzle jab into his back and chest.

"Dad told us what you'd try to do. Don't do it again, or we'll make Swiss cheese out of you. Put your hands behind your back."

Sheep Dog meekly gave up and complied. One of the youths put plastic band wrist binders on him, and the five men trudged into the dense under-brush on a trail that Sheep Dog had been unable to see before. They walked about a mile on a heavily used horse trail until they came into an open cleared spread of fields, checkerboarded with an assortment of crops. Ahead, there was a handsome large log house with five similar out buildings and a huge barn. There were several large reception discs facing solar south to catch satellite signals. A corral holding a dozen good looking quarter horses stood to the right of the house, and a fenced pasture on the left contained several hundred sheep, goats, and sturdy Hereford cattle.

As they approached closer to the house, Sheep Dog could see into several of the sheds and took note of the farm equipment—which was obviously in keeping with the rest of the ranch appearance—but also two large Hummers. Sheep Dog wondered to himself where they drove the large all-terrain vehicles. He had not seen any roads that led into the main dirt track where he had been obliged to leave his GMC. One of the sheds was a well constructed hangar. In it sat a sleek Bell Longranger helicopter painted with a deep-forest camouflage pattern.

Twenty yards from the house, a tall, very large man with a shock of white hair stepped out of the front door. Behind him and walking in his protective umbra came a small, dark-skinned Asian-Eskimo appearing woman of about thirty. The manwho looked to be around his same agegrew larger as he approached Sheep Dog. He was a real giant, the white giant ghost [*con ma da trang khong-lo*] whom Sheep Dog had known as Anders Bergstrom, only an older copy of the infamous killer.

"You don't look like Hunter Caulfield," he said by way of greeting.

"And you don't look like Anders Bergstrom. I have an excuse; I'm in disguise. What's yours?"

Steffan laughed, "I'm old. But I could still give you a run for your money, Hunter. Let's go inside. You can get out of those clothes and that head, and we'll get some supper and have us a good talk. Boys, be nice and put away your guns."

Sheep Dog was impressed at how immediately the youths obeyed. Steffan Johannson ran a tight ship.

"This is my daughter—step-daughter—actually, Candy Okobuk. She came down here with us when we left Kotzebue ten years ago. Her mom, Mary, got breast cancer and died after we moved."

"Sorry," Sheep Dog said.

He looked closer at the young woman. She was not Asian exactly, probably Inuit, maybe northern Alaskan Indian.

The Johannson ranch people were meat eaters. Candy, an Indian girl, and two Hmong girls served supper to sixteen ravenous workers: a huge pot roast, pork chops, a bushel basket sized bowl of steamed vegetables, apple sauce, boiled Russet potatoes, and two oversized platters of corn bread with slabs of butter and a serving bowl full of honey. Dessert was a peach cobbler served directly from the Dutch oven in which it was baked and two gallons of ice cream. Apple juice and whole milk sat in several large pitchers on top of the heavy table.

Sheep Dog thanked the girls and Candy and watched them and the hands clean up with an alacrity that the navy could learn from. Steffan bade Sheep Dog and three aging Asian men to follow him into his office.

"Hunter, these are the best men on earth. They are my most trusted friends. We all know about your troubles with the CIA. We have good TV news, and more than that, Daniel Perez—another real friend—clued us in. You're among friends. This is Nguyen Lui Tran," Tran gave a slight nod. "This is Phan Duy Ky, and that handsome devil is Fang Pao Xe."

He gestured at a thin, wiry Vietnamese man and to a Hmong who still wore his hair in a tightly braided queue. Their scarred faces and hard eyes attested to their murky past. They acknowledged Steffan's introduction of them.

"This is Hunter Caulfield, public enemy number one. Remember when I used to have that status. Kind of takes you back doesn't it?"

"Hunter, let's hear from you. Then you can wash up and get rid of that disguise. It's kind of unnerving to hear your voice coming out of a different person."

"Steffan, if you don't mind, I need to keep it on, because I don't have the materials to redo it, and I need to match my face with the picture on my documents to get back out of Canada. That okay?"

"Sure. Now, let's hear it."

Sheep Dog was at one of those rare points where he had to trust someone, and he instinctively felt trust for Steffan and his small band of Chinese pirates. He told them his whole story and concluded with the reason for which he had traveled to B.C.'s Caribou to see them. They nodded their understanding and approval. He handed Steffan a glossy 8 X 10 photograph of a girl.

The next day, Steffan had one of his boys fly Sheep Dog back to Vancouver and assured him that someone would drive the rental car back to the airport on time and full of gas to avoid drawing any attention to it. There was very little talk on the trip to the airport. When he got out, Sheep Dog thanked the young man, who merely nodded. By the time Sheep Dog was going in the doors of the South—International—Terminal, the Bell Longranger was back in the air.

CHAPTER SIXTY-ONE

15 Months After the Attack on Iran
White House Oval Office: Conference, 1345
Present: POTUS, VPOTUS, FULL CABINET, SECRETARY OF
STATE, JUNIOR DEPUTY UNDERMINISTER FOR FOREIGN
AFFAIRS, ISLAMIC REPUBLIC OF IRAN

The president's steward served Moroccan coffee, madjool dates from Saudi Arabia, freshly squeezed orange juice from Syria, and baklava from an old Persian recipe on a highly polished sterling silver platter to the men seated around the Oval Office. The unique aspect of this gathering was that it included an official representative—albeit an extremely minor one—of the Islamic Republic of Iran, the first such face-to-face encounter between officials of the two countries since the Iranian government sanctioned the student take-over of the U.S. Embassy in Tehran in 1979, and the ignominious failure by the Carter administration to take serious measures to rescue them or to retaliate against the Iranians.

"We are pleased to meet with the president in the Oval Office," the nervous and stiffly correct young diplomat, Amin Mir abu-Saab, said.

"And we are pleased that your government would be willing to take this step towards rapprochement and normalization. We trust that your government is satisfied with our overtures to date?"

"President Sofrekheneh, himself, asked me to convey that very sentiment. In return, we wish to suggest that our two nations mutually establish a small consular representation consisting of a deputy foreign affairs consultant and an office staff of five persons. We suggest that the offices be established in Washington D.C. and Tehran respectively."

"I see no particular hindrance to that proposal, do you Mr. Secretary?"

He directed his question to Jeremy Southem.

"No sir. I think we can persuade the Congress to go along."

"There is just one thing," abu-Saab said hesitantly.

"And that is…?"

"We have not yet been able to fund the work to complete covering the areas contaminated with radioactive waste. My president is unwilling to go ahead with normalization until that is done."

"How can we help?"

"I hesitate to ask, but we are in need of $5 billion to complete the work. The president would be much better able to concentrate on the issues of normalization if we could obtain funding from our new friends, the Americans."

It was blatant blackmail or begging or conniving or all three, but the president and the secretary of State felt pressured to make an historical breakthrough.

"I believe we could see our way clear to be of help. However, Mr. abu-Saab, we must have a gesture of good faith from your government."

"What form might that take?"

"The government of the Islamic Republic of Iran holds as prisoners nearly thirty members of Usama bin Laden's close family members who escaped into your country from Afghanistan immediately before the attack on New York City on September 11, 2001. You are—no doubt—familiar with the letters written by Khalid bin Laden to your government, to your president, and to Supreme Leader Ayatollah Ali Khamenei, himself. We have independent sources. Among those family members being held are Usama's sons Saad and Hamza, who are leaders of al-Qaeda, and their sister, 27 year old Eman, who escaped to and is being held in protective custody by the Saudis in their embassy in Tehran. Here is a complete list of the individuals. Mr. abu-Saab, we insist on these people being turned over the officials of the United States as a prerequisite for any further discussions about normalization."

"I have no authority to grant such a privilege, but I will carry your request back to my government. I am authorized to inform you that the government of Iran will not go further than what we offer today until the criminal— Hunter Caulfield—is turned over to our representatives for trial in Iran."

"We are not able to find the man, Mr. abu-Saab; and we don't yet know if he is the so-called terrorist you deem him to be. Furthermore, we have no direct proof that he committed crimes on Iranian soil or upon Iranian officials or citizens elsewhere, or that he is the person whom you dub "The Shadow". For that matter, we have no evidence that he is even alive. We have principles of due process here, and we will hold to them in the case of Captain Caulfield since he is an American citizen."

"Proof of his death would suffice," the stone faced Iranian said.

The Same Morning
Headquarters United States Marshal's Office, 600 Army Navy Drive, Arlington, Virginia
Present: ATTORNEY GENERAL, DUSMS, DDUSMS, ADFBI

The twenty-five year old USMS headquarters building is located in the sprawling Arlington, Virginia federal area where there is a concentration of United States Federal office buildings situated on a handsome campus adorned with a few remaining highly ascetic red oak and copper beech tree stands of those which once covered the area. The USMS HQ building is a huge eleven story behemoth made of bronze glass windows and their frames causing the casual observer wonder how the whole thing stands up. It is one of four such office towers that fill a full block a mile down the Potomac from the Pentagon. The other towers house offices of the DEA, DIA [Defense Intelligence Agency], ATF, IRS, and NSA, and a host of others that the public does not need to know about.

Four senior law enforcement officials occupied the plush chairs of the director's office with its view of the heart of the capital city, its monuments, the Jefferson Davis Highway, and the Arlington Memorial Bridge by which everyone from D.C. finds his or her way to the USMS HQ. USMS Director Colin McPherson presented the evidence that he considered to be the first breakthrough in the manhunt for the fugitive, Captain Hunter Caulfield.

Memo Begins

Interagency Fugitive Notice

Date: 04 May

Source: British Columbia Provincial Police Airport Security Detail to Interagency Fugitive Operations Office, Brooklyn Court Street Federal Building.

See BOLO-CIA internal communication US9164-CT 4779, 0107TWEP

Subject: International fugitive, U.S. citizen, Captain Hunter Caulfield, has been positively identified by facial recognition technology, as having passed through the Vancouver, British Columbia, International Airport. He was in disguise, but the facial recognition technicians consider their ID to be 92% certain. He was traveling under what is presumed to be a false identity in the name of Hyrum Edgar Poindexter from Port Coquitlam, British Columbia, a certified accountant. The name is that of a child who died forty-two years ago in Ontario, and the address—while genuine—was found to be that of an abandoned warehouse in a seedy section of Port Coquitlam. The owner lost the property to foreclosure five years ago and has since died. The Office of the RCMP for British Columbia has launched a quiet but extensive search and investigation. To this date, it has been established that the fugitive obtained a rental vehicle from the GMC Canada, airport outlet and returned it one week later. No evidence has been elucidated to indicate a travel route(s) or destination(s). He has been identified as having departed Canada via American Airlines flight 1432 the same day as the vehicle was returned. There is no videocam evidence of him having ever left that airplane and no surveillance data indicating that he—in fact—entered the United States.

Director McPherson played and replayed the remarkably clear surveillance footage. The subject made no effort to conceal his face, and no one in the room could convince himself or herself that they could tell that it was the fugitive.

"I suppose we'll just have to go along with the facial recognition techs and move aggressively. Director, this is an FBI case, especially since it is currently isolated to foreign soil or to cross international boundary movements. Can you go along with that?" Attorney General Gertrude Heimel asked.

"I suppose so. The USMS is fully ready to cooperate. Let us know what we can do. We have a lot of takedown teams who are itching to get on this guy's tail."

"You have any problems with the Bureau taking charge, Mr. Zikordov?" AG Heimel asked the ADFBI.

"We'll be on it as soon as I can get on my cell phone."

By the time the interagency fugitive notice was disseminated, The Sheep Dog had been in the United States for eight days. He was—at the moment—milling about with several hundred flea-market aficionados in Memphis, Tennessee. He stopped at seven different gun sellers booths and found everything from left hand guns, to women's small purse .22 "mouse guns", to a Smith and Wesson Model 500 .50 caliber Magnum double action revolver—essentially a handgun that fired an elephant gun round. That massive, nearly useless gun for a man of action—weighs 4.5 pounds and has an 8.37 inch barrel. Hefting the huge revolver gave Sheep Dog a good laugh.

He moved quickly between booths and finally found the most ill-kempt, most alcoholic, most devious gun dealer he could come up with. He bought three guns from the same dealer for a total of $480. The first was a Smith & Wesson Model 640 stainless steel snubby that fired .357 magnum rounds. Its limitation was that it could only hold five rounds. Its advantage for Sheep Dog was that he would be able to conceal it in a sack or satchel or even in the leg pocket of a pair of cargo pants. The second was a Springfield XDN 9 mm Black 19X1 modified to hold 13 rounds. The third was an Armscor M1911A1 .45 from which the serial number had been removed He bought a stock of the dealer's own wild cat—self-made—rounds, including a box of "cop-killers"—ammunition coated with polytetra-fluoroethylene [Teflon] for piercing Kevlar vests.

"You got any I-dee?" the sleepy bearded hillbilly asked.

"Nope," Sheep Dog said and looked down at the man sitting in his folding chair.

Maybe it was the eyes that convinced him. Maybe he just didn't care. The sale was concluded with cash and no paper.

There were things about the guns that Sheep Dog did not know and would not have learned had he even asked the right questions. Each of the weapons had been used in at least one murder; one was used in three separate murders. The three guns were first seized by the Memphis area sheriff's office, then were sold by the Sheriff's Department to a reputable gun dealer who sold them to a lawful concealed weapon holder who sold them to a friend of a friend at a flea market—all for a profit—and finally; they came into the possession of Emer Hadclif from Berryville, Arkansas, who was either drunk or did not care. Many states destroy such guns, but Tennessee and Kentucky—among a few others—sell or trade the guns for such things as Kevlar vests thanks to the lucrative efforts of the NRA. They can be resold legally in those states and are all but untraceable thereafter. Sheep Dog carried his guns and ammunition out of the flea market in a black canvas bag with a Lancome logo.

THE END-GAME

"If there's not any endgame, we're in quicksand.
We take one more step, and we're still there,
and there's no way out."

—Richard Shelby

CHAPTER SIXTY-TWO

"Patience is the most valuable trait of the endgame player."
—Pal Benko, speaking about chess

Yale senior Heather Prentissthe only daughter, the only child, of Oliver Prentiss—the assistant director of the Central Intelligence Agency and his wife Natalie, had a part-time job as a dorm floor supervisor in Silliman College on Old Campus. During the evening when Sheep Dog came for her, she was conducting a discussion group on the diversity of American cultural life for VISA—Vietnamese Student Association—for which she volunteered as a mentor two evenings a week.

Heather was intelligent and excelled at Yale in her chosen major, art history. She was not particularly attractive and did not have a boy-friend, nor did she date very often. She poured her enthusiasms into causes, not unlike most of her Yale contemporaries. She had flirted with socialism and militant women's lib which led her deep conviction of the value of activism to take Bella Abzug as her hero, to make sizable financial contributions to anti-war factions protesting the continuing involvement of the United States in Iraq well after the war was over, and to join a campus anti-gun coalition. She made friends with the leaders of SANE [National Committee for a Sane Nuclear Policy], the SPU [Student Peace Union], and especially VISA. She became interested in VISA when she attended an anti-U.S. seminar which focused on the atrocities committed by her country during the illegal Viet Nam invasion. She openly detested her father and his involvement with the CIA.

That Tuesday evening, the VISA discussion meeting was being held in the newer Georgian brick portion of the college in the Sillibrary—the college's library—located in the third floor of Byers Hall. Silliman College is a residential college at Yale which opened formally in 1940, the last of the original ten residential colleges. Silliman occupies a full city block in New Haven.

Sheep Dog met the two Johannson brothers—the same ones who had poked their rifle muzzles into his chest and back during his recent visit to Nazko—in the baggage area of Bradley International Airport Distance, 52 miles from New Haven. The elder of the two brothers, Xe Johannson, had graduated from Yale the previous year and was altogether familiar with the Hartford, Connecticut—technically, Windsor Locks—airport and the route to mid New Haven and the university. The younger brother, Tran, was in training for a career in the RCMP and considering an intelligence service option.

The three men parked their rental car in an alley off Wall Street and headed across the college courtyard, which covers almost an entire city block—the largest enclosed courtyard at Yale. It was a warm evening, and the three men walking through the gloaming attracted no attention from the crowds of excited students engaged in intense games of whiffle ball, flag football, and Frisbee golf. There were several cause booths with student orators shouting to dwindling on-lookers. The three climbed the stairs to the third floor. Sheep Dog and Tran found soft chairs outside the library, and Xe was chosen to go into the library after Heather because of his thorough knowledge of the building and the library facilities. All three men were dressed in campus police uniforms.

Xe carried a set of photographs of the girl which Sheep Dog had obtained during the past week while he surveilled her. He was able to approach the VISA group because he heard raised voices speaking Vietnamese, his birth language. He wandered through the stacks nearby the group meeting area and kept himself as unobtrusive as possible. The informal meeting began to break up half an hour later, and the young Vietnamese students drifted away in groups of two and three leaving Heather to clean up the debris from their pre-meeting visit to The Buttery, a student-run eatery in the basement that serves highly popular greasy happiness and beer on weekday nights.

He approached Heather and greeted her in Vietnamese, "*Chao co*, Miss Prentiss."

She responded with, "*Chao ba*, officer. But, I'm sorry, I really don't speak the language even though I lead the VISA group here."

"I don't mean to alarm you, Miss, but I have been sent by the campus police department to fetch you. It seems that the government feels that you are in danger from the federal fugitive, Hunter Caulfield. Maybe you have heard of him?"

"Who hasn't. What has he to do with me?"

"There have been threats from the terrorist's organization against your father and other officers of the CIA and their families. Your father, the CIA, and the FBI are taking these threats seriously. Please follow me to the campus police headquarters where you can call your parents, and they can tell you what measures have to be taken."

"I have a cell phone."

"Sorry, no cell phones; they are too easily traceable. We presume that Caulfield's terrorist ring is very savvy electronically."

That was sensible. Heather may have disliked her father and his profession, but she knew full well that it was a dangerous one. Despite her own opinion, she believed the young officer that she was in real danger from someone her father had offended or wronged. She left with him willingly. In the sitting area outside the library entrance, the two other officers stood and followed Heather and Xe out of the building. Xe led the party in the direction of the campus police HQ through what had become a dark, starless night. As they left the walled square and out onto the street, the three men looked carefully around for pedestrians; and seeing none at the moment, Sheep Dog produced a handkerchief soaked in chloroform and clapped it over the unsuspecting girl's face. She struggled but could not scream, and within seconds slumped unconscious. Xe and Tran supported her in an upright posture back to the Wall Street alley with Sheep Dog walking closely in head of them to obscure what they were doing.

They loaded her inert sleeping body into the trunk of the car, handcuffed her hands and feet, and put duct tape over her mouth and a black hood over her head. Sheep Dog left the two young Canadians and the girl at that point and caught a taxi to the New Haven Hotel. The sons of Steffan Johannson knew the plan precisely and did not need any further instruction from him.

Sheep Dog found a rest room and switched out of his campus police uniform and into a charcoal grey business suit to wear on his flight to Reagan International Airport in Washington D.C. He had taken the precaution to mail his guns to a PostNet postal service box in Fredericksburg, Virginia that he had secured online the week before. The boys drove straight through all that night and the next day on I-95 to the border crossing at Houlton, Maine. Heather was very uncomfortable and very angry, but frightened enough to keep quiet and to remain cooperative with the young men who were pleasant and kind to her, allowing bathroom breaks and providing food. They did not, however, allow her out of the trunk or to have her hood off except for the bathroom breaks. They kept her purse in the back seat, but threw away her cell phone. They crossed the border without incident and found the helicopter where they left it in the small private airport hanger. They seated the hapless girl uncomfortably in the rear seat and took four days to fly a circuitous route to Quesnel, nearly 3,000 miles away, landing in wilderness clearings for breaks, food, and sleep.

Two Days Later

Oliver Prentiss had a long day. Being the assistant director was too much like when he was a naval ship's executive officer. He had no direct control of anything, really; but he had to take the blame for all failures without whining—very really. It had been one of those days. He was to blame for the lack of intel on the new Greek financial crisis, for the intransigence of the Iranians who had delivered up only four of the bin Ladens to The Company; and—as on every other day—for not being able to capture his man, his protégé—Hunter Caulfield. He gritted his teeth every time he thought about Hunter. He would see him arrested or dead this year and succeed Gerald Lang in the DCIA's office, or he would have to take his pension and go plant posies for his wife and play golf with a bunch of bored duffers like himself.

Going up his driveway, he was wool-gathering about what he would do if he could just have the chance to meet Hunter face-to-face and have the drop on him. He put the Jag in the garage, picked up his briefcase and put it on his office desk, grabbed a Bud from the fridge, and headed upstairs to get a few winks before Natalie got on him about something that needed to be done.

The bedroom was dark. He flipped the light switch and did a double take at a scene that could not be real. Hunter Caulfield was sitting in the bedside easy chair. Hunter was aiming a .45 at his chest. It just did not fit into his world view. He took several seconds to take it all in.

When he had himself collected, he asked, "Hunter, what's up with this. You broke into my house, my bedroom. Why on earth are you pointing a .45 at me, huh?"

"Because they don't make .46s, Oliver. Sit down and shut up. I have news for you," Sheep Dog said tersely.

Oliver found the second easy chair. It had been moved so that it faced Hunter directly. He waited without speaking.

Chapter Sixty-Two

"Surprised to see me?"

He held up his hand to command continuing silence. It was clear that he was in charge, and his questions he was about to ask would be rhetorical.

"Surprised to see me alive? It's not any fault of yours that I am. It has been a difficult couple of years."

Oliver got out a, "But…" and Sheep Dog's uplifted hand shushed him.

The gun never wavered in its menace.

"Oliver, I want you to take out your guns, and your cell phone one at a time…verrrry carefully—and I mean delicately—like porcupines making love. I have no compunctions about finishing you right now. I think you want to live, and I want something you can do only if you are alive. You might just want to hear what I have to say."

Oliver removed his Beretta from the shoulder holster, holding it by the trigger guard with his thumb and index finger and set it gingerly on the ground and kicked it towards Hunter. He did the same with his ankle weapon and his cell phone.

"Good. The next thing we are going to do is check out the hallway by your wife's sewing room. After that, I will have something else to show you, and something to tell you. What you do after that is up to you; but, at least, you will have the facts to work with."

Oliver was both frightened and curious. He waited for Hunter to stand; then, he stood up. Hunter gestured to him to lead the way. The hall was dark; he should have noticed earlier. Of course, Hunter had doused the lights. They rounded the corner to the sewing room, and Hunter turned on the lights. What he saw was a scene from a bad horror movie.

Natalie was standing tip-toe on the top platform of their tall step ladder which Hunter must have brought up from the garage. A noose of heavy rope was tied at the side of her neck with a well constructed judicial hangman's knot. The rope was attached to a heavy screw-ring that had been screwed into a joist in the ceiling twelve feet above the landing. Natalie's eyes and mouth were taped shut, and her wrists were taped behind her. Her ankles were taped together, and a 25 pound exercise weight was taped to each ankle. Natalie was alert, terrified, and frozen in place, knowing that if she wearied or became faint, or lost focus, she would fall off the ladder and would be dead. She was stark naked and had humiliated herself by her bowels and bladder having released involuntarily in her terror.

Without saying a word, Sheep Dog pushed the distraught husband towards the bathroom. Theresitting in the sinkwas a large role of duct tape.

"Strip," Sheep Dog commanded.

"Hunter, don't do this. We can talk. We can talk this out."

Sheep Dog swiped the heavy steel of his .45 across Oliver's mouth breaking off two gleaming white front incisors and opening a visible cut on his upper lip.

"Shut up."

Oliver rushed out of his clothing. Maybe if he cooperated, Hunter would make his death quick and would have enough mercy left to spare Natalie. He determined not to lose hope.

Naked and completely at Hunter Caulfield's mercy, the man whom he knew considered him his friend; and he had nonetheless betrayed, looked at him with a malevolence he had not seen in any man since he had watched Jean-Luc DuParrier begin a torture session in Dà Nang those eons ago. He capitulated and gave himself over to death.

Sheep Dog taped Oliver's wrists and ankles and put him in a hog-tie position. He put tape over his mouth, then he lifted Oliver up and dumped him painfully into the tub. He twisted Oliver's head so that he could see what Sheep Dog wanted to show him. He opened a large envelope and extracted an 8 X 10 glossy of Heather Prentiss seated on a folding chair that could have come from any public building in the world. She was naked and holding the front page of the *New York Times* in her two hands, dated two days previously. Her lips were sealed shut as were her eyes. Her ankles were bound with plasticuff strips. She could well have had the word "TERROR" imprinted on her forehead.

Oliver was afraid that he would faint. He groaned through his gag. Hunter let him gaze at the terrifying picture for a few moments before he spoke.

"I trust you are impressed—old friend—the one man in the world that I trusted with my life. You will not find her in a million years; so, it is futile to look. I have left an envelope with instructions in the top left drawer of your dresser. Once you get out of these restraints, take a look at it; and, if you want to see Heather alive sometime in the future, follow those instructions to the letter. You can communicate with me by placing an encrypted message—the same one as you and I have been using—on your computer in The Company folder. I will get it. I have my ways. In fact, once you comply exactly, I won't have to get a message; it will be in all the papers."

Sheep Dog left Oliver writhing in the tub and walked back into the hall to the ladder where the exhausted and moaning Natalie was fighting to stave off 'Charley-horses' in her calves. She was nearing the end of her strength.

He climbed up the ladder along side her taking care not to touch her bare skin. He cut the rope just above the knot, and caught her over his shoulder as her legs gave way. He backed down the ladder carrying her fireman style and laid her on the bed in the master bedroom. He covered her nakedness with a blanket before leaving.

He said, "Make Oliver do what he's told, or I will be back. I have a skill set that you can't even imagine. I can get to you."

She was crying.

He dialed the number in Russia on Oliver's desk land line.

When it was picked up, Sheep Dog said only, "Yuri, proceed."

He went back to the ladder and gave it a brutal kick which sent it flying over the banister and onto the floor below with a frightful crashing noise. He could hear Oliver's muffled screams even with the tape covering his mouth. He slipped out the way he had come in.

Quesnel, Two Days Later

When the Bell Longranger put down behind the large barn, Heather was so exhausted that she no longer cared what happened to her. If they were going to rape her, so be it. She was a virgin, and at least she would know what it was like before she died. If they kept her as a slave or something, she would adapt. She demanded of herself to be strong.

Xe and Tran each took an arm and helped Heather out of the back seat of the helicopter. She was wobbly and uncertain at first, but had her sea legs back by the time they entered the house. She did not know where she was, not even the country. She had been kidnapped by two Orientals and was now in the center of a vast unpopulated forest. Her best guess was that they were in Siberia.

Candy Okobuk put her arms around the traumatized young woman and held her quietly for a few moments.

"I'm sorry. You're safe, dear. You will understand better in time, but just know that you are safe here. No harm will come to you, and one day you will go home."

Heather's voice quavered, "Will they rape me, torture me?"

"No, no, no, my dear girl. No one will molest you in any way. These young men will protect you with their lives. You are safe."

"What about that terrorist, Hunter Caulfield. He's awful. Is he going to kill me, or is it just to get ransom money?"

"In due time, in due time. Try to come to peace with it. I absolutely guarantee that you will be able to roam free here, to help if you want; but no one will force you in anything. Hunter Caulfield is nothing like what he is portrayed to be. In time you will come to know that. The man has been terribly wronged, and I'm afraid that much of that evil comes from your father."

"So, he'll get revenge by torturing me?"

She could not get that pervasive idea out of her mind.

"No, I repeat, no. My father will not let anything bad happen to you. You haven't seen him yet. When you do, you will know that you are safe. No one can go up against him. No one ever tries. Hunter Caulfield may seem scary, but my dad is the very definition of it if you are on his wrong side."

Tran took a digital photograph of Heather holding the *New York Times* newspaper edition he and Xe had bought on the way out of the U.S. He regretted having to make the girl take off her clothes; but Hunter had insisted, absolutely insisted. It was over in about a minute, and he quickly covered her up and no one ever did anything like that again.

It took three months for Heather to be convinced—three months of free roaming, long conversations with the large extended set of family and friends, and the mothering kindness of Candy. Initially Heather was dismayed about being jerked away from her life at Yale with all of its urbanity, vibrancy, and quirkiness. By three months, however, she rather enjoyed the tranquility of the pastoral life afforded her on the ranch. In all of that time, she did not even attempt to walk to the edge of the property, even though no one made a move to prevent her. She was certain that it would be futile for her to go out into the vastness that lay around her, and she was entirely correct. In the life on the ranch, she was safe.

CHAPTER SIXTY-THREE

Two Days After the Encounter at the Prentiss House

Oliver had worked feverishly to get himself free after Hunter had left. He was afraid of what he was going to see once he got loose, and almost as afraid that his maid, Cassandra, would be the first on the scene; and the story would be front page on the *Washington Post*. He developed the distinct feeling that Hunter had put the restraints on just loose enough that he would be able to work his way free in a few hours. It took six hours and twenty-three minutes to be exact.

He tore into the hallway and turned on all of the lights. The ladder was lying in a twisted heap on the floor of the story below. Natalie was not there. He panicked and ran down the stairs two at a time. There was no sign of Natalie—no blood, no hair, no clothes, no nothing. He was agonized that she had been killed and taken away to be buried in the woods or incinerated or thrown into the Potomac. He was exhausted, and it was almost impossible to think. He stank to high heaven from the stress-sweat he had worked up during the night, and his clothes were ruined. He was parched. He slowly climbed back up the stairs to his bed room to think, to shower, and to put on something clean.

There, he experienced a profound kaleidoscopic mix of emotions as he found his wife lying inert on the bed under a blanket. She was alive, filthy, terrified, traumatized, beautiful, and ecstatically happy to see her husband again, to have her bindings removed, and to get circulation moving again. She was confused at what had happened and why. She was deeply anxious about what they should do and what was going to happen. All she believed in, hoped for, and understood had been shattered. Oliver felt much the same way.

Much as it pained him to do so, he knew he had to tell her the truth about Heather and about Hunter's threats. He was going to have to confess that he was most unsure about what to do next.

Natalie showered and dressed, then she and Cassandra scrubbed the mess she had made in the hallway. She and Oliver had a light breakfast; and then, Oliver had gotten his courage up enough to broach the subject of Heather's kidnapping.

"Nat, I know you think you've been through the worst, and you've heard the worst; but there's something else you have to know."

"What? What more could there possibly be?"

He produced the photo of Heather holding the *New York Times* and showed it to her. She vomited before he could give even a word of explanation. He carried her to the bathroom where she emptied her stomach. She slid away from the toilet bowel and lay supine on the floor sweaty and ashen.

As gently as he could he told her everything that he knew from the previous night, leaving out any reference to Hunter as Sheep Dog or his complicity in the Sheep Dog's actions, or the demands Hunter had written out and included in the envelope with the photograph. She could not force herself up from the bathroom quite yet, but she was now calm.

"What do we do?"

"I have basically two options, Nat. I can cooperate with law enforcement and set them on his trail from here, or I can hope that our old friendship will prevent him from harming Heather. He didn't kill us, and he wants something specific from us. I'd guess that he wants me to make the manhunt go away, but he has to know that I am powerless to do that. I'm inclined to take the wait-and-see option. What do you think?"

She had not put in a second of vacillation.

She said emphatically, "We wait. If they catch up with him, he'll have her killed. That is one thing I am sure of. Then, we will never know what happened to her."

Oliver stewed and vacillated for two days before making a decision about what he should do. He based his decision on his gut feeling that—in the end—Hunter Caulfield would wreak revenge. He had to take the chance that the man could be caught and *persuaded* to reveal where Heather was being kept. He factored in the potential that Heather might become collateral damage. It was terrible to think about; but even her death could not compare to what would happen to Natalie and him, including the destruction that would result from his exposure in this whole messy business. He knew just the man for it. He made a call to The Farm.

"Salinger here."

"Ed, you recognize my voice?"

"Yeah. What's up?"

"Is this a secure line?"

"As secure as our government can make it."

"I have a job for you, an off-the-books sort of job."

"I hate conversations that start with that kind of caveat."

"You won't like this one, but it has to be done. I'll get right to the point. I need you to bring in Hunter Caulfield. I'm sure you have figured out that he is your very own John Smith and is the Sheep Dog. He trusts you, and he'll walk into a trap you set. I don't want to harm him, but I need for you to get some information vital to national security from him. Do what you have to do, but don't kill him. Call me when you have him in a secure situation. I'll give you further instructions then."

Edgar Liam Salinger had worked for the CIA since he was eighteen years old. He had been a full-fledged officer for forty-five years, and in all of that time it had never occurred to him to refuse a mission or to subvert one. Now, it occurred to him to retire—now, today. His sober and obedient side told him that The Company could never just let him go. He knew things that could bring down governments. Moreover, his compassionate side told him that Hunter Caulfield was a dead duck if he could not get to him before the cops did. He would be turned over to the CIA, which had the original jurisdiction; and he would disappear.

Ed remembered having been the instrument of disappearance of more than one traitor to the CIA. Ed did not want another one on his conscience. Ed Salinger did not have much of a conscience, he admitted to himself. His parents had been Unitarians, a sect which Ed called a cushion for back-sliding Christians to land on. He intended personally only to enter a church twice in his life—once when he was born; and he had already done that; and once when he died; and both times he would have to be carried in. He had done things people should not do, even *pro patria*. He had obeyed orders that should not be given. He could not talk about almost anything that he had experienced in his adult life. But, he felt somewhere back in his insular mind that what was about to happen involving Hunter Caulfield was a mortal sin.

"All right," he said, "I still have the codes. I'll send a message and see what comes of it."

Oliver called in sick for the two days immediately after the midnight encounter with Hunter. He opened his computer for the first time since the episode. What he saw was a very queer thing. Instead of his program opening to the agency counterterrorism page when he entered his password, a glossy color photograph of a beautiful, gleaming white Great Pyrenees Sheep Dog filled the desktop of his computer screen. It was not possible that anyone could have hacked into one of the most secure computer sites in the world. He had personally been responsible for having the electronic security updated. He had worked with…what was that company?…the Starbright Corporation, the best in the world, to install anti-hacking software.

He felt sick. He had made a colossal blunder, and when The Company tracked the transactions they would very quickly learn that the CEO of Starbright at the time had been none other than his current nemesis, Hunter Caulfield. The presence of the photo on his computer was another kiss of death from his former friend, and Oliver's resolve hardened. He was going to bring Hunter Caulfield down, no matter what the cost.

Every office and officer who had received the original 08, January Department of Justice message with the CIA BOLO attached also received the peculiar bit of hacking and every one of them had no explanation. When the DOJ got around to asking questions about what the sheep dog photo could mean, Oliver lied.

Sheep Dog stole a car in Arlington and drove to Fredericksburg, Virginia. At the PostNet office, he picked up the box he had shipped containing his three untraceable guns, closed his account, and drove to New York in a second stolen car. He parked in an open lot outside the city operated by a community volunteer group and called for a taxi into the city. He was disguised as a postman by the time he checked for messages on a computer in the Stephen

A. Schwarzman Building, the main New York Public Library on Fifth Avenue at 42nd Street. He was not surprised to find an encrypted message; neither was he surprised to find out that it came from Ed Salinger. It was simple and to the point, requesting a meeting of Ed and Sheep Dog alone.

Sheep Dog's danger antennae were in full operation. He trusted no one at this point; and since there is no such thing as a coincidence, the message coming this close to his late night tête-à-tête could only be construed that Oliver had gotten Ed to send it. That fact could mean either of two things: it was a trap, or it was the first step in Oliver's compliance with Sheep Dog's demands. He replied with a time and place of his choosing—in fact, of his choosing several days previously.

Several bulletin board notices and posters advertised a Red Cross blood donation drive being held in the library that morning. Sheep Dog filled out a form with a pack of lies and submitted to a cursory physical examination. He donated a pint of his blood. He carefully watched as the venipuncturist set aside the plastic bag of his blood among nearly a dozen other blood bags on the table between the recliner where Hunter was sitting, and the next recliner with the next donor.

"Take all the time you need, sir. Thanks for your help. Drink some OJ, and be careful when you stand up."

The venipuncturist set to work on the next donor and turned all of his attention to her. Sheep Dog got up slowly and found that he felt fine. What he did next was a curious thing. He took one step to the side and picked up his blood bag, tucked it under the flap of his postman jacket and walked away.

CHAPTER SIXTY-FOUR

Interagency Fugitive Operations Office, Brooklyn Court Street Federal Building.

Frank Jefferys and Linc Goodworth came in late from a day filled with two take-downs in the Bronx. There were two fewer drug vendors on the streets and two more back in custody. It felt good; getting mopes out of circulation *was* good. It was Miller-time and time to go home. The two marshals groaned as they watched the first of three faxes come off the printer.

Message Begins
Urgent

Message Origin: U.S. Marshals Squad, Bronx Borough, South Bronx; USMS HQ; DOJ

Date and time of Transmission: 18 September, 2215 hours

Message Recipients: IFO; FAT, NYPD; JTF-6, FBI Federal FAT of Greater New York; NYPD Traffic Dept.

See BOLO-CIA internal communication US9164-CT 4779, 0107TWEP

See VICAP and NCIC link to BOLO

Message: U.S. and International fugitive, Hunter Caulfield, positively identified in New York City, Manhattan between 1522 and 1630 18 September. Computerized facial recognition confirms two verified sightings, one for subject walking in front of Henderson's 24 Hour Grill on 42nd Street, and the second for subject leaving Stephen A. Schwarzman Building, the main New York Public Library on Fifth Avenue at 42nd Street, one hour later. At library, subject was wearing postal worker uniform.

Unconfirmed sighting, Daniel McGinty's 24 Hour Bar and Grill at 81 West 31st Street, Precinct 14, Midtown South at 2100 hours.

Request: Immediate emergency dispatch of available units. IFO, Brooklyn nearest and has the lead. Coordinate by telephone. Do not wait for backup. All units move with all haste—lights and sirens. NYPD traffic division to coordinate route and traffic control

Comment: Subject is extremely dangerous. Full riot gear mandatory. Expect heavy gun fire response to approach by officers. RTA [Return to Archive] notation-CIA, FBI, Interpol. Special note: Presidential Green Light

There are 2,397 security surveillance cameras in Manhattan, plus 55 sighted on the major traffic arteries and 4,313 on the subway system. The vast computerized network of interrelated cameras includes Visionics company software, Facelt—which automatically locates faces in complex scenes— and Software and Systems International software—Mandrake, with a truly remarkable ability to identify faces. Mandrake identifies, collates, and separates faces even in crowds, taking into account head orientation, lighting, conditions, facial expression, aging, and attempts at disguise. The cameras are found in doorways, alcoves and above garage doors. There are full and half sphere globe cameras on light poles, on the corners of buildings, outside stores, and on the vast majority of restaurants and bars.

The camera mounted between the first and second stories of the Lennox Palace Hotel and focused on the hotel's entrancewhich was also the entrance into Daniel McGinty's 24 Hour Bar and Grillregistered two separate facial identification images during the previous 48 hours that were decoded by the system's computer to correspond to the face of international fugitive, Hunter Caulfield. Close monitoring of the video feed from the hotel did not reveal the fugitive leaving.

The second message came immediately on the tail of the first printing:

Message Begins

Message Origin: RCMP Border Security Houlton, CPIC

Date and Time of Transmission: 18 September, 2128 hours

Message Recipient: IFO; FAT, NYPD; JTF-6, FBI Federal FAT of Greater New York; NYPD Traffic Dept., Interagency Fugitive Operations, Federal Building, Court Street, Brooklyn, NYC, Canadian CPIC [Canadian Police Information Centre] and FIRS-Canada-wide (Federal Information Relay Service)

See BOLO-CIA internal communication US9164-CT 4779, 0107TWEP

See VICAP and NCIC link to BOLO

Message: FYI. Possible sighting of subject of BOLO, Hunter Caulfield. Suspicious vehicle at border crossing late hours of 16 September, 2305 hours. Vehicle left in small private airport and suspicious persons entered helicopter and left without flight plan. Possible that one of the suspicious persons may be fugitive Caulfield entering Canada illegally.

"A day late and a dollar short," Linc said. "Grab the next one and let's get out of here. Hey, Franks and Tomlin, suit up, full gear, we have a big one. Expect action. We'll give details en route. Head for Midtown South."

The third transmission followed the first two, and was an automatic response to the RCMP message. That response had been prepared in advance by Yuri Yurievich Chopiak in faraway Khimki in the event that a new directive tied Sheep Dog to anyplace in Canada. It was directed to every federal agency involved in fugitive apprehension. Below the Message Recipient line the photograph of a Great Pyrenees sheep dog printed out. After that, the Interagency Fugitive Operations computer crashed. The same thing happened to the all 94 offices of the USMS FBI, ATF, DEA, JTF-6, NCIC, VICAP, FLO, NYPD FAT SQUAD, INS, CIA, NSC, all state and D.C. police and major city police offices, Canadian CPIC, FIRS-Nationwide, U.K.-Scotland Yard, U.K. wide Special Police Forces, SOCA-Serious Organized Crime Agency, French *Gendarmerie National and Police Nationale,* Russian Federal Security Service (FSB) and Ministry of Internal Affairs *Militsiya,* OMON: Russian—Отряд милиции особого назначения; *Otryad Militsii Osobogo Naznacheniya,* and Special Purpose Police Unit [*OMOH*] computers.

The result was a Chinese fire drill—or maybe a better analogy—is a Keystone Cop movie scenario involving blind lunatics in an unsupervised race to McGinty's.

CHAPTER SIXTY-FIVE

2200 Hours, 18 September
Daniel McGinty's 24 Hour Bar and Grill

When Sheep Dog arrived in New York City he searched for the most inconspicuous place to flop in Manhattan. He chose a room on the 15th floor of the Lennox Palace Hotel at 81 West 31st Street, 14 floors above a sleazy all night Irish bar and grill called Daniel McGinty's even though it was owned by a small time hood named Rodrigo "Bad Tooth" Delatante, a Sicilian. Sheep Dog scouted out the room and made sure he had a good view of 31st Street and Fashion Avenue below and an easy escape route up the elevator or fire escape to the roof. The hotel had a breeze way bridge across to the next door Harmony Franks Office Building and Factory.

At nine o'clock, he came down from his room and found a small booth and took a Naugahyde covered seat in the polluted atmosphere of the bar. He ordered a Bud Lite and a grilled cheese sandwich. The cigarette and cigar smoke in the air was thick enough to cut. The Southern black man sitting at the table next to him was eating a bowl of dry Golden Flake cereal and alternatively drinking from a bottle of chocolate milk and a bottle of Thunderbird Wine, one of the three vintages offered in McGintys. Three older addicts hunched in a darkened booth and cooked up "Chiva"—Spanish colloquialism for heroin—and a small group of young men prepared to shoot up DOI—2,5-Dimethoxy-4-Iodoamphetamine, an hallucinogenic. "*To each his own,*" Sheep Dog thought.

The dim view afforded the discerning late night patron of McGinty's included a Genesee Beer sign, a plastic reproduction of a green St. Pauli's Beer bottle—a beer that did not sell because it was expensive—a Muriel Cigar clock, two tired and world weary waitresses, and a huge black man in a sleeveless, dirty, once white undershirt who served as a bouncer and janitor. A few men were scattered at card tables playing Liars Dice and a variety of brands of poker—Omaha, 7-Card Stud, and Texas Holdem. There were two billiards tables with noisy and profane games of 8-ball and snooker underway. It was a room full of drunks—men and women—air full and hazy with cancerous cigarette and cigar smoke, the smell of stale beer and sweat mingled with Bay Rum, Old Spice, and a hint of sweetness from a marijuana joint. The sound of constant white noise punctuated with intermittent strains of a Tito Puente or a Garth Brooks song formed the background music for the scene.

Outside, the occasional ambulance or police siren whined; but otherwise McGinty's shut out the intrusions of the streets and real life. No one talked to anyone else, and no one could see all the way across the room. For a few days, it was Sheep Dog's kind of place. At quarter of eleven, he finished his beer and sandwich and paid cash for his meal and a tip. He rode the elevator nonstop to the 15th floor and entered his room and double chain locked the door. Being his usual overly cautious self, he took one last look out onto the streets below. A light rain had begun to fall, and the usually dark streets were now opaque in the gloom. The street light on the corner was out, and only the glow of lights from across the street gave any hint that there was a future on the lifeless streets.

As he was about to turn away and get into bed, he saw—for the first time—something out of place on the street below. It had not been there before. He looked intently now. What he was seeing was the furtive movements of men running in zigzag patterns towards the hotel carrying the faint lights of neon glow sticks—policemen holding the lights to identify each other in the murk of the night. Despite his tiredness, Sheep Dog sprang into action. He did not give a nanosecond's thought that this could have anything to do with anyone else but him.

It was his rule never to spread out his things in a hotel room or put anything into a drawer. He swept up his satchel of false passports, driver's licenses, three guns, and a change of clothes and sprinted to the door. He peered out of the peep-hole; and, seeing no one in the dimly lit hall, he quietly and quickly went out into the hall. He ran to the elevator jumping up to knock off the ceiling light bulbs as he went. He got on the elevator and hit the top floor button.

Below, in McGinty's 24 Hour Bar and Grill there was pandemonium. The first four U.S. Marshals entered through the doors and another set crashed through the street level window taking out the Beetle's poster from the sixties and the Red Hot Chili Peppers band sticker from the nineties in the crash. Gallon jugs of Thunderbird and Gallo crashed off the shelves screwed onto the mirror behind the bar. The drunks cowered under their seats, and the bouncer/janitor was run over like a high school freshman football guard in an NFL game.

The heavily armed marshals shouted orders and flashed Hunter Caulfield's photo to everyone in the room, none of whom could contribute a thing, and the only thing that came of that futile effort was a lot of blubbering and slurred denials. Linc Goodworth cornered the bar keep and shoved the photo in his face.

"I never seen him," the half-drunk Irishman whimpered.

"He lives here, punk. Try again."

The bartender wanted nothing more than to get the behemoth out of his face and away from his space.

He relented in his protestations of ignorance, "Yeah, maybe. There's a guy what stays upstairs who maybe looks somethin' like that. The book's over by the phone. Your guess is as good as mine which room he's stayin' in."

Linc hurried to the hotel register book and turned to the last page. He ran his index finger over each entry listing a man who booked into the hotel in the past four days. This yielded six men on as many floors. He shouted orders to five officerssome FBI, some ATF, and some USMSto head to the respective floors and gave each officer a name and room number. He took the one on the fifteenth floor himself. The elevator ride was a scene of frustrating chaos. Each officer pushed the button for his assigned floor, and the creaking old elevator moved with glacial celerity up the shaft, stopping at five floors and letting an officer out. The hotel shortly became a nightmare of door banging, shouting, and the tossing of several flash-bang grenades. The air filled with acrid smoke as the officers met the occupants in a cacophonous, blasphemous one-sided conflict.

On the sixth floor, a late-middle aged African American couple was startled out of their sleep by a marshal breaking down their door. The befuddled woman asked her husband, if it was the Dominos Pizza delivery man.

"No, Sophronia," her husband said, "it's the cavalry."

Marshal Goodworth finally got to the fifteenth floor. His psychological fuse was lit and sputtering by the time all of the stopping and scrambling to get out of the elevator and into action had come to an end. He burst out of the elevator and raced to the end of the hall to number 1521 and banged on the door.

"U.S. Marshals. Open up!" he shouted three times.

He waited a full second and then kicked the door in. The door reluctantly splintered open after four bone-jarring front kicks. Three seconds later, he was satisfied that the room was clear. The only evidence that the room had been occupied was the fact that the bed spread was rumpled. He decided to act on a hunch, having nothing else to go on. He raced back to the elevators and waited for what seemed like an interminable period of time before the middle elevator came back down from floors above the fifteenth.

That confirmed Linc's hunch, and he punched the topmost floor button— the 32nd—and rode to the top. He found the stairs and raced up the single flight of stairs to the metal door that led out onto the roof. He had to stop to catch his breath and to curse his own failure to keep in shape. He was hampered by the good forty-five pounds of gear he was packing. The order to suit up in full riot gear was roundly hated by every marshal and cop on the job because the gear was so hot and heavy to pack around that it impeded mobility. You had to be an Olympic marathoner and weight lifter to run in all that stuff.

In addition to his own not inconsiderable bulk, Linc was carrying a Kevlar second-chance vest with ceramic trauma plate. Around his waist he had a Sam Browne black webbed leather belt loaded with gear: a Beretta 9 mm semiautomatic, 2 sets of mat-black handcuffs, two extra 15 round magazines and a Smith & Wesson 9 mm on a shoulder holster rig, a can of Mace, a Mini-Maglite and a large Maglite with four D-cell batteries on belt hooks. He had a portable radio attached to a microphone mounted on his left shoulder, his gold Marshall's star badge on a leather clip next to his large belt buckle, and slung over his shoulder a Heckler and Koch MP-5K minisubmachine gun with a half moon shaped magazine of 30 mm full metal jacketed bullets. His armamentarium was topped off with four flash-bang stun grenades, and, for good measure a Monadnock billy club.

Linc took a deep breath and blasted himself through the door and onto the roof into a defensive crouch. He saw no one near the door, and he was equally convinced that no one was on the roof as he raced around the periphery in a very quick search. He was about to admit that his hunch had been wrong when he heard the faint clatter of feet. He looked across to the next building top just in time to see a fleeing figure approach the far side of that roof.

He ran at sprint speed to the breeze way bridge between the two roof tops and across to the other side puffing, sweating, and swearing as he went. Breaths were coming hard now. He reached the roof's edge and peered over at the fire escape in time to see his quarry descending with considerable speed and agility. He could not even tell if it was a man or a woman; but since he or she was running away from a cop, he or she had to be bad.

"Stop or I'll shoot," he choked out, having difficulty coming up with enough air to get out a good authoritarian order.

He didn't have the breath for another yell; so, he fired three quick shots. He knew it would be nothing short of a miracle if he hit the guy, and all that came of it was the high pitched metallic ping of ricochets bouncing off the metal fire escape steps. He bit the figurative bullet and started down the rickety ladder clinging on for dear life and afraid that the extra weight would put him off the ladder for a thirty story fall. He somehow made it to the bottom and was—by then, soaked in sweat—and heaving for breath. He placed his hands on his knees to catch enough wind to be able to get on. He shouted into his shoulder radio for back up.

Frank Jefferies responded, "Where are you Linc?"

Linc coughed into the radio, "Nearing the corner of West 30th and Fashion. Perp's headed west on 30th towards 8th Ave. Get everybody out of the Lennox and onto the street. I am in pursuit of a definite fleeing suspect who fits our guy."

He ran out onto 30th as fast as his lungs and his equipment would let him move. He hated all the stuff on his Sam Browne. For one thing, as he ran, all those heavy pieces of equipment banged bruises on his butt and—if he turned just right—gave him a good jab in midline places he would be embarrassed to mention in polite company. He moved along fast enough just to be able to see the perp round the corner of 8th Ave, a block below Penn Station, and head southwest towards 29th Street.

He called that information in to Frank and continued to run. Suddenly, he felt a crushing, overwhelming substernal chest pain that radiated down his left arm and up into his left jaw. Everything started to go black. He knew that he was experiencing the classical deadly symptoms of a heart attack. He presumed that he was a dead man as he pitched forward and landed on his face on the pavement.

Marshal Frank Jefferies came running down 30th behind Linc and was horrified to see his partner lying inert on the sidewalk. He assumed the worst.

He knelt over Linc's body and felt for a carotid pulse. It was there but thready. His partner was alive, but barely.

Frank caught his breath and called in the "officer down" code and Linc's location. He decided that there was nothing he really could do for his partner and took off after the perp. The figure rounded the corner on 29th still heading west. Frank called that fact in and ran as hard as he had ever done in his life. As he passed an alley in the middle of 29th, he heard a man's voice which startled him as if he had touched an electric wire.

"Stop!" the disembodied voice commanded.

Frank reflexively went for the Tec-Nine on his belt.

Sheep Dog had wanted to avoid at all costs what was going to happen next. He purposely held the Springfield XDN 9 mm hoping that he would be able to put a pursuing police officer out of commission without killing him by stunning the cop with a couple of well placed rounds in the man's Kevlar vest that knocked him down. Frank Jefferies was about to have further reason to thank the policy requiring the vest and ceramic insert. Sheep Dog fired another two rounds directly into Frank's vest stunning him and taking away his ability to breathe. He had not put in the "cop-killer" rounds; so, the marshal would have vividly memorable bruises when he came to; but neither round would penetrate into his chest; and he would live to work another day.

Sheep Dog took a quick look into the street. No one had as yet come to back up the two marshals, but he could hear the wailing sirens approaching. He sprinted to West 28th where he saw a Yellow Cab waiting on the street by Chelsea Park. The cab driver was taking a cell phone call. It is illegal for a professional driver to use a cell phone while driving, and the elderly Hungarian immigrant was not about to take a chance on losing his license. It was hot and muggy out and a fine rain still misted the air. He had opened the driver's side window to get some air into his environment of tobacco smoke and mugginess.

Sheep Dog jammed his gun in the old man's face and shouted, "Out. I'm taking the car."

He jerked the door open and hurled the startled and bemused cabbie out onto the wet street. The old man watched helplessly as the car-jacker drove away in his livelihood. He made the sign of the cross and thanked God that he was—at least—still alive.

Sheep Dog made a U-turn and drove away to the West putting ever more distance between himself and the hordes of law enforcement converging on the pitiful Lennox Palace Hotel. He made a right on 10th Avenue and drove to the exit leading to the Lincoln tunnel as the armadas of police cars raced into

Midtown South. They paid him no attention as they focused on their police vehicles' VDTs—Video Data Terminals—devices mounted on a swing-arm on the dashboard, with a bright orange screen which fades to black as it warms up, and an orange cursor. The officer in the shotgun seat punches in an access code, gets a menu list, hits a function button to get NCIC activated, while the driver tries to listen to his partner and to concentrate on not having a collision with all of the other police units heading towards the unmistakable crime scene illuminated even at that distance by the brilliant spot lights coming down from four police helicopters hovering over the corner of 31st and Fashion. There were too many flashing lights, orange cursors, and internal distractions for anyone to notice one of the thousands of Yellow Cabs plying its trade that night going in the opposite direction.

Sheep Dog eluded any would-be pursuers without them having any idea that they had passed right by Public Enemy Number One without even a passing glance in his direction. He held to the speed limit and drove steadily north. He found a place to hide and crash in the dark shrubbery of Morningside Park and stayed there until it started to get light.

CHAPTER SIXTY-SIX

The Next Day, 1800 Hours
Office of DFBI, J.Edgar Hoover Building, Washington, D.C.
Present: DFBI, ADFBI, DUSMS, DINTERPOL, DRCMP,
COMMANDER IFO

The six men sitting around the polished oak table were tired and glum. Sinclair Thompson, the DFBI, spoke first, "Gentlemen, we had a colossal SNAFU last night. We all but called out the National Guard, and Captain Caulfield still got away. One U.S. Marshal had a heart attack, and another took two in the chest. He's sore, but he's okay, just bruised up because he had on a vest. Civilian bystanders didn't fare so well. Two habitués of this place they raided, uh…McGinty's bar…got knocked around pretty badly; one died of a broken neck and another is in critical condition from a head injury. And neither of them had anything to do with the fugitive. In the excitement and confusion, an older neighborhood man was accidentally shot to death. The media are camped out at the bar, and it is the usual circus. I suppose you've had a chance to hear what they're saying about us."

They all nodded. It was teeth-gritting time.

"And the worst thing about the whole sorry affair is that Caulfield has vanished from the face of the earth. He has to have an army of co-conspirators. No one could move that far into the shadows without boocoo help. We have hundreds of leads we're following, but so far we've got bupkis."

"This is CIA's guy, right?" asked the commander of the Interagency Fugitive Operations office. "So, where are they today?"

Oliver Prentiss glared. He wanted to say that The Company's mandate only allowed them to work on foreign soil. He also wanted to say that his agents had been operating to the maximum degree possible during the whole manhunt, but they had to keep under the radar. He wanted to punch the IFO commander directly on his huge nose. But, he did none of that. Just glared.

"Conniving, I suppose," answered the disgruntled director of the FBI for Lang, giving Prentiss a reassuring sidelong glance. "Oh, that's not really fair. They are using up every asset all over the world in this hunt. They can't work here; so, Mr. Lang told me it would be a waste time for them to attend our get together."

Each director handed out a summary of his agency's efforts over the night, and a bulleted, tersely worded list of the historical events up to that day. They parted with promises to keep in touch by conference each day at the same hour until Caulfield was either caught or something better came of their efforts.

At three on the same day, Sheep Dog took a room at the Ritz Carlton Tysons Corner in McLean, Virginia. He had been able to get to a truck stop bathroom to apply the last bit of disguise material in his satchel to become an elderly tycoon. He completed the impersonation by walking into the highly touted men's clothiers—James Limited—and bought a full dark suit, red tie, white shirt, dress tasseled black loafers for a rather obese and stoop shouldered man. He was able to be fitted off the rack without alterations being required. He presented his American Express Gold Card for the clothing and the hotel booking and made himself scarce, hiding in maximum luxury. His name for the occasion was Peter Alan Webster from Oklahoma City, Oklahoma—one of Chun Lam Kong's creations. The first thing he did when he got into the room was to place the bag of his blood into the room's mini-fridge.

Immediately after eating a sumptuous early dinner, Sheep Dog checked his e-mails and found a note from "John I" requesting a meeting. Sheep Dog replied and agreed to meet his teacher in Loudon County. The message he sent to Ed, when decrypted, read:

Meet Great Falls, Loudon County, Va, Monday 0600: Come alone or not at all. Presence of any other person will result in great harm, and you will never see me again. I will always be out there with my skills and my secrets. Drive to the end of Seneca

Road, park on the shoulder in front of the locked gate. Pass the gate and walk down the paved road until it turns left 90 degrees. At this point turn north off the road and follow the Potomac Heritage National Scenic Trail [PHNST]. It is easy, just watch for the turquoise blaze marks until it goes into a passage through the large Lowe's Island Golf Course. Southbound, the PHNST follows the old road toward the Potomac River, and then turns downstream. Where the cliffs drop directly to the river, the trail climbs a series of switchbacks to the ridge. Stop there and do not go up towards the ridge. You will find a small historical marker pointing in the direction of the switchbacks telling you that the trail leads to the old bypass channel constructed by George Washington's Patowmack Company in the late 18th century and that this segment of the PHNST is now called the Ira Gabrielson Trail. Wear a bathing suit and water shoes. Set your clothes within sight of the historical marker and have nothing on but the bathing suit. I will be watching, and when you have complied, I will step out in a bathing suit as well. That way we will both be and feel safe. I look forward to seeing you and to getting something worked out with The CIA with your help.

"After a bad opening, there is hope for the middle game. After a bad middle game, there is hope for the endgame. But once you are in the endgame, the moment of truth has arrived."
—Edmar Mednis, speaking about chess

CHAPTER SIXTY-SEVEN

Sheep Dog had three advantages. He had spent most of the time he was courting Rosie in the very same area, hiking the very same trails. She was born and grew up in Sterling in a residential area just off Lowes Island Parkway and with a view of the golf course. He had played golf with her father and two brothers on the course and had taken some harrowing trips down the tempestuous river in a Combat Rubber Raiding Craft [CRRC]— best known as a Zodiac for its manufacturer—that he had managed to get listed as "excess equipment" and sent back to her parents' house during one of his Viet Nam tours. The family was probably never in any real danger. The Zodiac is a 15-foot, heavily reinforced, inflatable rubber boat that that is tough, reliable, and difficult to sink. He earned a bucket full of kudos from her family, and some rewards from Rosie that he really cared about. His last hike into the area of the cliffs had been with the whole family just prior to his daughter—Donna's—marriage. They had played hide-and-seek for hours, and Hunter came to know just about every hiding place there was along the river and in the dense adjacent woods and craggy rocks.

His second advantage was that Ed Salinger trusted him; he had every reason to do so, and no reasons not to. The third advantage, he would manufacture for himself. After checking out of the hotel and stealing another car, he bought some things he needed at Loudon Guns in southeast Leesburg. Loudon Guns is a very large and well stocked shop which carried everything he needed, and he was familiar with it from years past. He then waited until deep darkness that Friday night. He drove to Seneca Road and found a parking place about a mile from the locked fence which he had told Ed about. There were seven other cars parked there, and he found a place in between two of them. He was paranoid, but in his recent experience it appeared that it was the paranoics who survived. He hoped this tactic would make it too difficult for a car bomb to be placed with any hope of getting the right victim.

He carried a large MagLite in his hand and a backpack full of necessaries including food, water, and weapons for a long stay. He made his way carefully through the golf course and down along the rough winding trail. It was still dark when he arrived at the cliffs, but that was of no great concern since he was so familiar with the terrain. He found the crevice in the cliff walls that he remembered and set up camp deep inside it. He put down his new ghillie suit to ease his muscles and bony protrusions as he settled in that dark crawly den for a three day wait.

At the first hint of light on Saturday, he opened his pack and took out his four guns and the four new hunting knives he had bought at Loudon Guns. He took great pains to hide three guns and three knives within a ten foot radius of the historical marker and made them disappear from the unsuspecting eye. He had no plans to use any of the eight weapons, but he also had no intention of being caught nakedly devoid of a weapon. He placed little tell-tale markers on the locations of the weapons that only he would recognize. Before full light, he retired back to his den to wait unobserved.

School was back in session, and no hikers came down by the river, or visited the historical marker or went up to see the Ira Gabrielson Trail. The weather was overly warm, and he sweated up a healthy stink. He was wearing a bathing suit under his camouflage BDUs—as he had promised—and it was chafing his upper inner thighs like crazy. The bugs were bad, and it was an effort of almost heroic proportions not to scream or to flail at them. He could not make even the smallest fire; so, he ate all cold food as he had planned to do beforehand. For all of that, the worst thing was boredom. He forced himself to keep a lookout and to pay attention, but it was very trying. It was what he remembered from Viet Nam search-and-destroy missions: hurry up and wait; silently sing every song and recite every poem he had every memorized, and try not to think about sex. That—at least—was not an issue for Sheep Dog at this juncture in his life.

"It's always better to sacrifice your opponent's men."
—Tartakover, speaking about chess

It was not until close to midnight Saturday that he heard the first sounds of a man's footfalls coming down to the area where the cliffs meet the river. He froze in place and peeped out from under his ghillie suit cover with his night vision goggles. The silvery light of the full moon reflecting off the river gave the perfect background of limited light to make the figure of the new man in the area between the cliffs and the water's edge stand out in vivid green luminescent relief. The satisfaction gained from that positive finding was tempered by the fact that the intruder was also wearing night vision enhancing eyewear.

The man opened a back pack and took out an entrenching tool and began to dig a deep foxhole in the moist clay of the river's edge. When he had completed his digging, he spread a camouflage net over the opening and got inside to test the visibility of landmarks like the historical marker. He was not quite satisfied. He got back out and extracted a collapsible machete from his back pack and went along the edge of the river and into the brush hacking off a fairly large bundle of fresh branches. He expertly laid a haphazard roof of branches over his fox hole, replaced the camouflage netting over it, and slid under the camouflage via a clever sort of trap door he had included in his work. He rustled the branches a little, apparently adjusting his weapon.

The distance to where Sheep Dog would be standing tomorrow was so small, that it would be almost impossible to miss. In the semi-darkness—even with his night vision goggles—Sheep Dog would not have been able to find the hiding and killing place. He was grateful for the intuition or paranoia or both that had persuaded him to arrive so early to the killing site.

Around four in the morning, Sheep Dog dozed off despite the uncomfortable position he was in. He was aroused by the very quiet, but unmistakable squawk of a walkie-talkie. The sound of the river had become background by now, and the sound of the squawk was followed by a male voice reciting a series of numbers. The new player in this complex game of chess gave the code twice before the killer in the pit responded.

"One," he whispered.

"Two," the newcomer whispered back.

"In place," the man nearest to Sheep Dog—in fact less than twenty-five feet away—announced."

"I'll set up in the trees at the last bend before your hole. That's about 200 yards up, I reckon."

"Good hunting."

"A beer on it?"

"Make it Michelob. Out."

Silence returned, and the waiting game went on. "One" was almost as good at playing the game as Sheep Dog except for two things: Sheep Dog knew "One" was there, and "One" did not know that his opponent was there in the shadows. The second thing was that "One" had not been blessed with the fine bladder capacity enjoyed by Sheep Dog. As the pre-dawn first light began to be manifest, he slithered out of his hole and crawled to the water's edge to urinate. Sheep Dog admired the force of his stream. The man would probably be able to pee over a six foot fence.

"One" crawled back to his fox hole and began to lift his makeshift trap door to slither back into his uncomfortable place of safety. His vigorous bladder emptying and the sound of the strong urinary stream hitting the water had dulled his appreciation of his surroundings. By the time he was lying prone and beginning to lift the branches, he was unaware that another figure was lying along side him in the small adjacent clump of bushes. It was awkward working himself in under the branches, and he was moving head first like a centipede. Sheep Dog drove a hunting knife blade into the midline of the base of his neck between the sixth and seventh cervical vertebrae. The aim was perfect. A single hard thrust drove the knife through the space between the posterior elements of the spinal column and transected the man's lower cervical spinal cord with a surgically clean cut. The knife veered to the side and transected the left carotid artery for good measure. There was very little bleeding; the bulk of the hemorrhage occurred in the anterior part of the neck. Despite the transaction of the carotid, the bleeding was limited also because the hunter/killer was already dead from the cord injury before the artery was severed.

Aside from a muffled grunt, the murder had been very quiet. Sheep Dog pulled on the man's legs and dragged him out of the hole. He stabbed both lungs to facilitate sinking and tied the man's backpack, gun, food bag, and a couple of rocks to the corpse and eased it into the rushing water. In less than two seconds it was gone somewhere down river, likely to be missing for a fairly long time. Sheep Dog tidied up the camouflage over the hole, put on his ghillie suit, picked up his bag of weapons, and began his deadly cat and mouse game with "Two" who did not yet suspect that he had become the prey instead of the predator.

Sheep Dog moved fairly slowly along the trail for the first hundred yards, half the distance that "Two" had said he would be waiting for his and "One's" intended victim. He then moved into the trees walking very slowly, very carefully, and silently; it was the jungle highlands of Viet Nam all over again. It would take infinite patience, but he had a full day to go a hundred yards to get to the other predator. His night vision goggles made the going easy. There was very little dead-fall, and the ground was soft from millennia of accumulated fall leaves and from the frequent rain. It was too early for this year's leaves to fall and litter the ground with crackling debris.

It was getting light when he caught the scent of cologne. It was incongruous in the forest. He slowed down to a near crawl and squinted into the gathering light. Finally, his eyes fixed on a low mound among a collection of four large trees. Sheep Dog envisioned the view of the trail that passed below the mound and decided that this was the killer's vantage point. He now crawled on his abdomen, toes, and elbows, softly, silently, patiently, and inexorably as the morning light increased. Good as the camouflage was, the mound was still artificial, crafted. From the trail, no one would be able to see it, but Sheep Dog was on a level ten feet above in height and fifty feet further along the trail, the opposite direction from which the killer would expect him to come.

The cologne smell increased and was intermingled with the odor of sweat. No sound came from the mound. The man was good except for the foolish vanity to wear cologne. He was probably young, and maybe this was his first real field assignment, Sheep Dog imagined. He envisioned a young man full of piss and vinegar and his own invincibility. He took four hours to move forty feet. He was getting weary, and his concentration was beginning to wander. He bit his tongue hard to clear the cobwebs of his mind and relentlessly inched closer.

Eight feet…six feet…four feet. Slowly closer. Never a sound from the hunter. There was not a movement in the mound. It was now eight o'clock in the morning, and the sun was visible through the trees to the east. He had stripped to his shirt and pants and left the back pack and night vision equipment behind him at fifteen feet away. He made a calculation of risk. He could not afford the attention that a gunshot would bring. He would have to depend on surprise and his knife.

The brush lying over the mound moved very slightly. Sheep Dog could imagine the discomfort of his enemy's position. Maybe there were bugs annoying him. He moved towards the bundle of sticks hiding the man at the speed of an advancing glacier. He now had his K-bar knife in his right hand and ready. He stopped two feet from the mound and waited, as ready to spring as a praying mantis.

And waited still more to be certain of his own security and the security that only a killing would give him. It was enough to drive him crazy. Two full hours passed. A family of fourtwo of which were noisy childrenpassed the mound going down the river to the cliff edge. The mound moved a little. Sheep Dog mentally envisioned the killer taking a better look to be sure that his quarry was not with the noisy family. Sheep Dog's problem was that he could not tell sufficiently well how his prey was positioned to be able to attempt an attack on or through the amorphous mass of the camouflage. He waited.

Just before nine, he heard and smelled the flow of a man urinating. The branches rustled. The man was stretching his stiff joints. The branches lifted enough so the killer could get a better look along the trail. Sheep Dog stopped breathing. A camo gloved hand moved cautiously out followed in half a minute by the man's head which was covered by a camouflage patterned three hole ski mask. He was looking away from Sheep Dog, his gaze focused on the trail to his left. Sheep Dog tensed and concentrated on making his body into a coiled spring.

It was apparent that he would not get another chance; so, he exploded off the ground landing where he envisioned the man's body lay behind his slightly exposed head. The hole was deeper than Sheep Dog had anticipated and the man was protected by the deep pile of branches. He was also pinioned beneath the weight of Sheep Dog and the entanglement of the branches. He grunted from the impact and turned his head and neck to meet his attacker. Sheep Dog could only see that much of him and brought the point of the knife in a wide side-directed arc into the exposed neck. An arterial hemorrhage poured into the foxhole. The man had not had a chance. The element of surprise was far too great to allow either thinking or even an instinctual response. He died in a few seconds. And he died quietly.

Sheep Dog waited until he was certain, then he carefully extracted the body from the foxhole and kicked as much dirt as he could to cover the blood and its smell. He replaced the branches and lowered the profile of the mound to prevent it from attracting any attention. He stabbed the dead man in the chest to deflate the lungs then dragged the body to the river. At that point, the current was six feet below him. He weighted the body down with rocks stuffed into the shirt, under-clothes, and every pocket and slid it over the edge into the Potomac. It disappeared with nothing more than a soft splash. Sheep Dog took a quick look around and satisfied himself that no one had witnessed the killing.

He hurried back up the hill and retrieved his gear then headed in a zig-zag through the trees to his hiding place to wait. It was eleven fifteen. If Ed Salinger was punctual, he had nineteen hours to wait. He ate and drank lustily having decided that this would be the safest time, and he would only be able to nibble thereafter.

The wait seemed interminable. At two in the afternoon, a lone woman walked down the trail, stopped to examine the historical marker then turned and hiked briskly up the switch-back trail towards Washington's old by-pass channel. A pair of teenagers passed by at five thirty. After that, no one came by. The rest of the afternoon, evening, and the night were quiet, lonely, and painfully boring. Crouched in his crevice, he checked his digital watch dozens of times to alleviate the boredom and to give his mind something to do so that he could stay awake. Ed could come any time, and Sheep Dog could not afford to be surprised the way his two victims had been.

"The winner of the game is the player who makes the next-to-last mistake."
—Tartakover, speaking about chess

At twenty to six, he heard the out-of-place sound of a man whistling coming down the trail to his left. It was light out and crisply cool in the morning since the sun had not broken over the hills above. At five to six, he began to hear a man's voice—Ed Salinger's voice—speaking at a conversational level.

"Hunter, it's Ed. If you're here and looking at me, see that I'm unarmed."

He was wearing a tee shirt, Bermuda shorts, and Tevas. He held his hands above his head and twisted his wrists to demonstrate that he, indeed, was unarmed. He repeated his demonstration and his audible message every ten feet or so.

Sheep Dog watched him as he stopped by the historical marker and ascertained that he was in the right place. He checked his watch to be sure he was on time. Sheep Dog waited fifteen minutes to be sure that he was unaccompanied.

Finally, as Ed began to fidget, Sheep Dog called out softly from his hiding place, "Ed, keep your head down. I have an M-16 leveled at you. You don't have a chance. If you have friends out there, I'll kill you before they can get to me."

"I'm unarmed. I come in peace. Don't get nervous. Guns are dangerous, you know," Ed said in a friendly, mildly joking tone.

"Strip down to your bathing suit."

"Is that really necessary, Hunter? I mean you no harm. I'm about the only friend you have left in the world. I have a peace offering from The Company. Come on down and let's talk."

"Let's see your bathing suit."

"You, too."

"You first."

Ed slipped off his shirt and shorts and stood fully vulnerable in his bathing trunks.

"Turn all the way around slowly, Ed. No quick moves."

Ed complied.

"Now let's see you," he said.

Sheep Dog slowly stepped out of the crevice holding the .38 Chief hideway he had bought at Loudon Guns leveled at Ed's mid-chest. He carefully stripped down to his own swim trunks. Ed stood stock still, the quintessence of benign safety.

"Okay," Sheep Dog said as he walked down to where Ed was standing. "Let's talk."

Ed quickly told Sheep Dog about the deal Oliver Prentiss was making. He could come in out of the cold with full written immunity signed by the president. The manhunt would be called off with an announcement that it had all been an error. The news media would be fed a cock-and-bull story about an investigation having cleared him, and he would be able to ride off into the sunset and not have to look over his shoulder.

"And you give your personal word of honor as my friend that the offer is genuine, no strings, no new Sheep Dogs coming after me next week or next year, Ed?"

"I do. I'll step back, and you can check in the right hand pocket of my pants. You'll find a signed copy of the immunity guarantee."

Ed could not control his eyes perfectly. It saddened Sheep Dog when the CIA agent could not resist a quick look to his left at the expertly camouflaged mound where he knew that his ace-in-the-hole lay hidden.

Sheep Dog bent down and felt for the folder in Ed's pant pocket. He found a blue plastic folder envelope with the presidential seal. The immunity—written on embossed parchmen—was there including the famous signature of President Storebridge.

"See, no tricks, no sleight of hand. Come on in out of the cold. No one can survive out there forever."

Ed's cautious face betrayed a growing concern. He chanced another quick look at the mound. Seeing nothing except the haphazardly strewn branches, he made what he presumed would be a casual look up the trail to his right.

Sheep Dog did a better job controlling his face and eyes. He hesitated, his face a picture of concentration as he mulled the decision over in his mind. After a few moments he extended his right hand.

"Shake on it, Ed. I'm exhausted. You warned me about The Company betraying me, and I took what you said to heart. I want you with me when I go in. Deal?"

"Sure," Ed said and extended his hand.

Ed's eyes betrayed him. He looked quickly around in a 180° arc as quickly as possible; hoping Hunter would not notice but demonstrating a small but definite mixture of anxiety and hope.

Sheep Dog clasped Ed's hand firmly and pulled Ed towards him. Ed was not much of a man for hugging, but he moved in to clinch the deal with an embrace. From nowhere, Sheep Dog stabbed a knife hand strike into Ed's vulnerable throat with his left hand stunning him with both surprise and physical injury. He fought for breath and found it extremely difficult. Sheep Dog drove his other fist powerfully into Ed's solar plexus causing sudden nausea and a desperate fight to get air.

Absent the surprise, Ed would have been every bit the match for the Sheep Dog, but now he was crippled.

"Wha...?" he gasped.

Sheep Dog connected with a hard round house punch to the head and a pair of vicious kicks to each of Ed's lateral thighs making his legs buckle. Ed mounted a feeble defense with an attempted knee to Sheep Dog's groin, but Sheep Dog anticipated and deflected it. Ed's attempt at a punch was knocked aside with a numbing punch across his exposed forearm. Sheep Dog bore in and wrapped his right arm around Ed's back, swiveled his hips into place and held Ed's right arm in a vice grip above his elbow. He hurled Ed through the air in a lightening fast *Osae-Komi Uki-Goshi* hip throw. Ed hit the rocky ground from four feet in the air which knocked out all of the air reserves he had left.

Sheep Dog dropped his knee from three feet above into Ed's unprotected solar plexus then pounded his face with six rapid-fire hammer blows. Ed was helpless.

"Why? why?" he managed to get out, gurgling blood from the injuries to his nose and mouth..

"I've been here since Friday, my old friend," Sheep Dog said with maximum venom, "I killed your two ninja buddies and tossed them into the river."

Ed knew his deadly deception had failed and that there would be no last minute help and no mercy. This was his last moment alive, and he resigned himself. He could not mount a defense; so, he waited for the inevitable.

It came with devastating swiftness. Their struggle had unearthed one of the knives Sheep Dog had hidden three days ago. He plunged the blade deep into the side of Ed's neck and moved quickly away to avoid getting covered with the fountain of bright red blood. Ed's body was lying on an incline; his heart had been pumping furiously before the stabbing; and he exsanguinated almost completely in a few seconds.

Sheep Dog's adrenalin subsided, and the blood red tint to his vision cleared. He looked around hurriedly and seeing no one, set to work. The work was grisly. He cut off Ed's head and both hands, weighted the parts down with rocks and threw the head and one hand into the Potomac. He hauled the body up to his crevice hiding place and removed his gear and stuffed the headless handless corpse into the hole and covered it with branches. He opened his backpack and took out the bag of his blood which still seemed to be fluid and not severely deteriorated. He pushed the plastic bag in under the branches alongside Ed's corpse. He went back to the killing site and scuffed dirt over the blood until it was covered. He put Ed's other hand into a baggie and into his backpack along with his gear—including the two guns and the other knife he had buried for the upcoming fight—and took a final look around.

He gave a last nod in the direction of the crevice and said aloud, "You were right, Ed; and I learned well. If you let yourself get into a fair fight, your tactics suck."

With that he hiked back to his car for the next and hopefully the final round in his fight—the last move in the endgame.

Chapter Sixty-Eight

And that after this is accomplished, and the brave new world begins
When all men are paid for existing and no man must pay for his sins,
As surely as Water will wet us, as surely as Fire will burn,
The Gods of the Copybook Headings with terror and slaughter return!
—Rudyard Kipling, *The Gods of the Copybook Headings*

It was midnight. Oliver Prentiss had sent Natalie to her mother's house in Sterling and gave Cassandra a two week vacation to "thank her for her years of service". He was taking no chances that Hunter would return.

He was fast asleep in the master bedroom with the new double bolt lock system on his door engaged. He had had bars put on the windows. He was having a series of unpleasant dreams, but the Ambien he had taken was keeping him from his initial few days of insomnia.

The phone rang. He heard it but could not get the sound to register properly. It rang again. He came to enough to see the dreaded caller I.D. notation of "Wireless Caller" on the LED screen. He cursed and picked up the receiver.

He was about to give the telemarketer a piece of his mind when he heard, "Oliver, don't speak. Listen. You are stupid. You risked Heather's life. Our mutual friend and I had a meet. He brought two friends. Those two have taken a swim in the Potomac. Tomorrow morning you will receive a box delivered by courier to your door. In the box you will find all the evidence you need to confirm where our friend is and his condition. You will follow the instructions in the box about how to get to the next set of clues—sort of like a scavenger hunt, almost perfectly like a scavenger hunt. You will bring home the bag you find beside him, and you will then execute the plan I gave you when we had our last visit. Betray me again, and the next package will be the size of a hat box. You won't need DNA or finger prints to know who won't be coming back."

The phone clicked off as Oliver was stammering out his profuse apologies, his sincere promises, and his primeval panic.

At eight o'clock sharp that morning, the doorbell rang; and a Fed Ex delivery man presented Oliver with a neatly wrapped box for which a signature was required. They exchanged pleasantries, then Oliver calmly shut his door. He raced into the kitchen and tore open the box. It contained a neatly typed note of precise instructions and a severed hand. By noon, he had a match on the fingerprints and DNA. Oliver was on the verge of hysteria after he received the call from the CIA's lab. He called covert ops.

CHAPTER SIXTY-NINE

Five Days Later

Jean-Luc Le Croix sat on the veranda of his plantation home in Hué perusing the two day old copy of *The New York Times* that his houseman had fetched him from the airport newspaper shop.

The front page headline told Sheep Dog what he needed to know:

MANHUNT OVER
Most Wanted Fugitive Identified in Fiery Crash

The article told of "a massive firefight between federal officers and the fleeing fugitive traitor, U.S. Navy Captain, Hunter Caulfield. Caulfield was finally stopped by a hail of machine gun bullets outside the nation's capital which had turned his escape car into a roaring inferno. The bullet ridden charred corpse was identified by dental records and DNA obtained from some blood that had escaped incineration by seeping through the destroyed floor boards onto the automobile's frame. The D.C. Medical Examiner who performed the autopsy listed the cause of death as gun-shot wounds to the chest and head, and expressed his gratitude to federal officials for providing finger print and DNA data to confirm the identity. The long saga of one of the nation's— even the world's—most celebrated manhunts came to an end during the night of September 23rd. No officers were injured or killed, which—as one senior officer put it—was 'nothing short of a miracle'. Except for the federal officers involved, there were no witnesses. One senior federal officerspeaking on condition of anonymitydescribed the final encounter as 'spectacular as the ends for Bonnie and Clyde, and John Dillinger put together', but would not elaborate on details of how the fugitive was found."

The article gave a lengthy and detailed account of the extensive worldwide manhunt and of the massive efforts on the part of federal, state, and local U.S. law enforcement and by their counterparts throughout the world. The director of the FBI was quoted as saying that his bureau "could not have done it without the tremendous level of cooperation that the FBI—as lead law enforcement agency—received."

President Storebridge extended his hearty congratulations to the members of the law-enforcement community and to the regular citizens who had been so beneficial to the FBI's efforts. The world is "a safer place today", the president said.

Muslim leaders from five countries joined in praising the work of the Western police agencies, an almost unprecedented communication for nations usually considered hostile to most military and law enforcement activities in the West. The *Times* took special note of the fact that Iran joined its neighbors in extending its congratulations to the FBI and that this was—perhaps—one more evidence of the welcome thaw between the U.S. and Iran.

Sheep Dog had arrived in Viet Nam the previous afternoon, having traveled from Paris under the name of Asian art importer, Douglas Conroy Weaver from Atlantic City, New Jersey, whose set of identification papers he destroyed before leaving the Tan Son Nhat Airport. As he now sat on his own veranda, he mentally reviewed the instructions he had given Oliver. By now—he assumed—Oliver would have found Ed's body and Sheep Dog's blood and had been able to use his covert-ops resources to obtain a cadaver from somewhere, fake a firefight for the media, and to burn the corpse beyond recognition. Knowing the careful and incorruptible work ethic of the D.C. coroner, Sheep Dog's blood would have had to have been placed very carefully. Sheep Dog had been certain that Oliver would find a way once he had sufficient incentive to apply his sharp mind to the task.

He finished his martini and went inside to send an e-mail message. He let Steffan Johannson know that he would meet him in Quesnel in a year. That trip would provide full closure to the Sheep Dog saga. He arranged a wire transfer of funds to support Heather Prentiss for the year she would have to remain in Canada.

**One Year Later
Quesnel, British Columbia**

Candy sent Tran out to fetch Heather Prentiss when Hunter Caulfield landed in the back pasture of the ranch. Steffan, Xe, Tran, Heather, the Dakelh Indian ranch hands, and nine children watched the final approach. Heather was as excited as she had been for her fifth Christmas morning. Steffan and Candy had promised her for a month that she would be released the day the man the ranch workers called Hi Poindexter came back. Most of the hands knew next to nothing about the man on the helicopter, except that he had been there once before—a year or so ago—and that; on his account, they kept the location of the ranch a complete secret from the American girl, Heather.

Hunter was dressed in old ranch clothing and had a month old beard which aged him ten years. He wore opaque sun glasses and a wide-brimmed cowboy hat pulled low over his forehead. He had dyed his hair black and wore it long like the Dakelhs. His skin was either genuinely tan or he had a convincing make-up job. He greeted the Johannson's affectionately and took a moment to greet every ranch worker enthusiastically. The pilot—one of the cousins named Ben—had briefed Hunter on their names. His long history as a spy had given him a remarkable memory for names, and he impressed and delighted the ranch inhabitants with his easy facility with everyone.

After supper, Hunter and Steffan talked for an hour. Over Steffan's protests, Hunter forced him to take a $100,000 Canadian National Bank bearer's bond for the year's worth of service.

"Who knows, Steffan," Hunter said, "I might have need of your services again one day."

"Let's hope we meet again in less stressful circumstances," Steffan said.

"I'll drink to that."

The men shared a tall glass of Malviore Ice Wine that Hunter had brought from New York for the occasion. He explained the odd origin of the wine and let Steffan judge for himself the quality. The ice wine is harvested from frozen Reisling grapes picked at 14° F. along for the Niagara Peninsula. Steffan approved, so much so that he had another full glass.

In the morning Candy persuaded Heather to don the opaque hood for the trip back home. Hunter avoided talking to the girl who sat in the back seat of the Bell Longranger all the way to Creston, B.C. near the international border where they landed in a small private airport. Hunter then allowed her to remove her hood. She looked about anxiously and was still uncertain as to whether she was in Canada or Siberia. There were no telltale landmarks to convince her of either choice. The short drive from Creston to the Canadian/ US Border allowed her for the first time to know that she was in Canada. She remained uncertain about whether or not she had spent the entire past year in the huge country to the north of her own home country.

For the first time, Hunter spoke to Heather. He did so in a broad Canadian accent with 'ehs', and 'oots' and 'down souths' and a bit of overacting.

"Heather," he said. "You are almost home. You have been on vacation, and you are returning to school. We'll drive to Sand Point, and from then on you are safe and on your own. You can contact the police, and you can speak to the news media if you want. I suggest—however—that you talk to your parents before you do either. They may convince you to keep your recent year's experience to yourself. I am Hyrum Edgar Poindexter. I suggest you remember me and forget other names you know about."

Heather was still cowed by the forceful man who was apparently behind her kidnapping and confused about the reason for it all. She nodded her agreement.

The two drove the rent-a-car through the Rykerts-Porthill border crossing station without incident. Hunter drove south on Idaho Highway #1 to U.S. #95 and into Bonners Ferry—the gateway to north Idaho—where they had a quick hamburger lunch at McDonalds. Hunter let her off in front of the post office in Sand Point, fifty miles south of the border, gave her $10,000 dollars in cash, and told her to "have a nice life".

He drove away out of her life as enigmatically as he had entered it a year ago. She hurried to a Verizon store and purchased a throw-away cell phone and called home.

"Hello."

"Mom, it's me...it's me, Heather."

"Oh, sweetheart, I was afraid this day would never come. Are you all right? Did they hurt you? Are they still guarding you? Did they tell you why they kidnapped you? Oh, baby, are you okay?"

"One thing at a time, Mom. And yes, I'm perfectly okay. I've been a ranch hand, and I am in the best shape I have ever been in. I want to get back to school, but I've changed. I don't think I'll ever be the bratty selfish Yalie I was ever again. The man who dropped me off here told me I probably shouldn't talk to the cops or to the news media until I talked to you guys. Is that what I should do?"

"Your dad is absolute about that. I don't quite understand all the reasons why, but we should really go by what he says. This is one time for sure that we need to trust that he knows best."

"I'll keep quiet. But sometime I'm going to need some explanations. I've earned that privilege."

"You have. Right now what's important is where are you?"

"Some little burg called Sand Point, Idaho. It's right by the Canadian border. How do I get home?"

"Your dad will have a plane in the air within the hour. I think he can get to you before midnight. Check into a motel and call me again when you're settled. Oh, I didn't think, do you have any money?"

"Yeah, Mom, it was weird. The guy gave me ten thousand bucks. I could party hearty tonight."

"Get some food and rest. Dad'll be there before you know it. I will be able to start life all over again when we get you home. I feel like I've been holding my breath for the entire past year."

Heather found out from her father enough to convince her to let the past year's experience become a lost part of history.

"The people who took you are nobody to mess with. They do keep their bargains, and they have a very long reach. I want you to stay safe and live a happy life. You are more likely to be able to do that if you will keep this a secret."

The Same Day
Central Intelligence Building, Langley, Virginia
Office of the Director

DCIA Lang arranged for a black star to be placed in the official history of the Central Intelligence Agency. No one would ever know the name of Edgar Liam Salinger, but his star would at least be part of the noble heritage of agency heroism.

He spoke briefly to his ADCIA, "I'll handle the transfer of evidence to Afshin Baktiari myself. They won't accept anyone's word that the guy they call "The Shadow" is really dead. The evidence looks good, don't you think?"

Lang had reference to his counterpart, the head of The Ministry of Intelligence and Security of Iran—the VEVAK.

"I saw to it myself. We thought of everything. We won't run into any difficulties."

"Good work, Oliver, this had to be hard for you. You have always been a Company man to your core. I'm going to retire after this year, and I'll do my best to put you in my chair when I do."

"Thanks, Director. It's always been the Company and the country above everything else for me. It has been an honor to serve."

The moment was as close to a "warm-fuzzy" as happens in the Central Intelligence Agency.

CHAPTER SEVENTY

"A player can sometimes afford the luxury of an inaccurate move, or even a definite error, in the opening or middlegame without necessarily obtaining a lost position. In the endgame...an error can be decisive, and we are rarely presented with a second chance."

—Paul Keres, speaking about chess

One Year Later
White House Oval Office: Morning Briefing, 0630
Present: POTUS, DCIA

"Good morning, Mr. President. I trust you slept well."

"Thank you, Director Prentiss, tolerably well. What's new?"

"VEVAK handed over the rest of UBL's family members and threw in fourteen middle level agents—scapegoats, to use the Hebrew phrase—for good measure. These scapegoats, however—unlike the Biblical ones—will not be let out to wander alone in the desert. We plan a vigorous interrogation."

"No water boarding or anything not allowed by policy and law. We've all learned the danger of getting overly enthusiastic."

Oliver—like every one of his predecessors—thought that concept was rubbish pure and simple, but he kept his opinion to himself. He had taken elaborate measures to shield the president from ever being informed of Company procedures in dealing with the Iranian agents, whom he knew were already being hailed as martyrs for the jihad in Tehran.

"Maybe the best news is that the Iranians have been keeping a low profile ever since the attack by Israel. We are not getting any intel about them transporting missiles or trained terrorists. They don't act especially chastened, but the result is the same. It appears that your decision to rein in the Sheep Dog program was a wise one."

"Thanks, Oliver. Too bad I can't get a little political credit."

"While it would be nice, you don't really need a bunch more credit. Your administration will leave a sterling history, and you don't have to run again."

If the president was aware that the new DCIA was applying the flattery with a trowel, he did not show it. If the truth were known, he quite liked flattery and thought he deserved it.

"Where are you off to, next, Director?"

"Secretary Southem, Director Thompson, and I will be attending the Organization of American States in Montevideo in April. Besides the plenary sessions, I will be meeting with my counterparts separately to go over strategies for dealing with the 'facilitators of man-made disasters' who are increasingly finding their way into South America. It seems that the Middle-Eastern facilitators have discovered that South Americans have the wrong religion and they present soft targets galore. Our interest is to keep the infiltrators who have come to South America from heading north."

"Keep me up on developments, Oliver. I have to tell you I just don't feel up to going down there in all that heat and humidity this year. I'll depend on the three of you."

Meeting of the Israeli Cabinet-0900
Tel Aviv, Israel
Present-PM, FULL CABINET, FOREIGN MINISTER, DMOSSAD, COMMANDER IDF

"General Fürstenberg, your most recent reports from the overflights across Iran seem convincing. The Iranians do not appear to be starting up their nuclear program."

"Yet," said Ari Maor bar-Lev.

"Always the skeptic, Ari," PM ben Cohen said.

"That's why you pay me the big shekels," Director bar-Lev quipped.

"Do you have any evidence from our assets, Ari?"

"Hints, Ehud, just hints, but we are getting concerned."

"Nothing seems to change, really, does it? Israel appears doomed to repeat this cycle endlessly, going from catastrophe to catastrophe, fight to fight."

"Can you imagine what it would be like if we weren't Yahweh's chosen people?" Ari—the out-of-the-closet atheist—asked.

"I think I can, or at least the prophet Zephaniah could, 'That day is a day of wrath, a day of trouble and distress, a day of wasteness and desolation, a day of clouds and thick darkness'."

EPILOGUE

When the heavens shall be rent asunder,
And when the stars shall be dispersed...
Again, what will teach thee what the Day
of Judgment is?
It is a day when no soul will avail aught for
another soul..."
—Holy Qur'an, 82: 1-19

Get hence, the hearse is at your door—the grim black stallions wait—
They bear your clay to place today. Speed, lest ye come too late!
Go back to Earth with a lip unsealed—go back with an open eye,
And carry my word to the Sons of Men or ever ye come to die:
That the sin they do by two and two they must pay for one by one—

Rudyard Kipling, *Tomlinson*

The Same Year, April
New York Times, Front Page, Column A1

CIA Director Oliver Prentiss Assassinated
Official Murdered at Meeting of OAS
in Montevideo, Uruguay

Reuters News Service-Montevideo, Uruguay: This morning the recently appointed director of the United States Central Intelligence Agency was the victim of an assassination plot in the South American capital city of Uruguay. Details are sketchy, but preliminary reports indicate that he was the victim of an attack with a very swift acting poison. The police commissioner of Montevideo released information indicating that an unknown person was seen to walk up to the senior U.S. official, to speak to him briefly, then to strike him with the point of an umbrella he was carrying. Reports vary about the possible identity of the assassin, even as to his race. Most reports indicate that it appeared to be a well-dressed English gentleman, possibly one of the delegates to the OAS gathering. Others describe one of several disgruntled beggars. There is one report that a man dressed in Arab costume was seen talking to the U.S. official and gesturing with an umbrella. One sighting described a man of Negro extraction rushing at Director Prentiss. The police commissioner cautioned about rushing to hasty conclusions and assured the delegation and the Uruguayan people that a thorough investigation is underway and that the police have several useful leads.

Conspiracy buffs in the United States have suggested that this attack was very similar to one that occurred in England in 1978 when dissident Bulgarian journalist Georgi Markov was murdered. At that time, a Scotland Yard autopsy revealed, imbedded in his leg, a BB studded with tiny holes. It had been shot into Markov with an umbrella rigged as a pellet gun. The holes in the BB had been packed with ricin. Russian spies were thought to be the culprits, but no hard evidence was ever produced, and the murder remains unsolved. U.S. conspiracy theorists—led by Andrew Potter—strongly suggest a Russian plot.

The Times has described the deaths under suspicious circumstances of a total of at least twenty-eight agents considered to be clandestine operatives over the past two years. Although no direct link has been established among the separate incidences, a senior government official, who insisted on anonymity, told *The Times* that, "it strains credulity not to wonder about an organized attack on intelligence officers of the United States". Nevertheless, "the White House denies any known attack, coordinated or otherwise" according to Press Secretary Irwin Lloyd in yesterday's daily conference with the White House press.

Five Years Later
New York Times, Government Section

Washington, D.C.: The director of the Central Intelligence Agency announced today that Heather Prentiss, PhD (Harvard, International Relations) has been appointed as an officer of the agency. She will be part of the analysis division and will, reportedly, be involved in evaluation of Middle-Eastern security affairs. Dr. Prentiss is the daughter of the late director of the CIA—Oliver Prentiss—who was the victim of an assassination in South America five years ago. Director Prentiss's black star award is now one of those proudly displayed in the entryway of the CIA Headquarters in Langley, Virginia. The black star is awarded for agents killed in the line of duty. Dr. Prentiss stated during her appointment ceremony, "my father was a patriot of the first order. I hope to be able to make even a small contribution. I would be arrogant even to wish to be able to make a contribution to the country comparable to that of my father's. I will—however—do my level best to live up to his legacy."

Ten Years Later
New York Times, Front Page, A2-left column, below the fold

Washington, D.C.: President Mary Louise Hanover, Speaker of the House Henry Clay Davidson, and Senate Majority Leader Danny Rodriguez met the press on the West lawn of the White House at nine a.m. today to make a joint announcement that has shocked the world, both for the specific content of the message, and for the far-reaching implications of the underlying reasons for the announcement. President Hanover issued an order canceling all military and social aid to Israel and Egypt for the foreseeable future. The president told the *Times* White House reporter Stephen Prince that the main reason for the change in policy was to further the negotiations directed towards the establishment of a new State of Palestine, "in order to balance the playing field". Administration officials, speaking on condition of anonymity, and Congressional sources have privately informed the *Times* that they have grave concerns about the economic slow-down coming from the massive deficits inherited by this administration from entitlement program payouts that have come due recently. A senior administration official, speaking off the record, stated that "our debt to the Chinese alone requires drastic measures, and the cessation of all foreign aid is on the table". Military equipment subsidies to Israel were cancelled as of ten a.m. EST today. The Israeli ambassador to the United States has requested an urgent meeting with the president and the secretary of State.

New York Times, Section B

Washington, D.C.: More fallout from the deepening recession. President Hanover announced today sweeping changes in the intelligence services of the United States. Effective in one month, all major national intelligence agencies will be brought under one administration—the National Intelligence Service—and there will be "drastic" reductions in funding for all intelligence services. "They will have to do more and make do with less," The president told the *Times*. President Hanover has nominated Christine Dangerfield-Udall to be the new director and Dr. Heather Prentiss to be the deputy director.

Of the new director, President Hanover said, "Mrs. Dangerfield-Udall has a thirty year career in intelligence and was most recently the director of the NSA. She is an effective and frugal administrator, a set of abilities sorely needed now during the current serious recessionary crisis." The new director described her deputy as "the finest intelligence analyst I have known in my thirty years. Her contributions to counterintelligence efforts in the Middle and Far East have been invaluable. She will be a welcome addition to the upper echelons of the NIS." Informed sources tell the *Times* that the functions of the National Security Agency [NSA], Defense Office of Intelligence [DOI], The State Department Intelligence Service [DIS], the National Reconnaissance Office [NRO], the Central Intelligence Agency [CIA], the Bureau of Intelligence and Research [INR], the Official National Geospatial-Intelligence Agency [NGIA], and Treasury Department of Intelligence Support [TDIS] will all be subsumed by the parent National Intelligence Service. The administration states that the reason for the changes result from a year-long study aimed at achieving the greatest effectiveness and efficiency from the often duplicated services of the intelligence community. Insiders place the decision squarely on the need for cost-saving measures.

In related news, *The National Intelligence Report*—a bi-weekly non-classified newsletter which is widely regarded as being on the forefront of the gathering and collating of non-partisan factual data related to United States' interests—reported this week that the outlook for the next decade is negative and growing increasingly worse each year. Last year, for the first time, the United States lost its third place ranking among developed nations with regards socio/political influence, military preparedness, and financial dominance. This year the United States is likely to fall to fifth place with Germany assuming the fourth place position behind the Peoples Republic of China, Japan, and the U.K. According to *The National Intelligence Report*, the consequences are profound and appear to be irreversible. See Front Page, Column A2.

Twenty Years Later
New York Times, Front Page Special Edition

NUCLEAR ATTACK ON ISRAEL

Reuters News Service-Amman, Jordan: In a lightening multi-pronged thermonuclear attack on the tiny nation of Israel, the increasingly militant Islamic Republic of Iran wreaked wide-spread destruction. U.K. satellite intelligence reported at least four ICBMs armed with plutonium warheads landed on the four principle cities of Israel: Jerusalem—the capital city which dates back to 3,000 years ago when it was built by the biblical hero, King David; Tel Aviv-Yafo—the economical and cultural center of Israel; Rishon-LeZion, with a population of 480,000; Haifa, a major port and industrial city; and Ashdod—a city with a population of over a quarter of a million people. Ten major Israeli Defense bases were reportedly wiped out in the raid that came as a complete surprise to the rest of the world along with the catastrophic damage to the cities. Jordanian officials—who declined to be identified—reported that the nation of Israel was unable to mount any substantial response, and that the country is unlikely to be able to function as a cohesive nation in the future. King Hussein, VI was visibly shaken. He stated that "...our good neighbor has been bombed back into the 8th Century. Radioactive fallout has forced Jordan to evacuate to the west of the country, and many of our citizens have fled to Syria, Iraq, Egypt, Saudi Arabia, and some even to Europe. We have been unable to communicate with Lebanon and fear the worst."

U.S. President Yashon Rankowitz gave only a very limited response to the inquiries by the *Times* White House reporter, Sam Dorrity, "We are studying the situation." Many people in the United States have been complaining for ten years that America owes Israel protection. Succeeding presidential administrations and congresses have defended their penurious foreign policies on the persistent and deepening recession that has gripped the nation even as our Canadian neighbors and European and Asian friends have come out of the slump and have been thriving. An unnamed administration official blames the economic down fall for the failure of the United States to respond, "We cannot fully protect ourselves, let alone get involved in an endless foreign war".

New York's Beth Israel Chief Rabbi, speaking to a somber crowd in the synagogue, stated that, "This is the culmination of anti-Semitism in the United States and is the worst catastrophe to befall the Jewish people since the Holocaust. There was a time—not so long ago, that America had the respect of all the world—and Israel—with America's help—was fully capable of defending itself. There was a day when a lone agent was able to frustrate the plans for world destruction and domination by the Islamic maniacs, and he was branded a traitor and an international criminal. What have we come to?"

Hourly reports coming in to the news services all indicate that between 15 and 20 million people have died or are in critical condition without hope of medical help. The entire Israeli cabinet, the president, and the prime minister were in a building that was demolished and all are presumed dead. American Jews appear to be of one voice: America saved pennies, and lost Israel. "(פ')שייבל; טימהל זולק; ליפשהל; טורפל לע ישגר השובה" [For shame].

Thirty Years Later
Tiempos Del Mundo English Language Edition, Obituary Section

Asuncion: Neighbors found the body of an elderly man in his apartment in a senior citizen home in the *Salvador Del Mundo [Asunción] barrio* under unusual conditions. Residents report that Eduardo Perropastor Salvador—a man well into his late nineties— was discovered in his bed room dead. Señor Salvador was dressed in an expensive black suit, white silk French cuff shirt, expensive Mara tie, and expensive Gucci patent leather opera shoes. His hands were folded across his chest as neatly as if he had been placed in a coffin by a professional mortician. The room—which was immaculately clean—contained only bare furniture—no clothes, personal articles, and no papers or documents. There is no known next of kin.

Fellow residents describe Señor Salvador as a quiet man who kept to himself. One resident stated that she had known him for almost thirty years and found him to be friendly but a man of few words who may once have been in the import/export business. Workers at the city morgue—speaking with promise of anonymity—described the mandatory autopsy. There was no evidence of recent foul play. However, the elderly gentleman was described as having been covered with scars, many obviously inflicted as torture. It is suspected that he was one of the silent victims of the regime of Paraguayan military officer and dictator, Alfredo Strössner, who ruled country with a murderous tyranny from 1954 to 1989.

Eduardo Perropastor Salvador was known only for one thing in the city; he was a recent major benefactor of the *Sociadad de La Muy Noble y Leal Ciudad de Nuestra Señora Santa María de la Asunción*. He was buried in the capital city's place of rest for the poor by Potter's Field Ministries.

Deseret News, LDS Church News section
Salt Lake City, Utah

The Church of Jesus Christ of Latter-day Saints First Presidency announced yesterday that the Church had received an anonymous donation of $9.0 billion. An extensive investigation failed to reveal anything about the donor other than that the generous sum was transmitted through an investment bank in Vanuatu. President Yoshio Yamada called the gift, "a miracle that could only have come from the hand of our Lord and Savior." The gift was earmarked for the Church's far-flung humanitarian services and "will be put to great use in Heavenly Father's Kingdom".

-THE END-

www.ingramcontent.com/pod-product-compliance
Lightning Source LLC
Chambersburg PA
CBHW071341020726
47502CB00001B/195